P9-ASJ-267

Dragon Venom

Lawrence Watt-Evans

TOR®
fantasy

A TOM DOHERTY ASSOCIATES BOOK
NEW YORK

This is a work of fiction. All the characters and events portrayed in this book are either products of the author's imagination or are used fictitiously.

DRAGON VENOM

A Tor Book
Published by Tom Doherty Associates, LLC
175 Fifth Avenue
New York, NY 10010

www.tor.com

Tor® is a registered trademark of Tom Doherty Associates, LLC.

ISBN 0-765-34170-0
EAN 976-0765-34170-9

First edition: October 2003
First mass market edition: November 2004

Printed in the United States of America

0 9 8 7 6 5 4 3 2 1

Dedicated to Deborah Hogan,
who was always a joy to work with

The Dragons

1

In the Dragon's Lair

*T*he stench of venom and rotting dragon was over-whelming, and depressingly familiar. Arlian breathed shallowly as he raised his torch high and looked out into the darkness of the cavern, the long obsidian-tipped spear ready in his other hand.

The orange light of the flaring torch lit the upper end of a great sloping limestone chamber, perhaps a hundred feet wide and a quarter-mile long. Clustered nearby upon the vast claw-marked stone floor lay four dead dragons, their carcasses already collapsing in supernaturally rapid decay, their scaly black hide peeling back from white bone, their partially exposed spines arching well above Arlian's head.

A dozen soldiers wearing the white-and-blue uniforms of the Duke of Manfort's guards stood scattered around the dragons, spears and torches held ready; every so often one of them would glance expectantly at Arlian, awaiting orders. The fine wool of their winter coats would not have appeared white in the torchlight in any case, but was further discolored with smoke and streaked with dirt—they had been on campaign for months, out of reach of Manfort's tailors and cleaners. The mail shirts the men wore beneath their coats were smoke-stained and battered—but never rusty; polishing armor kept the soldiers busy and their equipment fit.

The piping on Arlian's own black wool cloak, once brilliant white, was now mottled brown and gray; the black had kept its color, but showed significant wear. His broad-brimmed hat was battered and shapeless, the plume that had once adorned it long since lost; his boots were scraped and scuffed, and his hair and beard needed brushing and trimming.

The fourteenth and final member of the party, however, remained clean and trim, his green-and-buff coat spotless. He stood near the cave entrance, staring at the dead dragons unhappily. He held neither torch nor spear. Arlian glanced at him, then turned his attention back to the remainder of the cavern.

He listened, and heard nothing but his own men, leather boots creaking or shuffling, woolen clothing or iron mail rustling, breath sighing gently. He looked, and saw nothing else moving but the dragons' remains collapsing in upon themselves.

There could be no question that the four dragons were dead. That was one good thing about the creatures, Arlian thought; one never need worry that a dragon was feigning death. If the flesh failed to sink inward, if the bones did not protrude through stretching hide, then the dragon was not dead. If the rot set in, the dragon was irrefutably gone.

Arlian and his twelve men had had no trouble in dispatching these four, despite their size and presumed ferocity—the dragons had been deeply asleep, as they always were in the winter, and none had awakened before they died. The last had been stirring slightly when four men had plunged the ten-foot black-tipped spear into its black heart, and had thrashed briefly as it died, but that was of no consequence. None of the slayers had been harmed, and the world was rid of four more of the foul beasts, four more added to the scores Arlian and his troops had dispatched.

It was odd how routine the task had become. For centuries, humanity had thought it impossible to kill a dragon; no known weapon could pierce that magical hide or harm the creatures in any way. Only recently had the late Lord Enziet's sorcery and Arlian's own experimentation revealed that the black volcanic glass called obsidian could cut easily through a dragon's flesh, and that a blow to the heart with an obsidian blade would kill a dragon instantly.

Once it was demonstrated that the dragons *could* be killed, Arlian had been appointed warlord by the Duke of Manfort, with instructions to exterminate the creatures—instructions he had been following enthusiastically every winter, when the dragons were dormant. In warmer weather, when entering the lairs of the great beasts verged on the suicidal, he attended to other matters.

The great obsidian-tipped spears and the knowledge of where and when the dragons slept had made killing them simple. Where harming a dragon in any way had once seemed miraculous, disposing of four of the monsters was now scarcely more than just another day's work.

Arlian frowned. Four. That equaled the most he had ever found in one place, but nonetheless, he had hoped for more; the report had been that at least *six* dragons dwelt in this region. The ancient documents he had inherited, files that described every recorded dragon sighting for the past eight hundred years, had said that half a dozen dragons, perhaps more, had swept down from these mountains some five centuries ago and laid waste to the town of Beggar's Oak.

That "half a dozen" report might have been exaggerated, of course—that was common. It seemed as if most of the reports he had followed in his fourteen years of dragonhunting had claimed more dragons than Arlian had actually found in the caves and caverns he located. In some cases he supposed that might be because some of the dragons had departed, either died or moved on to other locations, but he was fairly sure that many of the original stories were simply wrong. It was human nature to exaggerate, to think every large bird spotted in the vicinity of an attack was another dragon, or every glimpse of a dragon was a new monster, rather than the same one seen twice.

And the records for this particular lair did not come from a survivor, but only from people who had seen the attack on Beggar's Oak from afar. Such a description would inevitably be less reliable than the accounts by survivors in the destroyed village itself.

Of course, often there *were* no survivors. There had been no survivors in Beggar's Oak.

Arlian waved the torch gently overhead and considered the dead beasts. If there *had* been six dragons in that long-ago attack, it was possible there might be another cave somewhere in the vicinity, one that his sorcerers and soldiers had not yet located—but after all these years of experience, his people had learned their job well. The vaguest accounts would usually be enough to locate the right vicinity, and a little simple sorcery could then find any nearby cave mouth. His hired sorcerers said it grew easier every time.

They had only found one entrance here.

Besides, Arlian had never yet encountered a confirmed report of an isolated attack, like the one on Beggar's Oak, that involved more than one lair of dragons. The great battles of the Man-Dragon Wars had sometimes involved multiple lairs, but all that had ended seven hundred years ago.

For all Arlian knew, two of the six reported dragons could have died of old age in the intervening years—but while dragons definitely aged, he had never found any solid evidence that they *ever* died merely from the passage of time, and five centuries was nothing by draconic standards.

Perhaps two of the dragons had died, not of old age, but in attacking the wrong target; many of the important towns of the Lands of Man were now defended with the gigantic spear-throwing catapults Arlian had invented, and he knew of at least six instances in which those machines had brought down or driven away attacking dragons. Only two of those had resulted in confirmed kills—but perhaps both of those had come from this nest.

Or perhaps there had been six in the cave today after all. There might be more to this cavern than the entry tunnel and the single vast chamber where these four had slept. Those other two dragons might well be sleeping—or wait-

ing in ambush—just out of sight. The torchlight did not
penetrate everywhere in the miasmal gloom even in the
main chamber; the orange light illuminated large areas of
bare stone, but shadows and darkness extended still farther.

"Does anyone see further openings?" he called. "Anywhere there might be more?"

Armor jingled, weapons rattled, and other torches flared
in the cool, foul air as his dozen men peered around at the
cavern walls, at the flowstone formations and shadows
thrown by the stalactites overhead.

"Not here, my lord," someone replied; Arlian recognized
the voice of his junior lieutenant, a man universally known
by the nickname Stabber. He had earned his name today; it
had been he who thrust a ten-foot spear into the hearts of
two of the four dragons, three of his men helping him to
drive the point home.

"Nor here," answered Quickhand, the senior lieutenant.
He and his men had disposed of a dragon, as well; Arlian
himself, with help from others, had slain the fourth.

"Let us take our time, and look carefully," Arlian said. "I
do not care in the least for the possibility that a dragon
might come up on our heels as we leave."

He could almost hear the shudder his words evoked.

"Come on, you two," Stabber called, gesturing to his
nearest companions. "We'll do this right, walk along the
wall and inspect it inch by inch."

"A dragon needs more than a few inches to squeeze
through, sir!" one of the others protested.

"And there might be an opening up above, among those
stone spikes, where we wouldn't see it."

"Do as he says," Arlian ordered. "We do what we can, as
best we can. And a dragon can fit through a smaller opening
than you might think; their hide and bone is tough, but their
flesh is far less solid than our own." He gestured at the gigantic rotting carcasses to illustrate his point.

"Yes, my lord."

"Stabber, you take your two around to the right, and

Quickhand, you take two men to the left. Burn off any
smears of venom you find—no sense in leaving it for scav-
engers. The rest of you, spread out across the floor—there
could be pits below, or shafts above. Torches high!" He
waved his own torch to demonstrate, and the flame roared
and crackled; the air was still thick with flammable venom.

The venom fumes were why they carried torches, rather
than lanterns; a lantern might be shattered by a flare, or
smoked into uselessness. Torches were clumsier and did not
last as well, but were far more suited to the environment of
a dragon's lair.

The men obeyed, the two parties moving along the walls
while half a dozen others scattered.

The man in the green coat, however, stepped down from
the entrance, came up behind Arlian's shoulder, and said
quietly, "My lord?"

Arlian turned his head slightly. "Yes?"

"My lord, if any more dragons remain alive in this place,
surely they must be awake by now, and lurking in conceal-
ment, awaiting an appropriate moment to strike."

Arlian shifted his grip on his spear. "You may well be
right," he said.

"My lord, killing four dragons as they slept was a task
within our capabilities, but fighting a *waking* dragon? I
think we might do better to withdraw into the tunnel and
await events."

"I think not," Arlian said, studying the cavern ceiling for
openings. "I have fought dragons before. They are fierce
and mighty, but hardly indestructible."

The other grimaced—Arlian could see the expression
from the corner of his eye. "Our ancestors thought otherwise for centuries," he said.

"And we have repeatedly proven them wrong. Obsidian
can pierce the dragons' hides, and a blow to the heart can
kill. You saw as much not ten minutes ago."

"Indeed. But any other dragons would be *awake*. And

here, in these confined spaces, in foul-smelling darkness, can we hope to strike quickly to a moving beast's heart?"

"Quickly enough. I have done this before, my lord, more than once."

"We could lose several of our men to a draconic ambush, my lord."

"So we could. I have lost men several times in the past; some of those who accompany us today were present on such occasions, as you were not, and yet they have come here willingly, and they understand the risks. They know they might die today—but if we do not seek the dragons out and destroy them, Lord Rolinor, how many innocents will those dragons eventually slay?"

"Perhaps many, perhaps none. My lord Obsidian, we cannot accept the responsibility for every innocent life in the Lands of Man! We . . ."

"On the contrary," Arlian interrupted. "I have done exactly that in accepting the Duke's commission as warlord. It is my duty, my responsibility, to protect *every* innocent from the dragons, insofar as I am able, even if it cost my own life, or the lives of my men. It pains me that hundreds of innocents, perhaps thousands, have died beneath the claws and flame of the dragons in recent years, not only because any death is a loss, but because those lost lives *were* my responsibility. I have sworn to exterminate the dragons if I live long enough, and I mean to do so. We are all volunteers here, Rolinor—have you forgotten what we volunteered for?"

"*I* volunteered to slay dragons in the Duke's service, my lord, not to die!" Rolinor's voice was not entirely steady, his sibilants slightly slurred; Arlian wondered if the venomous atmosphere was affecting him.

"Then let us slay dragons, my lord, and try our very best not to die in the process." With that he turned away and raised his torch again, staring out into the cavern.

His two lieutenants were moving along the walls, long

spears held ready, spreading torchlight into the depths of the cave, each with two companions following close behind with their own torches and shorter spears. Every so often one of the men thrust a speartip into a crevice to test its dimensions, or put a torch to a glistening streak of poison, sending a vivid flare roaring up the stone as venom ignited.

Each such flare destroyed hundreds of ducats' worth of venom, venom that the lords of the Dragon Society could perhaps have used to add to their numbers and buy the loyalty of more troops; Arlian was pleased to see that his men did not hesitate to burn the foul stuff.

Elsewhere in the cavern, away from the walls, the other soldiers were scattered, moving more or less randomly down the vast chamber, each with a torch, two with the long killing spears and the rest with shorter defensive weapons.

"You in the center, form a line!" Arlian called. "You might miss an opening if you just wander about like dazed sheep!"

Some of the men glanced back at him; one called, "Yes, my lord!" Then they wandered on as they had before.

Arlian sighed. These were good men, for the most part, strong and brave and obedient; except for young Lord Rolinor they had all been with him for at least two or three years now, and he knew them and was proud to lead them. Still, they were not as disciplined and thoughtful as he might have wished.

He considered sending Rolinor down to direct them into a better line, but then rejected the idea; Rolinor was no more disciplined than the others, and a good bit less dedicated and eager.

Lord Rolinor was, in fact, the only one in the party who had not really volunteered. Oh, he had made a show of enthusiasm when he first arrived a week before, made a little speech about how pleased he was to join the great Lord Obsidian in his crusade against the dragons, but Arlian and Rolinor both knew it was all for show. Rolinor was here because he was trying to impress the Duke in order to establish himself in the government, and slaying dragons in their lairs was more impressive than overseeing fortifications or financing caravans—and probably safer than attacking the Dragon Society's strongholds, tracking down the Society's assassins, or attempting to capture the dragonhearts themselves.

Rolinor's family had sent him to court to carry on their long tradition of service to the Dukes of Manfort, and Rolinor was doing his best to cooperate, but his heart was not in it. Court intrigue suited him well enough, and he had no trouble playing the sycophant, but fighting dragons was clearly not something that held any appeal for him. He had not asked for a killing spear, and appeared to have lost even his short spear; he had not approached any of the dragons closely until after they were dead. He was here to advance his career, not because he hated the dragons.

Rolinor had not lost family or friends to dragons, as Arlian had. He had not twice seen his home destroyed by dragonfire. He had not conversed with dragons and felt their scorn and hatred. He had not seen a newborn dragon tear its way from a man's chest. While Arlian knew that another such monster was growing in his own tainted blood, Rolinor had never been thus polluted, never lived in dread of such a death. To Rolinor vengeance was only a word, an abstract concept.

To Arlian, vengeance upon the dragons was everything. Vengeance was why he lived, why he fought, the entire reason he had sought wealth and power, his purpose as warlord to the Duke of Manfort. Destroying the dragons and their human allies, protecting innocents from them, was far more important to him than his own survival.

"My lord!" One of the soldiers was bending down, waving his torch. He had found an opening in the cavern floor, and thrust his spear into it without striking bottom.

"I see it," Arlian called, starting forward down the sloping stone surface. "Stand clear! Spears ready!"

2

The Warlord's Mercy

*A*rlian knelt beside the hole, his torch high, peering down into the darkness beneath. The soldiers formed a ring around him, and he was vaguely aware that young Lord Rolinor was not among them.

"Surely, that's not big enough for a dragon!" one man said—one of the newer recruits, a fellow the others called Leather.

He had a point; the hole in the stone was no more than four feet across at its widest, perhaps six feet from end to end.

"Not for a *large* dragon, certainly," Arlian conceded.

"Are any so small as that?" Stabber asked.

"They can compress themselves most amazingly; remember that a newborn dragon rises from within a man's chest," Quickhand replied. "I have seen the smallest in one lair squeeze through an opening not so very much larger than this."

Arlian glanced at Quickhand. For centuries the knowledge that dragons spawned their young in human hosts had been the deepest and darkest of secrets, known only to one living man, but then Arlian had learned it, and had been far less adept at secrecy than the late Lord Enziet. Now it was common knowledge among the Duke of Manfort's soldiers, and throughout much of the Lands of Man.

Quickhand had never *seen* a dragon's birth, as Arlian had, but he had obviously heard the stories.

Quickhand met Arlian's gaze for an instant, and then both men returned their attention to the task at hand. Arlian lowered his torch down into the hole, as far as he could reach; the orange light shone only on bare stone and blackness. He could see no sign of a dragon, nor any indication that a dragon had ever dwelt therein—but he could not see the full extent of the chamber below.

"Stand ready," he said.

Around him the men stepped back, adjusting their black-tipped weapons; then Arlian dropped his torch.

He watched it fall for a second, strike a jagged chunk of rock and tumble down a slope—and at the last instant he saw the gleaming fluid and snatched his head back, away from the opening.

The pool of venom in the bottom of the pit ignited, and a swirling cloud of yellow flame filled the entire lower chamber, bursting up through the opening in a coil of light, heat, and smoke. Arlian could feel his hair and eyebrows singeing as he tumbled backward, away from the blinding, searing blaze. Around him his men cursed and mumbled and coughed.

And then the dragonfire was gone, almost as swiftly as it had erupted, and Arlian blinked at the darkness, his eyes struggling to readjust to the restored gloom. The stench of venom smoke and burned hair filled his nostrils, and sweat crawled on his brow and under his shirt. The weight of his mail suddenly seemed greater.

He coughed once, wiped soot from his eyes, then leaned forward to peer down into the hole.

Traces of burning venom still flickered here and there on the walls and floor of the lower chamber, seeping out of cracks in the rock, and these gave enough light to see that indeed, there were no dragons down there, nor room for them, nor further openings.

There were charred brown bones, however, many of them. Old bones, by the look of them—very old. None of them were big enough to be dragon bones; a few were unquestionably fragmentary human skulls.

"A charnel-pit," Stabber said, kneeling beside him.

"An oubliette, perhaps," a man called Edge suggested, as he, too, stepped forward and looked down.

"Or worse," Arlian said, not voicing his suspicion—near-certainty, really—that the dragons had used this hole simply for waste disposal, making no distinction between human remains and any other unwanted debris.

Although why the dragons would have brought humans here he was not entirely sure. The dragons, contrary to widespread belief, did not seem to actually eat people—or for that matter, anything else. They apparently subsisted on magic alone. Enziet had told him long ago, "They are the magic of the Lands of Man made flesh, a primal force drained from the earth and given shape," and whether that was the precise truth or not, it did appear that they did not need solid food.

On the other hand, they did seem to enjoy tormenting and killing people, and might well have dragged a few back to the lair as playthings—though Arlian had never heard any reliable reports of such a thing, nor found any evidence in the other lairs he had explored over the past fourteen years.

The thought occurred to Arlian that those bones down there might have once belonged to the very men and women who spawned the four dragons whose rotting carcasses lay a dozen yards away. It seemed incredible, though, that anything recognizable could still remain after so very long, even in the dry, dead air of a cave; the dragons here had surely been thousands of years old. Their hides had been entirely black, the sign of a fully mature, even elderly, dragon; newborns were blood-red, a color that faded swiftly to golden yellow, and then to green, before giving way to the final black.

Every adult dragon Arlian had ever seen had been black. At least one of the three that destroyed his village and slaughtered his family had still shown faint traces of green when sunlight caught its scales at the right angle, and as a much younger man Arlian had encountered two bright red newborns, but none he had seen since had been anything but utterly black. Arlian turned to glance at the dead monsters, as if he could still somehow judge their age from the rotting remains.

He froze for an instant at what he saw in the torchlight, then closed his eyes wearily. He sighed, and turned back to the others.

"There may be more openings," he said. "Let us continue our search."

"As you will, my lord," Quickhand said, lifting his torch. The circle of soldiers broke, the men scattering again.

"Form a line!" Arlian called uselessly after them, as he got to his feet.

He stood and watched as they once again failed to obey, but he made no effort to pursue and coax them into a proper formation. Instead he waited for a moment, then turned his attention back toward Lord Rolinor.

Arlian saw that the man—hardly more than a boy, really—had at least had the sense to move well clear of the dragons again. That did not alter what Arlian had seen. He wished he could have dismissed it as a trick of the poor light, an illusion, an unfortunate appearance of an innocent act, but he knew it was none of those. The light had been sufficient, the actions unmistakable.

Rolinor had been collecting venom. He had brought a bottle, and had been thrusting it into the rotting venom sac at the base of one dragon's sagging jaw. He had tucked the bottle out of sight now, but still wore the heavy gloves he had donned to handle it.

Dragon venom had only three known uses, and only one of those could not be achieved more easily with less precious fluids. It was a deadly and corrosive poison, and highly flammable, but its unique purpose lay in the fact that when venom was mixed with human blood, it became the elixir that turned an ordinary human being into a dragonheart.

A man with the heart of the dragon was immune to poisons, disease, and aging, and acquired a strength of personality that allowed him to command the attention of ordinary men. Dragonhearts also seemed to be a little stronger and a little faster than they should rightfully be, and to have superhuman endurance.

Dragonhearts were also unable to sire or bear children, and tended to grow cold and detached over time.

And after an incubation of roughly a thousand years, each dragonheart would die giving birth to a dragon. Only death or a hideously painful magical ritual that would cleanse the draconic taint and restore the dragonheart to normal humanity could prevent this eventual transformation.

The Duke of Manfort, ruler of all the Lands of Man, had decreed fourteen years ago that every dragonheart in his realm—or rather, every dragonheart but Arlian, who had been given a special exemption until such time as the dragons were destroyed—must either submit to the Aritheian purification spell or die.

Most of the dragonhearts had refused and fled Manfort, establishing a new headquarters for the Dragon Society in the eastern port city of Sarkan-Mendoth; the Duke's armies had waged constant war against them ever since, trying to enforce the edict. The Duke had law and tradition on his side, and all the legitimate forces of the Lands of Man, but the lords of the Dragon Society, who had had centuries to build their fortunes and who could to some extent communicate and cooperate with the dragons themselves, had considerable resources of their own.

The Dragon Society could also offer one very strong incentive to ensure the loyalty of their troops. It was said that those followers they deemed worthy were rewarded with the elixir, and became dragonhearts themselves, with a thousand years of life ahead of them.

That was a strong enticement. To Arlian and some of the others the prospect of becoming a dragon at the end took the appeal out of the idea, but not everyone thought the price too high.

And apparently Lord Rolinor had given in to the temptation. Now he stood on a rise in the cavern floor, watching
Arlian nervously.

Arlian began trudging slowly back up toward the nobleman, and Rolinor stood, waiting. At least, Arlian thought,
he did not embarrass himself further by fleeing.

"Lord Rolinor," Arlian said, "a word with you."

"Of course, my lord," Rolinor replied. He did a surprisingly good job of concealing his nervousness.

Arlian approached to a comfortable conversational distance, his spear held casually in his hand. He made no
threatening moves, and his tone was mild as he asked, "Did
you want the venom for yourself, or were you planning to
sell it?"

"My lord?" Rolinor's handsome face shaped itself into a
carefully crafted look of confusion.

"I believe I spoke plainly enough."

"I . . . Yet I fear I do not understand the question, my
lord." Rolinor's expression was becoming worried, but not
yet frightened.

Arlian sighed, and the point of his spear was suddenly
aimed at Rolinor's throat. Fear appeared in Rolinor's eyes,
but still he made no attempt at flight.

"You filled a bottle with this monster's venom," Arlian
said, jerking his head to indicate the nearest of the dead
dragons. "I want to know whether you intended to use it to
prepare an elixir for your own use, or whether you intended
to sell it to other would-be dragonhearts."

"I did not . . ."

The black stone point of the spear was under Rolinor's
chin, pressing into the soft flesh. "I saw you fill the bottle,"
Arlian said. "Now, answer my question, or die. The choice
is yours."

Rolinor swallowed. "And if I admitted that I *had* collected
venom, would I not die in any case? We are forbidden . . ."

"Indeed you are forbidden to collect venom, and as you

suggest, the penalty is death," Arlian interrupted, "but you are young, and I may show mercy. If I am forced to strip you naked to find the bottle, the urge to be merciful shall be tempered by irritation at the inconvenience. Now, answer my question—what did you intend?"

Rolinor drew himself up to his full height—several inches less than Arlian's own—and said, "I had not yet decided, my lord. I saw an opportunity that might not come again, and chose to avail myself of it . . ."

Arlian interrupted him again. "You had brought the bottle with you. This was no mere whim, no spur of the moment."

Rolinor grimaced. "The bottle was not empty when we came, my lord; it contained brandy, with which I fortified my courage before facing a caveful of dragons."

"Oh?" Arlian leaned forward to smell the younger man's breath.

"I had never seen a dragon, my lord, and the tales were hardly encouraging. The reality was daunting enough that I made good use of the brandy, and when I was done I had the bottle, and there was the dragon, and the rest of you were all looking the other way, and a sudden impulse . . ." He shrugged.

Despite the cavern's reek the faintest whiff of brandy was indeed just barely discernible, and Arlian could hear the slurring in the younger man's speech. Arlian lessened the pressure on the spear ever so slightly, held out his other hand, and demanded, "The bottle."

"More of a flask, really . . ." Rolinor said as he reached into his buff suede waistcoat and drew out a flat brown glass bottle.

Of course it was glass; few other substances could hold venom without corroding. Arlian snatched it away, then turned to glance at the rest of the party.

They had reached the far end of the cavern, the light of their torches illuminating a blank stone wall, and as Arlian looked, Stabber called, "Nothing here, my lord!"

"Then let us be out of here, before we smother in this foul air," Arlian called back. He lowered the spear and trotted quickly to the edge of the opening in the floor, where he tossed the bottle in.

The glass shattered with a satisfying crash, and a hiss sounded as its noxious content spilled across the stone.

That done, he marched back to Rolinor's side and took him by one arm, leading him toward the cavern mouth. "Come on, all of you!" he called back over one shoulder.

Then, without looking directly at Rolinor, he murmured, "You're young, and you were perhaps drunk—I have heard from my men that venom fumes can combine with alcohol in unfortunate ways, though I myself have never been fool enough to drink before entering a dragon's lair. I will assume your wits were addled, and once we are out in the open air we will say no more about this. But understand, my lord Rolinor, that addled wits or no, you gave your life entirely into my keeping today, and you still live only because I choose to allow it. Do not rely on any further mercy."

Rolinor threw him a quick, uneasy glance, then looked down at his own feet and the stone floor. "Thank you, Lord Obsidian," he said.

Arlian clapped him on the shoulder, and said loudly, "Not the half-dozen I hoped, but still, four dead dragons is a good day's work, is it not? And our young Lord Rolinor is blooded at last; even if the hand that struck the killing blow was never his, he stood at the ready every time, and did not hesitate to approach. Perhaps he *likes* the stench of venom, eh?"

A few of the soldiers laughed. Rolinor coughed, but said nothing.

And then they were in the steeply sloping passage that led up from the torchlit and reeking gloom of the cavern into the cold sunlit open air, and too busy watching their footing to speak further.

3

Wine and Conversation

*T*he long walk back down from the cave mouth through the pine forest to the camp was largely silent, save for the crunch of footsteps trudging through the crusted snow; the men were tired and somewhat nauseated by the fumes, and opening one's mouth to speak would let precious warmth escape into the bitter wind of late winter. The party stayed together until they had passed the pickets and been recognized, but then the others proceeded onward while Arlian paused to talk to a sentry.

"Any news?" he asked.

The guard straightened. "No, my lord; all's quiet."

"No sign of the Dragon Society's spies? No word from Manfort?"

"Not that I've seen or heard, my lord."

"Good man," Arlian said, clapping the soldier on the shoulder. He glanced after the rest of his company as they dispersed in the deepening gloom of early evening.

Although the party that had entered the cave had been a mere fourteen men, the camp held over a hundred—enough warriors to fend off any attack the Dragon Society was likely to send in winter, along with a couple of dozen cooks, drivers, smiths, armorers, clerks, grooms, and spencers, and of course the three sorcerers whose magic had helped locate the cave mouth. Thirty tents were arranged under the tall trees, the paths between them trodden almost free of snow. A score of horses were tethered in a clearing to one side, their breath fogging the air as they nosed at their hay, and to the other side a line of wagons held the expedition's supplies. The smell of woodsmoke and the faint murmur of voices filled the air; Arlian's men were returning to warm campfires and good company, not just cold wagons and empty tents.

Lord Rolinor was already almost at the door flap of his pavilion, where a young woman waited, shivering as she held up a welcoming lantern. Arlian was unsure just who the woman was, but he had seen her in the vicinity now and then since the expedition had passed Crackstone. He supposed she was just another local girl turned camp follower, and perhaps a bit more fortunate than most in her choice of targets; Rolinor was far wealthier than any of the ordinary soldiers, and would presumably be reasonably generous with his money.

The others were breaking into groups, Quickhand and Stabber bound for the wagons where the lieutenants slept, the others heading for their own respective tents. Quickhand's arms were wrapped around a bundle of spears, while Stabber was collecting the last few obsidian daggers into a leather bag before allowing the men to go their way; the precious black weapons were always returned to the arsenal wagon for safekeeping.

Rolinor's spear had not been lost after all, but left in the entry tunnel with the men's hats; now it was in the big bundle Quickhand bore. At least the lordling had not broken *every* rule.

Arlian still carried his own spear, and still wore his glassy stone dagger on his belt—retaining his personal weapons was one of the privileges of his rank. He grimaced. It was not so very long ago that spears and daggers had been seen as the mark of the commoner, and a lord had been expected to carry only a fine steel sword, and perhaps a matching swordbreaker.

Arlian had such a sword at his waist, of course, but had not drawn it in the cave; steel could not pierce dragonhide, only obsidian could. Still, the sword had seen use a few weeks before, when one of Lord Hardior's hired assassins had attempted to waylay Arlian outside a tavern in Upper Durlek; the man's first dagger thrust had been turned by the mail Arlian wore beneath his blouse, and that had given Arlian the time he needed to draw his own blade. The assassin had not had a chance to make a second thrust, and his skull now hung on a pike at the rear of Arlian's wagon.

The man had lived long enough before bleeding to death to confirm that Lord Hardior had recruited him, but little more—not that it mattered. The Dragon Society, presumably at the direction of their monstrous masters, had been sending assassins after Arlian and certain others for a dozen years now, and there were few surprises left in their stories. A contact by a trusted friend, a succession of meetings, and finally a promise from Lord Hardior that if the assassin could kill Lord Obsidian he would be given a dose of life-extending elixir—the tales did not vary in any important feature.

Lord Shatter was nominally the head of the Dragon Society, on the basis of seniority, but Lord Hardior seemed to be in charge of hiring killers, and Lady Pulzera clearly held a great deal of authority, as well. Hardior and Pulzera had wanted Arlian dead even before open warfare broke out between the Society and the Duke; it was hardly surprising they continued to do so.

Arlian took a modicum of pleasure in frustrating them. He smiled grimly at the memory as he marched across the frozen mud of the camp to his own pavilion.

He had no woman waiting for him as Rolinor had, but when he opened the flap he found his steward setting two glasses and an open bottle of good red wine on the little folding table between the camp chairs. A fire was already burning in the improvised earth-and-stone hearth, but while the flames took away the worst of the chill the tent's interior was not truly warm, merely less cold. Arlian's cloak stayed around his shoulders, his hat on his head.

The steward's true name was Beron, but he was known to all as Black; his hair and beard were black, and he usually dressed entirely in black as well, generally favoring leather garb more suited to the caravan guard he had once been than to the steward he had long since become. He was one of Arlian's oldest friends, as well as the head of his household staff, and Arlian regretted that they spent so little time together; ordinarily Black remained in Manfort with his family, overseeing Arlian's affairs, while Arlian ranged about the countryside battling dragons and dragonhearts. This visit to the dragonslayers' camp was highly unusual—but very welcome.

Black poured generous servings of wine, then waited while Arlian set his spear in its brackets, extending horizontally across almost the entire width of the pavilion, and hung his sword and obsidian dagger in their place above his cot, joining the swordbreaker he had not bothered to carry on the day's expedition.

Weapons secured, Arlian doffed his hat at last, brushed at the soot that had collected on the brim, then set it aside before turning back to Black. He accepted a glass as he sank onto one of the chairs and let his cloak fall open.

Black settled into the other chair and asked, "Did it go well?"

"Well enough," Arlian replied, stretching out his legs.

"Were there indeed six dragons, then? Did any wake?"

"Only four," Arlian said. "And we slew them all before they woke, though the last seemed to be stirring as Stabber approached; no one was hurt, no harm done."

"Except to the dragons."

"Except to the dragons, yes. And the venom supply. We ignited a sinkhole full of the foul stuff."

"And what of the poison sacs in the four corpses? Burned, or simply left untouched?"

"Neither, to be honest. There was . . . well, I said I would not speak of it further." He waved the matter away.

Black smiled. "Ah, now you've piqued my curiosity. Shall I remind you of your oath, these many years past, to keep no secrets from me?"

"I sometimes think I swear altogether too many oaths," Arlian said ruefully.

"Undoubtedly you do."

Arlian tasted his wine, considering the flavor carefully; there was a certain smokiness to it that he did not find particularly appealing after the day's events.

"I await the tale," Black said.

Arlian decided the wine would do well enough, and took another sip. "Ah, it seems our little lordling Rolinor was momentarily overcome by greed," he said. "I caught him filling his brandy flask with venom."

Black was silent for a long moment, all levity vanished. Then he asked, "Have you arranged to send word to his family, or to the Duke? Will the body be sent home?"

Arlian blinked at his steward, then said mildly, "He's not dead."

Black stared back. "He's not?"

"He's not."

"You let him live?"

"Indeed I did."

"But trafficking in venom—Ari, how could you let him live?"

Arlian sighed. "Black, he's a young fool of good family who lost his head under extraordinary circumstances—a head that was full of brandy and the stench of venom. I destroyed his flask, warned him sternly, and told him that was the end of it, that it would not be mentioned again."

"You let him live." Black's struggle with disbelief was obvious.

"The complications if I had not would be *most* unfortunate," Arlian remarked.

"But you're showing human weakness, Ari; how unlike you!"

"I prefer to think of it as the lingering traces of compassion in my makeup. Another century will surely burn them away, and then there will be no more of these embarrassing lapses."

"Ah, then you do plan to live another century?"

"I fear it will prove necessary. How many dragons have we slain, in fourteen years of war? How many yet remain?"

"With today's four I believe the count stands at eighty-eight confirmed slain; the numbers remaining are, of course, unknown, but your own last estimate, after going through those mysterious records of yours, was that another forty-six are suspected, and that an unknown number of others may exist, as well. But I would point out that these same records said we would find six in this area, and I assume you were your usual thorough self and there were in fact only four."

"Only forty-six?" Arlian stared over his wineglass at Black.

"Yes. If that. At the present rate another ten years should surely be enough, then."

"I wish I could believe that," Arlian muttered. "I don't. I suspect that so far we have been picking off the easy ones. Some of those other forty-six are probably well hidden and clever, and it *might* take a century to find them all. And then, when those have been disposed of, we will still need to deal with Lord Hardior and the other dragonhearts, old and new, to ensure that no new plague of dragons is ever unleashed. That will be unpleasant."

"It may not even be *possible*, Ari; true, we have numbers and tradition and law on our side, but the Dragon Society can offer followers a thousand years of life. That's a powerful inducement for any ordinary man—as we have seen often enough! Stamping them out will not be easy. All the Duke's men have been working on it for fourteen years, with only limited success."

"No, it won't be easy," Arlian agreed, "but I think it can be accomplished. Once the present dragons are all dead, our foes will have no source of fresh venom until the next dragon is born. That will limit their ability to recruit supporters."

"And how old is Lord Shatter? How long do we have until that next dragon bursts from his chest?"

"I believe he is not much past eight hundred years of age; we should have at *least* a century."

"And you just said that disposing of the other dragons now alive might take that century."

"Let us hope that it will not—and that we will be able to dispose of Lord Shatter, as well, in that time." He leaned back. "Black, there are only twenty-six dragonhearts older than myself remaining; no matter how much venom the dragons may give them, no matter how many others they may recruit, it will be a thousand years before a twenty-seventh new dragon can be born. I think that we can achieve our final victory in that time. It may take a century, it may take two or three, but I am ready to pursue it for however long it takes—assuming no one manages to assassinate me."

"Yes, we all know your mad dedication, Ari. Or perhaps not so mad, in this case; I suppose you are in no great hurry to have your own heart torn out and magically cleansed."

Arlian turned his head away for a moment, then said, "Lady Rime made that same accusation long ago. In truth, I do not look forward to undergoing that procedure—I saw how much Rime and Shard and Spider suffered, and how swiftly they seemed to age in the weeks after it was done. I am relieved I was not present when Lady Flute surrendered herself, as I do not wish to ever see the process again, let alone experience it. I think I might prefer to simply die, as Lord Wither did—after all, what awaits me if I am cleansed? Where would I fit in a world purged of dragons? What do I have to live for, save my revenge upon them? I am polluted with their magic, and have been since childhood. I have no place among humanity. Better to die than suffer such torment and live out an empty existence."

Black stared at Arlian for a long moment before replying.

"I think you should speak to Rime and Shard and Spider and Flute before making any choice so permanent," he said at last. "You have hardly said a word to any of them in longer than I can recall—they might have some comment on the emptiness of their existence." He shifted in his chair. "Why *haven't* you discussed this with them, if you harbor such doubts?"

"I *have* been rather busy," Arlian pointed out. "All of us have been traveling extensively, and going about our various businesses."

"As the deaths of eighty-eight dragons will attest."

"Indeed."

For a moment the two men sat silently, each lost in his own thoughts; the side of the tent rippled in the breeze, and Arlian watched the movement idly as he sipped his wine, noting the change in the fabric's color as the last sunlight faded and torches were lit.

Then Black rose to his feet. "I think I have had quite enough wine for now, my lord," he said. "Let me fetch our supper, such as it is."

"Very good," Arlian said. "Thank you, Black."

Black bowed, then slipped out of the tent into the torchlit twilight beyond.

Arlian remained in his chair, staring blindly at the tent wall.

"Eighty-eight dragons," he murmured to himself at last.

When he was a new-made orphan swearing revenge, and in all his seven years as a slave in the mines of Deep Delving, when he had been plotting and praying for that revenge, and on his journey through the Desolation to the Borderlands and Arithei, when he had been struggling to find the means to pursue his oath of vengeance, he had never dared believe he would ever kill so many of the monsters. He had become wealthy and powerful entirely so that he might have greater resources to devote to the task, but even so, even when he had succeeded at almost everything else, he had only hoped he might someday find a way to kill *one* of them.

But then Lord Enziet's death, in a cave beneath the Desolation, had shown him how the dragons were born, and how they could die.

And the dragon that destroyed his former home in Manfort had let him demonstrate to the entire city that an adult dragon could indeed be slain.

The Duke of Manfort had named him warlord and charged him with the destruction of the dragons and the extermination of those dragonhearts who would not allow themselves to be transformed back to ordinary men and women, and he had done the best he could to carry out his duties. He had chosen to concentrate his own efforts on the dragons first, deeming them the greater threat, leaving most of the fight against the Dragon Society to the Duke's other commanders.

He and his men—the Duke's men, really—and the defenders of certain villages had slain eighty-eight dragons.

And still they had not yet found the one that slew Arlian's grandfather, and tainted Arlian's blood with venom. As long as the three dragons that obliterated his village and slaughtered his family still lived, Arlian's vengeance was not complete.

He would find them in time, he told himself. There were still forty-six dragons listed in the records Wither and Enziet had left him, forty-six dragons that had been seen emerging from their caverns, forty-six dragons that could be tracked, by skill and sorcery, and killed as they slept in their underground lairs.

Surely, the ones that destroyed the village of Obsidian would be among them! He would find them and slay them in time.

And when those forty-six were slain, when the threat was ended forever—what then?

Ah, but the threat would *not* be ended while any dragonheart still lived. The twenty-six surviving members of the Dragon Society would be hunted down, by the Duke's order, and offered a choice of death or magical cleansing. And the underlings they had fed the elixir of blood and venom would be offered the same choice—there were probably dozens of them by now, though of course Arlian had no accurate count. They would all be found and dealt with; dragonhearts could be recognized by anyone familiar with the signs.

And then it would be done, the Lands of Man freed forever from the dragons' malign power, and Arlian could rest. He could choose a normal life, as Rime and Spider and Shard and Flute had, or he could choose death, as Lord Wither had.

He sat slumped in his chair, fingertips resting lightly on the cold earthen floor of his tent, as he considered which alternative he would pick.

He really ought to speak to Rime and the others, he thought; Black was right. And given how rapidly they seemed to be aging, he could not afford to put it off for very long.

He reviewed his plans. The next reported cave was about eighty miles to the northwest, deep in the Brokenback Mountains, and despite the cold and the lingering snow the first scent of spring was already in the air; he would have to hurry if he wanted to get there before the dragons could wake. Rolinor would need to be watched closely . . .

He stopped in midthought.

No, he told himself. No.

He had reached a decision. He had been on campaign constantly for more than four years this time, moving from one site to the next, tracking down reported sightings of dragons, searching out the caverns by means both mundane and magical. When the weather was cold enough to ensure the dragons would be asleep he had slaughtered his monstrous foes in their lairs; in warmer weather he had helped fortify and defend the towns he found himself in, and had sometimes found, fought, and slain dragonhearts who had refused the Duke's order to undergo the magical cleansing that Oeshir and her heirs offered—not to mention defending himself from the Dragon Society's attempts to kill him.

While messengers had brought news, supplies, and troops from Manfort, as well as occasional nuisances like

Lord Rolinor, he and his best men had remained afield—
well, most of his best men; Black only rarely joined the
campaign, and only for brief periods, preferring to spend as
much time as possible in Manfort with his wife and children, overseeing Arlian's various business concerns.

Arlian had not returned to Manfort, summers or winters,
for more than four years. In all that time he had lived in inns
and tents and guesthouses, and had not slept under his own
roof. He had not seen Black's children grow, nor Hasty's,
nor any of the others born to the women he had rescued
from slavery. He had not properly reviewed his holdings, or
spoken to his staff other than Black—he had no idea how
most of his various businesses were doing.

He glanced at the battered, plumeless hat he had set on a
nearby chest. He had not seen a decent tailor in four years,
either; he was unsure what the current fashions were. The
damnable fad for wearing masks seemed to have spread to
most of the Lands of Man now; might it have finally faded
away in Manfort? Black had not mentioned it. Observant as
Black might be, he could not tell Arlian everything as effectively as Arlian's own eyes could.

Arlian had noticed that Lord Rolinor's coat was cut differently from his own, with sharply tapered lapels—was
that the latest style, or merely an individual affectation?

Arlian did not like being out of touch with events. Styles
were not important in themselves, but what else might he be
missing? Was the Duke of Manfort steadfast in his support
for the war against the dragons? Might the Dragon Society's careful lies have undermined his determination, or
fourteen years of war sapped his courage? Was Lord Rolinor typical of the attitudes of the younger nobility? If the
Duke's support was to weaken or vanish, the campaign to
exterminate the dragons might never reach a successful
conclusion.

The remaining forty-six dragons, or whatever the actual
number might be, could wait until *next* winter, or subse-
quent winters, to die. Arlian had had enough for this season.

He resolved to spread the word this evening, as soon as he had eaten—they would break camp first thing in the morning, as expected, but not to travel farther into the northern wilderness. Instead he and his soldiers and sorcerers would be marching back to the Duke's Citadel in Manfort, and the camp followers, whether servants, whores, beggars, or entrepreneurs, would be turned out to find their own way home.

He would return to Manfort, report his progress to the Duke, and then pay a call on Lady Rime to discuss his future.

He looked up as Black reappeared at the flap, supper in hand. Arlian rose and took the platter, glanced at the unappetizing slices of boiled salt beef, and remarked, "At least it's warm."

4

A Bird in the Hand

*A*rlian came awake suddenly, muscles tensed, but did not move beyond a slight twitch. He lay on one side on his cot, wrapped in blankets, as he opened his eyes carefully and peered into the cold darkness, trying to make out what had awakened him.

The last carefully banked coals of the evening's fire still glowed on the crude stone hearth, and the distant glow of the sentry's lanterns seeped through the tent's canvas, so the darkness was not absolute; Arlian could see the slim figure standing at the tent's entry flap. Arlian realized that he had awakened because he had heard the flap opening, and had heard a footstep.

That was not Black, come to carry out some late-night errand; Black was twice the size of this person. The intruder lowered the flap and looked around, and as she turned, revealing her outline in silhouette, Arlian was left in no doubt that this was a woman, and one not dressed suitably for the wintry weather.

That was interesting. She could hardly have any legitimate business slipping into his pavilion in the middle of the night, but that did not mean her intent was hostile. Arlian did not consider himself a great beauty, but he knew many women found him attractive, and of course he was wealthy and powerful, and had the unnatural charisma of the heart of the dragon—the possibility that she had come seeking a harmless tryst did exist.

Also, in recent years a superstition had arisen that a dragonheart's seed conveyed longevity, that the life-giving potency that could no longer engender children had been transformed rather than destroyed. Arlian did not think there was any truth to the rumor; certainly members of the Dragon Society who had married ordinary mortals had always outlived them, and he could not recall any mention of extended lifespan among those spouses. Still, the belief persisted in some quarters, and some women therefore sought out dragonhearts as lovers.

On the other hand, most of the people sneaking into his tent or bedroom at night over the past several years had been would-be assassins sent by the Dragon Society.

His sword and two lesser blades were hanging from the pavilion's frame just a foot or so above him, but he was facing the wrong way and was too wrapped in his blankets to grab them quickly. He began easing his right hand upward, out of the bedclothes, as he watched the intruder.

She seemed unsure of herself—or perhaps she simply could not see much in the gloomy interior of the tent. She stood by the entrance, hands slightly raised from her sides, and stared into the darkness for a long moment. Then she apparently found her bearings, and moved slowly forward, circling around the table and chairs in the center of the pavilion.

He could see that her hands were empty; that was reassuring. Most assassins, especially the sort of amateur most tempted by the Dragon Society's offers, would be brandishing daggers or winding garrotes by this point. The exceptionally stupid might be uncorking poisons, unaware that dragonhearts were immune to virtually all natural toxins.

This woman, whoever she was, had her hands raised, fingers spread, as if to help her balance. If she was an assassin, she was a subtle one. Whoever she was, she was also either cold or nervous—he could see that she was trembling.

By the time she reached the side of the cot Arlian had both his hands out of the entangling blankets, ready to grab for either the woman or a weapon, but had not otherwise moved.

"Lord Obsidian?" she said, in a nervous, high-pitched whisper. "Are you awake?"

Arlian sighed, and rolled over on his back, no longer feigning sleep. "What is it?" he asked. "Who are you?"

"I'm called Wren," she said. Her voice was unsteady. "I'm sorry to trouble you, my lord, but I wondered whether I might sleep here tonight."

Arlian considered that, and as he did he reached up, without looking, and closed his hand on the first hilt his fingers encountered. Watching the woman as best he could in the darkness, he drew the blade and sat up, aware by the feel that he held his swordbreaker—probably the most practical weapon in this situation, really. The swordbreaker was a heavy knife with a leather-wrapped hilt and a blade slightly over a foot in length; the crosspiece between hilt and blade was curved into a U, its two arms paralleling the blade for almost half its length and ending in sharp points, giving the overall weapon almost the shape of a three-tined fork. It was designed to be held in the left hand when dueling, where it could be used to stab, to parry, or to catch the blade of an opponent's sword. With luck and skill a sword could be trapped between the swordbreaker's blade and one of the side pieces, and a twist of the wrist would then snap it off short—or at the very least, bend it into uselessness.

This woman had no sword to break, but the swordbreaker was handier in confined spaces than the sword, and less likely to chip or shatter than the brittle obsidian dagger.

"Who are you?" he repeated.

"Wren. I'm . . . I . . ." Her voice trailed off.

Arlian adjusted his grip on the swordbreaker, making sure she had seen it.

"Lord Rolinor threw me out," she said, on the verge of tears. "And I can't go to any of the other tents, because they . . . they would want to share, and I don't . . . I thought you . . ."

She did not need to complete her explanation; Arlian understood. Of the hundred men in camp, only three slept alone—himself and Lord Rolinor in their respective pavilions, and Black in Arlian's personal wagon. This woman clearly had only one form of payment to offer for lodging, and did not care to degrade herself further by compensating multiple landlords; Rolinor had evicted her, Black was a married man of uncertain temperament, and that left Arlian as her best prospect to avoid freezing to death in the open.

One important question remained, however. "Why did Rolinor send you away?" he asked. "Surely, if he had simply wearied of you, he would allow you to stay until morning."

"I . . . He was in a foul temper tonight, my lord. I don't know why. It seemed to worsen when we heard that you would be returning to Manfort, rather than continuing northward."

"Hmm." That was interesting. While the reason for his initial ill temper was obvious, why would it worsen? Had Rolinor perhaps hoped to fill another bottle of venom, and been disappointed to learn he would not have a chance to do so?

Or had he taken the change in plans as an indication that Arlian did not trust him?

"I tried to cheer him," Wren said, "but it didn't help. He was . . . It didn't help. It just made things worse." That required no further explanation. "I just want somewhere to sleep, my lord—I will not trouble you." Her voice dropped in pitch as she added, "Though of course, if there is anything I can do to please you, I will be happy to oblige."

"That won't be necessary," Arlian replied. He might have been tempted under other circumstances, but the day had been long and wearisome, and he wanted to be alert when breaking camp in the morning. Keeping the swordbreaker ready, he used his other hand to pull two of the blankets from his wrappings and toss them to the woman.

"Here," he said. "You can sleep in one of the chairs, and leave in the morning. You're from Crackstone, I believe?"

"Yes, my lord," she said, catching the blankets.

"Then you can go home tomorrow, and find a better way to earn your keep."

"Thank you, my lord," she said, but her gratitude did not sound especially sincere.

He watched as she settled into one of the camp chairs, wrapping the blankets around herself, and then allowed himself to sleep again. He kept the swordbreaker tucked at his side, however, rather than returning it to its sheath.

And then he awoke again at the sound of footsteps on the frozen ground, and turned to see that Wren had risen from her chair and was approaching him.

"Lord Obsidian?" she said.

Arlian did not immediately reply. He listened to her voice, considering her pronunciation of his name.

"My lord?" she asked again.

"Yes?"

"It's so cold—I can't keep warm in that chair, or on the ground. Can't I sleep on the bed with you?"

"No," he said flatly.

She stopped a pace away, but pleaded, "Oh, please, my lord—it's so cold!"

Up to that point he had been perfectly willing to give her

the benefit of any doubt, and to accept her story as genuine, but now his suspicions were aroused once more. The night was cold, but not so bitter as that; an ordinary camp follower would not press her case—and then there was her accent, which did not seem to be quite that of the region in which they found themselves. Rather, she seemed to be *imitating* the local accent.

"It would do you no good to cuddle with me," he said. "I am no warmer than the night air. Did you not know that dragonhearts are as cold-blooded as the dragons themselves?"

"No, they . . ." she began, startled. Then she stopped. "I never heard that," she said warily.

"And how would you know anything of dragonhearts?" he asked.

"Just . . . well, people talk."

"Yes, of course they do." He sat up, the swordbreaker in his hand again. "Fetch the lantern," he said, pointing at the lamp hanging from a hook on one of the pavilion's supports. "Light it from the coals on the hearth."

Uncertainly, Wren obeyed, and returned a moment later with the lantern aglow. Arlian finally got a decent look at her face, and saw that yes, this was the woman who had been living in Rolinor's tent; that much of her story was true.

"Take off your clothes," he said.

"But it's so cold!" she protested.

"I want to see what I am offered," Arlian replied.

"I would be happy to lift my skirts, my lord, but . . ."

"Take them off."

"But . . ."

"Mistress, you may either remove your clothing or remove yourself from my tent; the choice is yours."

Wren hesitated, then reluctantly cast aside the blankets and began to unbutton her coat. Arlian watched with unfeigned interest.

Beneath the inadequate fleece-lined coat she wore a green dress with an elaborate bodice trimmed with gold cord; when she turned to drape the coat across a chair he saw that the bodice laced up the back. She reached behind to untie the laces while still facing away from him.

"Turn around," he said.

Startled, she glanced over her shoulder at him.

"Turn around," he repeated.

"But the laces . . ."

"I don't want to see the laces," he said. "Face me."

Reluctantly, she obeyed, and faced him, her head down as she reached back to loosen the laces. He studied her closely.

"Stop," he said. "Stand up straight."

She sighed, and obeyed—and as Arlian had expected, a gold ornament at the base of her loosened bodice slipped down, revealing itself to be the hilt of a stiletto.

"Raise your arms," he said, as he rose from the cot and stepped forward, the swordbreaker at the ready. She obeyed, dislodging the concealed blade further; Arlian reached out and plucked it from its sheath, and looked it over while never taking his attention entirely off his guest.

The stiletto's narrow blade was six or seven inches long, ending in a needle-sharp point; the golden hilt was roughly teardrop-shaped and had hung just above Wren's navel, where she could have easily reached it while lying on her back.

"I need to be able to defend myself!" Wren said.

"Perhaps you do," Arlian said. "Perhaps you are indeed merely a girl from Crackstone who happens to own so elaborate a dress and concealed weapon, yet who chooses to become a camp follower; a girl who feels the need to defend herself by such means, yet tries to talk her way into my bed; a girl who does not give her true name, a whore reluctant to disrobe. We are funny creatures, we human beings, and it is indeed possible that you are just what you claim to be." He sighed, and raised the point of the swordbreaker to her throat. "On the other hand, I think it rather more likely that you are a would-be assassin, hoping to collect the bounty the Dragon Society has placed on my head and gain a thousand-year life expectancy. I think that you sought to gain my trust in order to get into my bed while I was unarmed, where you could draw this blade and thrust it into my heart before I would have time to react. You have undoubtedly heard how difficult it is to simply catch me unawares, as several of your predecessors discovered, and rather than try to stab me in my sleep you hoped to disarm my suspicions and render me vulnerable to your assault."

"I . . . I would never . . ." She stared down at the hand holding the swordbreaker, and tried to back away, but collided with a chair. Arlian stepped forward, keeping the blade at her throat.

"I further suspect, young lady, that you have been cozening Lord Rolinor, and that you were partially responsible for his near-fatal lapse in common sense in the cavern today—perhaps you thought there might be an easier way to obtain the elixir than through killing me. When you learned that Rolinor had failed in his attempt, and furthermore that we would not be providing another opportunity this season, you decided to kill me after all."

"No!" she shrieked. "I don't know what you're talking about!" Her false accent had vanished, though he could not immediately place her natural tones.

"Perhaps, as I said, you genuinely do not. There may be a simple enough way to determine whether you are a liar, young woman; in the morning we will be leaving this camp and proceeding to Crackstone, which you have said is your hometown. We should be there the following evening, if the weather holds, and we can then inquire of your friends and family, and if you have told the truth return you to their care. If you are *not* from Crackstone, then we must assume you are indeed an assassin. Now, if you cooperate, I might show mercy—Lord Rolinor will have told you that I sometimes do. If you force us to drag you to Crackstone in chains and pointlessly interrogate the townspeople there, then I'm afraid our resentment will impel us to execute you, and your head will adorn the pike at the rear of my wagon—the skull there at present has had its day."

At that she broke down in tears. The jerking of her head as she sobbed drove the tip of the swordbreaker into the skin of her neck, leaving a shallow scratch, but Arlian held the blade unwaveringly in place.

Arlian waited, and at last she regained sufficient control to say, "Please don't kill me, my lord. Please, I'll do anything."

"Simply tell me the truth, and we shall see whether your death is necessary."

"I'm not from Crackstone," she said. "No one there knows me. But I'm not an assassin, I swear it! I've never killed anyone."

"I was to be the first, then?"

"Not originally," she said. "I wasn't sent to kill you, but I . . ." She stopped and swallowed, the motion catching the skin of her throat against the point of Arlian's blade. "I didn't want to hurt you," she said, staring helplessly up at him.

"Tell me about it," he said gently. "Tell me the whole tale."

She swallowed again, struggled to compose herself, then said, "I'm from Siribel. I was at the market in Sarkan-Mendoth when the news came."

Arlian's lips tightened. Siribel was a coastal town the dragons had destroyed two summers back, when the town elders chose to side with the Duke of Manfort against the Dragon Society. Black's wife, Brook, had been born in Siribel—and that might mean she would be able to verify the accuracy, or lack thereof, of Wren's story, should it prove necessary.

The lilt of the coastal dialect was in Wren's speech, though.

"My whole family was dead," she continued. "I had no one to help me, no one to keep the slavers from taking me, so I went to Lord Shatter to beg his protection. I tried to shame him, saying the attack on Siribel was his responsibility."

Arlian smothered a derisive snort. "Shatter has never been one to live up to his responsibilities."

"He saved me, though. He took me in and fed me and hired me as a spy. He sent me here, to watch you, and to send word of your intended route. I could not catch *your* eye, so I seduced Lord Rolinor and coaxed your plans from him, and then reported them to one of Lord Shatter's messengers—but then tonight, when you changed them and said we would turn back to Crackstone . . . well, I had instructions for such an eventuality, and the dress and knife Lady Pulzera had given me."

"So there is an ambush waiting for us on the road north."

"I don't know. Not for certain."

"But you have no reason to think otherwise."

"No. I . . . There is a phrase I was taught. If bandits struck at us, I was to call out to Fate and the dead gods, and I would be spared."

Arlian nodded. "And if my forces prevailed, we would not have recognized that as anything out of place. So an ambush was planned. And what else? What of your connection with Lord Rolinor?"

"He . . . he was at hand, my lord; no more than that. I needed someone in your camp to take me in, and he is comely, he eats well, and he has his own pavilion."

"And the flask of venom?"

"I suggested he do that as if I were teasing, my lord. I told him I could find a buyer."

"Why? Surely Lord Shatter has all he needs."

"If I had the venom, my lord, I would not need to return to Lord Shatter—but furthermore, I do not believe his masters are generous with their elixir. He said he would be glad of any I could fetch to him, and generous in recompense."

"Interesting." For the first time Arlian let the swordbreaker's blade drop slightly. He believed Wren's story, believed that she had indeed told him the truth. The Dragon Society boasted of their access to dragon venom, but in fact he had heard before, from reliable sources, that the dragons had refused to supply their servants with the vile fluid.

So Wren was telling the truth. Now the question remained of what he should do about it.

5

The Defense of Ethinior

*I*n the end, Arlian decided to do nothing.

He had Wren bound and placed under guard, of course, and put her in his own wagon under Black's supervision, but he made no other changes in his plans. He said nothing more to Rolinor, and resolved to do nothing about the waiting ambush. After all, he had no idea what forces Lord Shatter might have committed to his trap; even with the benefit of the element of surprise transferred from his opponents to himself, he could not be sure of victory should he march up and confront the foe. Better to let Shatter's men sit in the snow and mud, eating their rations and burning their fuel, waiting for an enemy who never came.

For himself, he would return to Manfort, as quickly as he reasonably could. If the Dragon Society was planning to ambush a company of over a hundred men in winter they were growing either ambitious or desperate, and either way, Arlian wanted to discuss it with the Duke in time to make plans for the summer campaign.

The shortest route back to Manfort was not the way Arlian and his warriors had come, nor in fact along any roads that Arlian had ever traveled before; the local camp followers assured him that the best way to reach the city was to take the logging road from Crackstone down to Ethinior, and then the trade road from Ethinior to Westguard.

From Westguard, of course, Arlian knew the way to Manfort very well indeed; he owned property in Westguard. He had no objection to a route that would allow him, purely for his own self-interest, to inspect it.

Accordingly, once the camp had been cleared away he led the long line of wagons down the trail to Crackstone, where an assortment of women and boys were restored to their families or turned out to fend for themselves. Since the expedition had been planned to last another few weeks there was no real need to resupply, but a portion of the remaining contents of Arlian's strongbox was spent in the local markets as much to maintain goodwill as to equip the journey home.

The company stayed the night in Crackstone, and in the morning headed southward down the logging road to Ethinior.

Arlian estimated that a lone rider could have made the trip in three or four days; it took his little army almost a fortnight before their wagons rolled onto the ancient cobbles of Ethinior's town square. Keeping Wren safely confined became first a nuisance, then a routine.

News of her presence, and that she was a Society spy, gradually spread through the company, and Arlian knew that his men were curious as to just what he intended to do with her.

He was curious about that himself; he had still not decided her fate when they reached Ethinior.

That arrival was interesting; naturally, the company was spotted well before arrival, and there could be no mistaking it for anything but soldiery. The spears and other weapons were plainly in evidence and far too numerous for a caravan, and no ordinary caravan would have approached down the logging road without hauling lumber.

The identity of the soldiers, and their intent, was far less obvious, and apparently no advance word had reached

Ethinior from the three tiny villages Arlian's party had passed through on the way.

Accordingly the streets of Ethinior were deserted, the windows tightly shuttered, when the wagons rolled past the ancient and empty guard tower at the outskirts of town. Arlian was certain that dozens of eyes were watching, but at first he could neither see nor hear a single living soul other than his own party.

But then word of the Duke's arms and livery, the obsidian spearheads, and the general lack of signs of hostility must have circulated. Third-story shutters opened a crack; faces peered cautiously down.

Then upper-floor windows were flung wide, and the townspeople leaned out, calling and waving, and by the time the wagons rolled into the square and Black reined in the horses a heroes' welcome was under way. Crowds gathered in the side streets and children ran alongside the wagons, and the air echoed with singing and cheering.

Arlian adjusted his hat and sword, then climbed down from his wagon and looked about. As he had expected, an official emerged from the crowd to greet him—a plump man wearing a gray woolen cloak and a hat with the brim pinned up on one side, his breath clouding in the cold air.

The two exchanged bows and introductions, and Lord Obsidian found himself discussing accommodations with Monifin, Lord Mayor of Ethinior. The men were tired of sleeping in tents and wagons, and Arlian inquired about finding rooms, or at least beds, for them in the town's houses and inns. Lord Monifin was optimistic that arrangements could be made.

Arlian also, however, discovered a misunderstanding about the nature of the new arrivals.

"We have three old stone towers that should be your initial construction sites," Monifin said. "Of course, we know that won't be sufficient. I understand catapults can be mounted on ordinary rooftops, though—are your men equipped for this?"

Arlian paused before replying, then said, "My lord, I fear you misjudge the situation. We are not here to build catapults. We are merely passing through on our way home."

Monifin cast a quick look at the wagons, then turned back to Arlian. "But surely, my lord . . ."

Arlian held up a hand.

"My lord," he said, "while the Duke most certainly does send troops and equipment to fortify towns against the dragons, such work is generally not undertaken in winter, when most towns have enough difficulty in feeding their own without being asked to supply hundreds of soldiers. No, this is a company of dragon-hunters—we have rid the world of three lairs this season, for a total of nine dragons slain. This task can only be accomplished in safety when the weather is cold and the dragons are sound asleep, and thus, unlike the Duke's other armies, we are abroad in the snow."

Monifin blinked in surprise. "You have *slain* dragons?" he said.

"A good many of them, yes. Most recently we disposed of four dwelling in the ridge a dozen miles above Crackstone. However, we are done for the season, and on our way home to Manfort. Ethinior is not our destination, but merely a pleasant stop along the way. My sincere apologies for my failure to make this clear immediately; I plead fatigue from the journey."

Monifin hesitated, then began, "And should we expect . . ." He paused. Arlian waited politely. Monifin began again, "My lord, does this not make it even more pressing to defend Ethinior against retaliation?"

Arlian blinked. "Retaliation?" He glanced at his wagon, where Black sat on the driver's bench and Wren, he knew, was bound inside. "By whom?"

"By the surviving dragons, of course, or their human minions."

"The other dragons are all still asleep, my lord; unless the weather should warm in a truly astonishing manner, they will not wake for at least a fortnight and probably considerably longer. As for their servants . . ." He considered that, then said, "While I suppose they might be interested in avenging their masters' losses, why would they trouble Ethinior? They would far rather recruit you into their ranks than fight you."

"We have heard tales from the east, my lord, of how neighboring towns are destroyed in revenge for each lair of dragons you expunge."

"Do not put too much faith in travelers' tales, my lord." He sighed, and said, "We will speak of this at length later, but for the moment, we are tired and hungry . . ."

"Of course, of course! A thousand apologies, my lord!" Monifin spread his arms in an expansive gesture of welcome, and then turned to his townsfolk and began calling names, asking for families to host Arlian's men.

An hour later housing had been assigned to all; Black and Arlian were, of course, to be guests of the Lord Mayor and his wife.

The next question to be addressed was the disposition of the prisoner. Arlian had been considering this during the journey down from Crackstone, and had finally, as they entered the town, reached a conclusion. No good would be served by killing her, selling her into slavery violated his principles, and he doubted she posed any real threat to anyone's well-being. Simply turning her loose, however, would leave her prey to slavers and free to fall once again under the Dragon Society's sway. A place would have to be found for her—and Ethinior seemed as good as any.

To bring her into her new home as a bound prisoner would hardly enhance her chances for a decent life there. Accordingly, when the wagons had first rolled to a stop he had removed her bonds, after obtaining her promise that she would tell no one who she was or why she was there. He told her no more of his plans for her, preferring to observe her behavior for a time before saying anything he might later find it necessary to retract.

He also passed the word among the men to say nothing of Wren's history; should anyone inquire, they were merely to say that she was Lord Obsidian's business and not theirs.

On the second night of their stay a ball was held in their honor, despite the local disappointment that they had not come to establish the town's defenses against dragons. This seemed amazingly short notice to Arlian, but he was happy to attend; he had been to few social functions of any sort in recent years.

He observed that the fashion for wearing masks that had taken hold throughout much of the Lands of Man was still considered too extreme for ordinary pursuits in Ethinior, but entirely appropriate for a celebration of this sort—at least half the two dozen natives attending the dance covered their faces in one manner or another. While his own men had no masks, a few improvised with handkerchiefs or watchcaps.

At one point he found himself dancing with Wren, who took the opportunity to ask, "Why have you freed me? Aren't you worried I might flee, and return to Lord Shatter?"

"I am relying on your common sense to prevent that," he replied.

She stared up at him for a moment as they progressed through the figure of the dance, then said, "Thank you."

As they were about to part, she whispered, "Don't trust Lord Rolinor."

He stared after her as she danced away, but then a local noblewoman was demanding his attention for the next figure, and he let the matter drop.

Late in the afternoon of the third day, as Arlian and Black took inventory of their supplies in preparation for continuing to Manfort, Lord Monifin approached. He wore the city's seal on a chain around his neck to indicate that he was there on official business, rather than merely making conversation.

"Your pardon, my lord," Monifin elder said, bowing, "but it would appear you are preparing to depart."

"Indeed, I hope to leave at daybreak tomorrow," Arlian replied.

The mayor bowed again. "Can we not persuade you to stay? Our people are so honored by your presence . . ."

Arlian and Black exchanged glances.

"Is it still the dragons you fear, or the Dragon Society?" Arlian asked.

The man hesitated, and Arlian thought he could see a faint flush on his face. "Both, my lord. Even if there is no pattern of revenge or retaliation, certainly both have attacked undefended towns."

"True enough. Still, a few dozen soldiers, even soldiers as valiant and experienced as the men I have the honor to command, would probably be of little use against a waking, airborne dragon. We kill them in their lairs while they sleep because it is only there and under those conditions that we can be assured of any success. In the open air, fighting an alert and angry enemy, even with our spears we would be hard-pressed to survive, let alone triumph. And despite all this, my lord, I doubt the dragons would attack a town as large as this—they would be wary of traps and treachery, and of the sheer number of foes."

"Lord Obsidian, last summer Sellas-at-the-Falls was burned to the ground. Ethinior is not much larger than Sellas was."

"Ethinior is built mostly of stone, where Sellas was largely of that fine dark wood that burns so well when struck by flaming venom. No, I don't think this is an ideal target for the dragons—but I have been wrong before, and that's with no mention of the Dragon Society." He glanced at Black. "We must return to Manfort, my steward and I, but I will see if any of my men would like to stay here, to show you how to build defenses and to train your own men to fight. We have none of the materials to build catapults, neither the old wooden ones nor the fireproof iron kind we now prefer, nor do we have experts in their construction and use, but we will leave at least a few of our obsidian blades, so you will have something that can pierce a dragon's hide."

"*Thank* you, my lord." Monifin bowed yet again, then retreated.

Arlian watched him go, then turned to Black. "What do you think?"

"I think you have made an excellent decision," Black said. "If the people of Ethinior feel they have your support, they won't be tempted to turn their coats should Lord Hardior or one of the others come riding up with an ultimatum. We certainly won't need the men or obsidian in Manfort."

"You think some will volunteer, then?"

"Oh, certainly! They're heroes here, and it's a long, boring journey to Manfort. I wouldn't be surprised if they *all* volunteer."

"That might be awkward," Arlian said with a smile.

"On the contrary. We can travel faster alone, and fortifying Ethinior is a worthwhile task to occupy the men for the summer. I would think the Duke will commend your enterprise and efficiency if you leave the entire company here. And you can retrieve them in the fall, before proceeding up into the mountains."

Arlian nodded thoughtfully.

"They can build the catapults," he said. "They have wood and iron and rope here. The obsidian spearheads, though . . ."

"Perhaps you should send a messenger to the Smoking Mountain, to direct a shipment this way."

"A fine suggestion." He glanced at the bundles of supplies that he and Black had been tallying, and said, "I'll speak to Quickhand; you find Stabber. We'll pass the word that we're looking for volunteers to stay in Ethinior for the summer."

6

A Wearisome Journey

*T*he confusion of asking each soldier whether he preferred to stay or go, allowing them time to confer with their comrades, and making sure of their answers delayed Arlian's departure another full day—and in the end, almost all of them volunteered to stay, at least for a time. Several had hesitated, or initially chosen to go, but had in the end been swayed by the majority. Even the sorcerers, to Arlian's surprise, chose to remain in Ethinior—as much to avoid the strain of travel as for any other reason, as all three were elderly.

Of course, knowing that their campaigns would be long and dangerous, Arlian had deliberately recruited soldiers with few ties—not a one had a wife or children awaiting him in Manfort.

Not all would stay the summer, even so; the company was divided into two groups, one that would remain indefinitely, under Stabber's command, and the other, under Quickhand, that would linger until warmer weather, to aid in preparing Ethinior's defenses, before returning to Manfort. All the men seemed content to join one party or the other; even those with kin in the Duke's city were in no great rush.

The one exception was Lord Rolinor, who chose to continue directly to Manfort.

"I am not sure I would *allow* him to stay, had he asked," Arlian remarked to Black as they sat in his room in the mayor's house on their fourth and final night in Ethinior, reviewing their preparations. "I don't want him conspiring with Wren, or looking for a source of venom."

"I don't think you ever needed to worry about him staying here," Black replied. "He can get a hero's welcome anywhere, with his title and his looks, and he's eager to get back to the Citadel, where he can fawn on His Grace some more."

Arlian grimaced. He let the matter lie, and set about hiring a messenger to carry instructions to the Smoking Mountain.

That done, he then spoke to the Lord Mayor.

"My lord," he said, "we have with us a woman named Wren whose home was destroyed by the dragons; I would esteem it a personal favor if a home could be found for her here in Ethinior."

"Of course," Monifin said.

And Wren's future was decided.

It still remained to inform Wren of this; he found her chattering happily with some of the women she had met at the ball, and drew her aside, where he explained that he was freeing her, and leaving her in Ethinior.

For a moment she was silent. Then she asked, "Did you tell them I was a spy?"

"I saw no point in doing so," he replied. "I would rather have you made welcome here, so that you face no temptation to aid Lord Shatter further. I suppose most of my own men know, but I have asked them not to mention it to the townsfolk."

"I suppose your men will be watching me, to make sure I behave."

"I suppose they will. Is that so great a burden?"

"No." She reached up with both hands, catching him by surprise, and pulled his face down to her own, kissing him on the cheek. "Again, my lord, I thank you."

Then she released him, and they parted.

The following morning three men and a single wagon

continued down the trade road toward Westguard. Rolinor had previously ridden with the lieutenants, but Arlian had appointed Quickhand and Stabber to the command of Ethinior's temporary garrison, so Rolinor's belongings had been transferred to Arlian's wagon.

They rolled out of Ethinior's town square to the sound of cheering and shouted farewells, but by the time they passed the ancient guard tower that marked the town's nominal boundary the only sounds they heard were made by the wagon, the horses, and the wind. The chill air carried a dampness that soaked through their cloaks and devoured the lingering warmth of the mayor's hearthfire, and for a long time they huddled in cold silence as they rode.

At last, though, as Black drove and the others rode in the open area behind the driver's bench, Rolinor leaned over the side and stared back at the fog-softened outline of Ethinior vanishing behind them, then sat up and said, "So, my lord Obsidian, I understand your ancestors hail from Blackwater?"

Arlian blinked in surprise, and turned to look at the younger man.

"No," he said. "My family lived on the Smoking Mountain, where the obsidian workshops now stand."

"But there have never been any prominent families from the Smoking Mountain! I had heard you claimed to be from there, but I assumed it was merely a pretext to justify your nickname."

Arlian turned away again. "No. My family was not prominent. I was born in Obsidian, on the Smoking Mountain, and took my name from my origin."

"And you have no ancestors among the nobility of Blackwater?"

"None."

"Then perhaps your fathers served the Dukes of Manfort in some noteworthy capacity?"

Arlian was becoming annoyed at Rolinor's determination

to find some trace of noble blood in him, though he supposed it was intended as a compliment. "No. My fathers never set foot in Manfort."

"But you owned the Old Palace."

"I bought it from the Duke."

"And you own the Grey House."

"Lord Enziet bequeathed it to me in a momentary fit of perversity."

"Surely, it was more than that! He must have recognized some spark in you."

"He recognized that I was as stubborn and as damned as he was himself." He did not mention that he thought Enziet had intended the inheritance more as a burden than a reward; he doubted Rolinor would believe it.

"But you were a great lord before Enziet died, were you not?"

"I was wealthy, certainly."

"From your family's holdings?"

"From trading with Arithei."

"But you must have started with something . . ."

"I stole a keg of gold from a man named Kuruvan."

"Stole?" Rolinor appeared shaken.

"Of course. His favorite whore told me where to find it; she was one of the ones who taught me my courtly manners. I was an escaped slave, and the women of a brothel took me in." He glanced at Rolinor. "Had you never heard this tale? I thought it common gossip."

"I . . . There are many rumors, my lord. Most of them are lies."

"Never be too quick to dismiss the unlikely as lies. Fate plays strange tricks, and a good many unlikely things are absolutely true."

"Then . . . is it true that you have sworn to exterminate the dragons?"

"Yes."

"But if your family had no estates—why?"

Arlian blinked. "What?"

"I had heard that the dragons had laid waste your family's estate, and that you had taken the last of the ancestral money and parleyed it into a vast fortune so that you might avenge this loss. But if there *were* no estates . . ."

"True, the dragons killed my family—and that was quite enough to earn my hatred. Our 'estate' was a modest house in a mountain village, where I hid in the cellars while the dragons burned the town and its inhabitants to ash. The looters who combed through the ruins sold me into slavery; I escaped, and sought revenge."

"And swore to kill *all* the dragons?"

"Yes."

"But they didn't all attack your village."

"Three of them did. The others have slain innocents enough elsewhere."

"But how do you know that?"

"What?"

"Well, dragons are surely not all exactly the same—how do you know that all of them are killers? Perhaps a few evil individuals are responsible for all the attacks."

"No. They are all monsters."

"But how can you be sure of that? They are born of men's hearts, and men's hearts are not all of one sort."

Arlian sighed. "Men are not dragons," he said.

"Yet surely, you do not argue that all dragons behave identically!"

"No. There is variation among dragons, as among men—though not, I would say, as *much* variation."

"Perhaps—or perhaps they are just as individual as we, with a wide range of personalities. Perhaps there are dragons lurking in the earth beneath us who are as beneficent and kind as anyone could ask."

"It seems rather unlikely."

"But what if there are? Have you not sworn to exterminate the entire species?"

"I did," Arlian agreed.

"And for fourteen years, you have been hunting down

dragons and killing them, regardless of whether you knew them to be ruthless murderers or not."

"Ah, but there you err," Arlian said. He pointed to a small locked chest in the body of the wagon. "You forget that the only means we have of locating dragons in their lairs is by following the descriptions and hints in the old records that Lord Wither and the Dragon Society compiled. For more than six hundred years the Society noted every report, every sighting, and Lord Wither collected and organized and preserved those notes. It is those records we use to find their caverns—and for *every one* of those sightings and reports, the dragons that were seen attacked some human community and slaughtered dozens or hundreds of innocents. Any dragon we *find* is a killer, beyond question. If there are draconic innocents, we have no way of knowing it, and no way of finding them. And frankly, my lord, I doubt any exist. I think it is inherent in the very nature of dragons to amuse themselves every so often by killing people; certainly they have done so for each of the past fourteen summers, and hundreds of men, women, and children have died as a result."

"You declared war on them! You have been butchering their fellows as they sleep! How could they not fight back?"

"But they do not attack Manfort, or the towns I have fortified; they invariably choose undefended villages, where they can slaughter freely. They do not kill for any strategic or tactical purpose, but only because they delight in inflicting suffering and death."

"Or perhaps merely because they are hungry, my lord?"

Arlian shook his head. "They do not eat human flesh, my lord."

That startled Rolinor. "Do they not?"

"No. They do not. The occasional reports of half-eaten bodies are the result of corpses partially dissolved by venom. Dragons are creatures of pure magic, and require no material sustenance. They kill because they choose to kill, because they take pleasure in it."

"Perhaps they can be convinced not to, then!"

"Lord Enziet thought so. For centuries he bound them to a bargain, and their end of it required them not to harm humans—yet still, every few years, every decade or two, a village would be destroyed. They simply could not resist the temptation. This, to me, is an evil worthy of obliteration."

"If *all* of them do this, perhaps."

"All we have ever seen have done it."

"But perhaps there are some we have never seen, lurking deep in the earth, who do *not* yield to this temptation!"

"And if there are, we shall never find them, and therefore shall never harm them."

"Yet you still will not allow men to become dragonhearts."

"Ah! I was beginning to wonder why you chose to defend our ancient foes. You like the thought of a thousand years of life, and then giving birth to a benign creature, rather than an abomination, upon your death."

"Well—yes."

Arlian shook his head. "I do not believe in your benign dragons. All I have ever seen of them has been destruction, pain, and evil. I believe it to be their very nature."

"I am not entirely convinced, my lord."

"That does not particularly concern me."

"The dragons drove the old wild magic, the wizards and demons and monsters, from the Lands of Man—surely that was a beneficent act!"

"First, if that did in fact occur, it was thousands upon thousands of years ago, and anything we know of it is probably so garbled as to bear little resemblance to the truth. I would note that you attribute this to the dragons, as I suppose your parents taught you, while *I* was taught that it was the gods who drove out chaos before they died. Second, I would suppose the dragons did so, if they did, to remove any challenges to their own rule, and not out of any sort of altruism."

"Nonetheless, it was a benefit to humanity."

"If it happened, yes, it unquestionably was—the lands beyond the border are hellish chaos, and we are all blessed to be natives of the Lands of Man, rather than slaves in Tirikindaro or clansmen cowering behind iron and silver wards in Arithei. Even so, I hardly think that balances out the dragons' evil."

Rolinor had no immediate answer to that, and Arlian took the opportunity to move to the driver's bench, beside Black, and inquire about the road and the weather. That bench only seated two, leaving Rolinor to his own devices.

They camped by the roadside that night, and Rolinor wearied Arlian with further explication of how the dragons might actually be a benefit to humanity, and suggestions of how the Duke might choose his court more wisely by paying more attention to ancestry and less to charming words. Arlian, pleading fatigue, retired early.

The next day was no better, but there was no escape in the cramped space of the single wagon. Thrust irrevocably together as they were, Arlian quickly grew inexpressibly tired of Rolinor's company; by the third day of the journey he fervently wished they had brought a second wagon so that he could avoid conversation. By the time they reached Westguard, almost a month later, spring had washed away the snow and Arlian's boredom had washed away all interest in keeping an eye on the younger man, or worrying about any further attempts Rolinor might make to obtain dragon venom.

He tried to convince himself that since Rolinor had behaved himself on the journey and showed no untoward interest in dragon venom, he had demonstrated that he could be trusted to continue unsupervised. The truth was that Arlian was thoroughly sick of Rolinor's arrogance, his wishful theorizing about the nature of dragons, and his obsession with the minutiae of genealogy and court intrigue; he wanted to be rid of the youth.

Accordingly, as they rode through a cold drizzle past the ranked wooden catapults into Westguard, he said, "I want to stop in at an inn I own, my lord, and inspect the books, and I'm sure you would prefer not to delay; why don't you go on ahead to Manfort, and let His Grace know we're on our way, and that we left the others in Ethinior? Although we have no horse for you, the walk is easy enough, and the rain has melted the snow and ice from the road."

"I would be delighted to oblige you, my lord," Rolinor replied, with a bow; he appeared genuinely pleased, and Arlian wondered whether the youth was as weary of Arlian as Arlian was of him.

When Black brought the wagon to a stop Rolinor was in the back, collecting his belongings; a moment later Arlian helped him climb down and settle his packs in place. Then, with a final wave, the young nobleman marched off to the east, heedless of the thin rain.

Arlian watched him go, then muttered to Black, "I have rarely been so glad to see someone's back receding."

"While I would not ordinarily seek out his company, it would seem I find him less aggravating than do you," Black remarked, as the two men walked, hunched against the cold and damp, toward the now-badly-misnamed New Inn. Arlian had bought a new plume for his hat in Ethinior, but he had removed the feather before debarking and left it in the wagon rather than let the foul weather ruin it; with that gone, and his cloak pulled tightly about him, he was, like his companion, wrapped in black from head to toe.

"When he is not trying to convince me to spare a few dragons, he talks of little but the foolish power games in Manfort!" Arlian protested. "I can think of nothing more wearisome."

"Ah, he is obsessed," Black said, "just as you are. And the conflict lies in the simple fact that you are obsessed with different things."

"And if this is true, and an unshared obsession is as wearisome for you as for me, then how can you tolerate either of us?"

"Oh, easily—I am not obsessed, but I take an interest in both his obsession and your own. More importantly, though, I simply do not listen much of the time. I have learned to give the appearance of polite attention while in truth I'm remembering what I had for supper the night before, or what Brook told me on our wedding night, or some other unrelated matter."

"You *always* listen," Arlian said. "You remember every word spoken within a hundred yards of your ears, I swear it!"

"I *hear* every word, and I remember those I think might prove important, but I do not *listen*. It's a useful technique."

"You must teach it to me someday."

"Perhaps I will, when you are sufficiently free of your own obsessions to learn it."

And then they were at the door of the inn; Black swung open the unlocked door, and as Arlian stepped in his attention focused on business, and on getting warm and dry for a time.

7

A Debatable Homecoming

*T*hey reached Manfort late the following morning, passing unnoticed through the city gates; Arlian observed that the iron-framed catapults on the city ramparts appeared fully crewed, and were loaded with obsidian-tipped missiles, despite the lingering chill in the air.

The wagon rolled up the stone-paved, rain-drenched streets to the Upper City, where the city's nobility had built their mansions and palaces. The sun was peeking through thinning clouds, almost directly overhead, when Black and Arlian pulled up at the entrance to the Grey House.

Most of the homes of the lords and ladies of Manfort were grand edifices of wood and stone and glass and plaster, with broad windows and tidy lawns; the Grey House, however, had been built eight centuries ago, in the days of the Man-Dragon Wars, and resembled a fortress more than a palace. Its windows were few and narrow, its yards and courts entirely paved with gray stone; its every exposed surface was smoke-blackened stone or dark, heavy tile. Wood and thatch and greenery could burn when dragonfire splashed across the city, so the Grey House had none visible; even the exterior doors were sheathed in metal.

Arlian would not have chosen so forbidding an edifice as his home, but he had inherited this one from the late Lord Enziet—his sworn enemy who had nonetheless left Arlian all his worldly possessions, apparently in the belief that his foe could make better use of them than any of his surviving allies.

When he had first come to Manfort in his guise as the wealthy Lord Obsidian, Arlian had made a point of buying the most ostentatious housing available; he had lived for some time in the Old Palace, a former home of the Dukes of Manfort—but the Old Palace had been destroyed by fire, and Arlian had been left with the Grey House as his only residence in the city. He spent so little time in Manfort that he saw no point in replacing it with a more pleasant abode.

Arlian swung himself down from the wagon on one side while Black dismounted from the other; together they marched up to the door, but then Arlian had to stand and wait while Black found the right key and unlocked the forbidding iron gate.

Arlian looked around, puzzled.

"I thought there would be a guardsman here," he said.

The lock clicked, and Black looked up. "Why?" he asked.

"To let the Duke know we've arrived. Rolinor must have told him we were coming; I had half expected to find an escort waiting for us at the city gate, to fetch us to the Citadel."

Black held the gate open as Arlian stepped through. "Why would the Duke be in such a hurry as that?"

"I would think he would be eager for the latest news of our campaign."

"He has undoubtedly *heard* the latest news of our campaign," Black pointed out. "Rolinor has an active tongue."

"A good point," Arlian conceded. "Still, I am the Duke's warlord, and I would have thought that my arrival would command a certain level of ceremony."

"And I expect you'll have it—just not immediately."

They had reached the door of the house itself, and Black had found the appropriate key, but before he could apply it to the lock the door swung inward.

A thin, white-haired figure in Obsidian's black-and-white livery stood there, bowing deeply. "Welcome home, my lord," he said.

"Thank you, Ferrezin," Arlian replied, removing his hat. "It's good to be here."

Ferrezin started, then blinked. "Ah, Lord Obsidian," he said. "Do you know, for a moment I took you for Lord Enziet?"

Arlian froze in midstride and stared at the old man.

"Enziet's dead," he said at last. "Dead these what, sixteen years? Seventeen?"

"Of course, my lord, of course. I know that. But I served him twenty years as his steward, and lived forty years before that as his slave, like my mother before me, and in all those sixty years Lord Enziet never aged a day, and I did not see him die, nor did I see his body. I know in my mind that he died long ago in a cave beneath the Desolation, as you and Black and Lord Enziet's own sorcery told me as much, but my *heart* is not yet convinced, and I often find myself expecting to see him around the next corner, or stepping through the gate."

"He's dead," Arlian said sharply.

Ferrezin bowed again, but said no more. Arlian looked at the chamberlain, at his snow-white hair and bony face, and wondered whether it might be past time to retire him, give him a pension and find him somewhere quiet to live, some family to care for him. By Ferrezin's own reckoning, as just stated, he had lived over three-quarters of a century, without benefit of sorcery or dragon venom; he could scarcely be expected to simply labor on until he fell dead in his tracks.

Arlian wondered why the old fool's fancy had bothered him so much. He and Enziet were both tall, dark-haired, well-built men, scarred on the right cheek, and both habitually wore black—mistaking one for the other was not really so unreasonable.

But Enziet had trimmed his garb in gold, while Arlian used white; Enziet's face had been beardless and badly marred, while Arlian's scar was a single streak of red and he wore a neatly trimmed beard. Anyone with a working eye could surely see as much at a glance. Even with the white plume removed from his hat, the difference was obvious.

Perhaps Ferrezin's eyesight was failing. Yes, definitely time to consider a pension.

"Is my wife at home?" Black asked, interrupting Arlian's thoughts—and reminding him of yet another obvious difference between Enziet and himself; Enziet had had no companion who resembled Black in the slightest.

"I believe so, sir," Ferrezin replied, taking Arlian's cloak. "Shall I have the wagon emptied?"

"Please do," Arlian said. "We will be staying for some time, I hope."

Ferrezin bowed, and turned down a stone passage that led from the entryway to the kitchens, hurrying as best he could to find a footman or two. He carried Arlian's cloak draped across one arm; he had apparently forgotten its presence, as he had passed the entrance to the cloakroom without pausing.

The man was overdue for retirement; Arlian had no doubt of that now. Ferrezin's momentary confusion of masters had been just one more sign of encroaching age.

It was just as well Arlian had returned now, and not left the matter any longer. Four or five years was clearly too long an absence.

When Ferrezin was out of sight, Black and Arlian pro-

ceeded on into the parlor. There Arlian stopped, to look
about and reacquaint himself with his surroundings; after
his long absence the room was not as familiar as he might
have liked. Someone had made changes while he was away;
the cabinet by the door was gone, the draperies had been replaced, and he did not recognize a gilt-trimmed chair that
now stood in one corner.

Well, it had been years, and the house had not been
empty.

Behind him he heard Ferrezin calling orders, and booted
feet running. A door slammed somewhere.

"Brook!" Black called, striding on into the gallery. "I'm
home!"

Arlian wished he were so confident; this was nominally
his home, yes, and certainly he owned it, but he had spent
so little time actually living in this house, and it had been so
long ago . . .

He sank slowly onto a brown velvet settee, and dropped
his hat—which Ferrezin should have taken, along with his
cloak, but had not—onto a nearby table.

The Grey House, home to Lord Enziet for several centuries—could this ever truly be *Arlian's* home? This was the
house where Dove was murdered, where Sweet was tortured and fatally poisoned, where Enziet had conferred with
the dragons and experimented endlessly in sorcery in his attempts to secure true immortality for himself. Arlian had
acquired it as part of Enziet's legacy, and for fourteen years
he had lived in it when he was in Manfort—but he had been
in Manfort so rarely!

The Old Palace, where he had dwelt when he first came
to Manfort, had been his home in a way the Grey House
was not—but the Old Palace was gone, set ablaze by dragonfire and burned to the ground.

The stony walls and vaulted ceilings of the Grey House
could never burn; if the dragons sought to destroy this
place, they would have to smash it with brute force, not
merely spray it with flame. As long as he fought the drag-

ons, the Grey House befitted him—cold and hard, resistant to the monsters' threats—but he was not sure it was truly *home*.

And when the day came that the last dragon was dead, the last dragonheart dead or cleansed, what then? Would he stay in this fortress when there was no longer a foe to defend against?

He grimaced to himself. That assumed that he would live to see such a day, which was hardly a sure thing. Forty-six dragons still lived, and twenty-six dragonhearts older than himself—but he had come so far, so fast! The possibility that he would survive to see his campaign's end was quite real.

And if he did, he would not stay in this house. He would find another, a place less drenched in blood and sorrow and sorcery, less fraught with memories and meaning . . .

Or he would die. Suicide would be the simplest way to ensure that no dragon ever burst from his bosom. Having his heart ripped out, cleansed of its hideous taint, and then restored to his body hardly seemed worth the trouble; what would he have to live for, with his enemies gone? What future could he expect that would justify such pain?

And what need would he have for another home, in that case? No, the Grey House would serve him well enough.

He heard voices, and the sound of doors and footsteps and luggage bumping walls. His servants were attending to their duties.

He was shirking his, merely by being here—he should be in the northwestern mountains, hunting for that next lair, or he should be at the Citadel, reporting to the Duke. Coming here was self-indulgence, yielding to his doubts and fatigue.

Nonetheless, he told himself, he was here now; it was far too late to reach another of the dragons' hiding places before spring arrived and the monsters woke, and the Duke had not requested his presence. He might as well indulge himself.

He rose from the settee, glanced at his hat, then left it on the table as he followed Black deeper into the house.

8

Lord Obsidian's Guests

*B*lack had found his wife at the north end of the long gallery, and had scooped her up out of her wheeled chair; Arlian did not care to intrude on their reunion, nor to get in the way of the footmen hauling his belongings from the wagon to his second-floor apartment, so he took the stairs up to the third floor.

This had once been Lord Enziet's private domain, where even his own servants did not often venture; this had been where he imprisoned and tortured slaves for his own bitter amusement, and occasionally killed them. This had been, as well, where he practiced his sorcery, where he sought to stave off the inevitable birth of the dragon growing within him.

That was all gone. This was now the preserve of the Aritheian magicians Arlian had employed, the physicians who knew how to remove the draconic taint from anyone who had drunk the elixir of blood and venom. What Enziet had struggled so long and futilely to achieve, Arlian's hired magicians had mastered.

As Arlian strolled down the passageway a door opened, and a woman stepped out, closing the door behind her. She turned, and saw Arlian approaching.

"Lord Obsidian!" she said, smiling.

Arlian smiled back. "Isein."

She curtsied. Arlian bowed in return, and looked at her more closely.

Isein of Arithei, it appeared, had finally fully adopted the styles of the aristocracy of Manfort; she wore a bottle-green velvet vest laced tight over a white linen blouse, and a full green skirt flared from her waist to the floor. Her hair was done up in an elaborate construction of curls and feathers—or at any rate it had been; bits were beginning to come down now, trailing over her lace collar. Because her skin, even after so long in the north, was still darker than that of any native-born lady of Manfort, the effect was oddly exotic.

When she had first come to Manfort, Isein had continued to wear the short, loose, brightly colored robes of her homeland—until her first experience of a real winter, when she had come to see the utility of keeping her arms and legs covered. For years, though, she had preferred her garments looser than custom required, and had always worn her hair in the simple Aritheian style.

It seemed she had reconsidered.

"I was very sorry to hear of Oeshir's death," he said. "You have my deepest sympathies, and my sincerest apologies for missing the funeral. Her accomplishments brought great honor to the House of Deri, and were of great service to me and my people. I regret my failure to acknowledge that at her passing."

"Thank you, my lord. Death comes to everyone, in time, and she had lived long and well."

"Are her students still here, and well?"

"Lilsinir lives here, my lord, but Asaf and Tiviesh have made their homes at the Citadel, with Hlur, that they might be more convenient to His Grace."

"Very sensible." Arlian was relieved that all three students were still in Manfort; they were the only three magicians in the Lands of Man capable of performing the elaborate cleansing spell that would restore a dragonheart to mere mortality, and he preferred to know they were safe and near at hand. "And Qulu?"

"We expect his return from Arithei any day."

"Another buying expedition?"

"Yes, my lord."

"You did not accompany him?"

"No, my lord; I stayed to oversee matters here. We thought it unwise to risk both of us, in light of the rumors of unrest in the Borderlands."

Arlian gave her a sharp look. "I had not heard any rumors of unrest."

Isein appeared startled. "Had you not, my lord? We have been hearing for two or three years now of disturbances along the border. Wizards and other magical creatures have been harassing travelers; what's more, the master of Tirikindaro is said to be extending its reach into the Borderlands, and there are tales of hauntings and strange dreams as far north as Sweetwater."

"I had not heard. Is the road to Arithei still . . ." He stopped himself before he completed the sentence; the question was absurd, since the road to Arithei had *never* been safe.

"It's hard to say, my lord," Isein answered the unfinished question. "It is certainly no better, from the latest reports, but whether it's any worse I do not know."

Arlian nodded, and tried to maintain a façade of polite sociability, but the Aritheian's news had disturbed him. Rumors of foreign magic as far north as Sweetwater? That town was at the edge of the Desolation, deep inside the Lands of Man!

He hoped Qulu had taken no needless risks, and was safely on the road to Manfort. Of the magicians he had hired long ago in Arithei, Qulu and Isein were the last who were still in his employ; he had brought them here to sell Aritheian spells and talismans to the nobility of Manfort, and had made himself stupendously wealthy thereby.

He no longer needed that wealth, though; he had inherited Lord Enziet's extensive possessions and enterprises, and had his post as warlord, as well. The magic business had become largely irrelevant—at least, to him; it was still how Isein and Qulu earned their keep.

He realized that he should have made clear to them that

they were welcome to remain indefinitely as his guests, and need not maintain the flow of goods from the south. He owed them a debt for past services that would more than cover any living expenses they might incur.

When Qulu returned—if he did return safely—Arlian was determined to offer him and Isein an honorable retirement, as he would Ferrezin. If they chose to continue, he wanted it clear that they did so of their own choosing, and not his.

"What has the Duke said about these rumors?" Arlian asked. "After all, the safety of the roads within the Lands of Man is his responsibility."

"I do not know, my lord," Isein replied. "I am not in His Grace's confidence."

"No, I suppose not—but you said that Asaf and Tiviesh are now residents of the Citadel; surely, some word must trickle out."

"Not that I am aware of, my lord. Although if you wish, I might inquire when next I see them."

"I would appreciate it," Arlian said. "It not only affects my business interests, but might well bear some relation to the war against the dragons."

"There have been no reports of *dragons* in the Border-lands, my lord."

"No, I hadn't thought there were. Still, who knows what might have some connections to the dragons' schemes?"

Isein looked very doubtful of this suggestion.

"Well, I'm sure you must have other matters to attend to," Arlian said. "I did not wish to keep you from them."

Isein curtsied. "You are my host and my employer, my lord; whatever pleases you I am happy to provide. That said, yes, I have business that demands my attention."

"Then go to it, by all means, and thank you for your time." He stepped aside to let her pass.

"You are most welcome, my lord," she said as she walked by him; then she turned and added over her shoulder, "And it is a great pleasure to see you home once more."

Arlian smiled, and watched her go.

He would need to do whatever he could to make himself current on the gossip and rumors of Manfort, that was obvious. Stammer, the chief of his kitchen staff, would undoubtedly be a rich source for that; she had always maintained an elaborate network of friends and acquaintances with good ears and wagging tongues.

And these tales from the Borderlands—*could* they be connected with his campaign against the dragons? Had the Dragon Society perhaps begun stirring up foreign magicians to distract the Duke's attention? Or might this be part of some new scheme to halt Arlian?

He glanced at a nearby door, and stepped through it into an unused bedroom, where two broad casements gave a view of the courtyard at the center of the Grey House.

He looked out at the balconies, then down at the courtyard pavement and the gentle fountain at its center, then up at the sloping tile roof.

Eight oak-framed catapults were mounted on that roof, two to a side, each one loaded with four obsidian-tipped spears ready to be flung at any dragons that might come to put an end to their bitterest foe, or to threaten his establishment. From the bedroom Arlian could see the two machines on the far side of the courtyard, and one on the roof to his right; the angle was such that the others were invisible from his present position, but he assumed they were all still there, armed and ready.

Stone walls and obsidian blades guarded him, but might the dragons be attempting something subtler, something these defenses could not stop?

Well, if they were, he carried steel and silver and amethyst, as well. Long ago, an Aritheian mage had told him that creatures of darkness feared silver, creatures of air could not pass cold iron, and the creatures of dream could not approach amethyst; his studies in sorcery since then had confirmed the virtues of silver and steel, though no one in the Lands of Man had known of amethyst's value. He knew how to place sorcerous wards that would warn him of an enemy's approach, and thus he was guarded against magic, as well as against men and dragons.

But there were a thousand other ways to strike at him, and he knew it. He had faced more than a score of assassins over the years without even counting the ones as ineffectual as Wren, and he had survived a dozen other challenges of one sort or another, but he knew he was not safe, was never safe.

When he had slain all the dragons and dealt with the dragonhearts, that did not mean the Lands of Man would be safe. There were always other menaces. Perhaps the problems in the Borderlands were something new that had no connection with the dragons or himself.

Well, he would not learn any more standing here looking out the window; he turned, then marched back along the corridor and down the stairs.

On the ground floor he found Black and Brook in the little gallery, talking quietly; Brook was back in the wheeled chair Black had built for her. She looked up at the sound of his approach, and Black turned.

Arlian bowed to Brook. " 'Tis as always a delight to see you, mistress," he said.

"The pleasure is mine, my lord," Brook said; she made no pretense of bow or curtsy. Her feet had been amputated long ago, when she was a slave, to prevent any attempt at running away—and to add a certain exoticism to her services in the brothel that had owned her. She was free now, but she would never be free of her mutilation; even the most learned of Aritheian magicians had denied knowledge of any method that might make her whole or allow her to walk again. Inspired by the wheeled carriages of Arlian's first catapults, Black had devised and built her chair and given her some mobility, but she could still not manage the ceremonial expectations of polite society, and saw no reason to attempt an approximation.

"Where are your daughters?" Arlian asked. "I had thought

they would be eager to see their father, and I would like to see how they have grown in my long absence." His specification of daughters, rather than children, was an attempt at tact on his part; Brook had delivered two stillborn sons since her second child's birth, as well as suffering a few miscarriages over the years. "Kerzia is now . . . thirteen, is it?"

"Her fourteenth birthday was a few days ago, my lord," Brook said. "She and her sister have gone up to the Old Palace—they have friends among the children there."

"Do they?" Arlian shot Black a questioning glance; the steward shrugged in reply. "Perhaps we should go see if we can find them; I would not mind visiting the old grounds myself."

"I had intended to do exactly that, Ari," Black said.

"Then let us be off! And worry not, my dear Brook; I assure you I will bring both husband and offspring back to you in short order, and will not undertake any new ventures, nor allow any distractions, until our return."

Brook just nodded at that.

A moment later the two men were walking up the street toward the site of the Old Palace, on pavement that was drying rapidly in the sunlight that fought through the scattering clouds.

The Palace itself was gone, of course, burned fourteen years earlier, but Arlian still owned the land. He had neither the time nor the inclination to rebuild; instead, when people fleeing villages destroyed by the dragons or the battles between the Duke's men and the Dragon Society began to pour into Manfort, Arlian had announced that he would allow these refugees to camp on the grounds and in the ruins until more permanent homes could be found for them. Furthermore, he decreed that no slavers would be permitted on the grounds, so that the homeless and destitute need not fear capture there.

Most of the refugees did indeed find places after a few months, but some did not, and a steady trickle of new arrivals continued; the original tents and crude huts had gradually been replaced by more extensive structures, built from the ruins of the Old Palace.

These people were called "Lord Obsidian's guests"; the name had originally been applied derisively, but it had become the accepted term. After all, they *were* his guests, and Arlian welcomed them as such. If he had never disturbed the dragons, the refugees would not have come to Manfort; he felt that providing this temporary accommodation was the least he could do for them.

Arlian had made his hospitality dependent upon certain conditions, however; foremost among these was an insistence that a portion of the old garden, and the graves therein, remain undisturbed. So far that requirement had been met, but he still wanted to check while he was in town, and make certain that all was well. Finding Kerzia and Amberdine provided a perfect justification for undertaking this inspection immediately.

They rounded the corner and came in sight of the old gateposts. The gate itself was gone, but the gateposts and most of the wall still stood.

The soot had washed away after all these years of rain, but the stone gateposts were still lightly stained, streaked with dark gray where dragonfire had struck them.

Arlian took off his hat and paused to kneel by one post; this was where Lord Toribor had died, luring the dragon into position to be killed by the first of Arlian's catapults. For most of the time Arlian had known Toribor the two men were enemies; Arlian had sworn to kill the older dragonheart, and had twice faced him in duels. Nonetheless, when the dragon came, Toribor had worked closely with Arlian to defeat it.

"If your spirit lingers, Belly," Arlian murmured, "I want you to know that I have not forgotten—without your aid all would have been lost. I would be long dead, and eightysome dragons would still live. Thank you."

Then he got to his feet and brushed mud from his breeches before turning to look into the refugee camp.

The houses had improved since his last visit; in fact, some showed every sign of being permanent. The floor of his great mirrored gallery, where once the nobility of Manfort had danced, was now serving as a street, and the structures on either side, while eccentric, seemed quite substantial.

He would, he supposed, want to start collecting rents on them—these were no longer a refugee camp, but cottages. He would keep the rents minimal, but if he did not assert his claim to the land beneath he might eventually lose it.

No children were immediately in evidence; he marched across what had been his forecourt, past the spot where he had first slain an adult dragon and where its bones had long lain exposed, to the guardhouse that stood where his cloakroom once was.

"Ho!" he called.

A young guard in the Duke's livery appeared at the door, obsidian-tipped spear in hand. He peered at Arlian's face, clearly not recognizing it, and said, "This is private property, my lord."

Black snorted. "We're aware of that, boy," he said.

"Black?" The soldier started, then straightened.

"And this is Lord Obsidian, the *owner* of this private property," Black replied, gesturing at Arlian.

"Your pardon, my lord," the guard said, bowing.

Arlian acknowledged the bow with a nod of his head, but he studied the young man for a moment before he spoke. Greeting a wealthy stranger with a warning about trespassing seemed a peculiar thing to do, and Arlian tried to guess why the soldier had done it.

No obvious explanation occurred to him, and in the end he simply asked, "Might I inquire, sir, why you felt it necessary to assert that this is private property?"

The soldier flushed slightly. "Slavers, my lord. We have had some difficulties with the slavers. Refugees rarely have any money or family, after all, and sometimes the temptation is too great, despite your orders. Slavers slip in at night, when the guards are dozing, or climb over the wall in areas out of our sight."

"Surely, you did not mistake me for such a slaver."

"No, certainly not, but on occasion lords like yourself have come here to have a look at potential victims before sending in their hirelings."

"Not lords like myself," Arlian said. "I own no slaves, and have no truck with slavers."

"Of course not, my lord," the guard said, flushing more deeply and bowing again. "And you show your face—the slave takers are usually masked. But the brim of your hat hid your features at first, and . . ."

"No need to say more," Arlian interrupted. "I understand, and you acted rightly. Now that we have that out of the way, however, perhaps you could direct us to where we might find children at play? My steward's daughters are reported to be in this vicinity."

"Oh, back that way, in the gardens, my lord." He pointed. "I saw them come in this morning, and I believe they've been there ever since."

"Thank you." Arlian nodded, and led the way.

He did not speak as they walked through what had once been his home; he was deep in thought.

No one had ever mentioned slavers defying the ban to him before, and he wondered whether this was a recent development. He could have asked the guard—but he did not want to question the man as if he were judge and jury determining his fate; the young fellow was doing his job well enough, but seemed a trifle unsure of himself, and Arlian had no wish to add to that uncertainty.

Besides, he did not really want to speak of these matters aloud—or not yet, at any rate. He wanted to think.

He hated slavers and slavery. He had spent seven years as a mine slave, and slavery was what he loathed most in all the world after the dragons.

Perhaps, if by some miracle he were to succeed in exterminating the dragons and survive the experience, he would

then turn his attention to eliminating slavery entirely—
though that would be a far more difficult task, in truth.
Slavers were not venom-spitting monsters, easily recognizable by their size and scales, but instead hid in the skins of
men and women, pretending to humanity. Many people believed that slavery was a natural part of the world's order,
that some men and women were destined, by the weakness
of their minds and spirits, to serve the whims of others, and
that this was as it should be, that those weaklings would
otherwise starve in the streets at great detriment to public
sanitation. Lord Toribor had thought as much and considered slavery just, until Arlian had convinced him to listen to
the tales some slaves told of their lives. That had planted
seeds of doubt, but Belly had died before they grew into a
conviction that slavery was inherently wrong.

The dragons were, however magical they might be, tangible and finite; they could be destroyed, and the destruction
seen to be certain. Slavery was an idea, hidden and mutable,
something that might lurk in any soul, might spread from
one to another overnight, might lie dormant for years or decades only to spring forth anew.

Still, an idea could be countered, could be fought, and
Arlian could think of nothing better to do with his life
should he somehow survive the last dragon and the last
dragonheart.

That slavers were intruding on *his* land, preying on *his*
guests, in defiance of the law, was disturbing.

And they came wearing masks. That damnable fashion
had arisen years ago, and Arlian hated it. Its advocates excused it on several grounds, including history—supposedly
in the latter days of the *old* Man-Dragon Wars, those brave
men and women who resisted the dragons' rule and defied
the human servants who oversaw the dragons' empire had
sometimes gone masked so that their identities would not be
reported to the dragons, and their families would not be
harmed in retaliation. The present-day masks were alleged to

be worn in tribute to those heroes of old, as a reminder that humanity was once again openly at war with its ancient foe.

Those rebellious forefathers had also used false names to disguise their identities and protect their kin. *That* custom had survived all the intervening centuries, down to Beron being known to all and sundry as Black, and Arlian's own use of the name Obsidian, but the masks had been cast aside when the dragons retreated to their caves.

Now the masks were back—but Arlian suspected that this time they were not protecting the dragons' foes, but their allies. Someone who knew the signs could tell a dragonheart from an ordinary mortal merely by a good look at the eyes, the face, the movements—and masks hid the face and eyes, enabling dragonhearts, at least in theory, to move freely among the people of Manfort despite the Duke's edict requiring them to undergo the Aritheian cleansing. Magical disguises known as glamours could accomplish the same thing, but a simple mask was far cheaper, and much easier to maintain.

Unfortunately, Arlian had, so far, been unable to convince the arbiters of style of the significance of this point. New fads and fashions were notoriously difficult to discourage, and masks, with their air of intrigue and mystery, were simply so much *fun* for many people that Arlian's protests were as useless as steel against dragonhide.

The two men rounded the final hut, following the sounds of squealing, and found half a dozen girls chasing each other madly across an area of plowed ground that would probably be someone's vegetable patch in a few weeks.

"Kerzia!" Black bellowed, in a voice he usually reserved for issuing orders to armed men.

One of the taller girls stopped dead, and whirled on one foot; another smaller one stumbled, then also stopped and turned, somewhat less abruptly. Then the two of them shrieked in unison, "Daddy!" and began running toward Black.

Arlian watched silently as the pair jumped the low fence and sprang into their father's waiting arms. He stood, waiting, as they babbled cheerfully and Black listened intently.

The other girls paused long enough to acknowledge that their playmates were departing, then continued their game, whooping wildly as they charged around the old ash tree and headed for the gallery-floor street.

Kerzia, the older girl, finally calmed down enough to notice that her father had not come alone; she stepped back, out of Black's embrace, brushed her pinafore down into position, then essayed a quick curtsy.

Then she glanced at her father, clearly awaiting an introduction.

Black threw a smile over his shoulder at Arlian, then said, "My lord Obsidian, allow me to present my daughters. That young lady is Kerzia, my firstborn, and this squirming nuisance here is Amberdine."

"Daddy!" Amberdine protested, as Kerzia's eyes grew wide.

"Lord Obsidian," she said, curtsying again. "It is a great honor."

"It is a pleasure for me, mistress," Arlian said, with a bow. "We *have* met before, as you may recall."

"Oh, but it's been *years*!"

"Indeed it has. You were not much older then than your sister is now."

Amberdine had finally realized the situation and untangled herself to stand beside her sister. "Have *we* met, my lord?" she asked.

"We last spoke when you were not yet three years old, I believe," Arlian replied.

"I don't remember," Amberdine admitted.

Arlian smiled. "I would scarcely expect a person of your charms to remember every man who admired her."

Amberdine had no idea how to reply to that, and glanced at Kerzia, who giggled.

"Time to go home," Black said. "Your mother is waiting for all of us."

"Will you tell us all about slaying dragons?" Amberdine asked.

"*I* haven't been slaying dragons," Black said, "but Lord Obsidian has. Perhaps he can tell you about it."

"Perhaps I can," Arlian agreed. "If you would, mistress?" He held a hand out to Kerzia.

She accepted it, and together the two of them marched toward the gate, while Black and Amberdine walked at their heels.

9

Lady Rime at Home

*A*lthough his duty as warlord required Arlian to call upon the Duke at the first opportunity, Arlian had come to Manfort to rest, to restore himself, and to renew old acquaintances, as much as to report to his superior. At present he found himself not concerned as much with the next step in the campaign against the dragons as he was with what would become of him when the campaign had ended.

The remaining forty-six dragons, or whatever the actual number was, would undoubtedly take several years to find and slay, but there seemed little doubt that they would, in time, perish. The twenty-six lords and ladies of the Dragon Society would also in their turn die or be restored to normalcy.

And what would become of Arlian when that was accomplished? He would have served out the destiny Fate had apparently assigned him; was he to have any life beyond that?

This was not a question to discuss with the Duke of Manfort; instead, Arlian intended to visit Lady Rime, one of the handful of dragonhearts who had been cleansed by the Aritheian magicians and returned to mere humanity. She, more than anyone else in the world, could appreciate his situation, his uncertainty about his future.

He had thought that would need to wait until after he had conducted his official business with the Duke before calling on her; indeed, he had expected to find guardsmen at the Grey House, waiting to escort him to the Citadel, when he and Black arrived. After all, Lord Rolinor had undoubtedly returned to the Citadel and told the Duke that Lord Obsidian was on his way, unescorted by the soldiers he had left in Ethinior.

That no such guards had materialized led Arlian to suspect that the Duke, for one reason or another, was in no great hurry for this appointment. If the Duke saw no great urgency in it, then Arlian was not inclined to argue; he preferred to attend to more personal concerns.

Therefore, on the day after his arrival in the city, rather than going in person, Arlian dispatched a messenger to the Citadel to inform the Duke of his arrival and assure His Grace that Lord Obsidian awaited his pleasure.

That done, and immediate household matters having been dealt with, he strolled down the street to Lady Rime's estate, leaving Black to deal with any replies that might arrive.

Upon his arrival Arlian found that the interior of Lady Rime's mansion was not as he remembered it. When he had last visited, several years before, the halls and chambers had been lushly furnished, tidy and well kept, as quiet as a cellar, and inhabited only by Rime and half a dozen servants.

Now the servant who admitted him had something purple and sticky in his hair, and the minute Arlian set foot inside he heard children laughing. The coatrack by the door held a dozen garments in assorted small sizes, and the mirror beside it was freshly cracked.

Arlian looked about, startled, as he handed the footman his hat and coat.

Then the head of a girl, almost a young woman, a little older than Kerzia, appeared around a doorframe. "Hello," she said, smiling. "Are you here to see Grandmother Rime?" Then the smile vanished, and she stared at him. "I know you, don't I?"

Arlian bowed. "Lord Obsidian, here to see Lady Rime," he said. "And to whom do I have the pleasure of speaking?"

"Lord *Obsidian*? Uncle Triv?" Her eyes widened. "Is it really you?"

For a moment neither spoke, as Arlian realized that the girl's face was indeed familiar, and there was only one girl her age who would call him Triv. Still, it was the footman who, having disposed of Arlian's outer garments, broke the silence.

"My lord Obsidian," he said, "allow me to present Lady Rime's adopted granddaughter, Vanniari."

Vanniari stepped through the door and curtsied, and Arlian bowed again in acknowledgment.

"My lord Obsidian," Vanniari said. "It has been a long time."

"Five years, I believe," Arlian agreed. "Pardon me for not recognizing you at once, Vanniari, but you have grown wonderfully—and please, forgive my long absence, and do call me Ari."

"Of course, Uncle Triv," Vanniari said, grinning. "Call me Vanni."

Arlian smiled despite himself. No one had called him Triv since he had last seen Vanniari's mother, Hasty, almost five years before. He glanced at the footman. "Do you know, Vanni, I had forgotten you live here? When last I saw you you were still my guest at the Grey House."

"That was *years* ago!" She shuddered. "That gloomy

place. I didn't mind living there when I was little, but every time I go back to visit Kerzia and Amberdine, or Isein and Lilsinir, it seems darker and colder and nastier."

"It's not a good place," Arlian agreed. "I had intended to sell it when you were a baby . . ."

". . . but the dragon burned up your other house. I know, Uncle Triv."

"And since then I've simply been too busy," Arlian agreed.

"You could just tell old Ferrezin to sell it for you, and you could move your things and all the Aritheians to the Citadel. Or here."

"But I prefer not to do that," Arlian said. "It seems wise not to become *too* dependent on the Duke's goodwill, and I have already imposed on Lady Rime's goodwill far too much. Besides, I have just this morning begun arrangements for Ferrezin to retire—I would need to ask someone else to handle the transaction."

It was at that point that he noticed there were now more faces peering around the doorframe, several of them, all of them younger than Vanni's fifteen years.

"Vanni?" a young boy said, noticing Arlian's gaze.

Vanniari turned, beckoned to the others, then asked Arlian, "Shall I introduce you, my lord?"

"Please," Arlian said with a bow. "I believe I recognize your brother Kuron?"

"Kuron, this is Lord Obsidian."

Kuron, age eleven, the boy who had spoken his sister's name, stepped through the door and bowed.

"And our brother Bekerin, my lord."

Bekerin nodded an acknowledgment, but stayed where he was. Arlian did a quick calculation and decided that Bekerin was eight; it seemed very unlikely the boy had any firsthand memories of their previous meetings.

"And this is Rose."

The girl named waved shyly from the door, but did not approach. Arlian had never previously met her; she had not yet been born when he last set foot in Manfort. He had been informed of her arrival four years ago, and at the time he had wondered what her true name was. Knowing her mother, though, he suspected that Rose *was* her true name, in defiance of all custom—and in honor of a woman murdered by Enziet's men seventeen years ago, a woman both Hasty and Arlian had considered a friend, a woman who happened to have been Lady Rime's several-times-great granddaughter.

"And this is Halori," Vanniari continued, tugging at the arm of a boy of ten or so. Arlian knew this was Musk's son, not one of Hasty's children; Vanniari had completed the roster of her own half-siblings. Vanniari never mentioned that she did not share both parents with her mother's other children, but Arlian had killed Vanniari's own father in a duel some seven months before her birth, and the girl certainly knew it. He was grateful that neither Hasty nor Vanniari seemed to hold that against him—and he was unsure exactly who had sired the younger three.

Halori, on the other hand, was clearly Dovliril's child; even had Musk and Dovliril not been happily married these past twelve years, the child's resemblance to his father was unmistakable.

"And that's his brother Selsur—do you remember him?"

Arlian smiled at the boy, who had been taking his first steps when last Arlian saw him. "Of course I do," he said.

"And the little one there is Fanora," Vanniari concluded.

The girl, who was perhaps three, ducked out of sight at the sound of her name, but Bekerin caught her and dragged her back to visibility.

"Your servant, Mistress Fanora," Arlian said, bowing again. He hesitated, then admitted, "I do not believe I've had the pleasure of your acquaintance, even by proxy."

Vanniari understood his meaning, and said quickly, "She's Aunt Lily's daughter, Aunt Lily and Uncle Stone."

"Ah," Arlian said. He had known that Lily had married one of the Duke's guardsmen, but had not realized any children had resulted from the union. "Thank you." He glanced at Vanniari. "Did I hear correctly, that you are now Lady Rime's adopted granddaughter?"

Vanniari blinked at him in surprise. "Yes, of course," she said. "She adopted *all* of us. She adopted Mother and Aunt Cricket and Aunt Lily and Aunt Musk and Aunt Kitten as her daughters, and that makes us all her grandchildren."

And her heirs, Arlian thought. The dozen of them would inherit the estates and companies that Rime had spent four centuries acquiring. That explained why the offspring of Dovliril, a mere footman, were playing in the front rooms of the house—and it probably meant that one day that footman would be Lord Dovliril. Was he still a footman at all, then?

And it meant that all the survivors of the House of Carnal Society would be provided for. Five of them were now heirs to one of the Duke's advisors—and the sixth, Brook, was married to Black.

That hardly seemed fair to Brook, to be a mere steward's wife rather than the heir of a great noble—but then Arlian remembered that he had named Black as his own heir. If he were to die, Brook would be the wealthiest of all the women.

"My lord," the footman said from behind him, "shall I show you to Lady Rime?"

"By all means," Arlian said.

"Oh, I'll do it, Oril!" Vanniari said.

Oril the footman quite properly ignored her, and told Arlian, "This way, please."

Arlian followed—and so did Vanniari and Kuron, though the other five children suddenly burst into shrieks and giggles as they spun about poking at one another, and then ran off in another direction entirely.

Arlian had expected to be led up to Rime's bedchamber, where she had customarily spent most of her time, but instead the footman marched down the gallery and guided the party into a sunlit room Arlian did not recall from previous visits. He had expected to find Rime alone, perhaps reading, but instead his approach was greeted with happy laughter, and he found her surrounded by women.

"Grandmother!" Vanniari called, as the footman stepped aside. "Look who's come to visit!"

Four faces turned toward the door—Rime and Cricket and Lily and Musk, all of them seated, all but Rime in wheeled chairs of the sort Black had created for Brook. Like Brook, all Rime's adopted daughters had once been brothel slaves in Westguard, and had had their feet amputated.

Arlian bowed deeply, and when he straightened found all the women exclaiming happily. Rime had found her heavy ebony cane and was rising from her chair, a trifle unsteady on her one foot and wooden leg.

"Ari!" she said, holding out her free hand. "How lovely to see you!"

Arlian took the offered hand in both his own and kissed it. "Your servant, my lady," he said. As he raised his lips from her knuckles he studied her appearance.

Hers was still a strong face, plainly visible, her gray hair—now entirely gray, rather than the blend of black and gray she had maintained for four centuries—pulled back tightly into a waist-length ponytail. Her skin was weathered and brown, her eyes dark—but not as compelling as they were when Arlian first met her, long before. The larger-than-life glamour, the charisma, the special intensity of the dragonheart she had once been was gone.

As she smiled at him, though, Arlian thought he saw something else there instead, something new. He stared for a moment, and belatedly realized he was behaving rudely—though she seemed untroubled by his gaze.

The excited clamor of the other women died away, and Vanniari was able to interject, "I introduced him to everyone, Grandmother—all the children, I mean."

Rime turned her smile on Vanniari, and at that Arlian realized what was different.

Rime looked happy. Not just amused, or satisfied, or momentarily cheerful, but genuinely, sincerely happy.

And something else was different, something missing—a physical object. He released her hand, and looked swiftly about.

The bone was nowhere in sight.

For as long as Arlian had known her, Rime had carried a polished human shinbone with her everywhere she went, using it as a gavel, a prod, a toy; Arlian remembered how long it had taken him before he realized that it was her own, the bone from her lost left leg.

And it was not there, not in her hand, not on the table, not anywhere in the room.

"Well done, Vanni," Rime said. "So, Ari, what do you think of my family?" She gestured at the other women, and at Vanniari and Kuron.

"I think they are very fortunate indeed to have you as their patron, my lady."

"Patron? *Patron?*" She pulled her hand away and feigned a frown. "Arlian, I adopted them; I am their *mother*, not their patron!"

"And it clearly suits you well. I meant no offense, my lady."

"Of course you didn't—but I truly don't think you understand, Ari, that *I* am the fortunate one, to have found five such excellent daughters so late in life."

"And seven grandchildren," Kuron said.

Rime grinned. "And seven fine grandchildren," she agreed. "And I thank you, Ari, for freeing my daughters."

"It was my pleasure, Rime; I owed them all a debt. I just wish I could have saved the others."

"So do I," Rime said. "But you did what you could."

"Where are Hasty and Kitten?" Arlian asked, looking around.

"Hasty is probably in the kitchens, and Kitten is in the library," Cricket volunteered. "I'll go tell Kitten you're here." She grabbed the wheel of her chair and started it rolling.

"Have you eaten, my lord?" Musk asked.

"Vanni, have you seen Falora?" Lily asked. "Has she met Lord Obsidian?"

Arlian and Vanniari both started to speak at the same time, and the conversation collapsed into chaos. Arlian found himself caught in a series of misunderstandings, and forced to meet all seven members of the youngest generation anew before being sat down and fed cakes and wine. Hasty and Kitten appeared in the midst of it, rolling their chairs into the room and adding to the happy confusion.

Arlian gave up all hope of immediately managing a serious conversation with Rime, and let himself be swept up in the cheerful chaos.

10

Considerations for the Future

*I*t was more than two hours before Arlian was able to get away from the crowd and speak with Rime in private. When he did finally coax her into accompanying him elsewhere, he deliberately guided their steps up a flight of stairs, where the five adopted daughters could not follow without assistance.

He knew what he wanted to ask his old friend, but did not know quite how to broach the subject; they walked in silence along an upstairs corridor. At last he remarked, "I see you do not have your bone; I trust it hasn't been lost?"

She glanced at him, startled. "No, of course not; it's on the table by my bed."

"You no longer carry it with you?"

Rime smiled crookedly. "No, I don't. While I am not in

the least surprised you noticed, since you've always been an observant young man, I confess to some surprise that you ask about it. How, then, does an old woman's legbone relate to your plans for vengeance?"

"Not at all, my lady."

"Ah. When you said you had serious matters to discuss, I had assumed that these matters must be a part of your grand scheme to destroy the dragons; I have never known you to consider anything else to be serious. Certainly, the whereabouts of my shinbone would not seem to be a serious matter. Why, then, do you inquire about it?"

For a moment, Arlian did not answer. They reached the end of the passage and stepped out onto a balcony overlooking the gardens behind the house.

"Perhaps it *does* relate to my plans for vengeance in a way, my lady," Arlian said. "Leaving it aside is a change from habits you maintained for centuries, after all. I find myself curious about your reasons for that change, and about the state of your heart and health in general. I came here today not merely for the undeniable pleasure of your company and your hospitality, but to learn from you something of the nature of the transformations you have undergone in your lifetime; it may be that your decision to leave that bone at your bedside is indeed a part of what I came to ask."

Rime leaned on the balcony rail, her ebony cane in her hand, and looked out over the garden; tulips were in bloom, daffodils beginning to wither. Then she looked up at Arlian.

"So you think you might complete your vengeance, and are contemplating what might lie beyond?" she asked.

"You have always been perceptive," Arlian said.

"I would think this would be something you would discuss with Black, rather than with me."

"Black has never been cursed with dragon's venom; he has never experienced the transformation from mortal to dragonheart, nor the reverse. You have survived both."

"So has Spider. And Shard, and Flute, and Rope, and Di-nan, and Demdva, and Pori, and . . ."

"You need not list them all," Arlian interrupted. "And I think we may safely ignore Rope and all the others who were dragonhearts only briefly; their experience would not reflect mine. You, Spider, Shard, and Flute are my only re-sources in this research, and of those, only you do I trust to speak only the truth."

"I'm flattered." She looked out over the garden again. "What is it you want to know?"

"Simply, my lady—was it worth it, to be cleansed of the dragon's taint, or would a quick death have been better?"

She smiled crookedly, and peered sideways at him. "You have always been able to surprise me, Arlian, and to amuse me, as well. You do realize, I trust, that for most men the choice would not be between mortal life and quick death, but between a brief but clean life, and centuries as a tainted but powerful dragonspawn, undoubtedly making preparations to ensure the timely demise of your eventual progeny?"

"I am not most men, my lady. I have never *been* a normal man—I was only a boy when I swallowed my grandfather's blood and the dragon's venom, and grew to adulthood in this polluted state. I have never had a man's life, a man's knowledge, a man's heart. I have no family and few friends; material possessions and worldly power mean nothing to me. The only woman I ever thought I loved was poisoned, and died in my arms. I live only for revenge upon the drag-ons that made me what I am, and when that is accom-plished, why should I continue?"

"For the company of others, and the enjoyment of the earth's bounty. Even as you are, you can appreciate the beauty of flowers in the spring, or a young woman's body—why throw away a life that has such things in it?"

"Because of what grows within me. I am unclean, and any passing pleasure I might take is more than counterbal-anced by the constant awareness of the abomination I truly am. You know I care little for my own life; you have certainly known me to risk it often enough."

"Indeed I have."

"Then you know how little I value mere continuance in my present condition. You have experienced what it means to be a dragonheart, and what it means to be restored to true humanity, and you know the cost in pain that must be paid—the agony of having your heart torn from your chest as you helplessly watch, of seeing it flushed of its poison and restored, of spending weeks or months healing and recouping your strength to face the certainty that you will, regardless, be dead within a century and that your sacrifice has bought you only a little time. You *know* what I would face, as I do not. You were not ready to die when you were a dragonheart, nor are you ready to die now—but how great is the difference? Given that I scarcely care whether I live or die now, is there any reason to suffer through magical torment rather than simply plunge an obsidian blade into my heart?"

"Oh, Ari . . ." She shook her head sadly, and looked out over the garden again. "You poor child. You know so little of life."

Arlian started to speak, to protest—he had traveled widely, lived as slave and noble, fought against men and monsters and magic, while most people lived and died in a single village, as his parents had.

But then he remembered who he was speaking to. Lady Rime was more than four hundred years old—and had he not come to her because she *did* have experiences he did not?

And had he not himself said, just a few moments ago, that he had never known what it was to be a man?

He bit his tongue and waited for her to continue.

"When I was a young woman, before the dragons came," she said, "I had hardly seen anything of the world, yet I knew many things that you have never learned, or cannot remember. I knew what it was to love, to care—and I lost that when I drank my own blood from an envenomed wound, down in that well where I hid from the dragons.

"I thought at first that it was the shock, the loss of my family, that left me numb. I thought my coldness was a defense against grief. Later, when I joined the Dragon Society, I learned that all dragonhearts grow apart from humanity over time, but still, we believed it to be as much because of the separation caused by our extended lives as anything else. And we did not realize the depth of our detachment— it deepens so gradually over the years, and we all lived through horror at the start.

"But then I was cured. *You* cured me, Arlian—you and your Aritheian magicians—and I owe you a debt beyond your comprehension.

"It took time to heal, to recover; it was perhaps two years before I was entirely well. But that time passed, and as my heart healed, so did my soul. I relearned what I had lost and forgotten. I'm whole again, as I was before ever the dragons came; even with the scars on my chest, and my leg cut short, I am more whole now than I was in those centuries before we met. I remember now what it is to love, to feel joy, to take pleasure in simply being alive. I lost my husband and my four children four hundred years ago, and never remarried, never sought a new family, in all that time, because I could not love—that capacity had been killed by the poison that flowed in my veins.

"But now I *can* love again, and in fact I can hardly stop myself. My dear daughters—I find those women so brave, so charming—how could I fail to adore them? All those years I thought there was no good to be found in humanity, when in truth there was no good in *me* that could recognize its kin! I love them, as I loved my children four hundred years ago. For nine years I let them stay on as your guests at the Grey House because I did not want to hurt you, because I was not sure they cared for me, but in the end I took them in, and I wish I had done it sooner. I would have adopted

Brook as well, had she allowed it, but she chose her husband's side, as she should." She smiled.

"The children have brought new life to this old house, filled it with laughter and happiness—I have a new family, a large and boisterous one, as dear to me as the one the dragons slew. I have once again had lovers who were more than a few nights' amusement. Arlian, life is very precious to me now, but I would rather have only an hour as I am than another four hundred years as I was, and I would gladly pay with the pain of the transformation to get it. The air is sweeter, the sky more beautiful, than you can imagine. I need no old bone to remind me of what I have lost, for what I have is more than enough. Those among our former companions who fight against this, who cling to the prolonged existence the dragons have given them, have no idea how very foolish they're being; I wish I could tell them, but would they believe me? They would tell themselves that I lie, that having sacrificed my own years I would see theirs stolen, as well, to drag them down with me—but I am not below them, Arlian, I am flying so far above them they cannot conceive of it. I told Flute, and she listened, and I hope you will, in time, when you have completed the arduous task you have set yourself, but I knew most of them would not hear me. Spider and Shard gave themselves into Oeshir's care of their own choice before I could sway them, and Rope and the others were compelled by the Duke's men, but Flute—she was my doing, and I am very proud of that. I think you'll find her grateful, should you ask."

"I may do that," Arlian said.

"And perhaps you'll be my second victory?"

"Perhaps."

"You know, Ari, how so many of the Dragon Society have turned to cruelty and perversion? I believe that they do so because on some level they know that they should be feeling more than they are, that they know something is lacking, and they look for *anything* that can provide a new sensation. I remember how amusing I found it that you openly announced your intention to kill Enziet and the others, but now—now I would be appalled, rather than amused." She hesitated, then corrected herself. "No, I would still be amused—but I would *also* be appalled." She smiled. "It's such a shame that Wither did not live long enough to be treated!"

"It is," Arlian agreed. He stood, leaning on the rail, ostensibly looking at the garden, but in truth seeing nothing.

Rime's words had answered his question, but had inspired a hundred more.

If he took her at her word, then the cleansing was clearly worth the pain it would cost—but was it truly that simple? She had been a grown woman, a wife and mother, when the dragons came; he had been a boy of eleven. Would his heart, once purified, be the heart of a man, or of a child? He had learned many hard lessons since that day when the dragons swept down on the Smoking Mountain, and he did not want to lose them.

Rime had regained her ability to love, but what might she have lost? Did she truly remember everything she had been, everything she had known, as a dragonheart?

Would every dragonheart react as Rime had? Perhaps he should speak to Flute, and find out whether she agreed with Rime's assessment.

Rime said she had been unable to love when she was a dragonheart, but Arlian believed he had loved Sweet. Her loss still weighed upon him. He had thought that her memory was a part of why he had never found another woman to be more than a friend or a brief amusement, but perhaps it was entirely the taint in his blood that prevented it. Perhaps what he had felt for Sweet was not love at all, or perhaps it had burned out his venom-diminished capacity for love.

To be able to love again, to live without the hard obsession that anchored his soul, to know the security of a family as he had when he was a little boy—that was a prospect so appealing that the thought of it was almost painful.

And the idea that he might raise his hopes, and suffer

through weeks of pain, and then find that he could never again know ordinary human emotions—*that* possibility was both painful and terrifying.

Did the other dragonhearts know that Rime's experience had been so happy? Perhaps a letter could be written and copied and distributed; perhaps more might surrender themselves to the Aritheians' ministrations if the word were spread.

He would suggest it to the Duke when next they spoke.

And perhaps someday, when the last dragon had died, he would ask the Aritheians to cut out his heart and wash the dragon's venom from his veins.

11

Encounters at the Citadel

When he returned to the Grey House no message had arrived, and after further consideration, and a chat with Black, Arlian decided that he would not wait to be summoned; on the third day after his return to Manfort he presented himself at the Citadel's gate and requested an audience with His Grace, the Duke of Manfort.

He was shown in immediately, as befitted his station, and word was sent to the Duke while Arlian was escorted to an elegant waiting room.

He would have preferred to wait in his own office in the outer wall, but apparently the Duke had given orders to the contrary.

The waiting room, decorated in powder blue and off-white, was pleasant enough, and he discovered upon his arrival there that he was by no means the only one waiting; a dozen assorted courtiers and messengers were scattered about the chamber. They looked up at his entrance, but most, upon seeing it was merely an addition to their number and not an official summoning them to the audience chamber, then returned to what they had been doing before.

Three well-dressed men were clustered in a corner, talking quietly; a man and a masked woman stood looking out one of the three broad windows; another elegantly gowned woman was seated on a blue silk couch while a masked man in bottle-green velvet leaned over the back to speak to her. Two men sat silently in their chairs, one of them reading from a small book; another man leaned indolently against the wall, watching everyone else.

And in the center of the room a masked man had been speaking with a splendid young woman, and these two did *not* return to their conversation; instead they stared silently at Arlian.

Arlian returned their gaze calmly. He did not recognize the woman, and the white silk mask that covered the man's face from brow to chin concealed his identity quite effectively.

The masked man leaned over and whispered a few words in his companion's ear; she threw him a quick glance, then looked back at Arlian and smiled. She took a step toward him and held out one slim white hand.

"Lord Obsidian, I believe?"

Arlian looked her over quickly as he accepted her hand and bowed. He did not recognize her face, but she was so young that he could not be sure they had not met previously; when last he visited Manfort she would have been still a girl, rather than a woman, and her appearance might have been quite different. Certainly, she would have been too young to have worn the low-cut blue velvet gown that displayed her unquestionable charms so admirably, and the elaborate hairstyle framing her face had not yet come into fashion.

"You have the advantage of me, my lady," he said. "Although my ignorance of the identity of anyone so lovely as yourself is clearly a disgrace, I hope you will forgive me—I have been long away from Manfort."

"Of course, my lord. I am Lady Tiria of Gallows Hill, and I am but newly arrived in Manfort myself, so you could hardly be expected to know me."

Arlian bowed again.

As he did, however, he saw from the corner of his eye that the man in the white mask had backed away slightly, while keeping his attention on Arlian. Not on Tiria, whom he had presumably been flirting with a moment before, but on *Arlian*.

Arlian straightened up, released Tiria's hand, and reached out toward her companion. "And who is this, then?"

The man froze for an instant, then reluctantly held out a hand. "I'm, ah . . . Tooth," he said, as he essayed the quickest, most reluctant handshake Arlian had experienced in years.

"My pleasure, sir," Arlian said with a nod, noting that Tiria was suppressing a smile at the exchange. "I am Lord Obsidian, of the Grey House."

Arlian had known someone who went by the name Tooth once before, long ago—in fact, that Tooth had been one of the looters he had sworn to kill. She was also a woman, which this person clearly was not.

Something about the masked man—his voice, or his grip, or perhaps the way he moved—was familiar, but Arlian could not immediately place him. Presumably this was someone Arlian had known here in Manfort, but of course he had been away from the city for so long . . .

The man was of medium height, and black hair with an admixture of gray was visible around the mask's edge— that hardly narrowed the field of possibilities significantly. He was dressed well but not ostentatiously—his brown linsey-woolsy coat was plain but of excellent cut, while the white silk cravat at his throat precisely matched his mask but was not embroidered and bore just a single narrow edg-

ing of lace. It was not obvious from his attire whether he
was a lord or merely a successful tradesman—and Arlian
suspected the ambiguity was deliberate. Whoever this man
was, he clearly did not want to be recognized. Arlian did not
believe for an instant that he ordinarily called himself
Tooth, and the mask, ostensibly a mere fashion accessory,
was almost certainly intended to conceal his identity not
just from Arlian, but from everyone.

A perverse whim struck Arlian. "Have we met, Tooth?"
he asked, staring at the eyes behind the mask—eyes that
even when half-hidden seemed to have an odd depth and intensity to them.

Tooth essayed a nervous laugh, and replied, "We have
now, my lord."

"Of course," Arlian said, managing a polite chuckle.
Then he was suddenly at a loss for words as the pieces fell
into place and he realized who Tooth was.

It was the laugh that had done it. He could not recall exactly when he had heard it before, and it was not a particularly distinctive laugh, but nonetheless it had served as the
final puzzle piece to trigger something in his memory. He
glanced at Tiria, wondering if she knew who she had been
speaking with—and seeing the expression on her face, he
was certain she did.

Did that mean that she, too, was a dragonheart?

No, Arlian decided, her face did not have that ferocity
that marked the heart of the dragon. It seemed clear,
though, that in all probability she was in league with the
Society.

Just what that meant, why she was in Manfort and in the
Citadel, was another question entirely. Had he encountered
her at one of his camps in the course of the winter he would
have assumed she was, like Wren, at best a spy and more
likely an assassin, but here in the Duke's stronghold . . .

"What brings you to the Citadel, my lord?" Tiria asked,
breaking the moment of silence before it became noticeably
awkward.

"Oh, I am but recently returned from slaying dragons in the Duke's service, and came to give my report."

"Ah, the dragonslayer has been at work! And would you care to rehearse this report for us, my lord? I know that *I* am eager to hear it, whether His Grace is or not."

That she was indeed a spy in the service of the Dragon Society seemed possible. Everyone knew of the Duke's weakness for pretty women, and it was widely rumored that his marriage some ten years ago had merely tempered his enthusiasm and increased his circumspection, not ended his adventures. A lovely creature like Tiria might well wangle a few secrets out of His Grace.

And her interest in his report might appear innocent enough, might *be* innocent enough, but it might also be part of her assignment.

"I do not think that would be suitable, my lady," Arlian said. "But perhaps we can meet after our various appointments, and I might review for you what I will have told the Duke?"

"That would be delightful, my lord. Shall I come by your home this evening, perhaps?"

Perhaps she was an assassin after all, Arlian thought, rather than a spy; he doubted she would have come here to kill the Duke, since that would have been almost certain suicide, but she might well have come here to kill *him.*

In fact, she might have been here in this waiting room not in hopes of seeing the Duke, but waiting for Arlian to put in his inevitable appearance. The Society almost certainly knew he had headed back to Manfort; while Wren had presumably never reported in, Arlian's failure to walk into the ambush would have been noticed. A word or two with almost anyone in Ethinior would have told an informant where he was going instead, and sorcery could have conveyed the information to Manfort more quickly than Arlian had made the journey. Arranging to have an assassin waiting would not have been difficult.

Flirting with him, arranging an assignation—what better

way to get close enough to kill him? It had been tried often enough before.

"And would you be interested, as well, my dear Tooth?" Arlian asked, looking the masked man in the eye. He could see Tiria's pout, but he remained focused on "Tooth."

After an instant's hesitation, Tooth essayed a bow. "I would be delighted, my dear Obsidian," he said.

"Then I will look for you both at the Grey House this evening, if our business here is done by then. For supper, perhaps?"

Tiria and Tooth exchanged glances.

"Let us see what our circumstances permit, my lord," Tiria said.

"Of course." Arlian made a small bow. He smiled.

The smile would certainly appear to be directed at Tiria, but it was actually to himself. He believed he knew what was going through their minds, and he was fairly certain that he would not be dining with Lord Zaner—for he had identified the white-masked Tooth as no other—that evening. Zaner could scarcely hope to keep his identity hidden at the table; one did not wear a mask while eating. He would undoubtedly find some excuse to avoid the meal, but might arrive later—if he came at all.

There was no obvious reason for Tiria to delay, though. As a dragonheart Arlian did not need to fear poison in his wineglass, but she might consider supper an ideal opportunity to worm her way into his confidence.

She had clearly not expected him to invite Zaner; he had done that deliberately to tease her, to make plain that her attempts at seduction would not be as easy as she had clearly hoped, and her pout had been his reward. On the other hand, letting them both into his home would mean that if either of them intended an assassination, she or he would now have a ready accomplice.

Arlian thought he could handle any assassination attempt, since he had already survived so many over the years, but he would still want to be sure that Black or Isein, or other reliable employees, remained close at hand at all times while Tiria and Zaner were present.

All in all, though, he looked forward to matching wits with these two, and perhaps permanently disposing of one more dragonheart in the near future; that was why he smiled.

Of course, here in the Citadel he could easily have denounced Lord Zaner on the spot, and had him captured or killed; the man had real courage to come here, even disguised. If he were identified he would either be slain immediately, or given a choice between death and the Aritheian cleansing. Despite Rime's enthusiasm for her new life, Arlian doubted Zaner would see that cleansing as a desirable option—hours of excruciating torment, months of slow recovery, a few years of life as an ordinary man, then old age and death.

Long ago Zaner had called Arlian a coward to his face, perhaps hoping to provoke a challenge and duel, perhaps because he had believed it; Arlian had always been certain enough of his own goals and values that the accusation had not troubled him. He wondered, though, whether he would have been willing to march into his enemy's stronghold in so flimsy a disguise, with so much at risk and so little to gain. Perhaps Zaner truly *was* the braver man.

And just what *did* Zaner hope to gain by coming here?

That was why Arlian did not simply denounce him, and why Arlian had invited him to the Grey House—he hoped to learn why Lord Zaner of the Dragon Society had come to Manfort, as well as who and what Lady Tiria was.

"You have been in the north, my lord, have you not?" Tiria asked.

"Northwest, in the foothills of the Brokenback Mountains," Arlian replied.

"I have never been there," she said. "Pray tell me, what is the land there like?"

"Pleasant enough, in its way," Arlian began. "Wooded

country, for the most part, and much of it pines, with their needles thick on the ground beneath . . ."

At that moment he heard the door behind him open, and he turned to see a captain in the Duke's guard entering the room.

"Lord Obsidian?" the soldier called. "His Grace would see you now."

"Your pardon, my lady," Arlian said, with a final bow; then he turned and followed the officer.

A moment later he knelt before the Duke, performing the ritual obeisance appropriate to a formal audience as a dozen courtiers, Lord Rolinor among them, watched. Arlian was dismayed to see that half of them were masked.

Lord Spider, formerly a dragonheart and now the Duke's favored advisor, stood silently and unsmiling at the right of the ducal throne.

"Rise, my lord," the Duke said.

Arlian rose, and awaited the Duke's command.

"I am delighted to see you safely home again, Lord Obsidian," the Duke said, smiling an oddly unwelcoming smile. "Lord Rolinor had brought us much of your news, and other matters were consuming much of my attention, so I thought it best to allow you a few days' rest before summoning you to the Citadel; I see your patience wore thin."

"Not at all, Your Grace; say rather, my eagerness to serve you overcame my fatigue."

"Very good, then! I understand you disposed of nine of our ancient foes in the course of this past winter?"

"I am pleased to say that my men did indeed slay nine dragons, Your Grace, and without the loss of a single human life." Arlian allowed himself a small smile of satisfaction; the Duke, however, did not smile in return.

"And the year before . . ."

"Eight, Your Grace. My steward makes the total to be eighty-eight since you first named me to lead the campaign against the beasts. We estimate perhaps fifty more still survive."

"Eighty-eight! Remarkable." The Duke leaned back in his chair, frowning slightly—Arlian supposed he was calculating something, and mathematics had never been one of his strengths. "If your numbers are correct, then well over half have been exterminated!"

"At dreadful cost," someone said. Arlian glanced at a blue-masked face, a woman he did not recognize standing at Rolinor's right hand. "Scarce a week passes in the summer months that a village or hamlet is not devastated by the surviving dragons in retaliation for your depredations; why, the death toll must be in the thousands!"

Arlian bit his lip before saying, "Perhaps tens of thousands, my lady; I do not deny this cost, and my heart aches whenever I think on it. I have devoted much of my fortune, and as much time as I can spare from hunting the creatures, to the mining of obsidian, the building of catapults, and the fortification of as many towns as possible—and those fortifications have proven effective. While only two dragons have been confirmed slain by catapult bolt since the destruction of the Old Palace fourteen years ago, no town thus defended has been destroyed."

"Naturally, the dragons choose the easier targets!"

"And when all our towns are thus equipped, presumably the raids will cease," Arlian said. "Better still, when all the dragons are dead, the very *possibility* of raids will cease."

"But then we . . ."

The Duke cleared his throat.

The blue-masked woman clearly had more to say, but a glance at the Duke's expression forestalled any further comment; she left her sentence unfinished.

Arlian thought he could guess what the woman would have said: That no town that had sworn fealty to the Dragon Society had been attacked, any more than the fortified ones had been destroyed. That the Lands of Man had known seven centuries of peace before Arlian's arrival stirred the dragons from their caves, and perhaps a similar truce could be negotiated once again.

He supposed the Duke had heard it all before, and did not care to hear it again.

"I am impressed with the progress of the war against the dragons, my lord," the Duke said. "I would be interested in hearing your comments on another matter, however."

"I will endeavor to satisfy Your Grace's curiosity," Arlian said, with a slight bow. He did want to continue discussing the war, at least to the point of mentioning the planned ambush he had avoided and its possible significance, but that could wait until he had humored the Duke and dealt with whatever other subject he chose to address.

"You have traded in the Borderlands, and you were responsible for reopening the road to Arithei, I believe?"

Puzzled, Arlian nodded. "As you say."

"In fact, you made a large part of your fortune dealing in Aritheian magic, did you not?"

"I did, though I am no magician myself."

"And you have studied sorcery?"

"Only the merest dabbling, Your Grace; I would no more call myself a sorcerer than I would claim I can fly like a bird."

"Nonetheless, you know more of the southern lands and their magic than any other here. What, then, do you think of the latest news?"

Arlian blinked, and glanced at Spider, whose expressionless face was no help. "Your Grace, I have not *heard* the latest news; to what do you refer?"

"Surely, you know that there have been incursions into the Borderlands?"

Arlian recalled his conversation with Isein. "I had heard that there were rumors of such, just since my arrival in Manfort," he said carefully. "No word of anything like that had reached me in the north. I know no details. Have there been intrusions?"

"Oh, yes." The Duke looked over the courtiers, and beckoned to one of them. "Come forth, Lord Naran, and tell Obsidian what you told me. Perhaps with his experience in the south he will have a greater appreciation of the fine points."

Arlian turned.

Naran was a tall, thin young man clad in fine linen, his face darkened by the sun; he stepped forward and bowed to Arlian and the Duke. Arlian returned the bow.

"I am delighted to meet you, my lord Obsidian," Naran said. "I have heard much about you."

"The pleasure is mine," Arlian said. "Now, pray, do tell me your news."

"Of course. You see, I am a caravan master, just returned from what was intended as a trading expedition to the Borderlands—but we accomplished little trade."

"And why is that?"

"We arrived in Sweetwater on schedule—I believe you know the town? My partner in this journey, a fellow named Drens, said you had accompanied him there once."

"I did," Arlian acknowledged.

"It was our intention to split the caravan at that point; Lord Drens was to proceed to the southwest, perhaps as far as Skok's Falls, while I would make haste to Pon Ashti, in the east. I had some hope of meeting merchants from the southern coasts in the markets of Pon Ashti, you see."

Arlian struggled to recall the geography of the Borderlands. He knew that Skok's Falls stood atop a gigantic cliff that formed a portion of the southernmost border of the Lands of Man, overlooking wild jungle reportedly inhabited by semi-human creatures, but no true men; adventurers sometimes climbed down into the jungle, at great risk to their own lives, and brought out various exotic goods that could be sold to the caravan merchants at outrageous prices. The merchants could then sell these herbs and creatures for even more outrageous prices once they were north of the Desolation.

Pon Ashti, on the other hand, was a city-state in the marshy southeast whose relationship with the Lands of Man had long been somewhat vexed. Since it was far enough to the north that magic was weak and easily regulated within its confines, and it was built upon land that had unquestionably been under the dragons' sway during at least a part of the long millennia of their rule, it should by rights have been considered a part of the Lands of Man—but its ruling council had never acknowledged the supremacy of the Duke of Manfort, or indeed any authority higher than itself. The city's location at the head of the Darambar estuary made it a center of trade, and every so often one of the present Duke's ancestors had attempted to collect tariffs or taxes on that trade, but never with much result.

Arlian had never visited either of them. "Yes," he said, "I see."

"We were in the process of dividing the caravan when word came from the east, with the first refugees—the Blue Mage had claimed Pon Ashti as her own, and attempts to repel her had utterly failed. All the eastern Borderlands were in turmoil as a result, and it appeared that the city had indeed fallen to the wizard's magic."

"But Pon Ashti is warded," Arlian protested. "The walls are sheathed in iron!"

"Say rather, the city walls are augmented with iron," Naran corrected. "They had insufficient metal for full sheathing. A strip of black iron every three paces—which had sufficed for these seven centuries, yes. Why that was no longer enough to withstand the Blue Mage, I do not know. I merely tell you what the refugees told us."

Arlian glanced at the Duke, who was sitting back in his throne with an uneasy smile upon his face, and then at Lord Spider, whose face seemed frozen into immobility, and who had not yet said a word in the entire course of the audience. Clearly, there were political currents here Arlian did not understand; that worried him. He looked back at Naran.

"Go on," he said.

12

The Border Aflame

"**O**bviously, we could not split the caravan under such circumstances," Naran continued. "We therefore resolved to carry out Drens's original plans, and proceed to the southwest, toward Skok's Falls—though we were not at all certain how far we would go. I do not know whether you are aware of it, Lord Obsidian, but in recent years Skok's Falls has been haunted—nightmares trouble the inhabitants' sleep, there are things glimpsed from the corner of the eye, and any number of odd occurrences have been reported. Herbs that once could only be found beyond the border now grow in the town's gardens, and unnatural creatures roam the streets. Fewer and fewer merchants dare venture there, and even some of the town's natives have been relocating to more northerly areas of late."

"I had not heard," Arlian said.

He was not happy to hear it now. He was reminded that the sorcerers he employed to locate openings into the caverns where the dragons slept had remarked on occasion that sorcery was becoming easier, magical energy more plentiful, in recent years; for the most part he had dismissed this as the result of improvement with practice, but had also worried sometimes that it was an inadvertent result of his own heavy importation of Aritheian magic into the Lands of Man. His meager studies in sorcery had taught him that when magic was used the energy did not simply cease to exist; rather, it dissipated into the surrounding air and soil. The energy expended by the Aritheian magic had been brought from the plentiful supplies beyond the border, and had presumably been added to the very feeble energies of the Lands of Man, augmenting the power the sorcerers drew on.

When dissipated over such a large area his imports should not have been sufficient to make a noticeable difference for even the most sensitive sorcerer, though, and could certainly not be responsible for events as distant as the Blue Mage's conquest of Pon Ashti, or the haunting of Skok's Falls. Some other factor was surely at work. The sorcerers' words should have warned him long ago.

Lord Naran continued, "Nonetheless, we set out along the southwestern road, and two days from Sweetwater we arrived in Redgate, only to find the town jammed with people driven from their homes. It would seem that the naked, screaming hordes of Tirikindaro had overrun the walled cities of Shenneyd and Talolo. We would have done far better to have brought grain and fruit than the wool and silk and tin that we had—many of these poor folks were starving. We did what we could, and then pressed on.

"Our next stop beyond Redgate was to have been Sazar, on the border of Shei, but the road was so infested with night-creatures and firebirds that we altered our plans—and later we heard that the wizards of Shei had annexed Sazar, in any case, and would quite likely have impounded all our goods. Instead we made our way to Galadas, and then Yellowfield.

"And there we gave up, and turned back."

"Why?" Arlian asked.

"Because there we met some of the survivors from farther south." Naran took a deep breath, then said, "My lord, Skok's Falls no longer exists. And some of its people, even those who fled, are no longer human. I saw a woman with eyes like a cat's, a boy with gleaming purple scales on his arms . . ." He shuddered. "The sky in Yellowfield was awash in magic—colors that should not exist flickered across it, and at night it glowed unnaturally, allowing us to see shapes flying overhead that still trouble me."

"I have seen the sky over Tirikindaro, or the Dreaming Mountains," Arlian said. "You need say no more."

"The towns between Yellowfield and Skok's Falls were in chaos," Naran said. "There were riots, battles between those who wanted to flee northward, and those who wanted to stand and fight—and those who had been corrupted by the magical forces from beyond the border."

"It would seem that *all* the Borderlands are in chaos," Arlian remarked.

"Indeed," said the Duke, before Naran could say any more. Arlian turned back to the throne.

"And I would know, Lord Obsidian, why this should be happening," the Duke continued. "The creatures beyond the border have always sought to intrude upon the Lands of Man, but never before, in all the centuries of recorded history, have they been able to make significant inroads. Why are they doing so *now*?"

"I do not know, Your Grace," Arlian said—and in truth, he did not *know,* but a ghastly suspicion was forming.

His Aritheian imports were not the only magic in the Lands of Man, after all.

"You are my expert on magic, Obsidian—have you no idea at all? No possibility to suggest?"

"Alas, Your Grace, I do not. Have you spoken to the Aritheian magicians—Asaf and Tiviesh and Isein? Or Hlur, the ambassador? The people of Arithei live with wild magic as a matter of course, and surely know more about it than I."

"I have spoken with Hlur and Tiviesh, and with my own sorcerers—though decent sorcerers are scarce in Manfort now that the old lords have died or fled."

"The dragonhearts, you mean."

"Yes. The lords who have lived long enough to *learn* sorcery. And three of our best remaining sorcerers accompanied you this past winter—have you brought them back with you?"

"Alas, Your Grace, I left them in Ethinior for the summer. But there is Lady Rime, here in Manfort. And Lady Flute knows more of sorcerous healing than any other who has lived these past five hundred years."

"Do you think they might know more than you?"

"Your Grace, I am a mere child by comparison, not yet forty years old where Rime has lived four hundred!"

The Duke frowned. "Lady Rime was among my advisors of old, Obsidian, and she abandoned me years ago, retiring to the bosom of her adopted family; I do not especially fancy the idea of going to her asking favors."

Arlian spread his hands. "Indeed, you must do as you see best, Your Grace; I did not mean to instruct you, but merely to assure you of my own ignorance."

And in fact, he did not really want the Duke to talk to Rime, or anyone else who might tell him what Arlian guessed to be the reason—not until Arlian had had time to consider the situation.

He seemed to hear Black's voice in his ears repeating what he had told Arlian long ago, when first they were preparing to join a caravan to the Borderlands. Arlian had been a mere youth, little more than half his present age, but he remembered it well. Black had been telling him what ruled the lands beyond the border.

"Gods here and there, perhaps, and certainly a few magicians elsewhere, but mostly . . . mostly it's *other* things. Things that neither men nor dragons conquered."

Those were the things that were now spreading north, into the Lands of Man, the lands men had taken from the dragons.

And Black had said, "They're things that *couldn't conquer the dragons.*"

But now, thanks to Arlian and his compatriots, more than half those dragons were gone, and the survivors, when they were awake, were busily destroying human settlements. Whatever the dragons had been doing to keep out those other things, the wild magic and the creatures from beyond the border, they were apparently doing no longer.

This made any discussion of avoided ambushes trivial and irrelevant; this could mean the entire nature of the conflict between humanity and the dragons must change.

"There is a theory that has been put forth, my lord," the Duke said, interrupting Arlian's thoughts. "I said I had spoken to some of the sorcerers and Aritheians, and I have; I did not say they had no answers. They do have theories, and one of them seems to be quite popular."

Arlian's heart sank. "Oh? And what would that be, Your Grace?"

"That your slaughter of dragons has weakened the magical defenses of the Lands of Man."

And there it was, then, out in the open. Arlian realized for the first time that the Duke had said he was impressed by Arlian's success in killing dragons, but he had not said he was pleased; he had called it remarkable, but never said it was *good.* And Lord Spider, who would ordinarily have congratulated Arlian on his successes, had said nothing at all.

Arlian upbraided himself for not noticing and correctly interpreting this sooner.

"In fact, we have a message from Sarkan-Mendoth, from the surviving members of the Dragon Society," the Duke said, gesturing. Arlian hardly needed to bother looking; he knew the Duke was indicating the woman in the blue mask as the messenger. "Their letter tells us the same—that the dragons, destructive though they may be, embody the magical essence of all the lands we call ours, and that their mere existence is enough to keep the wizards and monsters beyond the border."

That made a distressing amount of sense, but Arlian was momentarily distracted from the information by its source. The dragonhearts had sent a representative openly—then were Tiria and Zaner also in the Citadel legitimately? If so, why did Zaner bother with the mask?

No, those two probably were spies, operating clandestinely while this blue-masked woman served to distract the Duke. She was not a dragonheart, Arlian was sure; the Society would not risk openly sending someone whose mere presence in Manfort carried a possible death sentence. Whoever this woman was, she had not tasted the foul mixture of blood and venom.

At least, not yet; perhaps running this errand would earn her that false reward.

"Today we know of catastrophes in the Borderlands," the Duke said. "Pon Ashti and Skok's Falls and who knows where else fallen to wizards, the thing in Tirikindaro expanding, sending its slave-soldiers everywhere . . . it's a *disaster*, Obsidian. Bad enough that we have been losing hundreds of innocent lives to the dragons every summer— at least we could see an end in sight, and we had your obsidian weapons to defend us. But *these* things? If they cross the Desolation, will obsidian defend against *them*?"

"Cold iron will fend off some of them," Arlian said, without thinking. "Silver is proof against others, and there are certain stones . . ."

"*I don't care!*" the Duke bellowed, rising from his chair. "Do you think I want to live the way the Aritheians do, beset by nightmares, every road lined with iron posts to keep back the monsters? Hlur has told me what it was like there, and I will not have that in my lands!"

Arlian bowed a silent acknowledgment, but the Duke was not finished.

"And that's just the south," he said. "There is said to be wild magic beyond the western deserts as well, and in the icefields to the north, and beyond the mountains to the northwest— what's to stop *all* of it from pouring in on us if the dragons are all gone?"

"I do not know, Your Grace," Arlian said quietly.

"Much as I hate to say this, Obsidian, we *need* the dragons. Better those monsters than the *things* beyond the borders! Unless you can offer an alternative, and prove that it will work, you are not to slay any more dragons! Is that clear?"

"Utterly, Your Grace." Arlian turned to the blue-masked woman. "And will the Dragon Society undertake to arrange a truce in exchange, and ensure that no more innocents are slaughtered this summer?"

"I am only a messenger, my lord," the woman said. "I am sure they will do what they can, but they are the dragons' servants, not their masters."

"Do they admit that?" Arlian asked, startled.

"Perhaps 'partners' would be a better term than 'servants'? I do not think they are slaves, but all who live under their administration recognize that the dragons are more powerful than any humans, and that for the most part the dragonhearts obey the dragons, and not the reverse."

Arlian decided to withhold further comment; he had his own opinions as to power and humanity, but saw no point in arguing the matter here and now. He turned back to the Duke.

"Your Grace, you have my word that I will not hunt down any more of our draconic enemies without your permission until we have some solution to the situation beyond the Desolation. I trust I may be permitted to defend against any that emerge from their lairs, however? That I may continue to fortify the cities and towns of your realm against them?"

The Duke glanced at the messenger, then at Lord Spider, and finally Spider spoke. "I think that should be acceptable," he said. "The dragons must restrain themselves if we are to put an end to these invasions in the south."

"Then that will do," the Duke said. His expression softened. "Lord Obsidian, I know you hate the dragons for what they did to your family and your home; I know you hoped to exterminate them entirely. This must be hard for you to accept—but there are worse things than dragons. We have all lived with the dragons all our lives; we can live with them longer. You had no way of knowing what would happen."

"Thank you, Your Grace," Arlian said. He was unsure what he was thanking the Duke for, but could think of no better reply.

"You have fought hard for many years; go home and rest, and let the rest of us arrange matters." He waved in dismissal.

Arlian bowed; the audience was clearly at an end. Anything else he might want to discuss with the Duke—and with the altered circumstances, Arlian was no longer sure what that might be—would have to wait. He retreated quickly, and left the room.

He hesitated in the corridor, debating whether to go about any other business while he was in the Citadel, but decided he was in no mood to deal with the mundane concerns of the city's warlord.

Besides, he told himself, he had arranged to meet with Tiria and Zaner. He had thought that was to be a duel of wits, but now it appeared more likely to be merely settling the terms of his surrender.

He already regretted making his promise to the Duke; he still wanted to hunt down and kill the three dragons that had destroyed his home on the Smoking Mountain when he was a boy. Sparing the others in exchange for their services in magically defending the borders and an agreement not to raid undefended villages was hard, but perhaps something he could learn to live with; sparing the monster that had killed his parents, his grandfather, and his brother . . .

Well, he told himself, he would just have to bear it—or find some other means of defending the Lands of Man from the wizards and monsters.

Perhaps there *was* some means; perhaps he would find it. After all, Enziet had found the secret of the dragons' vulnerability to obsidian.

And as a dragonheart, he had plenty of time.

13

A Visit from Lord Zaner

*A*rlian was not surprised when a footman brought word
that his dinner guest had arrived at the Grey House; he
was startled to discover that the arrival was Lord Zaner, still
masked and calling himself Tooth, and not Lady Tiria.

They met in the passage by the foyer. "My dear Tooth!"
Arlian said, taking his hand. "A pleasure to see you!"

"Is there somewhere we could speak privately, my lord?"
Zaner asked nervously.

"Of course." He gestured to Wolt, the footman who had
escorted Zaner from the gate. "Where might we speak
undisturbed without inconveniencing anyone?"

The footman glanced down the passage toward the
kitchens, where the household staff was bustling about
preparing the evening meal, then toward the gallery, where
Amberdine could be heard laughing gaily over some new
game her sister had devised. "Perhaps upstairs, my lord?
Your study?"

Arlian had left Isein and Black in his study, where they
were going over some of Enziet's old papers on sorcery in
hopes of finding some hint about just how the dragons kept
other magic beyond the borders.

With Isein there, Qulu still not returned from Arithei, and
Lilsinir up at the Citadel comparing notes with Tiviesh and
Asaf, the third floor was uninhabited for the moment—
and a sudden whim struck Arlian.

"This way, my lord," he said, momentarily forgetting that
he was not supposed to know Lord Zaner's identity or sta-

tus. He led the way up two flights, his white-masked guest close behind; at the top he took a lit candle from one of the wall niches, and then marched down the length of the corridor to a heavy wooden door set with black iron brackets.

The bar that had once rested in those brackets was gone, but Arlian had deliberately kept the room otherwise much as he had found it upon first inheriting the Grey House. He opened the door and gestured for Zaner to precede him.

Zaner started in, then stopped. "What is this, Arlian?" he asked.

"This is a room where we may speak undisturbed," Arlian replied.

"It looks like a prison!"

"And so it was, when Lord Enziet owned this house. Now it is a memorial." He stepped into the room himself, his free hand taking Zaner's arm and urging him forward.

Once inside, Arlian closed the door and set the candle atop a crude, massive table that stood nearby. The candlelight vividly illuminated several dark stains on the table's rough surface.

The room they had entered was good-sized and appallingly bare; the only furnishings besides the table were two large chests pushed up against one wall. A long-unused fireplace filled one end of the chamber, and the opposite wall had two sets of heavy chains bolted to it. The walls were stone, and the floor bare and ancient planks, stained in several places.

"Why is this here?" Zaner asked. "What did Enziet *want* with it?"

"You might say he used it as a playroom," Arlian said, leaning against the table. "When I first saw it he had two women imprisoned here—one still alive, though he had already poisoned her, and one very, very dead. Both of them were my friends, one of them perhaps more than a friend; they are now buried in the garden of the Old Palace."

Zaner shuddered, the movement plainly visible despite the mask, even in the dim light. "That's *horrible.*"

"Worse than you know—but I will spare you the details. This was one reason I pursued Enziet with such determination, into the Desolation and to the cave where he died."

"Why did you bring me up here? Surely there must have been another room we could have used!"

"Oh, most likely, but I thought it fitting to show you this, to remind you that I have very real and personal reasons for loathing the dragons and their pawns."

"There I think I can equal you, Arlian. Just as you haven't told me everything, there are things I haven't told *you*!"

"I hope you don't simply mean your identity, my lord; I recognized you at the Citadel this morning. Please, my dear Zaner, feel free to remove your mask; I can't believe it's comfortable."

"I *thought* you might have," he said, as he pulled the mask up and off. "But no, that's not what I meant."

"Then what is it that you've come to tell me? I confess to some surprise that you came; I had thought you would want to keep your face hidden, which is hardly possible at the dinner table..What is so urgent that you gave up your secret for it, and wanted to assure our privacy before revealing it to me?"

"I want you to cure me," Zaner said. "That's what's urgent, and why I don't care if you see my face—I'm taking you and the Duke up on your offer. And I came early and alone so Lady Tiria wouldn't find out."

This was not at all what Arlian had expected; he had assumed that it would be *he* who yielded, thanks to the situation in the Borderlands. "You mean you want your heart to be cleansed of its taint? You want the Aritheian magicians to restore you to mere humanity, and remove the dragonspawn in your blood?"

"Yes, exactly."

"You know what's involved?"

"Not every little detail, but I think I have the *gist* of it. What does that matter?"

"I'm told it's excruciatingly painful."

"I don't care."

"You could have arranged this more easily by other means," Arlian said. "You could have surrendered to the guards at the Citadel today."

"But I wanted to talk to you," Zaner said. "I *needed* to talk to you."

"Now, my lord, I confess myself confused. Suppose we sit down upon these chests—I'm sorry now I did not choose a room with better seating—and you tell me everything you came to tell me. I admit I am *very* curious about your motives—after fourteen years of war, why do you decide *now,* when it appears that your compatriots in the Dragon Society have found a way to sway the Duke and compel a truce in your favor, to surrender yourself?"

"I don't think of it as surrendering," Zaner protested. "I'm asking to be purified. That's hardly the same thing."

"As you will, then. Tell me, in your own words, what brings you here today."

"I will." He looked around, but despite Arlian's suggestion he remained standing, while Arlian remained where he was, leaning against the table. He took a deep breath and began.

"You understand, Arlian, that I know the dragons are monsters. They killed everyone in Oginathi while I watched, more than five hundred years ago—I was a merchant, passing through town on my way home to Lorigol, and I hid in the watering trough in the stable beside the inn. I cut my forehead on the rim one time when I was ducking back down out of sight, and venom from the burning inn had gotten into the water, and here I am, centuries later, still alive—but I remember what I saw there. Men and women and children burned to death, or torn apart . . ." He shuddered again.

Arlian had never heard of Oginathi—but then, it had been destroyed five hundred years ago. Towns that the dragons chose were only rarely rebuilt; after all, whatever had drawn one attack might draw another. "Go on," he said.

"I thought they were beasts," Zaner said. "Like cats playing with mice. When I found out they were intelligent, and could communicate with us—well, I was horrified, but it didn't really change anything." He gestured at the hanging chains. "By then I had seen what my fellow man could do. I didn't *understand* it, but I had seen it, and how could I blame the dragons for inhumanity when I had seen what Drisheen and Horim did for amusement?" He glanced at the chains. "I hadn't known Enziet did that sort of thing, though—he was a little more discreet."

"Lord Enziet had many secrets," Arlian said.

"Indeed he did! And you seem to have discovered most of them."

Arlian nodded an acknowledgment. "He named me his heir."

Zaner grimaced. "I was shaken, you know, when you told us all how dragons reproduce—but at the same time, it seemed to explain a great deal. I thought that explained why they attacked villages, and killed all those poor people—they were trying to impregnate a few."

"If that were it, they were hardly efficient," Arlian remarked.

"Yes, I know, I realize that now, but I didn't see it *then*. I don't think I *wanted* to see it. And Pulzera had her theories about how all we dragonhearts by rights should be on the dragons' side, and how we weren't really even going to die, how we would be transformed into dragons, and it all seemed to make *sense* at the time, and *you* weren't being very convincing. Killing Horim and Enziet and Drisheen and the rest, and saying right out in the open that you wanted to kill *all* of us—how was I supposed to work with *you*?"

"I may have been excessively blunt," Arlian agreed. "I was young and foolish." He grimaced. "I am *still* young and foolish, but not quite as young, and perhaps not quite as foolish."

"We can hope, eh, Arlian? A little less foolish every year,

perhaps." He leaned against the table, a foot or so from his host. "Well, I went with the others to Sarkan-Mendoth, and I used my ships and coaches and warehouses to do my part in the war, and when Hardior and Shatter and Pulzera finally managed to talk to the dragons with that sorcery of yours I thought that we would be able to settle everything peacefully—make a deal, the way Enziet did seven hundred years ago."

"What sort of a deal?" Arlian asked, honestly puzzled. "The secrets are out, and cannot be called back—everyone knows now how dragons are born, and what a dragonheart is, and the names of the lords of the Dragon Society. What could you offer?"

"That's simple enough; we could offer their lives. We could find you and stop you, and agree that humans would kill no more dragons, and in exchange the dragons would promise to kill no more humans. What could be easier?"

"Indeed," Arlian agreed. "And if you had offered such a bargain after those first massacres, after Bentbridge and Kandarag and Upper Toniva, I believe the Duke would have taken it. I might have agreed myself, and if I did not, the Duke could have had me killed easily enough. The carnage that first summer . . ."

"I know," Zaner said. "I was sick about it. I think we all were. But the dragons were adamant. Even when we said that if they agreed to a truce we would use their venom to make more dragonhearts for them, all the dragonhearts they wanted, they wouldn't have it. Oh, they wanted us to use the venom, if only sparingly, and they wanted us to kill you—you know about that . . ."

"All too well," Arlian agreed dryly. "I know of about thirty assassins; were there others who failed without my knowledge?"

Zaner shrugged. "I don't know; that wasn't my concern. Hardior was the enthusiast for assassins. But my point is that no matter what terms we offered, the dragons would not agree to stop the killing. Ever."

"What?"

"Arlian, they didn't *want* a deal. They wouldn't hear of it. They wouldn't agree."

"But that's . . . but we've killed more than half of them since then. Why would they refuse a truce that could have prevented that?" He suddenly remembered the day's audience at the Citadel. "And why would they accept one *now*?"

"They were hungry. And now they aren't."

Arlian stared at him; then he reached down and shifted the candle to better illuminate his guest's face. "Hungry for *what*?" he asked. "What do dragons eat? There is no food in their lairs. When they emerge they burn their victims to death, or tear them to pieces, but they do not *eat* them—I know that, whatever the folktales may say. And what else could you mean? I had assumed they did not *need* to eat, that that was a part of their magic."

"That was what we *all* thought," Zaner agreed. "But it's not true. They eat *souls*."

"What?" Arlian said again.

"I only found out about six weeks ago. Hardior said something, and I asked, and . . ."

"They eat *souls*?"

Zaner nodded. "That's why they would never give up their attacks entirely, in all those years since Enziet bargained with them. They would have starved. They devour the souls of everyone they kill, and that sustains them. They fasted for a very long time during the Years of Man, waiting for Enziet to die, only emerging at long intervals, when they could stand no more, and even then restricting themselves to small, obscure villages—such as Oginathi or Obsidian. But then Enziet *did* die, and they came out to feast. First Kirial's Rocks and Tiapol, and then the next year, after you slew that first one, they went to Bentbridge, and . . . well, you know the rest as well as I do."

"But they told me . . . They offered to continue Enziet's bargain with me! They said they would stay in their caves if I agreed!"

"They lied, Arlian. They move slowly, and had not yet decided what to do about you, but they wanted you to keep their secrets secret until they were ready, so they told you what they thought might achieve that."

"And they let me destroy so many of their comrades?"

"Oh, they *tried* to stop you often enough! Those thirty assassins weren't all just friends of Lord Drisheen or Lord Hardior, you know. And after that first year you never spent a single warm day more than fifty yards from a dozen obsidian-tipped spears and heavy catapults, so they didn't want to go after you themselves. Not after what happened at the Old Palace."

"Yes, but to allow me to kill so many . . ."

"Arlian, you had the old records, didn't you?"

"Yes, of course."

"How often did they say there were more dragons than you found?"

"Often," Arlian admitted. "The last lair had four where I expected six, the one before that three where four were reported."

"They had moved. The younger ones. They left the old and tired ones, the ones who scarcely wake at all anymore, while the youngest and strongest moved to new lairs, safer lairs that aren't in your lists and maps."

"Still, to give up so many . . ." Then he stopped, and stared at Lord Zaner. "Those counts were accurate?"

"Probably. Most of them, anyway."

"But we were assuming that if the count was off, those others did not exist. That means . . ." He stopped again.

That meant that his estimate of forty-six remaining was horribly short of the truth. He had believed he had slain at least three-fifths of the world's dragons, but the actual fraction might be no more than half—perhaps *less* than half!

And the ones he had slain had been the old and feeble?

"Go on with your tale," he said.

"They never expected you to do so well," Zaner said. "You should be proud of that."

"Go on," Arlian repeated.

"They knew about the powers beyond the borders," Zaner said. They knew *all* of it. They didn't tell us much, but things gradually leaked out. They didn't want peace until they could make it on *their* terms. They feasted and feasted and feasted, and let you kill their old and sick until the decline in their numbers let the border magic decay, and *then* they sent us all here to Manfort."

"All?"

"The messenger—she's called Wing, and once she's safely back in Sarkan-Mendoth she'll be paid for this with a dose of blood and venom. Assuming, of course, that any venom is to be had. And Lady Tiria, of course . . ."

"Another assassin."

"Yes, but not for you," Zaner said. "She's been sent to kill as many of the Aritheian magicians as she can, to earn *her* dose of elixir. That's part of the dragons' price—not for you or the Duke, but for us, the Dragon Society. We are to bear their young to term, whether we like it or not, and anyone who might prevent that must die. All your Aritheian magicians are targets."

Arlian stood up straight. "And did you come here to the Grey House to kill Lilsinir, then?"

"Who?" Zaner looked baffled. "Oh, no, I'm no assassin. I'm just in Manfort as an overseer. We never trust anyone with anything this important without a dragonheart along to keep an eye on things."

"So you're distracting me, while your Tiria seduces Asaf or Tiviesh and stabs him in the back?"

"I *hope* not," Zaner said. "When you showed up in the waiting room we changed our plans—or, well, I had already been hoping to meet you somewhere and arrange to speak with you. When you came to the Citadel, it was the perfect opportunity. I thought I would have to ask Tiria to set up a meeting, but then you invited me, as well, and here we are."

"And where is Tiria?"

"Probably on her way here, after getting some last-minute instructions. I told her that talking to you was more important, and killing the magicians could wait. Frankly, I don't think she has what it takes to be an assassin, in any case; I doubt she could have killed any of them even if I *weren't* working to make it more difficult."

"Let us hope you judge her correctly," Arlian said coldly. "The Aritheians came here at my behest, and I do not want my guests murdered."

"Don't *worry*," Zaner said, slapping Arlian on the back. "They'll be fine. She won't dare do anything tonight—the whole Citadel is in an uproar about the news from the Borderlands."

"And that uproar might provide excellent cover."

"But it won't. I told you, Arlian, I'm here because I want the magicians to cure me, and they can't do that if they're dead. I've done everything I can to slow Tiria down and make her job difficult without giving myself away, and I really don't think she'll try anything tonight. She may be waiting downstairs right now."

"And where is the last member of your party, this Wing? Is *she* an assassin, too?"

"No, she's a messenger, and she probably has a dozen guards watching her every move. But who said she's the last? There were five of us."

Arlian closed his eyes and put his fingertips to his forehead. "Five," he said. "You, Wing, Tiria—who else?"

"Lady Opal," Zaner said. "She was chosen to oversee this expedition, and I had to speak fast and well to have myself included. I pointed out that a party of three women and a mere boy might draw unwelcome attention, and a mature man would look well . . ."

"That's four," Arlian interrupted.

"Ferret," Zaner said. "You don't know him; he's a boy from Lorigol, just turned seventeen. He's to spy on . . . well, on anyone he can. Get a feel for the mood in the city."

"So the Dragon Society, at the behest of their unspeakable inhuman masters, sent the five of you here to negotiate a peace with the Duke, and incidentally to assassinate the Aritheian magicians who know how to cleanse dragonhearts of their taint, and to spy out whatever you can about the city's morale."

"And the defenses," Zaner added. "And Opal seems to have some other plans of her own, but I don't know what they are."

"And you managed to have yourself included in this party—why?"

"Because I have seen and heard enough, Lord Obsidian. The dragons are the monsters you have always said they are; they kill so that they can eat the souls of their victims, and they deliberately prolonged this war to provide themselves with a banquet, even at the cost of their own elder brethren. When I found this out, on top of all these years of unnecessary bloodshed, it was too much for me. I could *not* continue in their service."

"But you've known this . . ."

"Just six weeks. And did I say that when a new dragon is born, it is *not* its human parent transformed? What you see in its eyes is not its own identity, but its first meal." He shuddered. "I do not want my soul to be eaten by some horrible parasite that's nourished itself on my heart and blood. I want my soul to go wherever souls *should* go when I die, whether that's to the realm of the dead gods or somewhere else. I'll give up half my thousand years for that."

"And you are doing this now, rather than waiting, because our fellow dragonhearts are endeavoring to eliminate the magicians capable of the operation."

"Yes, exactly. I certainly *hope* the Aritheians will survive, but the Society does have its resources, and I prefer not to take chances."

"Of course."

"Can you arrange it, then?"

"You'll need somewhere safe to stay for some weeks after the operation; where are you staying?"

"Ferret and I share a room at the Flapping Crow."

"That won't do. Perhaps I can find a room for you here—but I think I know an old friend who might help, if you would prefer."

"Either would be fine."

It was Arlian's turn to clap Zaner on the back. "I'll see to it, then. Now, let us go downstairs and see what my staff has prepared for us."

He opened the door while Zaner retrieved the candle, and the two walked out side by side.

14

An Awkward Supper

Wolt was waiting for them at the foot of the stairs.

"A lady has arrived, my lord, and we have seated her in the dining hall," he said. "Dinner will be served momentarily."

"Excellent," Arlian said. He glanced at Zaner. "This way, my lord."

"I can't let her see me here, with my face exposed in your presence!" Zaner said, tugging his mask back into position.

Arlian could hardly argue with that; he had wondered earlier how Zaner intended to join them at table. It appeared he didn't.

"Wolt, find someone to escort our friend Tooth to my study," Arlian said. "I believe he might appreciate a chance to speak to Isein—in private, but let his escort wait by the door. And send my steward down to dine with us, if you would." Arlian suspected that Zaner would prefer privacy while discussing the details of the cleansing spell with the Aritheian magician. Isein could not perform the ritual herself, but she had seen it done, and had assisted Oeshir and Lilsinir; she would be able to tell Zaner what was involved.

As for the escort, he did not yet trust Zaner enough to leave him unattended so close to any Aritheian magician.

Wolt bowed. "Of course, my lord."

A grateful Zaner turned and followed Wolt back up the first flight of stairs, while Arlian made his way to the dining hall.

That hall was perhaps the largest room in the Grey House, but no less gloomy than any other; the vaulted ceiling was unadorned stone, the tapestries on the stone walls had long since faded into beige incomprehensibility, and the massive oaken table was blackened with age. Its primary virtue was providing a place sufficiently formal that guests would not presume, simply because they had been admitted, that they were being welcomed into Arlian's home as friends.

There he found Lady Tiria seated at the foot of the great black table, with three or four servants standing uncomfortably about the room.

"I thought you were in Tooth's company, my lord," Tiria said, as Arlian bowed to her. "That was what your man said."

"Indeed I was, but I'm afraid he was called away on some urgent matter," Arlian replied. He turned to the most senior of the hovering servants—his chief footman, as it happened, a man not much younger than the retiring Ferrezin and soon to replace Ferrezin as chamberlain. "Venlin, would you see that some supper is taken up to my study, for Isein and her new assistant? I believe it would be best if they ate there, rather than interrupt their work."

Venlin bowed, and hurried into the kitchen, out of sight.

"Isein?" Tiria asked, accepting a wineglass from the tray a footman offered.

"A guest," Arlian replied, making his way to the head of the table. "One of my employees. She has been in my service many years now, and I consider her a friend. She is upstairs, attending to certain urgent business."

"The name is a curious one," Tiria said, turning the wineglass in her hand and eyeing the length of the table between herself and her host. The distance was not unmanageable—the table was meant to seat ten—but neither was it conducive to romantic whispers.

"I believe the name is Aritheian," Arlian said.

"Ah! And is Isein Aritheian, then? One of your famous magicians?"

"You are as clever as you are beautiful, my lady," Arlian said, lifting his own wineglass as he seated himself.

"I would like to meet her. I'm *fascinated* by Aritheian magic!"

Arlian smiled. Of course she was interested in the Aritheians—she had been sent to kill them. Isein was not trained in the physician's arts, and had never learned Oeshir's cleansing spell, but Tiria would not know that and might well not care about such distinctions. "Perhaps it can be arranged at some point, but her studies are at a critical stage tonight," Arlian said. He was not about to allow Tiria in the same room with any of her intended targets. Indeed, he would need to send warnings to the others at the first opportunity, before he allowed Tiria to leave, and make certain that all the Aritheians were provided with guards.

In fact, if he could find an excuse to leave her presence for a moment, he would attend to it immediately.

He turned at the sound of voices and clattering cutlery from the kitchen, and when he turned back he saw his steward standing in the far doorway, dressed in the black and white household livery and wearing the gold seal of his office around his neck for the occasion.

Arlian had not seen the seal in years, and had not been sure it still existed. "Ah, Black! Do join us!" he called.

"Of course, my lord," Black said. "I have taken the liberty of sending my children to eat in the kitchen, however."

That explained the giggling Arlian could hear from the kitchen.

"And your wife?"

"I thought it best she keep an eye on her daughters."

"Then I fear it will be just the three of us, my lady; I can have your plate brought to another seat, if you would prefer, so that we need not shout at one another."

Tiria smiled a smile Arlian supposed was meant to be seductive, but to his rather jaundiced eye she did not quite have the womanly grace yet to manage anything more than a rather forced playfulness. Perhaps in a few years she would do better—if she lived a few years, and did not distort her growth by becoming host to an embryonic dragon.

"I would be delighted," she said, rising. "I almost said something when your man seated me, but I did not want to presume."

A moment later Tiria was settled on Arlian's left and Black on his right, at one end of the table, while footmen set bowls of steaming turtle soup before them.

Tiria and Arlian spoke at length as the meal progressed, but Black limited his contributions to the conversation to occasional wry comments. Tiria coaxed Arlian into describing dragons' lairs, and the killing of their occupants, in some detail; he was unsure whether her interest was sincere, or simply carrying through on her alleged reason for taking an interest in him.

He described burning the venom from the cave walls, and Tiria's expression changed from her usual attentive smile to poorly suppressed shock.

"You know, I suppose," she said, "that in some circles that venom might bring as much as three hundred ducats for a single drop."

"So I have heard," Arlian replied, smiling, and knowing that his smile was cruel. This woman, hardly more than a girl, had become an assassin, had bartered away her ethics and perhaps her life, for a chance at such a drop.

"They say that even that little, just a single drop mixed in human blood, is enough to bestow the heart of the dragon."

"So they say," Arlian said. "In my own experience, the dose mixed in my grandfather's blood was considerably more than a single drop. It had eaten the flesh from his face and dissolved his left eye down to the bony socket before it dripped into my mouth."

Tiria swallowed, her face suddenly pale, and put down her fork.

"Ah, my apologies!" Arlian said, feeling a curious mix of vindictive pleasure and genuine remorse at her obvious discomfort. "This is no way to speak when dining with a beautiful lady! We should be speaking of life and beauty, not death and disfigurement."

"Yes," Tiria said, looking down at the fish on her plate but not picking up her discarded fork.

"Let us say no more about the foul dragons and their loathsome servants, the human incubators impregnated with their masters' monstrous spawn. Surely, there is something more pleasant that interests you?"

"But not all of them are loathsome," she protested, her eyes rising from the plate to meet his. "I . . . I have met a dragonheart, in Gallows Hill, and she seemed entirely charming—and of course, are *you* not an unwilling carrier of a dragon's offspring?"

"I have that disgrace," Arlian agreed. "It shames me that I have not yet taken advantage of the miracles of Aritheian magic to have the taint removed from my flesh, but I find the advantages it gives me too useful in the pursuit of my war against the perpetrators of this abomination. I will yield it up in time, when I am sure that the war can be successfully prosecuted without it—or when the war has *been* successfully prosecuted, and the dragons are no more."

"But you aren't at all loathsome or unclean, my lord!"

"How little you know him," Black muttered around a mouthful of bread.

"But *think* of the advantages it gives you! A lifespan a dozen times greater than we ordinary mortals, immunity to poison and disease . . ."

"Sterility, and a deadening of the emotions . . ."

". . . that superhuman charm—why, I can hardly keep

from flinging my arms around you! And they say that dragonhearts are stronger and faster than mere men, and gifted in sorcery . . ."

"Sorcery is but a matter of study and practice," Arlian said. "As for the rest, I cannot say whether there is **any** truth to it, but I think it a poor trade for the knowledge **that one** has a monster growing in one's heart."

"A monster that will only emerge after a *thousand years*!"

"Even a thousand years will pass in the end, and I would rather leave posterity a better legacy than one more vicious beast."

"I cannot even *imagine* the world a thousand years hence!"

"Nonetheless, it will come about."

"And what if, after nine hundred years, a dragonheart submits to the Aritheian rituals? Is that not the best of all worlds, living so very long, yet destroying the unborn dragon before it can do any harm?"

"It may be; I really cannot say. I am also uncertain whether those Aritheian rituals will still be known centuries from now. I believe the Dragon Society would like to see every Aritheian magician in the Lands of Man slain."

That was perhaps a dangerous direction for the conversation, coming as close as it did to Tiria's actual purpose in Manfort, and indeed, she did throw Arlian a sideways glance before apparently deciding it was mere coincidence.

"Well, what if they *were* slain?" Tiria asked. "Surely, more could be brought from Arithei."

"And of course, they would be *delighted* to come," Black said. "After all, simply because their predecessors were murdered . . ."

Tiria's sharp glance cut short his sarcasm; then she turned back to Arlian. "But wouldn't they come?" she asked. "If they were paid enough, given enough reason?"

"Indeed, given enough people, there are often fools who assume *they* will survive what their fellows could not," Arlian agreed. "But Arithei is a small country, and not every Aritheian is a magician, and not every magician knows the cleansing rituals. The secret could well be lost, in time."

Tiria looked sincerely troubled. "Do you think so?"

Arlian studied her for a moment, his fork poised in midair.

Obviously, she had intended to pursue exactly the course she had described—pay for a dose of dragon venom and blood, spend nine hundred years enjoying the benefits of its effects, and then have her full humanity restored, the infant dragon removed and killed. She had intended to pay for her prize in Aritheian blood, rather than golden ducats, but otherwise . . .

The loss of fertility and the chilling of her emotions did not seem to trouble her at all—but that was hardly surprising; Arlian had encountered that often enough in the past. Many people did not appear to believe in the emotional effects at all, and sacrificing unborn progeny seemed a small enough price.

"You realize, of course," he said, "that the dragons themselves do not want their young to be cast out and destroyed?"

"Of course they don't," she agreed, "but what can they do?"

"Quite a bit," Black said.

"We have your obsidian weapons to protect us," Tiria continued, ignoring the steward.

Arlian took a bite of fish and chewed it thoroughly, then swallowed and said, "The dragons, ancient though they are, still have centuries to find ways around our defenses and prevent us from destroying their spawn."

"And we have centuries to counter them. Really, Lord Obsidian, I think you underrate human ingenuity!"

"Rather, I think *you* forget that there are humans working on the dragons' behalf, and they are no less ingenious than the Aritheian magicians, or whoever else might conspire to cleanse dragonhearts of their corruption."

"No, I . . ." Tiria stopped, fork raised, as she realized that *she* was one of the people working on the dragons' behalf.

Arlian smiled at her. "A thousand years ago, at the very start of the rebellion against the dragons' rule and the beginning of the first Man-Dragon War, there was a group that learned how the dragons reproduce, and set about to put an eventual end to the dragons by the simple expedient of killing all the dragonhearts," he said. "This Order of the Dragon, as they called themselves, did not know of any way to kill dragons—the secret of obsidian was only discovered a quarter-century ago—but they could kill dragonhearts easily enough, and they did so, hoping that their distant descendants might be free of their draconic masters. The Man-Dragon Wars were the result, as the dragons struggled to produce dragonhearts faster than the Order could kill them."

"What?" Tiria said. "I never heard that!"

"Of course not," Arlian said. "It was kept secret. If everyone had known that the Order existed, and what it was doing, then the dragonhearts would have hidden themselves away, or fought back. And if the secret of how the dragons breed had been revealed, then there would have been hundreds, perhaps thousands, of eager volunteers lining up to drink the venomous elixir, trading their humanity for a thousand years of life. The Order revealed nothing—and neither did the dragons or their servants, for they were unsure who would win in the end if the conflict were to be entirely out in the open. Both sides preferred the real war to be fought surreptitiously, while the famous battles our legends recall were meaningless distractions."

"Why are you telling me this?"

"Because I want you to consider that what we see around us now is only the latest phase in a conflict that has been going on since the dawn of history. We had a respite of seven hundred years because Lord Enziet betrayed and murdered the Order of the Dragon, then blackmailed the dragons into withdrawing into their caverns beneath the earth—and the dragons agreed because they knew they would outlive him.

To them, that seven-hundred-year pause we call the Years of Man was trivial."

He leaned back in his chair.

"Now, do you really think that creatures that have fought to dominate humanity for so very long, creatures that can plan seven centuries ahead, creatures who managed to subvert a member of the Order of the Dragon and lead him to murdering his companions, won't have devised some way to ensure that most of their young *are* born on schedule?"

"They didn't know about the Aritheian magic!"

"They know about it now, and I'm sure they're trying to destroy it."

Tiria could hardly argue with that. "But there are other ways!" she insisted. "Look at Lord Wither, who killed himself with an obsidian dagger rather than release a dragon!"

Arlian winced at the memory—he had *seen* Lord Wither's suicide, and even provided the blade. "My lady, will you concede that there are those in the Lands of Man who would do almost anything for those additional nine centuries of life?"

"I suppose . . ."

"Let us further suppose, then, that as payment for their venom, the dragons require each would-be dragonheart to capture an existing dragonheart, one who is nearing the end of his requisite millennium. Let us suppose that the captor then amputates the prisoner's hands and feet to prevent escape or suicide, and holds him until the birth, and only then receives his reward. How, then, would the arising of a new dragon be prevented?"

"It wouldn't," Tiria admitted. "But chopping off hands and feet—how could anyone even *think* . . ."

"Have you met my wife?" Black interrupted, his anger only imperfectly hidden.

Startled, Tiria looked at him. "No, I . . ."

"Let us just say that there are those in this world who would not balk at such measures," Arlian said quickly.

Tiria appeared unconvinced—and that, Arlian thought, was perhaps the worst sign of all. She did not want to believe that she could not have it all, the thousand-year life *and* the restoration of her humanity.

And perhaps she *could* manage it—but not everyone would. Unless something was done to prevent the distribution of venom, there might soon be hundreds or thousands of dragonhearts in the Lands of Man, and a thousand years from now there would be hundreds or thousands of dragons.

The significance of this was just beginning to register on Arlian. He had had all the facts for hours, but had not really had the time to put them all together.

Now, though, with Lady Tiria's example before him, the pieces were falling into place.

The dragons had allowed the war, and Arlian's slaughter, to continue until the damage in the Borderlands was too great to ignore. They had been appallingly destructive themselves to further drive the point home—the Duke *must* make peace with them, or see the Lands of Man ruined. Exterminating the dragons would *not* bring peace; instead it would bring even greater disaster. A truce, allowing the remaining dragons to live so that their influence would keep the wild magicks at bay, was the only acceptable option.

And any truce would mean that their venom would be circulating, new dragonhearts being created. A ducal edict forbidding it would be worthless; any number of people would happily disobey such an order if it meant living for centuries.

The foul stuff was apparently already in circulation, at three hundred ducats a dose—there would be no established price if there were no supply. Arlian knew that the dragons had, for reasons of their own, not directly provided their followers with a supply, but presumably traces had been collected from destroyed villages or imperfectly cleaned lairs.

And if that supply should prove insufficient the dragons might, of course, change their minds and begin to deliver barrels of the stuff—well, no, not barrels, since venom would corrode its way through wooden staves, but bottles and jars.

A thousand years from now a new generation of dragons would be born—and that generation would dwarf any that had come before, would far outnumber the seven dozen Arlian and his men had slain. If the dragons chose there might be hundreds of new dragons every year, beginning in a thousand years and lasting indefinitely, until the Lands of Man were so choked with dragons that there was no more room for men.

Everything that the Order of the Dragon, Lord Enziet, and Lord Obsidian had done would be undone. The Lands of Man would once again be ruled by dragons.

The alternative was to continue Arlian's campaign until the dragons were extinct—and if Lord Zaner was to be believed, there were far more than forty-six remaining, so exterminating them would be no easy task. Then, when that had been accomplished, Arlian and his supporters would need to hunt down and kill or cleanse the hundreds of dragonhearts who would have come into existence by that point. That task was immense and daunting, and made all the more so because by doing so Arlian or his successors would unleash all the wizards, monsters, and nightmares that lurked beyond the borders, plunging the Lands of Man into utter chaos.

Domination by dragons, or descent into chaos.

Neither was acceptable, Arlian told himself.

He would have to find a third choice—some *other* magic that would protect the Lands of Man, as the dragons did, without killing innocents and devouring their souls.

But what that might be, he had no idea.

15

The Third Alternative

*B*y mid-evening Lady Tiria had, to her disappointment, been sent back to the inn where her party was lodged. She had learned little, if anything, about the Aritheian magicians, and if she had made any progress toward assassinating Arlian instead, he was unaware of it. Messengers had been sent to ensure that all the Aritheians were guarded, and that Tiria would not be permitted near them.

Lord Zaner was another matter; he and Isein had discussed the gruesome details of the purification rite. When Arlian came upstairs after Tiria's departure he found Zaner shaken, but still determined.

"It has to be done," he said. "The dragons are evil, and I can't be a party to their evil any longer."

"Has it taken you this long, then, to realize their evil?" Arlian asked.

"It has taken me this long to understand and accept the *extent* of their evil. I didn't want to admit it, but I can deny it no longer."

Arlian stared at him.

If Zaner, who had served them for these past fourteen years, could no longer tolerate the dragons, then how could Arlian, who had sworn to destroy them, consider a truce? The dragons *must* be obliterated.

Yet the wild magic must also be kept out, if the Lands of Man were to survive in anything like their present form.

But then, perhaps another form would suffice. Arlian looked at Isein, the Aritheian, who had grown up in the lands beyond the borders, where creatures of air and darkness prowled the sky, and nightmares stalked the hills.

Perhaps the magic could be controlled, could be made acceptable.

Arlian had visited Arithei once, long ago, and had found the experience harrowing. Arithei itself had been strange and uncomfortable, but not really bad; it had been the journey across the Dreaming Mountains that had been horrific. When Lord Naran and the Duke had spoken of the wild magic of the south loosed in the Lands of Man, Arlian and everyone else had thought in terms of the Dreaming Mountains, or the jungles below Skok's Falls, or the wizard-ruled realms of Furza and Shei, or Tirikindaro and its abominable master—but Arithei and Stiva were human realms, albeit ones where magic was omnipresent. If the Lands of Man were to learn how those two nations survived . . .

"I commend you, my lord," he said to Zaner, "and I beg your pardon, but I find that I need to speak privately to Isein."

Startled, Isein looked at him. "I will not be performing the ritual, my lord," she said. "You know I have never learned it; I have suggested that Lilsinir undertake it, and of course she will need a day or two to prepare."

"I know," Arlian said. "What I wish to discuss has nothing to do with Lord Zaner, which is why I do not wish to bore him with it. This is another matter entirely. Lord Zaner, if it would please you to stay here as my guest, by all means consider my home your own; my staff will find you appropriate accommodations. I regret to say that they will not be luxurious; this house was built in those ancient days when defense was considered more important than comfort."

"Maybe I should return to the inn, so that my companions will not realize anything is amiss."

Arlian bowed. "If you prefer, certainly—whatever you think best. I will have Lilsinir make the preparations and await your convenience."

Arlian saw Zaner to the door, and when Zaner was gone

Arlian stared after him for a moment, wondering whether he would indeed return to be restored to mere humanity, or whether he would lose his nerve and accompany Opal and Tiria and Ferret and Wing back to Sarkan-Mendoth, or wherever the Dragon Society was currently headquartered.

Then he turned and made his way back to the study, where he seated himself facing Isein and began questioning her about her homeland.

"How is it that Arithei has never been conquered by wizards, or overrun by other monsters?" he asked.

"It *has* been conquered," she replied. "Several times. The last wizard-king was killed when my grandmother was a girl—his slaves broke the protective circle around his bedroom and lured in a nightstalker."

Arlian blinked. "Why?"

"To kill him, of course. The nightstalker ate his eyes and brain from his head, and even a wizard cannot survive that without preparation."

Arlian's mouth opened, then closed again; the implication that a prepared wizard *could* survive it was deeply disturbing. He knew that wizards were not human, despite their usual appearance, but he had still thought of them as merely mortal.

"He tried to claim the nightstalker's body as his own, but the slaves were able to disrupt the spell," Isein continued. "Eight of them died preventing it, and three of the others were mortally wounded driving the nightstalker back out. Their faces have been carved in iron on the wall of the House of Indé in memory of their courage."

"I see," Arlian said.

"That wizard was not as bad as some," Isein continued. "He at least wore human form much of the time, and only killed those who displeased him. A hundred years earlier there had been a . . . I don't know the word in Man's Tongue. A single being with three bodies. *That* one depopulated an entire city before its heart was found and shattered.

Its death throes laid waste to so much land that hundreds of people starved for want of the crops thus lost."

"Oh," Arlian said, staring at her. How could she speak so calmly of such horrors?

But then, those who had never seen them spoke of the dragons' depredations with equal calm.

"There are stories of worse, long ago, but I cannot say how reliable they are."

"Yet in the end, the wizards and monsters are always driven out or slain?"

"So far," Isein said. "The struggle is constant. You have seen Arithei; you know the iron wards that guard the roads and towns. Our magicians spend much of their time weaving other protections and driving back magical creatures that venture near. The entire House of Shalien is devoted to keeping the thing in Tirikindaro from taking an interest in Arithei; their magicians know more of distractions and misdirection than all others combined."

"What *is* the thing in Tirikindaro?" Arlian asked. "I don't believe anyone has ever told me, in so many words."

"No one knows."

"Is it a wizard-king, then?"

"No. No wizard could live as long as that thing has. We don't know what it is."

"Could it . . ."

"*We don't know,* my lord."

Arlian glowered at her.

"My lord," she said, "I understand why you are asking me this; you are trying to decide whether the Lands of Man would be better off with the dragons, or the wild magic. My answer is that I do not know that, any more than I know what the thing in Tirikindaro is—but despite the dragons I prefer life in Manfort to my home in Arithei. Here my dreams are my own, and I need not fear gaunts crawling into my bedroom while I sleep; I know that when I wake up I will still be me, still be human. Children and sheep are never carried off by nightbeasts. People who stray from the roads are not found days or weeks later with their hearts or bellies eaten out from inside, their faces frozen in expressions of terror—nor do they come home marked with magic, clearly doomed, so that their families can spend the next several months waiting to see what sort of wizard or other monstrosity might in time be born from their kinsman's flesh. Yes, in the Lands of Man the dragons may come, entire villages may be slaughtered in a matter of moments, but it is an *understandable* threat, one that can be confronted."

"Then why does *anyone* stay in Arithei, or the other lands beyond the border?" Arlian asked, trying to understand. If Isein spoke the truth, as he did not doubt she did, then how could anyone prefer to remain in the magical realms?

"Well, no one can leave Shei or Furza because the mages do not allow it, and of *course* no one can leave Tirikindaro without permission. Leaving Arithei would mean crossing the Dreaming Mountains, which cannot be done without amethyst and silver—not to mention a good steel blade! As for Stiva, I know nothing about it; perhaps a compulsion spell keeps them from traveling."

"Thirif and Shibiel went home to Arithei, rather than stay here."

"Indeed they did—but they have family in Theyani. And Thirif told me he could no longer stand the cold here in the winter."

It took Arlian a moment to remember that Theyani was the capital of Arithei. He had visited that sunbaked city, long ago. "I can sympathize about the cold," he said.

"I rather like it," Isein said. "I like the north."

"Then you would accept a bargain with the dragons, even though it would mean that a thousand years from now, when the new dragonhearts hatch, there will be hundreds of dragons roaming the earth?"

"A thousand years from now I will be long dead," Isein

said. "What does that matter to me? Who knows what might happen in a thousand years?"

"The longer a truce holds, the more dragonhearts there will be in the end."

Isein spread her empty hands. "My lord," she said, "while I honor the memory of the slaves of the House of Indé, I admit I would not have had the courage to join them, to give up my life for the good of others who would come after me. And they, at least, hoped that the wizard-king's death would benefit their own friends and family, while you are asking me to concern myself with the people of a future a thousand years away. I cannot bring myself to believe that their eventual doom is important enough, and inevitable enough, to justify destroying the dragons and unleashing wild magic upon the Lands of Man."

"And what if we could find some way to hold the magic back, without the dragons?"

"Why, that would be the best of both worlds, surely—but how can it be done? My people have struggled for centuries to keep Arithei safe, and their success, while real, is a very limited one. Arithei is a very small land, and the Lands of Man are vast—all of Arithei would fit easily into the Borderlands, which are the merest corner of your nation. Every town, every city, every farmstead would need magicians protecting it; every road would require iron warding posts along its entire length. And the Desolation—no one can *live* there, so how could it be protected? It would become your equivalent of the Dreaming Mountains, the vast haunted wasteland that would be forever spilling its horrors down upon its neighbors."

Arlian knew she spoke the truth, but he refused to accept it.

This was hardly a new experience for him. He had sworn vengeance on the dragons when he was a mere boy, and for years he had been told he was mad, reminded that no man had ever slain a dragon—but he had found a way, all the same. Lord Enziet's six hundred years of research into sorcery and the nature of dragons had paid off in the identification of obsidian as the one substance that could pierce a dragon's flesh, and Arlian had put that discovery to good use.

Surely, there had to be some way to drive both the dragons *and* the wild magic from the Lands of Man!

And he had somewhere between nine hundred and a thousand years to find it.

And he knew where to start looking; Isein had told him. The Aritheians surely knew more about defending against hostile magic than anyone else. They had not yet found the one great key that would let them keep their land completely safe, but they could still tell Arlian what would *not* work, what would provide a partial solution.

He would go to Arithei. He would talk to the magicians. If necessary, he would learn their language so he could speak to them in their own tongue—at present he knew only a few half-remembered words in Aritheian. He would learn as much as he could, and he would seek some final solution.

And if the people of Arithei could not provide it, he would go to Stiva, or even to the wizards of Furza and Shei. In time, if all else failed, he might approach the Blue Mage, or perhaps even the master of Tirikindaro.

Somehow, he *would* find a way to defend the Lands of Man against hostile magic.

And when he had, he would resume where he had left off. He would exterminate the dragons once and for all.

The Magicians

16

Plans and Preparations

*T*he long-overdue Qulu never returned from Arithei, and after a month's stay in Manfort Arlian reluctantly concluded that he probably never would. Even in the best of times the road was hazardous, and these times were anything but the best.

That month had been an odd and troublesome one. Arlian had carried through on his intention to retire Ferrezin, though the old man had protested. In the end he had accepted the pension, packed up his few possessions, and departed—though he would not say where he was bound.

Lord Zaner had carried through on his promises, as well. In one of the upstairs rooms in the Grey House Lilsinir had removed Zaner's heart, driven the dragon taint from it, and then restored the purged organ to Zaner's body. Arlian had watched the whole thing, and had killed the misshapen horror thus expelled from Zaner's heart; the loathsome little thing, still five centuries short of its full growth, was no larger than a kitten and barely recognizable as a dragon when it took form from the bloody talisman Lilsinir had placed in Zaner's chest to draw out the poison in his blood. It mewled piteously as it crawled across the bedclothes and tumbled awkwardly to the floor, and it had scarcely struck the carpet when Arlian drove an obsidian dagger through it, reducing it to broken shards in a puddle of blood, venom, and offal.

The carpet, as well as the ruined bedding, was burned in the courtyard; the resulting stench took several days to fade.

Despite the stupefying herbs the Aritheians had provided the procedure had been agonizing, and Lord Zaner had lost consciousness. When he awoke he wanted nothing more to do with Arlian—apparently the mere sight of him was now associated with unbearable pain.

The Duke of Manfort, although generally preoccupied with negotiations with the Dragon Society and reports from the Borderlands, had formally pardoned Lord Zaner for any offenses he might have committed while in the thrall of the dragons, and had furthermore restored to him all his lands and properties that had been confiscated during the fourteen years he was outcast from Manfort.

His wealth and welcome renewed, and any fondness for Arlian destroyed, Lord Zaner was now recovering in his own old mansion—which had been standing empty for fourteen years, and was therefore badly in need of extensive repairs, repairs Zaner was supervising from his sickbed.

Zaner made it known that no dragonhearts, nor any of the servants of the Dragon Society, were welcome there—though those he called "my fellow victims of the southern witches" were cordially invited to call. Rime accepted that invitation, and reported back to Arlian that all in all, Zaner seemed to be adjusting to his altered circumstances quite well.

He had, for one thing, hired old Ferrezin as his steward. Whether Zaner had ulterior motives or simply wished to have an experienced man heading his staff, Arlian could not guess.

While the Duke was publicly pleased about Lord Zaner's submission, in private he informed Arlian that he and his magicians were not to solicit any further purifications.

"Your Grace's will is my own, of course," Arlian replied, bowing, "but I do wonder why that will should take such a direction."

"Because I'm in the middle of trying to make peace with the dragons and convince them to drive the invaders out of the Borderlands, and they don't *like* it when we abort their children!"

"Your Grace, might I suggest that further cleansings would serve to put pressure on the dragons, and convince them to agree to your terms?"

"Obsidian, I don't *dare* do that! We *need* them. I can't risk the possibility that they might simply abandon the negotiations and resume the war, or worse, join forces with the monsters beyond the border. Yes, you've been *remarkably* successful against them thus far, and I truly do commend and admire your actions, but Lady Opal tells me that the surviving dragons have retreated to new, deeper lairs where you cannot find them . . ."

"I can find them," Arlian broke in. "One way or another, I can find them."

"Perhaps you can, and perhaps you cannot," the Duke replied, annoyed by the interruption, "but my *point,* my lord, is that I want the war against the dragons to *end,* so that we can deal with those nightmares in the south."

"Perhaps, Your Grace, there is some other way to defend the Borderlands without giving in to the dragons."

"And perhaps there isn't. *I* don't know of any; do you?"

"No, Your Grace, but I am contemplating a journey to Arithei to discuss the possibility with the magicians there."

"Well, you're free to do that, my lord—I grant you leave. Your presence here does complicate the negotiations, as I'm sure you can imagine."

Arlian could indeed imagine it. He had a few uncomfortable encounters in the Citadel over the weeks of preparation; he and Lady Opal had been bitter foes for a decade and a half, and now she had been acknowledged as the Dragon Society's envoy to the Duke and given the freedom of the city, so it was not unexpected that they ran into each other on occasion, in the corridors of the Citadel or on the surrounding streets.

He remembered the first such meeting; he had rounded a

corner while hurrying, deep in thought, through the Citadel, and had found himself staring directly into Opal's green eyes.

They had both stopped dead in their tracks, and stood face-to-face, scarcely a yard apart. Arlian had been only dimly aware of the guard at Lady Opal's elbow as he met her gaze.

He recalled how when he had first met her, over Lord Nail's deathbed, he had thought her eyes dull and lifeless; that was certainly no longer the case. She had not yet tasted venom then, had not yet gained the heart of the dragon. Now her eyes shone.

The silence between them had begun to grow awkward, his staring rude; he forced himself to bow slightly and say, "My lady Marasa."

"Lord Obsidian," she replied, her voice strained.

"Your pardon; my thoughts were elsewhere."

"Of course." She did not smile, nor make any of the customary flirtatious responses an unmarried woman might ordinarily offer in such circumstances—but then, this situation was not ordinary.

Arlian thought of any number of things he could say, subtle insults he could direct at her, but as both were the Duke's guests in the Citadel, protocol required them to be polite to one another. No warmth was called for, and no one expected a pair of known enemies to express pleasure in each other's company, but civility was still necessary.

"If you will forgive me, I have business I must attend."

"Of course," she said again. She nodded, and he bowed again before stepping aside and striding past her.

That was not their only meeting, but it set the tone for all that followed. They continued to coldly acknowledge each other, but no more than that.

Even such minimal politeness required a considerable effort, apparently from both of them. Arlian did not enjoy those occasions, nor did he believe Opal liked them any better.

Of the others in her entourage, only Wing was openly acknowledged as her companion; Ferret and Lady Tiria were allegedly simple travelers, unconnected with the Society or Lady Opal. Tiria, however, could hardly help but realize that Lord Zaner had betrayed her identity and mission to Arlian, and she now avoided him—but not always successfully. That, too, caused some awkward moments.

Arlian had, of course, warned the Aritheians of Tiria's presence, and provided them with all the guards they wanted—or really, more than they wanted; he took the threat more seriously than did the Aritheians. Tiviesh, in particular, found the idea of an assassin targeting him absurd, and none of Arlian's protestations could sway him. Arlian hoped that the Aritheian would never realize that his food was being surreptitiously tested for poisons, his apartments carefully observed and occasionally searched for infernal devices.

Arlian had also set spies upon all of Opal's party, so that he might receive warning of any noteworthy activities. This yielded little, in truth, but some of the reports proved interesting.

For one, it seemed that Lord Rolinor had developed an infatuation with Wing, and was also spending what Arlian considered an unhealthy amount of time with Lady Opal in private conversation. This caused Arlian to doubt, more than ever, that Rolinor's earlier involvement with Wren had been entirely innocent; it was clear the young nobleman could not be trusted, and might well be hoping, even now, to earn a cup of blood and venom.

Not that Opal or Wing could necessarily provide one readily; while the dragons did communicate with the leaders of the Society, they did so only by sorcerous means over long distances, never face-to-face, and they did not freely supply their followers with venom. The dragonhearts were always eager to obtain more venom from any source they could find, to use in rewarding their followers—that had been part of Wren's assignment, after all.

Wing and Opal were reasonably attractive women, of course, as was Wren, so Lord Rolinor might attribute his interest in all of them to a normal young man's lusty nature, but there were plenty of comely young women in Manfort who did not have such unfortunate connections. Rolinor did not seem to spend an inordinate amount of time pursuing those others.

Whatever the reason for Rolinor's current attachments, Arlian was not pleased. "I should have killed the young fool there in the cave," he muttered.

"It wouldn't have mattered in the long run," Black pointed out. "There will be *hundreds* of eager buyers once it becomes generally known that the Duke is no longer having dragonhearts put to death on sight. Where there is a demand, there will be those who find ways to supply the desired goods."

"I know," Arlian conceded. "I still should have killed him."

Rolinor's activities aside, other reports led Arlian to conclude that Lady Opal had been sent as the Society's representative because the Society's leaders—Lord Shatter, Lord Hardior, and Lady Pulzera—considered her expendable; had she been killed, it would have been seen as no great loss. Now that she had succeeded, her position in the Society was, despite her youth, enhanced.

For centuries, rank within the Dragon Society had been determined by seniority; Lady Opal, as the youngest known dragonheart, should have been the lowest of the low. Instead, because she was the first to deliberately *choose* the heart of the dragon, and because she had been active and ambitious in pursuing the Society's ends, she seemed to have built up considerable influence.

Fourteen years before, Arlian, then the youngest dragonheart, had broken the Society into several factions with his actions and discoveries; the current reduced Society was the only surviving one of those factions, and now it appeared that Opal's actions might be splitting it anew.

That was not really surprising. The situations were complex, and the individuals involved varied. There were never simply two sides anymore. The Dragon Society nominally served the dragons, while the Duke and all Manfort nominally opposed them, but there were always complications, ways in which the Society's wants diverged from the dragons, ways in which the Duke's needs converged with the dragons, reasons for divided loyalties in individuals on either side.

Arlian hated that. He wanted the dragons dead, gone, abolished; he wanted vengeance for what they had done to his family, and he wanted to spare all the other villages the dragons would destroy in the future if they were permitted to survive. He wanted to save those souls the dragons would devour, if Zaner was right in his understanding of the beasts' diet. Arlian did not *want* any complications to this simple, albeit extremely difficult, goal.

Unfortunately, there *were* complications, as even he had to admit. He found it maddening.

He spent many evenings visiting Lady Rime and her household, enjoying the sound of childish laughter and the cheerful chatter of Rime's adopted family, and trying to distract himself from thoughts of magic and dragons and death.

It never worked for long.

And when the last trace of snow had melted, the spring flowers come and largely gone, the days grown warm, and Qulu had still not returned from Arithei with word of circumstances there, Arlian could stand it no longer. He had made preparations, and now he put them into effect.

"I am going to Arithei," he told Black at the supper table. "I leave tomorrow."

Black glanced at Brook, who sat on his right.

"I hope you will remain here, to tend to my affairs and keep a watch on events," Arlian added.

Brook smiled.

"How can I refuse?" Black asked, smiling back. Then the smile vanished. "I would accompany you, if you asked me,"

he said. "If you thought an old man's sword might be of
use."

"I'd rather have someone with common sense looking after things in Manfort," Arlian said. "Swordsmen are far
more easily found than sensible men."

Brook's smile widened. "I've told him that," she said.

Arlian nodded. "Though swordsmen of *his* caliber, I am
sure, are far less common."

That settled, the question of who Arlian *would* take with
him arose; after all, a lone man, even one of Arlian's experience, could not reasonably hope to cross the Desolation
unassisted. The remainder of the evening was spent in considering the possibilities.

In the end, there were three men aboard the wagon that
rolled out of Manfort two days later: Arlian and two young
soldiers from the Duke's guard, men known as Double and
Poke. For now, all three rode behind the oxen; Arlian intended to buy a horse or two in Stonebreak, so that one of
the soldiers could scout the surrounding area thereafter.

The party also included a woman: Isein.

"I thought you preferred Manfort," Arlian had teased
when she volunteered.

"I do," she said. "I don't intend to *stay* in the south. I do
hope to hear what became of Qulu, though, and to see for
myself just how bad things have gotten. Besides, my lord,
you will need a translator and guide."

"Indeed I will," Arlian agreed; despite his months of
study, his Aritheian remained quite limited. "Thank you."

The wagon itself was large and heavily built, its painted
sides reinforced with strips of black iron; fine silver filigree
decorated the gaps between iron bars, adding another layer
of protection against magic, and an amethyst was concealed
in each of its four corner joints. Each of the four travelers
carried at least two steel blades at all times; each wore a
good-sized amethyst around his or her throat on a heavy silver chain.

The interior was jammed with supplies, much of their volume simply water—they were going to be crossing the Desolation in summer, after all. There was almost no room for trade goods, but that did not concern Arlian; this was no money-making venture, no miniature caravan.

This was a scouting expedition.

He was, after all, the duly-appointed warlord of the Lands of Man. The Duke of Manfort might hope to make peace, to arrange a compromise with the dragons, but Arlian preferred to find a way to win the war against them.

17

Into the Borderlands

*T*he journey south was not a happy one. Rumors of the magical disasters in the Borderlands had reached every town and village along the road, and were the universal topic of discussion in the inns and taverns Arlian visited.

In the towns where he admitted his identity openly he was questioned to the point of harassment about what he and the Duke intended to do to rid the Lands of Man of both dragons and wild magic, and his insistence that no final decisions had been made provoked anger and derision.

"So the warlord himself is going to personally scout out the situation, with just two men and a wizard to help him?" one villager sneered in Benth-in-Tara, as Arlian looked over the town's array of half a dozen catapults.

"She isn't a wizard," Arlian corrected idly. "She's a magician, an Aritheian magician."

That provoked an argument that escalated rapidly and

eventually led to drawn blades, though in the end tempers were calmed without drawing blood; several of the villagers seemed to feel that all Aritheians were wizards, rather than human beings, and varied only in how well they hid their true nature. Other villagers considered this a side issue, and only wanted to know more about the Duke's intentions, and whether Arlian was genuinely scouting, or being sent into exile. Arlian's explanations failed to satisfy them or quell their suspicions.

At first Arlian had assumed this incident to be a fluke, but when roughly similar events occurred in Jumpwater and Blasted Oak he resolved not to admit his identity further. In Sadar he claimed to be a messenger in the Duke's service, forbidden to reveal his destination or the contents of his message. Astute natives noted the iron and silver on the wagon, and concluded he was bound for somewhere beyond the border.

The resultant prying for hints was maddening; Isein was reduced to tears and fled back to the wagon, while Poke resorted to drinking himself insensible in silence to avoid letting anything slip.

The overgrown ruins of Cork Tree, while depressing, at least did not demand explanations from the travelers. Arlian picked his way through the stones by the roadside, identifying the foundation of the tavern where he had run Lord Drisheen through, and locating the site of his nighttime duel with Lord Toribor, before settling to sleep in the wagon.

This was the one town on the route where no obsidian-armed catapults stood ready to defend against dragons; none had been ready in time. The meager remnants of Cork Tree served as a stern reminder of why those catapults loomed over the other villages.

In Stonebreak Arlian required Poke and Double to wear ordinary clothing, rather than their white and blue uniforms, and refused to give any account of himself whatsoever. That proved the best course yet—the townsfolk seemed far more willing to accept a completely mysterious

stranger than an imperfectly explained ducal representative.
The party stayed two days in town, and Arlian took the opportunity to buy a pair of horses, so that one or two of the
men would be able to scout ahead of the wagon in the
wilder lands to the south. He first chose a big chestnut gelding, a calm-tempered and well-trained beast, and then a
somewhat more skittish bay mare who showed a promising
turn of speed.

The negotiations for the horses went smoothly; the
seller, not wanting to lose the sale, did not pry into Arlian's
intentions nor make any mention of magic loose in the
Borderlands.

The horse trader was perhaps the only person in Stonebreak who did *not* warn the travelers against venturing further south; wild rumors and thirdhand reports of magic
filtering northward, of horrific happenings in the Desolation or the lands beyond, were everywhere. Arlian tried to
tease out fact from gossip, asking for names and dates and
places, and could find no reason to believe any of these
tales.

Despite the rumors and arguments and nervousness in
the various towns, Arlian and Isein found no evidence at
all that any wild magic had intruded into the surrounding
territory. Everything seemed entirely normal until they
were well into the harsh uplands of the Desolation. Arlian
dared hope, as they wended their way into the stony wasteland, that the reports received at the Citadel had been exaggerated.

By the time the wagon rolled down the rocky defile that
led from the Desolation into the Borderlands, however, Arlian had known for days that the situation ahead was very
bad indeed. He had seen the magic flickering across the
southern skies while still deep in the Desolation, and he
suspected that the uneasy dreams that had troubled any of
them who slept outside the amethyst-guarded wagon were
not entirely the natural product of their apprehensions.

Although they had taken the East Road, as Arlian had on

his previous visit to the Borderlands, the terrain had not looked familiar for the last few days; the sands of the Desolation often shifted, drifting in the wind, and he was fairly sure he had come down a different canyon than had his previous expedition.

That meant that the village ahead was probably not Sweetwater. Arlian remembered that there were three routes down from the Desolation in the vicinity, one of which ended at Sweetwater, and he was fairly sure the steepest and least likely did not emerge near any settlement at all; unfortunately, he could not recall the name of the town at the foot of the third.

Well, he would find out soon enough. He urged the oxen forward.

Double was riding ahead on their surviving horse, the big chestnut gelding; the bay mare had died ten days earlier and been left lying on the stony ground, as they could not spare the time and effort to bury her. They had never figured out exactly what had killed her, and Double had expressed doubts about the honesty of the trader in Stonebreak.

Poke was seated beside Arlian on the wagon—he had done most of the driving, but Arlian had taken the reins when he glimpsed the rooftops ahead.

Isein was staying inside the wagon, out of the sun—and out of bowshot of any foolish bandits who might decide to see what a lone wagon arriving out of season was carrying. She had abandoned her northern blouses and velvets for the vivid robes of Arithei, which were far more practical in the hotter climes of the south.

The two soldiers were back in the Duke's uniform, though with coats removed, sleeves rolled up, and buttons undone in deference to the warmer temperatures; Arlian had resolved to try revealing his true identity and purpose again, in hopes that matters were different here in the Borderlands than on the northern side of the Desolation.

"What are those trees?" Poke asked, as they emerged

from the defile onto the track between two tightly packed groves, a track too faint to be called a road.

"Orange groves," Arlian answered—he had seen such groves before. He scarcely bothered to look at them, however; his attention was on that seething, unnatural sky, where shadowy shapes fluttered through glittering purple clouds. He did glance to either side to make sure that the farmers gathering fruit were not obviously hostile, and was reassured to see that they waved cheerfully at the wagon. That settled, he returned to trying to estimate the distance to the aerial manifestations, and the nature of the things flying there.

Poke, on the other hand, stared into the groves, watching the workers, plainly fascinated. "Oranges grow on trees?" he asked.

Arlian turned, grinning, to stare at Poke. "Where did you *think* they came from?"

"Vines, like pumpkins," Poke explained. "I thought they were miniature pumpkins."

"No, they grow on the trees you see here," Arlian said. "Which, alas, cannot survive the winters back north. I think you'll find they taste even better fresh from the tree than they do back home."

"I've never tasted one at all," Poke said. "We couldn't afford *oranges*! If my family had that kind of money I wouldn't have become a soldier."

"Well, you'll eat them here," Arlian told him, smiling. Then he looked forward again. The conversation had reminded him of the village's name, which had previously eluded him: Orange River.

"I believe this is Orange River," he called over his shoulder to Isein. "Are you familiar with it?"

"No," she called back. "We always went by way of Sweetwater."

That was hardly surprising; Orange River was well east of the best route to Arithei.

On the other hand, if he remembered his geography correctly, they were only about four days from Pon Ashti. That city was reportedly now under the sway of the Blue Mage, but it might still be safe enough to make a visit there. Perhaps he could talk to magicians there, or even arrange an audience with the Blue Mage herself.

He and Isein had discussed various possibilities during the long ride across the Desolation, and Arlian had questioned her at length about the nature of magic, and of wizards.

"Wizards were all created from human beings," she had explained, "or at least so we believe. Those whose origins we know were people who were consumed by magic, and became something other than human."

"Magicians who lost control of their magic, then?" Arlian had asked her. "Are *you* at risk, if we venture beyond the border?"

"No," she said. "Previous knowledge of magic doesn't seem to matter; some wizards had been magicians, some were not. Rather, they were people who became infected with wild magic, which then overwhelmed and destroyed them, creating wizards from their flesh. The last wizard-king of Arithei had been a mushroom farmer—going about his business one day, then awakening transformed the next."

That had aroused Arlian's curiosity. What were wizards, and how did they come to be? Could their nature be the key to what he sought? Now he wondered whether a wizard like the Blue Mage might know everything he needed to safeguard the Lands of Man without the dragons, and whether she might be willing to talk to him.

He had briefly entertained the notion that allowing wizards to rule the Lands of Man might be acceptable; presumably they would keep the other wild magic at bay. Isein had done her best to disabuse him of this notion, however, and had largely succeeded—wizards, according to Aritheian history, were capricious and violent, thoroughly untrustworthy, and not particularly long-lived, so that any wizard-king of Manfort would need to be replaced fairly often. Finding *one* tolerable wizard-king would be extremely difficult, if it was possible at all; finding a regular supply of them was presumably out of the question.

"Wizards do not breed after the fashion of men or beasts?" he had asked.

"Nothing magical does," Isein had replied.

Somehow, that did not surprise him.

He had already learned a few principles of sorcery from Rime, years ago; his conversations with Isein had now confirmed that southern magic, however chaotic it might appear, also had certain underlying laws and patterns and limits. The magicians of Arithei knew some of the patterns and limits, but most of the deepest laws they could still only guess at.

When he had set out Arlian had intended to head directly to Arithei, to talk to the magicians there, but after months of conversation with Isein on the journey, he now thought he might do better elsewhere. There were undoubtedly Aritheians who knew more than she did, but she had given him an idea of the limits of Aritheian knowledge.

The Blue Mage spoke human languages, and could sometimes be reasoned with, and surely knew secrets the Aritheians could not imagine; perhaps she could be coaxed to reveal some of those secrets. She had taken Pon Ashti from the Lands of Man, in defiance of the dragons' power; perhaps if Arlian offered her further acquisitions . . .

But that would hardly improve the situation.

Double had stopped in a plaza ahead, at the heart of the little village, and spoken with one of the natives there; now he held his arm upraised in one of the signals Arlian had taught him.

"Double says that there's an inn ahead," Arlian called over his shoulder. "I know it's still early, but I think we should stop and hear the latest news."

"As you please, my lord," Isein called back.

Poke smiled. "I think it wise, my lord."

"Go tell Double, then," Arlian said, prodding Poke. "Get the innkeeper started."

Poke jumped down from the slow-moving wagon and trotted ahead. By the time the oxen plodded into the plaza both guards and half a dozen townsfolk were waiting. The two stableboys ran up, one on either side, and reached for the buckles.

"Wait until we stop," Arlian called, as he pulled on the reins.

"Of course, my lord," the taller boy replied, ignoring Arlian's order and tugging at the straps.

No harm was done; the oxen stopped, and Arlian was able to transfer the reins to one hand and pull the brake lever with the other before the wagon had rolled another foot. A moment later the boys were leading the oxen away to the stable while Poke and Double maneuvered the wagon up against the rail; Arlian had lifted Isein to the ground, and now he turned and bowed to the innkeeper.

"Lord Obsidian of Manfort, at your service," he said.

"Haddrew of Orange River, my lord," the innkeeper replied, returning the bow. He showed no sign of recognizing Arlian's title. "May I inquire after the remainder of your caravan? Will they be arriving today, or has some mishap befallen them?"

"Did a monster get them?" the taller of the local women called. "We've heard there are monsters in the Desolation now."

"We have no caravan," Arlian replied, glancing from the innkeeper to the woman and back. "I have not come to the Borderlands to trade, but on other business." He doffed his hat to the woman and added, "And we have seen no monsters, save those in the sky to the south."

Some of the townsfolk cast quick, uneasy glances at the southern sky.

"Nor were we troubled by bandits," Double remarked. "I had always heard that the Desolation was full of them."

Arlian suppressed a sigh. It seemed impolitic to mention
bandits in this particular place; the notorious raiders who
made crossing the Desolation so dangerous probably included several of the men of this village and the surrounding farms. Bandits could not *live* in the wastes; they came
from towns in the Borderlands. Caravans generally arrived
after the harvest; preying on them was seen here as a way to
keep young men busy and augment the household coffers.
The risks were considerable—the first man Arlian had ever
killed had been such a bandit—but the profits could be, as
well.

Fortunately, the townspeople did not take offense at Double's comment. A woman, one who had not previously spoken, said, "I think all of them have gone south to help fight
the monsters, or guard against the wizard of Pon Ashti."

Arlian turned. "The Blue Mage, you mean?"

"Yes, that's what they call her, my lord. You have heard
of her?"

"I fear I have. Then it's true? She has taken Pon Ashti?"

"She has." Both women nodded.

The wagon was secure, the oxen out of sight, and Poke
and Double were strolling over to join the group. Arlian and
Haddrew began to speak simultaneously, then stopped.
Haddrew bowed. "My lord?"

"I was going to suggest, sir, that we have come a long
way through some very dry terrain, and would be pleased to
take advantage of your hospitality . . ."

"Something to drink—of course, my lord!"He gestured
at the door.

A moment later the four travelers were seated at a table
in the inn, just inside the broad glassless window; the shutters were folded all the way back, but a wide canvas awning
provided shade. Haddrew, the two women, and an old man
who had not yet contributed to the conversation all pulled
up chairs nearby, while the two boys fetched water and wine
from the cellars.

"We had reports that magic had spread north of the border," Arlian remarked. "I'm sorry to see that they were accurate. How bad is it?"

"Bad," the shorter woman said. "We dare not go out at night."

"And even in our own beds, our dreams are troubled!" the taller said. "We pay taxes to the Duke of Manfort; can't he do something?"

"The Duke is a very long way from here," the shorter said.

"Nonetheless, his family claims to be responsible for protecting all the Lands of Man," Arlian said. "You have a right to expect something in return for your taxes." He did not mention that in fact, most of the Borderlands did not actually pay any taxes; he had heard the Duke's comments on the subject on occasion.

"He only heard about the problems a few weeks before we left," Poke said.

The southerners exchanged glances. "Then he *has* heard?"

"Indeed he has," Arlian said. "I am here in part as the Duke's representative, sent to assess the situation."

"Good!" the tall woman said.

"We have had no word from the north in months," Haddrew said. "We heard from Sweetwater that messages had been sent, but we had no way of knowing whether they had reached Manfort. I'm relieved to know that they did."

"Lord Naran encountered no serious delays on his way north," Arlian said. "All the same, several months have passed, and I'm sure matters have changed. Tell me, then, how things stand—the Blue Mage still holds Pon Ashti? What of Skok's Falls?"

Everyone began to speak at once, eager to pass on the news.

Several hours and several drinks later the torrent of gossip finally dried up, leaving Arlian with a clearer, albeit depressing, picture of the situation.

For centuries there had been a natural border, invisible but definite, that magical creatures did not cross. Oh, people who slept too close to the line might experience visions or nightmares, or glimpse unnatural movements from the corners of their eyes, and of course they could see the bizarre phenomena in the southern skies, but nothing more tangible, from the flittering nothings to the near-human wizards to the towering stalking horrors, had ventured into the Lands of Man.

The border's exact location might drift back and forth slightly; the city of Pon Ashti was built so close to it that at times its southern and western walls had been subject to the attacks of nightstalkers and gaunts, so that protective bands of iron had been mounted to repel infringing magic. That had worked well, and the border had been maintained. Any northward drift had always been balanced by a southward bulge somewhere else, and had reversed after a season or two in any case.

But a few years ago that had begun to change. Fields that had always been safe suddenly sprouted misshapen weeds that spoke in incomprehensible tongues; the flying monstrosities that circled perpetually over Tirikindaro swept through the skies of border towns, sometimes flapping at people's windows; drovers who used the southernmost roads found shadowy little creatures hiding in their wagons. There was still a border, but it was creeping northward, yard by yard, day by day, and the lands newly excluded were gradually absorbed into the magical wilderness, or were invaded and annexed by their southern neighbors. Most of the people who had lived and worked in those lands fought for their homes, but the magical assaults kept coming, traders became ever more reluctant to venture near, and more and more farmers and tradesmen were giving up and moving north.

There were humans dwelling beyond the border, but most of them were ruled by wizards, or lived in uneasy states of truce or stalemate with the wild magic. A few of the people of the Borderlands had tried to make common cause with these foreigners, but that had only made matters worse—if

they had felt any kinship to the inhabitants of the Lands of
Man and had any freedom to act upon it, they would not
have been outside the borders in the first place. Admitting to
them that the border was failing had resulted in raids by human foreigners, as well as the magical varieties.

Those raids had turned into full-fledged invasions two
years ago. All the lands beyond the new border had now
been usurped by one foreign power or another—Shei and
Furza and Tirikindaro had been especially greedy. The Blue
Mage, a uniquely powerful wizard who had never before
bothered to establish permanent rule over a specific place but
had simply moved about, occupying whatever settlement
took her fancy, had now taken a fancy to Pon Ashti and settled into the council palace there, establishing a miniature
kingdom. She had had the iron stripped from the walls, and
reports from the city spoke of inhuman creatures freely
roaming the streets, and handsome youths who caught the
Mage's eye vanishing into the palace, never to be seen again.

The Darambar River, which flowed through Pon Ashti on
its way to its tangled and swampy delta, had always been
clean and natural upstream of the city; now there were strange
many-eyed fish in it that would stare up at anyone who
came near, and the water seemed to glow at night. The true
border was now judged by some to be a good three miles
north of the city.

Other towns and villages had fallen as well, dozens of
them, but the people of Orange River considered the loss of
Pon Ashti to be the most significant disaster, since that had
been their major center of trade. The river for which their
town was named joined the Darambar just a day's travel to
the south.

It was widely feared throughout the Borderlands that the
wild magic's advance would continue until it reached the
Desolation, and all the inhabitants would be forced to either
flee or subject themselves to the whims of some wizard.

The reason for the border's retreat, which had seemed so
obvious in Manfort, was unknown here; these people sim-

ply didn't think about the dragons. No dragon had been seen in the Borderlands for three hundred years, and the stories that came from the north of villages burned and dragons slain in their lairs were merely stories that had no connection with the world these people lived in. No one here understood how a catapult worked, nor saw any reason to want one built in their village.

In fact, careful questioning led Arlian to conclude that the people of Orange River had never heard of dragon-hearts, had no idea how dragons reproduced, and knew of no uses for dragon venom. They knew that obsidian had been discovered to be effective in piercing draconic armor, but found this of purely academic interest—after all, none of them had ever seen obsidian or had a clear idea what it was, nor had any of them ever seen a dragon.

Arlian took a moment to show them the obsidian dagger he carried, which was passed around and marveled at.

"I want to see Pon Ashti for myself," he said. "How can I get in?"

The villagers looked at him and at one another, puzzled; then the tall woman said, "Just walk in. They won't stop you."

"They don't guard the walls?"

"The gates stand open day and night, now that the Blue Mage rules there; after all, what's left to keep out?"

"Ah, I see," Arlian said.

"Of course, it's dangerous. Wear gloves, lest a gaunt or night-thing bite you, and keep your back to a wall whenever you can. A plastered wall, if you can, as some things can seep through the cracks between stones or boards."

"Indeed." He hesitated, then said, "Many years ago I crossed the Dreaming Mountains to Arithei; should I expect anything worse in Pon Ashti than I faced there?"

Again the villagers exchanged glances.

"I suppose not," the short woman reluctantly admitted.

"Good!" Arlian said, slapping the table and pushing back his chair. "Then I will leave for Pon Ashti in the morning!"

18

The Gates of Pon Ashti

*A*rlian studied the terrain ahead with interest; he had never seen anything quite like it.

Directly ahead, to the southeast, his view was blocked by the golden-brown walls of Pon Ashti, speckled and striped by the marks where the protective iron had been stripped away, leaving snapped rivets, streaks of rust, and discolored stone.

To either side of the city, though, marshland stretched out to the horizon. At the moment the tide was out, and the gray-green marsh grasses lay stretched out flat, drawn seaward and woven into graceful patterns by the retreating waters. Here and there creatures of one sort or another flickered in and out of the grass blades—some of them the normal coastal wildlife, others shadowy or sparkling in ways that made Arlian quite sure they would not ordinarily be found in the Lands of Man. Every so often a wave of unnatural color flashed across the marsh to the south, and the southern sky was seething with magic. The air smelled of salt and storms.

The marshes were what made any sea trade here impractical, forcing merchants to send caravans across the Desolation instead. Arlian knew that somewhere to the east lay the sea, near enough that the tides washed up to the walls of Pon Ashti and raised those grasses up, but he could not see it; the marsh grass seemed endless.

And somewhere to the south the Darambar made its way through a hundred shallow, twisting channels in the marshes to the sea—but it also passed through miles of territory that had always been outside the borders, even when the dragons had been at their mightiest. Foreigners sometimes sailed their little flat-bottomed boats up through that maze, but no northern merchant had attempted it in centuries.

Beside Arlian the Darambar flowed smoothly over polished stone, water and stone glittering in the afternoon sunlight; behind him the land and the road rose up gently, well above the marshes, and houses and cultivated fields lined the road and covered the land.

Those farms were almost ordinary, while the marshes were utterly strange. Arlian reined in his mount for a moment, to take a better look.

He was astride the chestnut gelding, approaching Pon Ashti alone, and he did not care to ride directly into some sort of magical trap or ambush. He wished once again that Isein had accompanied him, but she had flatly refused.

"I came south with you because you said you were going to Arithei," she said. "I have no interest in Pon Ashti or the Blue Mage, except as things best avoided."

He had tried to persuade her, to convince her that knowing more about the Blue Mage could help Arithei, but she would have none of it.

Once that was settled, the decision to leave the wagon and his two men behind had been easy; without a magician along, his best course was to be unobtrusive. One man on a horse was less noticeable than three men in a wagon.

No one seemed inclined to notice him, however; he could see no guards on the ramparts of Pon Ashti, and several of the houses he had passed on the way had been standing empty and deserted, while the inhabitants of the others were going about their business and ignoring the passing horseman.

This lack of interest could be a problem, he thought. Despite what the people of Orange River had told him, the city gates were closed—at least, the set directly ahead of him; he knew there were others, and in fact could see the next to the west, on the far side of the river. If there were no guards to open the gate, how was he to enter the city?

He supposed he could wade out into the Darambar and scale the great stone lattice that allowed the water to flow freely through the wall, but the openings were not large enough for a man his size to squeeze through, and the overhanging rampart at the top would make climbing over a challenge—not to mention that his horse could hardly take that route.

Well, perhaps there *were* guards concealed somewhere, watching him. He shook the reins and urged the horse forward with his knees.

Sure enough, the gates swung open as he approached, and a man's voice called, "State your business in Pon Ashti!"

Arlian still did not *see* anyone manning the defenses; he could see a few people on the street beyond the gate, hurrying about their own affairs, but he could not see who spoke, nor anyone on the ramparts or moving the gates.

"I'm here to discuss trade agreements," he replied. He had settled on this as his best approach, and it was arguably true—he wanted information, and was willing to trade his own knowledge for it.

"Discuss with whom?" the voice asked—though the tone gave no indication that the speaker actually cared about Arlian's answer.

"With anyone interested," he replied.

"Do you carry cold iron or steel?"

Arlian blinked at the sudden change in subject. "I have a sword," he said. "And a swordbreaker, and a knife, and, oh, some of my mount's harness, and a steel with my flint . . ." He suspected he was about to be asked to surrender them all, and he did not like the idea—but it was not entirely unexpected.

"Do you carry silver?"

"A few coins, and the chain about my neck."

"Then there are places in the city forbidden to you—but

enter freely, and of your own will, and be welcome in the name of Her Majesty the Blue Mage."

That was interesting. "Her Majesty?" Parts of the city forbidden, but not all of it?

He noticed no one had asked about amethysts or obsidian; was that because those substances had no power against the Blue Mage and her minions, or simply because they were so rare that travelers were assumed not to carry them?

He carried them; he had an obsidian dagger in his blouse, a large amethyst on the silver chain about his throat, and a smaller amethyst in his pocket. He saw no need to say so, however.

He rode forward through the gates, and still saw no guards until at last, as the gates started to close behind him, he saw something from the corner of one eye. He whirled as best he could in the saddle and caught a fleeting glimpse, and then it was gone again.

He was unsure what it was, but it was big and yellow, with wings and horns, and oddly insubstantial. It moved impossibly fast—but then, it was clearly magic.

"You are forbidden the water steps, and the Mage's palace," the voice said from somewhere behind him. "The granaries and fisheries you may only approach if you have first disarmed and given up flint and steel, but you may keep your silver in those."

"Thank you," Arlian called back, still unsure who he was addressing; then he rode on, into the empty plaza inside the gate.

This, he thought, should have been a busy market, but instead it was a bare expanse of brown brick pavement, bounded to the north by the city wall, to the west by the river, and to the south and east by tall, narrow houses. Three streets led out of the square, one along the waterfront, the others piercing the rows of houses.

Beyond the plaza people were moving about the streets, clad in the loose robes common in the southern lands, though the robes here were cut longer than the Aritheian style, and bleached to white or pale, subtle hues where the Aritheians preferred vivid reds and oranges. Arlian noticed that most of the city's inhabitants seemed to be barefoot; he had expected to see sandals. Any more solid footwear was scarce this far south, but sandals were common.

Some of the people glanced at him, then quickly looked away.

That seemed odd; was it not permitted to look upon strangers here? If strangers were allowed into the city, it hardly seemed reasonable to expect the natives to ignore them.

He directed the gelding toward the river, thinking that would give him the best view.

"Remember, the water steps are forbidden!" the voice he thought belonged to the yellow creature called from behind.

"I remember," Arlian called back. He was not sure just what these "water steps" were, but he assumed he would recognize them when he saw them. The name and the timing of the guardian's shout implied that there was a connection with the river. He peered ahead, looking for some indication.

Soon enough the gelding's steady walk brought him around the corner, where he could see down the street and down the river, and the name was suddenly clear.

The Darambar cut straight through the center of the city, paved streets along either bank; Arlian counted four arched stone bridges crossing it, all of them in the upper half, where the river was perhaps thirty or forty feet across.

Beyond the fourth bridge, however, the river widened—and dropped down over a low fall, perhaps three or four feet. Below that, although it was hard to make out the details at such a distance even from horseback, he could see that it widened more, and more, and more, descending more sudden drops, all of them even shallower than the first . . .

Steps. The river, Arlian realized, flowed down an immense staircase, spreading out as it went, until at the very bottom, where it vanished through several hundred pipes through the city wall and flowed out into the marsh, it was half a mile wide and no more than a few inches deep.

And people were wading on these water steps, walking about, or crossing the river with no need of bridges, or going about other business, or simply standing in the cool water. Arlian could see men talking, gesticulating as they spoke, ignoring the greenish water eddying around their ankles; he could see women rinsing clothes in the steady flow, and children splashing each other as they ran shrieking through the water. Here was the life of the city that the plaza at the gate had lacked.

And he was forbidden to set foot in the water, by command of the Blue Mage. He frowned.

Well, perhaps if he disarmed himself, and left his steel and silver somewhere safe, he could join the natives—or perhaps he could accomplish his purposes on dry land.

That reminded him that he needed to find somewhere to stay, an inn or guesthouse; he had rented floor space from farmers on the ride from Orange River, but wanted something a little more formal inside the city. He had intended to ask at the gate, but had been so distracted by the guardian's discussion of cold iron and silver, water steps and palaces, that he had forgotten.

That was easily remedied, though. He called to a nearby woman as she passed, "Your pardon, my lady—is there an inn nearby?"

She looked up at him, then pointedly looked away and walked faster.

Puzzled and annoyed, Arlian let her go, then chose another pedestrian and repeated his question, with similar results.

It wasn't until his fifth attempt that he got an answer.

"You're human, then?" the man asked.

Arlian considered this question for a moment before replying, "I believe so, yes." He doffed his broad-brimmed hat, thinking that sunlight illuminating his features might be helpful.

"And that's just a horse?"

"To the best of my knowledge, yes," Arlian said mildly. "It was certainly sold to me as such back in Stonebreak, and I'm not aware of any change in species it might have undergone since then."

The Pon Ashtian looked quickly to either side, then stepped closer and asked in a loud whisper, "How did you get *in*?"

"I rode in, not half an hour ago," Arlian said. "The gate opened, and a voice challenged me, and was satisfied with my answers. I'm not to enter the palace, the fisheries, or the granaries, nor set foot on the water steps, but otherwise I am unfettered."

"But you wear a sword."

"Indeed I do, and as a gentleman in the service of the Duke of Manfort I am entitled to do so."

"Not *here*," the man said. "She doesn't *like* steel."

There was no need to ask who "she" was. "I presume that is why the palace is forbidden me."

"Yes." The man looked Arlian over, from his black-haired bare head to his black leather boots. "You're a northerner," he said.

"That fact had not escaped my attention," Arlian said dryly.

"I don't understand why the demon let you in."

"Demon?" Arlian glanced back toward the gate. "That yellow creature?"

"Yes. It's a demon. She summoned it to serve as her gatekeeper."

Arlian shrugged. "It admitted me."

"Then she's changed the rules *again*." Arlian was startled by the depth of despair plain in the man's voice as he spoke that single sentence.

"I wouldn't know," Arlian said. "Has she?"

"She must have. Swords, horses, northerners—those were all forbidden a week ago. Anyone found carrying a sword was destroyed, and she sometimes included others in the vicinity, as if they shared the guilt by their mere presence."

That accounted for the hostile reception Arlian had received from the city's human population, and spoke well for this man's courage.

"Nonetheless, I told the creature I carried a sword and other blades, and it allowed me to enter the city, with some restrictions made."

"She's changed it."

"In any case, my good man, could you direct me to someplace I might find lodging during my stay in Pon Ashti?"

"The inns are closed," the man replied. "Centers of unrest luring foreign troublemakers, she called them. I saw what she did to Hulimir—he was the innkeeper at the Broken Wheel." He shuddered.

Arlian was curious. "What *did* she do to him?"

"He was strangled by his own gut," the man said. "Like a snake choking him. His belly just opened up, and it crawled out and climbed up to his throat."

The mental image left Arlian wishing he had not asked. He sighed. "Then I suppose I'll have to make do with a patch of ground, or a quiet street. A pity; I had hoped for a good bed."

"Or you might find someone willing to share his roof— she has voiced no objection to that."

"Do you know of anyone who would be willing?"

The man looked up at Arlian, considering. "Can you pay?"

The man to whom Arlian spoke in the street turned out to be known as Broom; the widow who rented him a room called herself Twilight.

"I hadn't known that the custom of nicknames was common this far south," Arlian remarked, as he brushed down his horse for the night. Twilight had no proper stable, but there was sufficient space in her garden shed to provide the gelding with shelter.

"It wasn't," Twilight said from the garden bench. "It is now, though."

Arlian threw her a glance, then finished currying the horse in silence.

19

The Servants of the Blue Mage

Arlian had been in Pon Ashti for four days when the Mage's creatures came for him.

He had been half expecting something of the sort. While he had obeyed the injunction not to enter the palace or cross the water steps, nor bring iron or silver into the fisheries and storehouses, he had explored much of the rest of the city, and spoken freely with several of its citizens.

Far more dared not speak with him, and fled if he persisted in addressing them, but some answered his questions and discussed the situation with him. Twilight had been reasonably forthcoming so long as he did not specifically mention wizards in general, or the Blue Mage in specific; he learned that she had been widowed when the city's new overlord first arrived. Her husband had been a junior member of the old city council, and the Mage had seen no reason to leave alive any participants in the government she was deposing.

Broom apparently felt he had worn out his luck in talking to Arlian that first time and leading him to Twilight; he refused all further attempts at conversation, and actively avoided Arlian.

Others in the city, however, were eager to tell the northerner all about the Blue Mage's atrocities, often regardless of whether they had witnessed these acts themselves or merely heard vague rumors. Arlian spoke with people on the streets and in the squares—though he perforce avoided the city's preferred social venue and stayed off the water steps, as he did not intend to violate the restrictions the gate guard had placed upon him. However vile the Blue Mage might be, he had come here to learn from her, not to antagonize her.

He discovered, though, that if he regularly sat on a bench by the street overlooking the steps, people going about their business would notice him and grow accustomed to him, and he could then address them as they left the water and receive polite responses.

He also spoke to merchants and to other customers in the shops he patronized, sometimes continuing the conversations out into the streets. Many of the inhabitants of Pon Ashti were happy to chat at length with the exotic stranger as they walked, or even to invite him into their homes to talk.

Thus Arlian heard several descriptions of how the Blue Mage had captured the city by first subverting several of Pon Ashti's own guardsmen, placing spells upon them so that upon command they removed much of the city's magical protection—not just some of the iron bands upon the walls, but other, more hidden devices, the exact nature of which had never been made public. Then she and her creatures, her demons and apes and shadows, had swept in, overwhelming all resistance.

"But surely, some of your people fought back!" Arlian said, sitting at a small table in a sunlit yard. "And did they not have good steel blades?"

"Iron is proof against the creatures of the air, but it cannot harm the wizard herself," his interlocutor—who would not give any name at all—told him. "Her magic cannot move or break iron, but neither does it repel her, nor can steel blades cut her. She had chosen her servants with the iron wards and the guards' steel in mind, and brought only those that steel could not stymie."

Further details and other conversations made it plain to Arlian that the Blue Mage had planned her assault carefully, and had known what to expect. Despite her reputation for whimsicality, she was clearly not stupid or overconfident; she had thought through her actions, rather than relying on surprise and sheer power.

It also became clear, from any number of sources, that the Blue Mage had effective methods of acquiring information, as well as incredible magical resources. That was why the arrival of her servants did not surprise him, and why he did not bother to resist them.

Alone at the time, he had been walking down a momentarily deserted street with a sausage roll in one hand, planning to once again sit by the river and enjoy the view of the water steps while he ate, when the shadows around him began to move unnaturally, sliding away from the alleys and doorways and following him across the pavement. He slowed his pace, but did not stop immediately.

But then the gray ape-things appeared around the corner ahead, four of them, each the size of a man, and spaced themselves across the width of the street.

They were not true apes, but he could think of no better description for them; they stood crookedly on massive gray-furred legs, their long bony arms dangling clawed fingers a few inches from the street, their flat black eyes staring at him from flat gray faces.

He transferred the sausage roll to his left hand, in case he needed to draw his sword, and stopped walking. He waited. From the corner of his eye he could see the shadows gathering at either side; a glance at a nearby glass window showed him that more ape-things were blocking the street behind him. No other humans were in the hundred yards between the two lines enclosing him, so there was no question as to whether he was actually their intended target.

No one he had spoken to had specifically described these ape-creatures, so he did not know whether steel would be effective against them. If they were, as seemed likely, the

same apes that had been part of the force that had swept
into the city a year ago and left the water steps awash in
blood, then metal blades would not touch them.

"Did you want something of me?" he asked.

To his surprise, one of the apes replied, in a growling but
clear voice.

"Our mistress wishes you to accompany us."

"Did she say why? I was about to eat my lunch . . ."

"Our mistress wishes you to accompany us *now.*"

Arlian decided against further argument. "Lead the way,"
he said.

The apes did not appear to be armed, and he might have
been able to cut his way out, but why should he? He had
come here to learn from the magicians and creatures of the
south, and the Blue Mage was among the most powerful of
those; he had come to Pon Ashti to speak with her. Here,
then, was just the opportunity he needed.

Furthermore, there was no real reason for hostility between the two of them. Yes, she had conquered Pon Ashti,
killed dozens or hundreds of people, and oppressed the survivors, but what was that to the Duke of Manfort or his loyal
warlord? Pon Ashti had always defied the Duke, refused his
demands for taxes and tariffs and tribute. If it had fallen to
another, less tolerant master, what was that to Arlian?

In truth, it was a great deal—he did not care to see anyone slaughtering innocents, whether the killer was dragon,
human, wizard, or something else entirely. He did not think
much of overlords who set down arbitrary rules whose
breach was punishable by death. It offended his sense of
justice to see Pon Ashti as it was—but the Blue Mage presumably did not know that Arlian felt this way. Unless she
could read his thoughts, how would she have any hint?

And he did very much want to question her.

Accordingly, he strode unhesitatingly along as the ape-
things led the way to the Mage's palace, and kept his
weapons in their sheaths. He marched through the streets,
eating his sausage roll—after all, he could not be sure when

he might receive his next meal. It was drier and spicier than was customary in Manfort, but not unpleasant; he had grown to like the local fare since his arrival.

The apes kept up a good pace, walking along in an odd loping gait that used both hands and feet; he would not have thought they could maintain their speed so easily. It was scarcely ten minutes later when they guided him through a fantastical crystal gate—one that he was quite sure was of magical origin, and which he suspected had only recently replaced one of wrought iron—into the palace forecourt.

There, however, the ape-things abruptly stopped, forming a circle around him, forcing him to stop, as well, if he did not wish to collide with their furry backs. He hastily swallowed the final bite of sausage and brushed the last flakes of pastry from his beard, then stood straight and waited.

Something red and gray and black, with horns and golden eyes but with a shape Arlian could not focus on, emerged from the palace and loomed over him; the sunlight seemed to fade as it approached, the sky to darken and the hum of wind and water, the sounds of the city, to fade. Arlian was a tall man, and could easily see over the heads of the crouching apes, but this creature towered above him as if he were a child. It spoke—though Arlian was unsure of the exact words, or the sound of its voice. He simply knew that it had spoken, and the meaning it had conveyed.

He was to remove his iron weapons before proceeding further.

"Of course," he said with a bow. That was the protocol among the lords of Manfort, as well—one did not wear a sword into someone's home when making a friendly call, if only because it might scrape the furniture. He unbuckled his sword belt, then took his common knife from its sheath, and proffered them.

One of the ape-creatures turned and accepted the weapons, then carried them out of sight—Arlian could not see whither. Its movements were somewhat awkward, as it was forced to walk entirely on its hind legs while carrying the blades and would plainly have been more comfortable using all four limbs.

When the ape was gone the towering being loomed forward again, and the sky dimmed so that Arlian, without thinking, glanced up to see whether a cloud had passed over the sun.

The sky was clear, but its color was wrong, a sort of dull indigo streaked with reddish brown. The sun itself was the color of new-cut copper.

Arlian had seen magic discoloring the sky several times before, but never quite so close as this, so near overhead. He swallowed uneasily.

The creature spoke. Arlian was to remove any silver from his person, and give it into the servants' keeping.

This was not the custom in Manfort, but Arlian had been expecting it. Reluctantly, he took the silver chain from around his neck and tucked it into the purse on his belt, then untied that purse and offered it to the nearest ape.

The creature accepted it, and waddled clumsily away, holding the purse up at arm's length as if it were a loathsome and dangerous burden.

Arlian watched it go with unease. It was not the loss of his silver that concerned him, but the loss of the amethyst on that chain; he had not had any way to remove the stone from its silver mounting. He did still have a smaller amethyst tucked away in his pocket, but if he slept here he was not sure it would be enough to guard his dreams.

The redness-and-darkness spoke again, and the remaining ape-things parted—to either side this time, rather than front and rear; Arlian was to enter the palace.

He took a deep breath, and marched up the three yellow marble steps and through the brass-trimmed door.

Neither the apes nor the yellow-eyed creature followed, but his way was clear enough—a single passage led deeper into the palace. He strode forward.

The corridor was unlit and windowless, and the doors closed behind him, but light came from somewhere ahead—blue light that made it impossible to judge the natural colors of anything he saw. He headed toward it, ignoring the faint whisperings and rustlings around him. The passage smelled of damp stone, but he saw no sign of moisture, and the air felt dry.

He wondered who or what he would meet. His captors had not said the Mage herself wanted to speak with him, only that she had wanted him to accompany them—but why else would she have summoned him?

And what else could be the source of that unnatural light ahead?

20

A Meeting with the Mage

A moment later he emerged into what he at first took for a large room, but then recognized as a courtyard—he had been fooled by the blue light that washed over everything, shutting out the sunlight as ordinary light would drive away the dark. The court was perhaps twenty feet square, with a single palm tree at its center and fountains in each of its four corners, the tree and the fountains all surrounded by flowerbeds; Arlian suspected that the flowers would ordinarily have been a dozen bright tropical colors, reds and golds and yellows, but now they were all various shades of blue.

Benches stood around each flowerbed, and on one of the benches around the central tree sat a woman—and it was from this woman that the blue glow came.

This, obviously, was the Blue Mage, and any question about the origin of her name was answered. She turned to look at Arlian as he approached, and smiled; her teeth glittered like sapphires, and her eyes glowed as brightly as blue flame.

The glow and the distorted colors made it difficult to discern her features clearly, but Arlian judged her to have the appearance of a young woman, certainly one no older than himself—but he knew she had been a major power in the lands beyond the border since before he was born. Her hair flowed in rippling blue waves down across her shoulders and her back, reaching to the bench, and then not so much ending as fading away, like smoke, before reaching the courtyard pavement. She wore a dark blue gown that seemed to sparkle when she moved, but which had no perceptible jewels or ornaments anywhere upon it.

She was beautiful, but Arlian reminded himself that despite her shape, she was not a woman at all. She was a wizard, a creature of magic.

"Lord Obsidian," she said, as she rose from the bench. "Welcome to my realm." Her voice was low and musical and very, very beautiful, and she stood almost as tall as Arlian himself. He had never met a woman taller.

Arlian bowed deeply. "I am honored by your invitation, my lady—or is it, perhaps, Your Majesty?"

"I am not concerned with titles, my lord; call me what you will."

"Thank you, my lady."

She stepped forward, then stopped perhaps two paces away as he straightened from his bow.

"You *are* Lord Obsidian, the Duke of Manfort's warlord, known to some as the Dragonslayer?" she asked.

"I am, my lady." If she knew this much already, he saw no point in lying. Her magic could probably detect or defeat any attempt at deception.

"So the spy told me, and I wondered at this. Why would the Dragonslayer come to Pon Ashti? There are no dragons here."

"That, my lady, is why I have come—to learn *why* there are no dragons here."

She tipped her head to one side. "Indeed? What a very interesting question to ask!" She gestured at a bench—not the one she had just departed, but one to Arlian's right, adjoining one of the corner flowerbeds. "Please make yourself comfortable, and we will discuss this, for so long as it amuses us both to do so."

"Thank you, my lady," Arlian said, seating himself on the indicated bench. The Blue Mage moved to an adjoining bench—not so much walking to it as drifting—and sat down again.

This was beginning to confuse Arlian; it all seemed too easy, in a way. Was the Blue Mage really going to tell him what he wanted to know? Could it be that simple?

But at the same time, there were unforeseen complications. He had not expected her to know who he was; her reference to a spy puzzled him. Furthermore, simply *looking* at her, beautiful as she unquestionably was, was becoming painful. Trying to focus on her face was oddly tiring, and the glow she emitted, the only light in the courtyard despite the daytime sky overhead, was giving him a headache.

"You are sworn to destroy the dragons entirely, I am told," the Mage said.

"I have so sworn, my lady, yes—I have vowed to destroy them, or to die in the attempt."

"Why?"

"They killed my family, my lady. They burned my parents' home to the ground, burned my grandfather's flesh from his bones with their venom, killed my mother and my father and my brother Korian and all the village save myself. They kill at whim, destroying entire communities in mere moments. They prey upon my people as if we were cattle to be slaughtered. They have polluted me with one of their accursed offspring, and stolen away a part of my soul. Until they are exterminated humanity lives at their mercy, and I will not have it."

"Interesting," the Mage said, leaning back slightly as if to gain a new perspective on him. "You seem very determined."

"I am a dragonheart, my lady, polluted by the monsters' venom. Even as that damns me, it gives me certain advantages. Perhaps determination is one of them."

"An intriguing theory. If true, the dragons have brought their own doom upon themselves."

"I most assuredly hope so."

"As do I, Lord Obsidian, as do I. Perhaps you have realized that I have no love for the dragons?"

"I suspected as much, my lady; after all, is it not their puissance that keeps you from exploring the northern lands, should it please you to do so?"

"So it is, though I had not realized this was widely known in your homeland."

"It is not widely known, my lady, but I have taken a special interest in these matters."

"Of course you have. Fascinating." She studied him silently for a moment, then asked, "Why have you come to Pon Ashti? Why are you not hunting the dragons in the northern mountains where they lair?"

"Because my master has betrayed me," Arlian said, startled by the bitterness in his own voice, and the bluntness of his own words. "The Duke of Manfort has made peace with the dragons, in order to prevent further incursions upon the Borderlands."

"*Has* he? The spy did not mention *that*!"

Arlian hesitated, then asked, "My lady, who is this spy of whom you speak?"

The Mage smiled again, and blue light glittered from her teeth and shone from her eyes. "Did you not know? Can you not guess?" She paused, but Arlian merely looked at her expectantly until she said, "He is the dragons' spy in Pon Ashti, sent here to watch their borders."

"The *dragons*?"

Arlian had not considered that possibility. This city was

so far from any known habitation of either dragons or dragonhearts that he had simply assumed their reach did not extend here in any way. Surely, they had not had a man
following him all the way from Manfort!

"Yes. This fool somehow believed he could use sorcery
here, in my own stronghold, without my knowledge. I
demonstrated to him the error of his belief, and convinced
him to tell me his purpose here, and what he had reported to
his abominable masters."

"Then he followed me across the Desolation?"

"Oh, no!" She laughed, an inhuman sound that made Arlian's skin crawl and significantly worsened his headache.
"Do not think yourself so important as that! He is a native
of Pon Ashti, recruited some years ago and supplied with
the means to converse with the dragons regardless of the intervening distance."

"Ah," Arlian said. He supposed that the means of communication was the simple sorcery of human blood in a
bowl of water—he had used that himself in the past. He had
thought that the blood had to be that of a dragonheart, but
perhaps he had erred in that assumption.

"I suppose this is some dark northern magic," the wizard
said. "Certainly, I know of no such device."

"I believe I have heard such a thing mentioned," Arlian
admitted. "It operates only at the dragons' whim."

As he spoke he was trying to think. Did this mean that the
Dragon Society had agents scattered *everywhere*? They
could not have known he would come to Pon Ashti; he had
not known it himself until he reached Orange River. This
spy must have been positioned here for reasons having
nothing to do with him.

Well, in this case, he could see no reason not to ask.
While he knew that his enemy's enemy was not necessarily
his friend, there was no reason to assume that the Blue
Mage was openly hostile. So far, she had treated him well
enough.

"Why did the dragons want a spy in Pon Ashti?" he asked.

"He claims not to know," she replied, all trace of her smile gone; she watched Arlian intently. "He maintains this position even under very noticeable duress. Given his interest in you, I thought you might have a guess to offer."

"I might," Arlian said, "but no more than a guess. My lady, I will tell you my guess, but might I beg a favor from you in exchange?"

"And what would be the nature of this favor?"

"Nothing untoward, I assure you. I wish only to learn more of the nature of wizards."

"The better to slay them, I suppose? This is not untoward?" She did not rise from the bench, but somehow she seemed larger and more threatening; the blue glow of her eyes changed to a darker hue, almost indigo. Her hair stirred, as if in a wind, though the air in the courtyard was utterly still.

"No, no, my lady! I promise you, that is by no means my intent! On the contrary, I would learn more so that I might better *aid* you!"

"Aid me in what fashion?" Her form remained swollen, her eyes dark.

"In encompassing the destruction of our common foe! I do not want to harm *you*; I want to destroy the *dragons*!"

"It was my understanding that you already know methods for slaying dragons, and have in fact killed a significant number of them."

"Of course, my lady—and if you will forgive my bluntness, we both know that if I had not done so, you could not rule freely in Pon Ashti. The dragons' magic and your own would appear to be antithetical, unable to coexist."

She stared at him for a moment, then seemed to shrink again.

"An oversimplification," she said mildly, "but one with some basis in truth. Then you seek to learn more of wizards to turn our power against the dragons? But why would you need to do this, when you have your own proven methods?"

"I told you I have been betrayed, my lady; the Duke of Manfort makes peace with the dragons. He does so because he fears that you and the other creatures of the south will sweep northward across the Lands of Man as the dragons perish, and he prefers the familiar, however evil, to the unfamiliar. I came here to learn whether your rule might be so clearly superior to that of the dragons that he can be convinced to reconsider."

She stared at him silently for a moment, then said, "Tell me your guess as to why the dragons placed a spy among my people."

"To observe the decline in their own power, my lady. To measure, by the effectiveness of the sorcery he uses to communicate with them, how much their losses had weakened their control over these lands, so that they would be able to anticipate the inroads made by you and the other great powers of the south and act accordingly. Their embassy to the Duke was superbly timed, and surely your spy was one of the elements making such precision possible."

"I believe you might have hit upon it," she said, her eyes now a warm turquoise.

Hoping to take advantage of her apparent pleasure, he said quickly, "I have told you my guess, my lady; might you grant me the boon I asked in return?"

"Tell you more of the nature of wizards?" She laughed again. "You will need to be more specific than *that*!"

"My lady, let us begin at the very beginning, then—what *is* a wizard?"

She laughed again, and Arlian thought his throbbing skull would crack. "*I* am a wizard," she said. "A creature of magic, spawned of earth and fire through a human host."

"Then you were human once? A mortal woman?"

"No. I grew within a woman's body, and then emerged as you see me now, in a semblance of her shape, but I am not that woman; I cast her flesh aside to die, her mind and body ruined by my birth, when I sprang from her mouth."

The pain in Arlian's temples was piercing and intense now, and he could not help raising one hand to his brow. "Do you mean . . ." He stopped and took a deep breath.

The Blue Mage's description of her origin sounded appallingly familiar, and he wondered why he had never guessed at this. After all, to some extent magic was magic, whether the subtle and delicate sorcery of Manfort or the flamboyant exercises of Arithei, whether incarnate in a dragon or manifest in a wizard.

He let his breath out, then said, "Do you mean that wizards incubate in human flesh, then burst forth, killing their hosts? All of them do this?"

"You have grasped it exactly."

"And what is it that first quickens a wizard in a human body? Is there some ichor that . . ." He stopped and closed his eyes without finishing the sentence; the pain in his head was unbearable.

"No ichor nor venom, no seed nor egg, save the raw magic of the earth and sky," the wizard replied. "The natural world is *full* of magic, Lord Obsidian, ever seeking an outlet and a form, and when any wisp or current of that ubiquitous force chances upon a living thing, it seeps into it and takes form therein. If the host is man, woman, or child, and the power sufficient that the body's natural defenses cannot absorb it, then in a year and a day the magic bursts forth as a wizard; if it is a beast then a monster is spawned. The mindlessness of plants will yield mindless magical things that haunt the land to no purpose; the shapeless spreading of fungus or moss gives us bodiless dreams and figments."

Trying to think was becoming impossible; Arlian could no longer form complete sentences. "But the dragons," he said. "They . . . their venom. A thousand years."

"The dragons are different," the Blue Mage said. "They suck all the magic from the land, and pass it to their offspring directly. I don't understand how—if I could do the same, I would. I can have no children, Obsidian, not by any means known to me. I can transform other creatures to suit my whims, guide the land's magic to manufacture demons and gaunts from men and animals, turn beasts to nightstalkers—I created your escort today from shadows and squirrels. But these things live only to serve me, they have no will of their own, and none can work magic in their turn. When I die my magic will disperse and return to the earth, until such time as its eddies and currents again collect it and carry the bits and pieces that were once me into contact with other living things, to spawn a hundred new creatures, none of them like me. The dragons, though—the dragons can spawn more dragons, damn them all."

She rose abruptly.

"My presence pains you," she said. "Rest; we will speak again later."

Arlian tried to make a polite protest, but the only sound that emerged was a dry croak.

Then the Blue Mage was gone, and sunlight flared up, and he lost consciousness.

21

The Spy

*A*rlian awoke stretched on a stone bench in a courtyard, the night sky above him strewn with bright stars; he stared up at them for a moment, trying to remember where he was.

And then he saw a figure standing over him, a dark shape

blocking out the stars. Arlian sat up quickly, reaching for his common knife, only to find the sheath empty.

That brought the memories back, and he knew where he was: in the courtyard of the palace in Pon Ashti, the palace the Blue Mage had taken as her own—or perhaps, he thought, despite appearances, he should say *its* own. By the wizard's own description it had no true sex, and could not reproduce its kind.

The stars overhead meant that he had clearly been unconscious for hours; the last moment he remembered was early afternoon. His back was stiff from sleeping on the hard bench, and his head still throbbed dully, but the ghastly piercing pain the Mage's presence had caused was gone. The dim light in the courtyard was not blue, but the natural orange of torchlight—he could see brands set in brackets on each of the four walls.

And he could see the shadowy figure of a man holding a cord between his hands. He had stepped back when Arlian awoke, and now stood a yard away, watching Arlian intently.

"What is it?" Arlian asked. "Who are you? Step into the light where I can see you." Even as he said this his eyes were adjusting, and Arlian could see that he was addressing a paunchy, middle-aged man in a pale robe.

The man cleared his throat. "Felicitations, my lord," he said. "I trust you slept well, and your headache is better?"

"Well enough, thank you," Arlian said. "I fear you have the advantage of me; to whom do I have the honor of speaking?"

"My name is unimportant," the man with the cord said, fidgeting.

Arlian smiled crookedly. There had been a time, long ago, when he had said the same thing, and had thereby acquired the nickname Trivial. He was not inclined to share that name with this person.

"Say rather, you do not choose to give it," Arlian said. "As you will. Are you in the Blue Mage's service, then?"

"I serve the rulers of this realm."

That plural seemed to confirm Arlian's suspicion—this

man was almost certainly the dragons' spy. And that cord in his hands had doubtlessly been intended for Arlian's throat, but one did not survive fourteen years of war and attempted assassinations without learning to maintain a certain wariness even when asleep.

"And do you think, sir, that the Blue Mage will permit you to live if you kill me beneath her roof?"

"You know?" The man lunged forward, cord stretched taut.

Arlian raised a hand to intercept it, but the man was quicker and stronger than he looked, and pushed the cord up over Arlian's fingers before Arlian could get a good hold. The cord caught Arlian under the chin, and pushed him back; the bench on which he sat rocked backward under this pressure, and Arlian toppled over. The two men tumbled down into the flowerbed, the would-be assassin atop his intended victim, the cord pressing into Arlian's throat.

This was a worse situation than Arlian had anticipated; he had assumed he would be able to hold his attacker off easily, but had misjudged both his opponent's prowess and his own stability on the stone bench. He was not seriously worried yet, though, as he pressed at his foe with his left hand and reached for the buttons of his blouse with his right.

No one in this palace would have a steel blade, nor silver, which was presumably why the spy was using a garrote, but that did not mean Arlian was unarmed—and his weapon was one that he very much doubted anyone in service to the Dragon Society would carry.

The man's weight bearing him down onto the flowers made it difficult to reach his knife, but even the strongest strangler needed a few minutes to kill; he had time.

"I'm sorry, Obsidian," the spy grunted, as he struggled to cross the ends of his cord behind Arlian's back. "They promised me venom if I killed you—a thousand years of life!"

Arlian's hand finally slid into his blouse, groping for the

hilt, but then blue light flooded over the pair, and all motion ceased.

Arlian found himself staring upward into the spy's eyes, and he could see utter terror there—but he could not move. The pressure on his throat was less—though not gone.

Then gray, inhuman hands, the furred hands of the Mage's ape-things, closed on the spy's arms and shoulders and legs, and he was lifted off Arlian and carried away, the strangler's cord still in his hands. Arlian tried to turn his head to see where the man was taken, and who or what had taken him, but he could not; the Mage's magic held him where he was, staring upward at a sky where all the stars were now deep blue.

The pain in his throat was gone—but now his head was throbbing again.

Obviously, the Blue Mage had returned.

And then he heard her voice, that rich and beautiful voice.

"Did you think I would not know what was happening in my own home?" she asked.

"I hoped," the spy replied. "I thought perhaps the dragons' magic . . ."

"The dragons have no power here!" she shouted, and Arlian felt an involuntary tremor run through him, and through the broken plants upon which he rested. "And the dragons have no magic in *you*—it is *he*, Lord Obsidian, who is seething with their essence! It pains him merely to be near me because I have rejected your bestial masters and shut their power away from me; he suffers intensely, while *you* stand there unscathed!"

That, then, explained the headache, Arlian thought.

Her voice seemed to echo from the courtyard walls, but then the echoes died away and silence descended. Arlian was beginning to wonder whether the spy and the wizard were still there when she spoke again, in a quiet, musing tone.

"I find it curious," she said. "This Lord Obsidian is

ablaze with draconic magic, destined for a thousand years of life, and when that millennium is passed his heart and soul will go to nourish one of the mightiest magical beings to walk the earth since the days of the dead gods—yet he is sworn to destroy the dragons, to cast them down and prevent this fate. *You,* in turn, are untouched by magic in any form, though you have learned a few of the simple tricks you call sorcery, and yet you *serve* the dragons."

"I want what he has," the spy said.

"Yet he rejects it; what if, upon receiving it, you, too, reject it?"

"I won't. There are many who do not, and I would join them."

"Can you be sure?"

"I think so."

"And what if, rather than allow you your brew of human blood and dragon venom, I were to take you deep into the southern wilds, and arrange for you to be saturated with the wild magic of earth and fire? Would it please you as much to engender a wizard as to inculcate a dragon?"

Arlian could hear the uncertainty in the man's reply. "How long would that take? I mean, how long would I live?"

"For a year and a day you would live, though the magic would manifest itself about you in various ways—you might grow wings or scales or horns, you might gain the gift of second sight or a healer's touch. And then the mature wizard would emerge and cast your body aside."

"A *year*? Just one year?"

"And a day. Did you think you might have found another way to claim a thousand years of existence?"

"I . . . Maybe."

"No. Duration and longevity and continuity are the dragons' greatest magics. No one knows how long they live— thousands of years, perhaps tens of thousands, perhaps *forever,* while we wizards have only fifty years of existence, sixty if we are very fortunate, before we dissolve back into the chaos from which we sprang. And our spells dissolve with us—I could not grant you eternal life even if I wanted to, for any invulnerability I might bestow would vanish when *I* do."

Arlian listened to this carefully—this was important information, and fascinating in its own right.

It was especially noteworthy since he knew that the Blue Mage had been active well before he was born, probably at least a dozen years before, and he was thirty-seven. If it was true that she could expect only fifty years of life, then she was nearing the end of her time.

Then he felt cold hands closing on his arms, and he was pulled upright, heaved up and over the bench until he was standing on the pavement, ape-things supporting him on either side. He remembered that the Mage had said she had made them from squirrels, but their grip was as strong as any man's.

The spy stood a dozen feet away, similarly restrained, and the Blue Mage stood between them. She was looking directly at Arlian. Even though he knew she was a sterile, inhuman thing, he could not help thinking of her as female; save for their color and luminescence, her face and body were those of a beautiful woman.

"Yes, I am nearing my end," she said. "And yes, I can hear your unspoken thoughts, under certain circumstances." Her head tilted as she studied him. "You intrigue me, Lord Obsidian."

He could not bow while the squirrel-apes held him, but he nodded a polite acknowledgment. "I am pleased to entertain you in whatever way I might, my lady."

"This man was willing to risk my ire to kill you, yet I sense in you no anger at his actions, no hatred of him."

"He sought what he mistakenly sees as a great reward, my lady; he does not hate either of us. Why, then, should I hate in return?"

"The dragons did not hate your family, but slew them merely because they were there—yet you hate the dragons with a rare intensity. This distinction puzzles me."

"I loved my family. They had done no harm to anyone; they were innocents. The dragons had no *right* to kill them." Arlian was startled to hear the vehemence in his own voice.

"And this assassin has a right to kill you?"

Arlian fought down his anger, then shrugged. "He has a *reason,* in any case, and I can make no claims of innocence. I have assisted in the slaying of more than fourscore dragons; I have killed a dozen men. Nor is my life so very precious to me, in any case. I must in time yield it up, and while I am in no hurry to do so, neither do I believe it would be so very great a loss."

"Such resignation!" Wonderment was plain in the wizard's voice. "Can you teach it to me?"

"My lady?"

"My own dispersal draws near, Obsidian—my death, insofar as a being like myself can die. I dread it, but I know I cannot prevent it; already I feel myself becoming less focused, less cohesive. My light escapes me whether I will it or no, and there is nothing I can do to alter this. I cannot drink blood and venom and imbue myself with an extended existence, as a human might; I am neither human nor dragon, nor can I become either one. I came to Pon Ashti in hopes that the environment here, far poorer in wild magic than my native land while still outside the dragons' reach, might serve to prolong my time a little, but I can detect little or no improvement. It may even have worsened my situation; it is a very difficult thing to judge. So whether here in Pon Ashti, or roaming the wilderness, I am dying—and I do not *want* to die. If I could learn not to care, as you have, it would ease my passage."

"I am sorry," Arlian said, sincerely. "I am what I am because I have lived the life I have lived; I have nothing I can teach you in the time remaining." He hesitated, unsure why he was considering assisting this creature, then said, "I have heard of a wizard in Arithei, long ago, that attempted to transfer its essence into another body when its own was destroyed. Might you be able to perform such a transference, and thereby extend your life?"

The Blue Mage laughed unhappily.

"I could take a new body," she said. "I could put myself into one of those creatures holding you, or into one of the demons I have created, or even into the body of this man who tried to kill you—we wizards are not tied to a single form. It would not help. It's not my *body* that is weakening." She raised her arms and shifted her weight to one leg, displaying her not-inconsiderable charms. "Does this look like a body about to die of old age? No, it is my *soul* that now verges on disintegration, my magical essence, and transferring it to another, less familiar form would only hasten that dispersal."

"Maybe the dragons . . ." the spy said from behind her.

She whirled, one hand thrust out, and he was flung back against the courtyard wall; one of the two ape-things that held him was carried with him, the two of them slamming against the stone side by side, while his right arm was pulled from the other ape's grasp, leaving ragged, bleeding claw marks and sending the ape tumbling to the pavement.

The Blue Mage had grown as she turned, and now towered twice a man's height, glowing more brightly than ever. "The *dragons* will not help me," she bellowed, in a voice that was terrible and inhuman, far deeper than her previous tones, yet still beautiful. "The dragons are by their very nature the foes of all wild magic. We are the creatures of chaos and change, while they are the essence of order and stagnation! We and they cannot exist in the same realm—no wizard nor other magical creature can set foot in the Dragon Lands without suffering for it, nor can the dragons cross the borders into our territory."

So much, Arlian thought, for any possibility of some compromise whereby the dragons might be allowed to live somewhere other than the Lands of Man. The only comfort he found was that at least this meant any alliance of dragons and wizards against him and the rest of humanity was unlikely in the extreme.

The Mage turned, looking down over her shoulder at Arlian—though her shoulder seemed somewhat lower again.

"My lord," she said, in a voice returning gradually to its normal tones, "while you do not hate this man, do you see any reason I should let him live?"

"He is a human being," Arlian said.

"You think that reason enough?" Arlian opened his mouth to reply, but before he could speak she continued, "I do not!"

Blue light flared, and the dragons' hireling was smashed against the wall; Arlian could hear the crunch of breaking bones, could see blood, deep purple in the blue light, spurt from the man's mouth and the back of his skull. His face distorted as his head was flattened.

For an instant he hung there, as if pinned in place, then slid down the stone, leaving a smear of blood and hair, and lay in a heap at the bottom of the wall.

"If I cannot live," the Mage said, "why should he?" Then she turned back to face Arlian. "Now, tell me, Lord Obsidian—if I cannot live, why should *you*?"

22

A Change of Regime

"*I* am your enemy's enemy," Arlian said calmly—though he did not *feel* calm. He suspected he had erred in coming to Pon Ashti. The spy's death had convinced him that in all likelihood he was about to die. The prospect did not frighten him, but neither did it please him. "While that need not make us friends, nor even allies," he continued, "surely it means I can be useful to you, and am not a tool to be lightly cast aside?"

The Blue Mage stared at him, shrinking slowly. "You are not frightened," she said. "You truly are not frightened by death."

"I truly am not," Arlian agreed. "I have despaired of ever being able to live free of the burdens that weigh perpetually on my spirit and preclude all happiness; what terrors, then, lie in death?"

"The unknown," the wizard replied. "Dissolution. The loss of self. How can you not fear these? Everything that lives fears death!"

Arlian turned out empty palms. "I do not," he said.

The Mage, once again the size of an ordinary woman, gestured; the squirrel-apes released Arlian and stepped away, and the wizard drifted nearer. Glancing down, Arlian noticed that she apparently had no feet, or at any rate none that extended below the hem of her gown; she was floating a few inches above the paving stones. He was almost certain he had seen feet before, feet in blue velvet slippers, but there was no sign of them now.

"Yet there are things you want," she said. "Things that you need, things you urgently desire."

"Indeed there are," Arlian agreed. "And those that are not simply impossible often contradict one another. I want the dragons destroyed, yet I do not want the Lands of Man to be overrun with the wild magic that prevails elsewhere. I want my friends to be safe and well, yet I endanger them constantly by my actions in opposing the dragons. I want justice, yet I know that true justice is impossible in this life, that justice for one is cruelty to another."

"I want the impossible, too," she said, hanging a few feet away. "I want to be what I am, the mightiest of wizards, and yet I want to live forever—and wizards cannot. We are creatures of chaos and change, of death and renewal—so I must die. If I must die, I want to not *fear* it so. There are things I want, and if I die, I will never have them. If you die, here and now, you will never have your revenge, never destroy the dragons, never find justice for your family—do you not dread such a thing?"

"My lady," Arlian said, "I have never truly believed I could have justice, and I have learned that revenge is not enough. To destroy the dragons would be satisfying, but it would lay the Lands of Man open to you and your kind, and can you honestly say that would be an improvement for the ordinary villager or townsman? I will never have what I want, regardless of whether I live or die. I have accepted that."

"Then why do you live? Why do you bother? Why did you not allow the assassin to strangle you, to squeeze the life from you?" Her hands moved uneasily, and Arlian suspected she was on the verge of blasting him, as she had the spy.

He did not want to die, but he had no clever answer to give her, and simply spoke the truth.

"Because I have made promises," he said.

"Merely that?"

"Merely that. That, and perhaps a lingering hope that things can be better than they are, that while I cannot ever fully achieve my goals, I may yet achieve *something*."

"Other than life itself, I have achieved my goals in this life," the wizard said. "I have done as I pleased; I have taken Pon Ashti and made it mine, as I did a dozen other realms. I have cast down those who opposed me, and exalted those who honored me. I have shaped the world around me to suit my whims. I have no unmet goals, save my own preservation. Should I then simply allow myself to die?"

"This is surely something you must decide for yourself," Arlian said. "I cannot say what a wizard should do; I have quite enough to do in remembering how to be human."

"Perhaps I should die now, and get it over with, rather than live with fear."

Arlian hesitated. "*Can* you die whenever you wish?"

She laughed. "Not by wishing for it, but there are things that can destroy me."

"Iron? Silver?"

"No, neither of those—those are the banes of air and darkness, and I am a creature of earth and fire. I could scarcely have taken Pon Ashti if iron could harm me! A steel blade will shatter my illusions, reverse my transformations, for I weave those of the air around us, and for that reason I forbid such weapons in places where my creatures dwell, but no mere metal can harm *me*. Your sword, if you had it here, would pass through me without leaving a mark—or if I preferred, rebound from my flesh as if from stone."

The mention of earth and fire, air and darkness, stirred certain memories in Arlian.

"But there are weapons that can hurt you?" he asked.

"There are indeed," she said. "No wizard is truly indestructible, though I am more nearly so than most."

Arlian reached into his blouse and pulled out his black dagger—though even as he did he was unsure of the reason for his action. "Would this be one such weapon?" he asked.

She stared. "A knife? How did you bring a knife . . ."

"'Tis neither steel nor silver," Arlian interrupted. "Your creature said nothing of glass."

"Glass?" She drifted forward. "What sort of glass?"

At that moment Arlian's thoughts seemed to rush forward at impossible speed, despite the crushing pain in his head. He knew the Blue Mage had not deliberately harmed him, that there were still things she could teach him, but she was a wizard, unpredictable and deadly, and had slain dozens, perhaps hundreds, of innocent citizens of Pon Ashti—not to mention the assassin-spy. She deserved to die, and the weapon he held might be capable of killing her.

Arlian knew he would never have a better opportunity; he lunged, thrusting his right arm out while he stepped toward the Blue Mage, throwing all his weight onto his right foot, pushing himself into full extension and driving the obsidian dagger forward.

The black blade plunged into her chest as if she were no more than a shadow.

"Oh," she said, looking down. "Obsidian . . ."

And then light and movement burst forth, flinging Arlian backward; the world seemed to whirl about him in a tangle of blueness and darkness and torchlight, and then he slammed against a fountain, his left foot tangled in a vine, and he tumbled sideways. Wind whickered and swirled, and blue and orange light flickered.

Dazed, Arlian struggled to right himself, and finally managed a sitting position.

The Blue Mage was gone. The blue glow that had heralded her presence was gone. The stars above shone white and clear; the torches on the walls flamed yellow and red.

A squirrel stood in the nearest doorway, looking about in confusion, and another scampered up the palm tree. The assassin's corpse still lay slumped against the far wall of the little courtyard.

Arlian's headache was fading, replaced by the pain of various bumps and bruises and a soreness in his neck where the spy's cord had pressed. Bracing himself on the fountain and a flowering shrub, he pulled himself upright.

His hands were empty, he noticed. He looked over toward the spot where the Blue Mage had been, and saw that slivers of black glass were strewn across several square yards of pavement.

He looked at the squirrels.

The Blue Mage was gone. Her magic had died with her.

He was unsure just what had happened. Perhaps the obsidian had killed her, as obsidian thrust into a dragon's heart would slay; perhaps her time had arrived quite coincidentally at the instant he struck. Her last word might have been his name, or might have meant she recognized the material stabbing into her—he supposed he would never know which.

And there were so many other unanswered questions! The Blue Mage had been ruthless and erratic and unpredictable—was that inherent in the nature of wizards, or was it just her? Had her knowledge of her own impending death helped to drive her to such a state? She had been unique even among wizards in her blue radiance—what had that actually signified, if anything?

If it had been his knife that slew her, would obsidian kill *any* wizard, or had that been a peculiarity of the Blue Mage?

Could wizards be controlled? Could the magic of the Lands of Man be bound up in a few wizards, rather than in the dragons, and the wizards constrained not to harm anyone? Did wizards eat souls, as Lord Zaner had told him the dragons did? If so, they would be no improvement.

Or perhaps a diet of human souls was what gave the dragons their longevity, and it was only because the southern wizards had not learned this that they died after no more than a human lifetime. Arlian had no desire whatsoever to see a wizard test this theory.

Was there perhaps some way to bind the magic into something inanimate? Could obsidian perhaps be enchanted to absorb it?

Need there be magic at all? Was there no way the magic could be destroyed altogether, or at least reduced to harmless levels? Arlian had wanted to ask her that. Isein had not thought it possible, but the Blue Mage might well have known secrets not given to an Aritheian magician.

He looked at the dead spy, the man who had hoped to trade Arlian's life for a dose of dragon venom. Did the Dragon Society have other agents in the Borderlands? Could they, too, be seeking greater knowledge of the nature of magic?

Was it even true that the deaths of all those dragons had

been what allowed the creatures beyond the border to press northward? Could the dragons have somehow deliberately withdrawn their protection to provoke the Duke into making peace? Had Arlian been deliberately lured south in hopes that assassins here might be more successful than those in the north?

Somehow, that seemed too baroque for the dragons or the Society. Enziet might have arranged it, if he still lived, but Enziet was unquestionably dead—Arlian had seen the man's heart lying lifeless on the stone. And those eighty-eight dragons were just as unquestionably gone, so the loss of draconic power was in all probability real.

The Blue Mage had called the Lands of Man by their old name, the Dragon Lands, a name the people of the Duke's realm had rejected seven centuries ago; she had clearly believed that it was the dragons and only the dragons that defined the borders that excluded her.

But she had lived only fifty or sixty years; how had she known what she knew? Was it inherent in her nature as a wizard, or had she learned it during those fifty or sixty years?

Fifty or sixty years, no more. Until now, Arlian had not known that wizardly lifespans were so brief. The sorcerers of the Dragon Society considered seventy years the minimum necessary to really master the arcane arts—but then, sorcerers were human, and wizards were not.

There were other wizards out there, dozens of them—an entire council of them ruled the land of Shei, for example. Perhaps they had accumulated other knowledge that a solitary creature like the Blue Mage had not.

And there was the thing in Tirikindaro . . .

Arlian frowned, and looked down at the brittle shards of his knife.

Whatever it was that ruled Tirikindaro had been there for centuries, or at least so the stories claimed. If it was a wizard, then either it had found some way of surviving much longer than the norm, or it was not a single creature at all, but a succession of them.

More likely it wasn't a wizard at all, but something else, something that lived much longer—maybe not as long as a dragon, maybe not even as long as a dragonheart, but far longer than a wizard or an ordinary man.

There were those who said it was a god. Arlian was not sure what that meant; what *was* a god, really? Was a being that lived in the material world and reigned over a physical kingdom a god? That did not seem right. Certainly the dead gods Arlian had always prayed to, the gods that had once watched over the Lands of Man and might still protect it in some fashion, were not the same as the thing in Tirikindaro.

God or not, that being was a tyrant, as everyone knew; the people of Tirikindaro lived as slaves, sweating their lives away in hard labor, dressed in rags or less, eating only when and what their ruler permitted them. It hated the sun, and Tirikindaro was therefore perpetually shadowed by thick unnatural clouds.

A long-lived magical being that loathed sunlight and could alter the weather to accommodate that hatred—that was much like a dragon, really. But the thing in Tirikindaro was no dragon.

Nor, apparently, was it a wizard.

Arlian did not want to allow either dragons or wizards to dominate the Lands of Man, nor did he want to see his fellow men enslaved—but was the thing's tyrannical nature inherent? Might a more beneficent version be created? Could a dozen or a hundred such beings perhaps replace the dragons as the manifestation of the magic of the Lands of Man, and do so benignly?

There was nothing more of what he sought to be learned in Pon Ashti, that was clear—the Blue Mage had tolerated no rivals and accepted no comrades, and with her death the city was free of magic, if only for a moment. Arlian saw no reason to linger within the walls. He studied the exits from the courtyard, and eventually decided that one of the four was the passage by which he had entered; he took a torch from its bracket and made his way back down the corridor.

The rustlings were gone; the damp odor had faded away. There was no trace of the red-and-black demon that had guarded the entrance, nor of the ape-things; the forecourt was deserted.

The crystal gate was standing open, but he did not want to leave anything behind; he turned aside and conducted a quick exploration before leaving the palace. He found his sword belt, knife, and purse in a small side chamber and restored them to their usual places, and only then did he march back out into the night-shrouded city.

The dark streets were largely deserted, and he made his way unimpeded to the most southerly of the four bridges across the Darambar. There he looked southward, at the water steps.

The water's glow as it flowed over the stone was faint and uneven; on the previous nights of his stay it had been smooth and bright. The women and children who worked and played there by daylight were gone, but a few groups of men stood in the ankle-deep water, talking among themselves. A few looked up at him, their attention drawn by the light of his torch.

"Your attention, good people!" he shouted, in his best commanding-officer bellow.

More of the men fell silent and looked up at him.

"The Blue Mage is dead!" he called. "The palace stands vacant, and the city is yours once again!"

That said, he turned and proceeded across the bridge. He had delivered his message, and saw no reason to elaborate needlessly, nor make suggestions. The city of Pon Ashti was not his own.

He ignored the bustle behind him, the shouted argument and hurrying feet and wild splashing, as he made his way through the streets to Twilight's home.

When he rode out the gate the following morning the news had been confirmed and had spread everywhere, and there were vigorous debates under way on every street corner as to the ideal composition of the city's new government. No demon guarded the gate, no squirrel-apes roamed the streets, and the shadows lay where the sun cast them— but the water of the Darambar sparked and glittered at the roadside, and three-eyed fish watched him solemnly from just below the surface.

23

Under the Tyrant's Heel

*Y*ou're mad," Isein said.

"Yes, I know," Arlian agreed, as he checked the leather ties holding his supplies on the gelding's back. He was reasonably sure he had removed every trace of silver from his packs; the metal was not permitted in Tirikindaro. Iron could be carried in, so long as it was also carried back out.

He had arrived safely back in Orange River two days before, and was preparing to depart again—and once more, he intended to travel alone.

"No, my lord, you are *mad,*" Isein insisted. "Genuinely insane."

He tugged at the strap. "Yes, Isein, I *know.* I went mad when I was eleven. I have never said otherwise."

"Arlian, this is different. You have always been obsessed with your vengeance, and you have always been daring and fearless, but this . . ."

Arlian turned to look at her. As best he could recall, Isein had never before called him by his true name. "How is it different?" he asked.

"This is *Tirikindaro*."

"Isein, I survived a dragon attack when I was just a boy, then became the first man in recorded history to kill a dragon. To prove that was no mere fluke, I then slew fourscore more in their own lairs. I now appear to have slain the Blue Mage as well, and have emerged unscathed from that adventure. I have fought a dozen duels and survived, if not won, them all. I have survived more attempted assassinations than I can count. I have crossed the Dreaming Mountains alone, and survived the Desolation more than once. I have fought bandits and monsters and wizards and Manfort's finest swordsmen. What is Tirikindaro that makes it any madder to approach than all the rest?"

"It's a *god*, Arlian. And it's as mad as you are."

He stared at her for a moment, then turned back to the horse. "The gods are dead, Isein," he said. "I don't know what the thing in Tirikindaro is, and it may indeed be mad, but I doubt it is any sort of god."

"The gods of the Lands of Man are dead, or so you all say, but this is the god of Tirikindaro."

"Your origins are showing," Arlian replied. "You grew up with this thing just across the mountains, so near that sometimes you could see its magic in the sky; childhood fears are strong. I grew up on the Smoking Mountain, hundreds of miles from here, and do not share those fears. Whatever it is, even if it *is* a godling of some sort, what can it do to me that a dragon could not?"

"Anything it wants to. Any ghastly thing you can imagine."

"And is that any more than the Blue Mage could do?"

"*Yes!*"

Arlian stopped his work, closed his eyes, and sighed.

"I'm not going to fight it," he said. "I bear it no ill will— well, no, I lie; I *do* think its tyranny over its people an evil thing that should be ended. Aside from that, however, I do not hate it, I do not seek any sort of vengeance against it; I merely wish to speak to it, ask a few questions."

"And if an ant crawls up your arm, do you worry about whether it means you harm or was simply exploring, or do you flick it aside, perhaps squash it, without troubling yourself about its motives?"

"Ants do not ask questions in any tongue a man can hear; surely, the thing in Tirikindaro can hear its supplicants?"

"When it bothers to listen, perhaps."

He sighed again. "However mad you think it, Isein, I am going to Tirikindaro to speak to the ruler of that land. I do not expect you to accompany me, and I have ordered Double and Poke not to, but I am going."

"I thought you came south to go to Arithei, not Tirikindaro!"

"If I survive Tirikindaro, I intend to continue on to Shei and Arithei and Stiva and Baratu and Skok's Falls, and wherever else my quest may take me, until I find the answers I seek."

She stared at him for a moment, then said, "I had not truly realized until now what you seek."

Puzzled, he glanced at her. "I have said it often enough. I seek a means whereby the Lands of Man may exist free of hostile and dangerous magic, whether that magic is the dragons or the wild magic from beyond the borders."

Isein shook her head. "You seek death, Arlian," she said. "Whenever you accomplish one impossible task without dying, you begin another. You set yourself the task of escaping from slavery, though it was far more likely you would die in the mines. You set out to become wealthy, though it was first more likely you would be caught stealing Lord Kuruvan's gold and put to death, and then more likely you would die on the journey to Arithei. You determined to avenge your lost childhood by slaying Lord Enziet and his partners and hirelings—and what were the chances you would survive that? You tried to exterminate the dragons, walking into their very lairs, knowing they could easily kill you. You went to face the Blue Mage, and now Tirikindaro . . ."

"It is all the same task, Isein; I want to rid the world of the dragons to avenge my murdered family and ensure that no more innocents will be slaughtered as they were. *That* is what I seek."

"I think you seek to *join* your family, not avenge them—and that Fate has let you live this long, and come as close to success in your insane quest as you have, out of sheer perversity."

"If I wanted to die, Isein, I could have done so a hundred times over. I could have sought out a dragon's lair in summer, rather than winter; I could have let Enziet or Toribor run me through."

"You want to die without accepting the responsibility; you don't want to *admit* you want to die. Fate is playing with you until you admit that you seek death—and confronting the thing in Tirikindaro may well be admission enough."

"I think I know my own motivations better than you know them, Isein. I do not fear death, but neither do I seek it; I seek a better world for us all, one free of dragons. Tirikindaro may hold the knowledge I need to bring such a world into being."

"It very well may, but what makes you think you can take it thence?"

Arlian frowned at her. "Believe what you will, then. I see no reason I should *not* bring forth that knowledge. I am going to Tirikindaro; you are free to come or not, as you please, but I am going." He set his foot in the stirrup.

"Then I will never see you again, and I regret that."

Arlian swung himself onto the gelding's back. "Do not be too certain; I have survived the impossible before. Wait here a month, and if I have not returned, then go back to Arithei or to Manfort, as you choose. If you return to Manfort with Poke and Double, then be sure at least one of you tells Black of my fate, and urges him to continue my campaign."

"I will wait a month," she agreed. "No more."

"Good enough." He shook the reins and urged his mount forward.

He glanced back a moment later and saw Isein still standing in front of the inn, watching him. A second look, as he drew away from the village of Orange River, found the street empty, with no indication where she had gone.

He devised his route to avoid the city of Talolo, which Lord Naran had reported fallen to Tirikindaro's hordes, as he did not care to get involved in any of the conflicts likely to be taking place there; instead he directed his steps toward Tirikindaro's heartland. This detour meant the journey should have taken seven or eight days to reach the border, but it was only the fifth when he saw the sky overhead, as well as ahead, streaked with magic and obscured by clouds.

It was early in the afternoon of the sixth day when he found a dozen naked men working a field, men who ignored his shouted greeting. He had heard that the enslaved people of Tirikindaro often went without clothing, as their master did not care to waste resources on unnecessary garments, but he had never seen this at first hand until now. It seemed the stories were true—and the presence of these men meant that he was now past the new border, out of the Lands of Man and in Tirikindaro.

He was fairly certain that this area had still been a part of the Borderlands when last he traveled through the region, but it clearly was no longer.

He did not halt his mount, but rode on past, keeping one eye on the road and one on the men. They ignored him as they hacked at weeds with crude wooden hoes, and picked through their crop, as if looking for something. The stalks around them sometimes rippled in odd branching patterns that Arlian did not think were made by any natural wind.

He reached a deserted village early on the seventh day, and took a few moments to look through some of the roofless buildings. This had evidently been a small border town, one where travelers or caravans could stop and rest and regroup before entering Tirikindaro, but now the caravanserai was a burned-out shell, and the dozen houses surrounding it stood empty and abandoned.

At least, he thought as he looked down into the rubble-filled pit that had been the inn's cellar, he saw no bones, no corpses, nothing to indicate that anyone had died here. The beer barrels had been stove in, and there were several broken wine bottles, but the devastation was far less complete than dragons would have left. With any luck, the villagers had all fled safely to the north.

He looked up, and the sky above him was dark gray streaked with vivid pink, rolling and throbbing as if it were alive; he had trouble focusing on it.

He rode on. He passed more fields, more workers—some clothed, some naked—and a few oddly proportioned barracks. There were no more villages as such, no inns; Tirikindaro's people did not bother with such niceties as families, or individual homes, or accommodations that distinguished between resident and traveler. Their ruler saw no need for any of these things.

No one spoke to Arlian as he rode by, and when at last he reached a fork in the road where he could not be certain of his route simply by looking at the sky and directing his horse toward the highest concentration of magic, he had to dismount, grab a man from a nearby field, pry the two-foot cane-cutter from his hand, and put a chokehold on his throat before he would respond to a simple question.

The man struggled, but made no attempt to recover his blade or use it as a weapon. None of the other workers moved to intervene as Arlian dragged his captive to the fork, one arm around the man's neck, and pointed with his free hand at the roads.

"Which road leads to your master?" Arlian demanded again, in Man's Tongue—he had previously tried both Man's Tongue and pidgin Aritheian, without response. It was possible the man simply had no language in common with him, but Arlian was not yet willing to admit that.

"Let me go," the man replied, speaking at last. "I have work to do." His accent was odd, and his voice husky, as if he was not accustomed to using it.

"So do I," Arlian said, "and it requires a meeting with the thing that rules this land." The air around him seemed to ripple at the sound of his voice, and blue sparkled at the edges of his vision.

The man pointed at the left-hand path, and Arlian released him; he quickly hurried back to the field, picked up his blade, and resumed chopping at the brownish stalks. Arlian did not recognize the crop being grown here, and did not think he wanted to.

He looked at the two branches of the road ahead, then back at the field-workers. The man could have been lying, or could have chosen randomly if he didn't know which way to go—but he hadn't *said* that he didn't know, and he seemed too mechanical to be capable of subtlety or deception.

Arlian looked at the sky, where midnight-blue clouds seethed constantly, streaked with half a dozen bright colors that flashed and twisted through them; the density *might* be a little greater to the left.

He swung himself back into the saddle and urged his horse forward, along the left-hand road.

The gelding clearly did not want to go any farther; it kept trying to turn, but Arlian kept forcing its head back in line, and eventually the beast yielded and resumed its steady walk.

And then, with no feeling of transition or change, Arlian was riding down a marble-walled corridor, beneath painted arches. Ahead of him a golden glow obscured the far end of the passageway.

"Whoa," he said softly, tugging at the reins.

The horse stopped, but Arlian did not dismount immediately; he looked around at his surroundings.

The corridor seemed to extend perhaps sixty feet ahead of him, and an infinite distance behind; the walls were of fine marble of various hues, arranged in pleasing patterns of varying stripes—a broad expanse of black would be bordered by red or yellow or green, then a complementary border would be followed by a broad expanse of white. The floor was of some utterly black stone Arlian did not recognize, one that seemed to give back no light at all. Plastered arches a dozen feet above that floor were decorated with painted vines and flowers, and the ceilings between the arches depicted scenes of robed men and women lounging in sunlit gardens. While the only visible source of light was that golden glow far ahead, there were no shadows anywhere; everything was plainly visible.

Arlian suspected that that meant none of this was real.

"I would be honored if you would show yourself, dear host," he called.

I show myself now, said unspoken words, *but you do not see.*

24

Conversing with That Which Has No Name

Arlian looked about, but still saw only the bright palace walls. He saw no movement, no sign of life, nothing that could be the master of Tirikindaro—unless it meant the palace itself, or that glow ahead of him.

The voice that had addressed him had been plain enough, though. Arlian had encountered a variety of magical means of communication over the years, from the sorcerous transmissions of dragons to the wordless commands of the Blue Mage's demonic doorkeeper, and whatever had spoken to him now had been as clear as any of them.

"I beg your pardon," Arlian said. "My perceptions are feeble, I know. As you say, I do not see. How can I do better?"

You see what I choose, the unspoken voice said.

"And you have chosen to show me a passageway of stone, leading to a formless golden light." Arlian swung himself out of the saddle, dropping to the black stone floor. "If this is the shape in which it pleases you to be seen, I have no quarrel with that. I would not ordinarily ride through such a corridor, so I take it you wish me to dismount."

It matters not.

His horse was suddenly gone, along with his remaining supplies, and he was alone on the black stone floor, completely at the mercy of his magical host.

At least he had no headache this time.

"I see," he said. "It doesn't matter, but my mount is gone."

The steed lives. Your belongings exist. You do not need them here.

"It would appear I need nothing here but your sufferance."

Precisely. While I choose, you live.

"And you choose to let me live? My thanks, O mighty being."

Say rather, I have not yet chosen to destroy you.

"Ah. Is there, perhaps, some means by which I might ensure that you do not make such a choice? Some method by which I might earn your sufferance? Shall I beg and plead? Shall I bluster and threaten, or bargain? I am here as your humble petitioner, seeking knowledge, but I have no guidance in earning your generosity. You have me utterly in your power. What can I do to gain your favor?"

It is traditional, I suppose, to set a supplicant a task, one where successful performance means you may live a while longer, and where failure means swift and painful death. Is this not what the stories report?

"I have heard such tales," Arlian admitted cautiously, "though not about you, in specific."

It suits my whim to play the role on this occasion.

"Indeed—then how can I please you? What task would you have me perform, what test to prove me worthy of your tolerance? How can I demonstrate my valor?"

For a moment there was no response; then the being answered.

Sing to me.

Arlian blinked; his mouth opened, then closed.

"What?" he asked.

Sing to me. Sing songs of praise and thanksgiving, perhaps, as the priests of old sang to their gods, or songs of mourning for what you have lost and what more you may lose. I see that you are strong and swift, that Fate has favored you, and you have slain many foes, overcome many obstacles, so I would not waste our time by sending you into combat; any merely physical feat would be uninteresting. Instead I charge you to please me with song, as if I were your god.

"I am neither priest nor mourner, and have no skill at music," Arlian protested—but then he realized what he was doing, what he was refusing, and hastily added, "I must have a moment to compose myself."

Nothing answered; he stood alone in the corridor. He closed his eyes for a moment as he tried to recollect an appropriate song.

He had not sung in many years; in fact, he could not recall *ever* having sung since his parents' death. He knew no songs by heart. He had listened to several over the years, under various circumstances, but he had never attempted to join in, had never troubled himself to learn the lyrics.

He could remember a few tunes—though the ones that came to mind were all children's nonsense songs he had heard his mother sing when he was very young. He struggled to fit words to one of them.

"I am a foe of the dragons," he sang at last, in a voice that rasped unpleasantly. He stopped, cleared his throat, and began again.

"I am a foe of the dragons
Who has come to you seeking your aid.
I know not what coin I can offer
Should you demand to be paid.

"My houses are at your disposal
My gold I would lay at your feet
But surely you need no such baubles;
Your wealth is forever complete."

Arlian was not at all happy with the last line of that second stanza, nor with his tendency to slip out of key at the end of each line, but he was doing the best he could. Even as he was aware that his performance was inept, he found a certain pleasure in using his voice this way, and in fitting words to his chosen tune—even if the tune was a children's song originally about a lover gone to sea, and completely inappropriate for propitiating a demigod.

"Your power, the subject of legends
Is said to be almost divine
And I can but hope that your mercy
Extends to these few needs of mine."

And with that, he stopped; his invention had exhausted itself, and he had no idea what to say in a fourth stanza, nor how to say it. He was rather pleasantly surprised he had managed to get through three, strained meter and off-key voice notwithstanding, without completely losing control of his song. He took a deep breath, and let it out slowly.

How curious, that the gods of old took such pleasure in songs of praise. Your improvisation is clumsy, but so were many of the prayer songs of old. The gods reveled in such music; I find nothing exalting in it.

"I'm sorry," Arlian said. "I am no singer. Perhaps I could arrange for musicians . . ."

No.

He bowed toward the golden light. "As you please."

Always.

Arlian straightened. "If I may ask, does it please you now to hear my request?"

I know your request. You have come seeking knowledge that will permit you to rid your homeland of the dragons without subjecting it to the indignities of wild magic.

"Indeed," Arlian agreed. "You come directly to the heart of the matter."

I loathe the dragons that drove me here, and have no great love for the foolish chaos of the lands surrounding my own, but I have little aid to give you.

Arlian looked around again, at the apparently solid marble walls and the elaborate painting overhead, and said, "I find it hard to believe that a being as powerful as yourself can mean that."

To doubt me in my place of power is not wise.

Arlian managed a crooked smile. "I have never claimed to be wise," he said.

You amuse me, you and your awkward little song, and our shared hatred of dragons has bought you my brief indulgence. Ask questions, if you like.

"And you will answer?"

Until I grow bored and cast you out, or become angry and destroy you.

That was hardly an appealing choice, but Arlian supposed it was the best he was going to get. "What *are* you?"

I am that which has no name.

"Some say your name is Tirikindaro."

Arlian could sense the smile in the reply. *In the tongue of my native land, a tongue a thousand years dead,* tir i kin daró *means simply "that which has no name."*

"Dead a thousand years? How long have you existed, and how long have you ruled here?"

I no longer remember. Thousands of years, possibly tens of thousands.

"How can that be? The Blue Mage told me that no wizard can exist for more than sixty years."

I am no mere wizard.

"My Aritheian associate believes you to be a god."

There was a pause before the reply.

I do not believe I am truly a god.

That was interestingly equivocal, Arlian thought. "Then how can you live so long?"

There are dragons as ancient as I; one need not be a god.

"Nonetheless, such longevity is surely extremely rare; how did you achieve it? Was it a mere happenstance, a part of your nature?"

No. Long ago, perhaps ten thousand years, I drank the blood of a dying god, one of the dead gods you swear by, and became what I am now.

That was an intriguing answer, one with any number of possible ramifications, but Arlian did not allow himself to be distracted. He wanted to learn the nature of a magical being that was neither a dragon nor a true god, yet lived for millennia. "And what *is* that?" he asked. "What were you before you drank this divine essence? How did you happen upon this bleeding deity?"

There is no name for what I was, nor for what I am. I had been a creature of magic, a parasite of minds and dreams, and I dreamed of being more. I had taken the form of a man, imposing that shape and as much of human characteristics as I could on the body of a nightstalker, a body I had stolen. I had fought my way up as far as I could through my own devices, consuming wizards and possessing the nightstalker, and I was not satisfied. I petitioned the gods for aid, and when the dragons betrayed the gods and destroyed them I was there, and I drank the blood that spilled from a god's torn throat. Then I fled, lest the dragons turn on me, as well.

Arlian sensed a sort of hesitation, a thoughtfulness, and then the thing spoke again.

Do you know, O man, I have not remembered those times

*in centuries? You have reminded me of where I came from,
and I am unsure whether to thank you for it, or condemn
you to decades of torment.*

"I would prefer the former," Arlian replied, as he tried to
comprehend what the thing had said.

I am aware of that.

Arlian ignored that as he attempted to match the creature's words— or thoughts, or whatever he was receiving—
with what he had thought he knew of the ancient past. The
old tales spoke of a time when gods strode the earth, and
the dragons were their dark and sometimes rebellious servants; then the gods had departed or died, and the dragons
had reigned over the land for thousands of years, oppressing
humanity, holding all the Lands of Man in bitter servitude.
For centuries men and women had hoped and prayed for the
return of the gods, but eventually most understood that the
gods were never coming back; then a few brave men had
risen up and begun the Man-Dragon Wars, which in time
drove the dragons into their caves and left humanity free at
last.

But no one had ever explained how the gods died. Arlian
had always assumed no one knew.

Apparently, no one had asked the master of Tirikindaro.

"You said the dragons betrayed the gods?" Arlian said.
"We have no record of such an event."

*There were no human observers. Only the gods, the drag-
ons, and myself. The dragons would hardly tell you what
they had done, and the gods could not—and until now, no
one had asked me.*

"I find that hard to believe, given how long you have
lived."

*Few dare question me. Few dare address me at all. Even
fewer of those who attempt it survive to tell the tale.*

"If you will forgive me, you do not seem so very dreadful; so far I have found you delightfully accommodating."

I am not always so. You amuse me—your fearlessness is

most unusual, and your song was comical. Your actions please me—you have slain dragons. Thus, I speak freely with you—though I may yet kill you, or transform you, or imprison you. I have lived long and seen much, and thus I can foresee many things, but I do not predict my own whims.

"Thank you for the warning."

It will do you no good.

"Nonetheless, I am glad to have it, and hope I will have no use for it."

You begin to bore me now. What is it you would have of me, beyond your own life?

"You said it yourself—I want a way to destroy the dragons without unleashing wild magic in the Lands of Man."

I know of none.

"But you do not deny that one is possible?"

There was of old a time when the gods ruled your lands, and dragons did not. Perhaps such a time can come again. I have no knowledge to the contrary.

"Gods?" That was not anything Arlian had considered.

Or some other beings. The magic of your lands, even when ordered, is not restricted to the form of dragons.

"Can the magic be destroyed, or removed and sent elsewhere? Must every land have magic?"

I am magic, given form, just as the dragons are, or wizards, or demons, or any of the lesser creatures—do you think I would tell you how I might be destroyed, even if I knew? The corridor shimmered, and the golden glow was shot through with red. Arlian decided not to pursue that particular line of inquiry.

"Then is there some difference between the magic of the dragons and the magic of the southern lands? Why is our northern magic always bound up in dragons, while the southern magic takes thousands of different forms?"

At root it is all magic, all the same essence of the land—I have tasted it in both realms and know this to be true. In the north the dragons pass it from parent to child, while in the south it arises spontaneously from the earth and air, and returns to air and earth when each magical creature dies.

"But why? How did this difference come about?"

How it began I do not know; that happened long before I arose myself. How it continues is plain enough; the dragons' greatest magic is not their long lives, nor their strength, their armor, their wings, their flame, nor even their mastery of the weather, but their venom, the venom that permits them to pass on their form to a new generation. No southern creature has any such gift. It is from this venom that all else derives.

"But . . . then other magical creatures cannot reproduce their own kind?"

They cannot. We cannot.

"Then why do the same forms recur? How can we tell a wizard from a demon, or a nightstalker from a nightmare? I know they vary far more than dragons, but why are there *any* patterns? Or if they all arise in the same fashion, why are they not all the same?"

Magic cannot take form from nothing, the thing replied. *Some, such as demons, are deliberately created by wizards or magicians, but those that arise naturally, like natural creatures, must have two parents. Where natural creatures are born of a male and female of the same kind, magical creatures are born of one magical parent and one natural one. In the north the parents are always dragon and human, and the result is thus always a dragon; in the south the magical parent is always the land itself, but the natural parent can be a man, a serpent, a tree—any living thing at all, down to the lowliest weed or worm. The form of the new creature, as with any species, is determined by its parentage—a human will produce a wizard, a predatory beast will yield a nightstalker, and so on.*

That accorded so well with what Arlian already knew— what he had been taught of the dragons by Enziet, what he had been taught of wizards by Isein and the Blue Mage—

that he could not doubt it, and instead wondered why he had never guessed it himself.

"And these creatures contain the magic that created them? They use it up? And when they die, the magic returns to the earth, to begin the cycle anew?"

You seem to understand.

"And the dragons use up so much magic that nothing else can arise in the Lands of Man? And this is why the only magic humans can use there is either sorcery, which draws on the tiny remnant of power the dragons have left unused, or magic that has been carried in from other realms?"

Obviously.

"So if I could find some *other* magical creature, some benign one, that could reproduce itself, then that could replace the dragons?"

As the dragons long ago replaced the gods, yes—if such a benign creature existed, which to the best of my knowledge it does not.

"Because the only way any magical creature can reproduce itself is the way the dragons use their venom, combining it with human blood and having a person swallow it? And no other creature can do that?"

No other means is known to me, nor do I know of any other magical creature that produces such a venom—nor do I know of a benign magical creature of any sort, not since the gods died.

"But why are there no benign magical creatures?"

I do not know.

That was a profoundly unsatisfactory answer. This nameless thing that ruled Tirikindaro was the closest Arlian ever expected to come to finding a living god, or a reliable oracle, and to be told that it could not answer a question was thoroughly frustrating. He tried to think of some other way to approach the issue.

"So all the magical creatures except dragons are completely sterile?"

Magic is inherently sterile, yes.

"But dragons aren't."

Their unique magic allows them to reproduce their kind, yes—but even then, it takes centuries to reshape a human soul into a dragon, and the human's own fertility is destroyed. Dragons are destroyers, not creators, and must be born of destruction.

"How do you know that, when you admit you do not know so many other things?"

I lived among the dragons. I spoke to the gods before they died. I sought to extend my own life, and therefore inquired at length about the nature of gods and dragons, and why they lived so much longer than all other magical beings.

"And they told you?"

Or I drank the knowledge from them.

"In the god's blood?"

Or a dragon's.

"You drank *their* blood, too?"

It was in my nature. The golden glow was growing redder, and the light in the corridor was starting to dim. Arlian began to wish he had a blade—silver, steel, obsidian, anything. He had left his silver behind, his steel was in the bundles on his vanished horse, and his obsidian lay in scattered shards on the Blue Mage's courtyard pavement.

"Why is that?" he asked.

You heard what I said of my origin. Have you not wondered what my natural parent was, or why I keep my human slaves?

"I . . . was more interested in other matters," Arlian admitted. "I did not wish to intrude on your privacy."

I said that the earth's magic could impregnate even the lowest living thing, and my beginnings were low indeed. I was born of a leech. An ordinary leech.

"And you have transcended your birth magnificently."

You hope to save yourself from my hunger—but I see you also speak your honest belief, and are not disgusted, as most men would be. Yes, I have transcended my origins; I have drunk the blood and knowledge and power and magic of a million more exalted creatures, and made it all mine. I have made the essence of those myriad beings my own essence. That is my magic, as venom is the dragons'—and I have used it as no other before or since. No other leech-thing has ever risen to even a fraction the heights I have attained.

The glow was golden once again, the red fading, and Arlian could feel the creature's pride—pride that Arlian thought was entirely justified. To start out as the magical spawn of a loathsome little bloodsucker and grow into something many believed to be a god—that was an accomplishment to be proud of indeed!

I had thought a dragonheart's blood might be an interesting new taste, but now I think I will spare you, it said. *I think you might well serve me better if I set you free. If anyone can destroy the dragons that drove me here, I think Fate has chosen you for the task.*

"I will certainly try," Arlian replied.

The dragons cast me out; now, in turn, I cast you out, Arlian of the Smoking Mountain. Complete the circle, and earn this life I grant you.

And then Arlian found himself standing in a deserted, sloping field, beneath thick clouds that flickered with purple and gold; clumps of brownish mist rolled across the dried stalks and bare earth. The air was hot and moist, and his sweat-soaked blouse clung to his back.

His horse stood a few yards away, pawing the ground uneasily but not fleeing; the remaining bundles of supplies were still in place.

Arlian turned slowly, looking for some trace of the "palace," or the being that had transported him back and forth and spoken to him without ever making a sign.

He and the gelding stood at the foot of a mountain, its peak lost in a seething mass of something that was not exactly cloud.

Arlian looked up the stony mountainside for a moment, then decided that he had probably learned everything worthwhile that Tirikindaro could teach him.

And the leech-god had certainly given him plenty to think about. If he could find some other magical creature that could breed true, some less harmful creature, then he could use it to replace the dragons.

But what could it be?

He spoke quiet, soothing nonsense as he walked up to the horse and caught the reins, and a moment later he was riding away from the mountain, down the slope in the direction he hoped was north.

25

The Lands of Wild Magic

Although he regretted any delay in exploring further beyond the border, Arlian rode directly from Tirikindaro to Orange River, back into the Borderlands to collect Isein, Double, and Poke. He had said he would return within a month, so he intended to return.

He had also said he would bring the magician to her homeland, and he thought that Arithei might as well be his next stop—he doubted that the wizards of Shei or Furza would tell him anything significant that he had not already learned from the Blue Mage or the thing in Tirikindaro, while the human magicians of Arithei might provide a different perspective.

As he rode past the orange groves into the village he saw Isein standing by the roadside, talking to one of the natives.

He recognized her immediately by her Aritheian attire, its colors so much brighter than the local garb.

"Hello there!" he called.

She and her companion turned at the sound; Isein's eyes widened, and she screamed, clapping her hands to her mouth. The Borderlander started at the sound, and stared at her, obviously astonished by her reaction. He began babbling at her, trying to calm her, as Arlian swung down out of the saddle and ran up.

"Isein!" he called. "Isein, I'm just Arlian!"

"You're . . ." she gasped. Then she caught herself, took a deep breath, and straightened up.

"You said you were going to Tirikindaro," she said accusingly. "You *said* you were going to talk to the thing that rules there."

"I did," Arlian said, stopping a pace away from her while the man accompanying her held her arm—Arlian was unsure whether he was comforting her or restraining her.

"But here you are alive! Did they stop you at the border? Couldn't you find it?"

"I found it," Arlian said. "I spoke to it."

"But you're alive—aren't you?" She reached out to touch him, but he was a few inches too far away. He stepped forward and took her hand. "It didn't enslave you, or kill you, or . . . or transform you?"

"I'm alive," he said, holding her hand reassuringly in both of his. "Alive, free, and untransformed."

"It . . . it didn't do *anything* to you?"

"I amused it," Arlian said wryly. "And we have a common foe. It let me live and go free."

Her astonishment suddenly transformed to anger, and she snatched her hand away. "How could you *do* that?" she said. "Just leave the three of us here, while you go off to do something insane?"

"I assumed you could take care of yourselves," Arlian replied. "And my life is my own, to risk as I please."

"You are inconsiderate, as well as mad," she said.

"I am a dragonheart," Arlian answered. "A monster, without true human warmth. You have known this for years."

"Ordinarily you do a better job of concealing it," Isein replied, but she spoke more calmly now.

"My apologies," Arlian said. "I was indeed inconsiderate. Nonetheless, it is done now, and I have survived, and the time has come to journey to Arithei, so that I might speak with the scholars and magicians there."

She considered that for a moment, then glanced at the man who had stood silently by throughout this exchange.

"Doni, it appears I will be traveling on on the morrow," she said. "I must therefore decline your offer, at least for the present." She threw Arlian a glance that let him know her anger had not entirely abated. "However, I will undoubtedly be returning this way eventually, and as I am not at all certain that I wish to continue in Lord Obsidian's employ, I may well reconsider at that time."

"As you please, Isein," the Borderlander replied, with a slight bow. His own glance at Arlian was more confused than angry. "If there is anything I can do to be of service to you, you need but ask, and it will be done."

Isein returned his bow.

Arlian decided that this would be a good time to retrieve his horse, in case the two had anything more to say to one another that his presence might inhibit; by the time he had found and recaptured the gelding, which had wandered a few yards into the grove, and returned to the road with the animal, Dori had departed and Isein was waiting impatiently.

No words were spoken as they walked on into Orange River, Arlian leading his mount. They were almost to the inn when Isein said, "Dori wanted to hire me as the town's defender against the spread of magic. I told him I wasn't sure how much I could do, but I could try."

"Very commendable," Arlian said.

"I had considered trying to reach Arithei on my own, of course—well, with Double and Poke, really. They don't know any better, and would have come if I asked."

"Indeed."

"I didn't want to rush into anything, though."

"Wise of you."

"We were in the South Groves so that I might attempt to sense how close the border has come; it didn't have anything to do with *you*."

Arlian tied the gelding's reins to the inn's rail and said, "I hadn't supposed otherwise."

"I assumed you were dead."

"As you had every reason to." He patted the horse, then turned to the door of the inn.

For a moment Isein was silent; then she burst out, "What did it *say*? What was it like?"

Arlian smiled. "I will be delighted to tell you all about it, once the horse has been tended to and we have let the innkeeper know that I'm here, and in need of food and drink."

He swung the door open as he spoke, and any further discussion was momentarily lost in the shouts of greeting from Poke and Double, who had been seated, beer mugs in hand, just inside the inn.

Arlian did describe his adventures in Tirikindaro at great length that night, to a rapt audience composed not merely of his three traveling companions, but of a dozen locals as well.

That delayed making any preparations for departure until morning, and in fact the four northerners spent another full day in Orange River, resting, planning, and loading, before setting out for Arithei.

The traditional route to Arithei led first westward, then south, then southeast, to avoid Tirikindaro and other established magical demesnes—but the borders had changed, and furthermore, Arlian felt he had an understanding with Tirikindaro. He suggested taking a more direct route.

The others argued against such an action. "We don't want to miss Qulu on his way north," Isein said.

"We need a road for the wagon," Double pointed out.

Arlian was forced to concede that these arguments were sound, and after further discussion tradition eventually prevailed.

Thus the wagon, guarded by steel and silver and amethyst, took the familiar route—but it was not familiar at first. The Borderlands had changed. Magic streaked across the sky, the wind laughed and muttered, and after just three days' travel they found deserted villages. In one of them peculiar trees grew in the streets, short thick trees that seemed to have human faces in the bark and that writhed and rustled without any wind; Arlian suspected that these had once been the village's normal inhabitants.

From that point on strange beasts stalked the nights, and marvels and wonders seemed to lurk around every corner. Flowers watched them pass with wide blue eyes, and birds spoke to them in several languages—one bright-plumaged creature followed them for a time, calling Arlian's name in his long-dead mother's voice. All of the travelers often glimpsed things from the corners of their eyes that were not there when looked at directly.

Oddly, once they were across the *old* border, some eight days from Orange River, the chaos subsided and a semblance of normalcy returned. The villages they passed now were inhabited by brown-skinned people in flowing bright robes, people who spoke Man's Tongue with strange accents if they spoke it at all—but they were inhabited, and the people, however foreign they might appear, were human.

Isein inquired once or twice whether anyone remembered seeing an Aritheian of Qulu's description passing through a year or so back, but received only shrugs in reply.

"Nothing has changed here," Isein explained when Poke commented on the unremarkable appearance of this area. "These lands have the same magic they have always had. The magic here is no stronger; the difference is that a part of the dragons' magic has been freed in the Borderlands, not that the wild magic beyond the old border has grown."

"But it seems so *strange* there," Poke protested. "Why should it be stranger than here?"

"Because the magic there has only recently been freed, and has not yet found its proper form," Isein replied. "No one there has learned to tame it, and nothing has yet restrained it. In time, it will settle down . . ."

If she had intended to say more, she did not get the chance; at that moment a roaring green monstrosity sprang from the roadside ahead, lunging toward the lead ox. Arlian had been walking nearby; his sword seemed to leap into his hand as he sprang to the animal's defense. Double, riding guard ahead, swung around as well, drawing his own blade, cursing himself for not having seen the creature as he passed.

The two swordsmen dispatched it in short order, chopping it into twitching, bloodless chunks, but a stop was required to tend to four long gashes its claws had inflicted on one of the oxen.

"It's no worse than before," Isein said, as she worked a quick healing spell, "but that doesn't mean it's safe. It has never been safe."

Arlian grimaced at the reminder, but said nothing.

A fortnight into the journey they passed the last village and began the climb into the Dreaming Mountains. On the third night thereafter the attacks began in earnest; the green thing had been only the first faint taste.

Fortunately, most of the nightmares and monstrosities fled or crumbled or faded away when stabbed with good steel; a few burst like soap bubbles. Some that were not especially vulnerable to steel blades were driven off by the touch of the silver necklaces all four travelers wore, and after one especially close call Arlian pried some of the silver ornamentation from the wagon and looped it around the oxen's throats.

The gelding now wore a harness trimmed with silver,

rather than the plain leather that Arlian had used in visiting
Pon Ashti and Tirikindaro—but that did not save it; on the
fourth night in the mountains, while the travelers were slaughtering a swarm of venomous black rat-things on the other
side of the wagon, something tore the poor beast's throat
open, and it bled to death before help could come.

Two nights later Poke lost two fingers off his left hand
while fending off an insectile horror that shrieked like a
woman when stabbed. The other two men dispatched the
monster while Isein tended to Poke's wound; while the
creature did not flee from cold iron, well-handled steel
could still pierce its chitinous armor.

Its blood was bright red. When it finally turned and fled,
Double suggested pursuing it to finish it off, but Arlian, seeing the red blood and hearing the woman's voice, remembered an incident from his first passage through the
Dreaming Mountains. He held Double back, and the beast
escaped.

That was the worst of it; five days later they came down
out of the mountains and saw the black iron gates of the
Aritheian town of Ilusali ahead. Late the following afternoon they arrived in Theyani, the Aritheian capital.

There they finally received some word of Qulu, though
hardly a satisfying report; he had arrived in good order over
a year before, and departed on schedule. No news of him
had been heard since.

"What *happened* to him?" Isein demanded—but no one
could tell her.

It was all too easy to make unpleasant guesses, though.

And then, for a time, the party disbanded. Isein sought
out her own family, to reacquaint herself with the affairs of
her clan, to seek advice on Qulu's fate, and to share her
concerns with others who had known and cared about him.
Since the party was in a civilized land and under the protection of the House of Deri, Arlian and Isein no longer required guards; therefore Double and Poke were free of their
duties. The two soldiers took the opportunity to relax, and

to familiarize themselves with the fabled magical land of Arithei—most particularly with its women and its strange southern liquors. Poke alternated between inquiring fruitlessly after magicians who might be able to restore his lost fingers, and using their absence to gain the sympathy of the local female population.

And Arlian spent his days talking to the greatest magicians and scholars of the House of Deri, and the House of Shalien, and the House of Peol, and even the House of Indé. He had not come this time to carry yet more of their best physicians away to Manfort as he had Oeshir and Lilsinir and Tiviesh and Asaf, nor was he interested in how the magicians created their spells, nor in the history of Arithei's occasional wizard-kings, nor in the nature of Arithei's defenses; he wanted only to know how magic could be bound up, as the dragons bound it, by something other than dragons.

And none of them could tell him. In fact, much of what he had learned from the Blue Mage and the leech-god of Tirikindaro had been unknown to them, so he taught as much as he learned.

Still, he did learn.

"The essence of every natural creature is found in its blood," old Epheil, one of the leading scholars of the realm, told him as they sat cross-legged on the tiled floor of a tower room in the clanhouse of Peol. "That is why cleansing the blood, rather than flesh or bone, transforms a dragonheart back to an ordinary man. We have studied this question extensively in the years since Oeshir's reports were first brought to us, and of course we knew a great deal about it from the wizards and magicians of old. We are certain of our conclusions. It is contamination of the blood that permits the creation of a new dragon or wizard, and it is this use of blood by the infecting magic that determines the consistent form of the offspring. Wild magic that inhabits the skin or flesh or any other thing than blood will spawn monstrosities, as we often see in the lands surrounding Arithei, and will commonly transform the affected host, rather than creating a new being."

"Wizards are more or less human in form," Arlian said. "Dragons are not, yet they are born of human blood. How does this accord with your theories?"

"This is still a matter of conjecture," Epheil replied. "It has been suggested that this is why the gestation of a dragon requires so very much longer than that of any other creature—the magic does not *want* to take the form being forced upon it, and the host's blood must first be altered, drop by drop, from human to dragon. Something in the venom causes this slow transformation, and only when it has been completed can the magic take on its final draconic form."

Arlian considered that for a long moment, then said, "Someone told me that dragons eat human souls."

"We have no knowledge of this," Epheil said, meeting Arlian's gaze. "It may well be true."

"If they do, then perhaps the first souls they eat are those of their hosts—perhaps, in fact, the taint in the blood gradually destroys the human soul, and this is why dragonhearts are incapable of human warmth." Unpleasant memories stirred. "And perhaps that is why, when a new dragon is born, its eyes hold something of its human parent—it has just finished eating that soul."

"Perhaps."

"And with the soul destroyed—that natural essence in the blood you spoke of—the dragon's form can prevail."

"This would be consistent with my understanding," Epheil agreed. "But we are merely guessing."

"So dragon venom is, perhaps, a sort of refined and constrained magic—it simultaneously attempts to transform its host into a creature of magic, as does the wild magic of the south, while being prevented from completing the transformation until every trace of humanity has been burned out of the blood."

"Again, this is mere theory," Epheil warned. "Remember

that dragon venom by itself is a virulent poison, and only in combination with human blood does it cause any transformation at all; there is clearly something more going on here than we know. Still, it is undoubtedly a very powerfully magical substance."

"And is there any other known substance, any potion or elixir, that acts similarly? Perhaps we might learn by comparing . . ."

Epheil shook his head. "I can think of nothing that causes so slow a process. There are potions that will transform a person into something else, either temporarily or permanently, as the Blue Mage transformed those squirrels you described, but these do not alter the underlying nature of a being, only its outward manifestation—as you saw, when the Blue Mage died the squirrels reverted to their natural form. This is a fundamentally different process."

"I would *prefer* a transformation that left the underlying nature unchanged," Arlian said. "Could I perhaps hire a wizard to transform thousands of creatures in harmless ways, and therefore absorb a portion of the magic inherent in the Lands of Man?"

"But you would be using the *wizard's* magic, imposed from without," Epheil pointed out. "There would be no inherent magic in your altered creatures. You could use only the magic the wizard already controls, and it would dissipate upon the wizard's death."

"I have slain dragons that had created dragonhearts, and the dragonhearts did not revert to ordinary men and women."

"A fundamentally different process, as I said. It is a quality of dragon venom that is unlike anything else with which I am familiar."

"Dragon venom," Arlian mused. "Always dragon venom. What if there were some way to transfer the magic inherent in dragon venom to some other form?"

"Then you would have your solution, I suppose—though you must be very careful indeed that this new form is no worse than the dragons."

"What could be worse?" Arlian asked—but then he remembered some of the things he had seen in the Dreaming Mountains, and in the fields of Tirikindaro, and even in the streets of Pon Ashti. He grimaced.

"Don't answer that," he said.

26

The Failed Quest

*A*rlian stayed in Theyani for a fortnight—long enough to convince himself that the magicians of Arithei did not have any easy solution for him. He learned a great deal of theory about the nature of magic, from Epheil and a dozen others, but no one could tell him what he wanted to know.

He did learn that as he had suspected, magical spells and devices served to concentrate natural magic, and move it temporarily from one place to another—his magic-importing business had transported a quantity of magical energy from Arithei to the Lands of Man. The Aritheians, who had an immense surplus, had considered this a good thing, and had believed the natural magic of the Lands of Man so depleted that any increase would be harmless; Arlian, however, no longer thought it wise to transfer *any* sort of magic to the Lands of Man, and resolved to shut down his enterprise.

No one could tell him how to remove magic from the Lands of Man, however, or how to bind it in a stable form other than dragons.

Therefore at the end of that two weeks he began preparations for further explorations, and three days later he set out for Stiva, another land where men ruled and magic was extensively studied. Double and Poke accompanied him, as did an Aritheian named Uilieh he had hired as a translator; Isein stayed in Arithei, further reacquainting herself with her homeland.

Upon their arrival in Stiva a week later they were initially received with suspicion—the only northerners who had ever traveled to that land were traders, and Arlian had no banners, no displays, on his single half-empty wagon; he had brought nothing to trade save information, and the people of Stiva placed no great value on that. In the end Arlian found it necessary to strip a few ounces of silver and several pounds of iron from his wagon's protective devices to pay for food, lodging, and the knowledge he sought.

He learned more of magical theory, some of it interestingly different from what he had been taught in Arithei, but still nothing immediately useful.

"After all," as one Stivan magician said, and Uilieh translated, "if we could create stable and harmless magic, would we not have done so ourselves, and drained our own realm of its dangers, rather than living huddled behind wards and hexes and protective runes?"

That simple statement of the obvious struck Arlian hard; he had somehow failed to consider that. Clearly, he was not going to have his solution handed to him on a silver platter, ready to apply to the Lands of Man; if such a solution were known, it would have been implemented somewhere, and it had not. In all the known world, from the western deserts to the Eastern Isles, only the Lands of Man were free of wild magic, gaunts, wizards, rogue magicians, stalking nightmares, and the like, and that distinction was due, it seemed, entirely to the presence of the dragons.

But, he told himself, no one had ever before combined *all* the scattered knowledge of the southern lands. No one else had spoken with the master of Tirikindaro and the scholars of Arithei and the magicians of Stiva and a wizard like the Blue Mage, and put all that together. None of the southerners had studied the subtleties of northern sorcery—though, Arlian admitted privately, he had only scratched the outermost surface of sorcery himself.

Lord Enziet had spent centuries studying sorcery and dragons, and had arrived at the secret of their vulnerability to obsidian; if he had ventured into the lands beyond the border, might he have learned that centuries sooner?

Perhaps, and perhaps not—Arlian would probably never know. He did know, however, from his inherited notes, that Enziet had never sought an alternative to the dragons; he had not lived long enough to concern himself with that.

That problem was entirely Arlian's.

He hoped very much that he would not need six hundred years, the length of time Enziet had taken to learn about obsidian, to find that alternative.

He stayed a little over a month in Stiva—he needed longer than he had in Arithei because of difficulties with the language, and because he had not spent years dealing in Stivan magic, nor crossed the Desolation in company with a Stivan magician. His initial ignorance of Stiva was impressively complete, though he did his best to relieve it as swiftly and thoroughly as possible.

In the end, though, he concluded that he had reached the point at which further gains would not be worth the investment of time and money. He had, he thought, learned all he could profitably learn of the Stivan understanding of magic. It might be that some missed tidbit, some obscure detail, held the answer he sought, but he did not care to spend years hoping to stumble across it. He found Poke and Double, loaded them and Uilieh back into the wagon, and headed west.

The guards were happy to go; the women of Stiva were far less cooperative than those of Arithei, their menfolk more protective and suspicious. Further, the only local liquor was a bitter wine neither of the soldiers cared for.

From Stiva Arlian set out to Lur Dalaket, a land in the southern jungles that had never traded with the Lands of Man; he hoped that this would mean there were untapped

insights there. Instead he found an unhappy huddle of prim-
itive villages and runaway superstition where the natives
were simply waiting for the next wizard who might choose
to rule them and impose a semblance of order on their mis-
erable existence. A week was more than enough time to
sicken of the place and move on to Baratu, a land that, he
discovered, had kept itself relatively free of wizards and the
like by slaughtering anyone or anything suspected of har-
boring any magical taint. The result was a tiny and dwin-
dling population living in an atmosphere so thick with
formless magic in some places that Arlian found it hard to
breathe; the air seemed to flicker constantly.

From there, Arlian turned northward to Shei, where a
council of thirteen wizards ruled over a reasonably healthy
human population. No human magicians were permitted, nor
were magical protections such as those on Arlian's wagon;
he left the wagon and oxen, as well as his three companions,
at the border while he ventured into the council's territory.

The wizards were sufficiently civilized and curious to
grant Arlian a brief and unsatisfactory audience, which was
largely spent arguing over whether the Lands of Man would
be better off ruled by wizards than by the current mix of humans and dragons. Arlian was relieved that the wizards
eventually agreed to disagree, and made no effort to change
his opinion with anything other than words.

Still alone and on foot he crossed from Shei through the
roadless jungles south of Skok's Falls to the city-state of
Kaltai Ol, where the magicians had taken charge of their
environment by learning spells that allowed them to enslave
nightstalkers, which were then used to defend them from all
other dangers. Arlian was initially intrigued by the concept,
and wondered about the possibility of scaling the spells up
to control dragons, until he discovered that the magicians
had been unable to alter the nightstalkers' diet. The women
of Kaltai Ol were kept perpetually pregnant to ensure a
steady supply of surplus babies, whose brains were fed to
the nightstalkers.

Arlian did not consider this acceptable, and said so, emphasizing his displeasure with his sword. He killed three of the eight court magicians before fleeing from some two dozen of their outraged and pregnant wives.

From there, rather than make his way through the jungles, he returned to the Borderlands—or at any rate, the lands that had once been north of the border, and had not yet been claimed by any other government. There he turned east once more, then south, revisiting Shei before returning to his wagon and rejoining the three companions he had left there.

In Arlian's absence Double had contracted a fever, so that the guard had spent several days lying in the wagon, soaked in sweat and tended by Poke and Uilieh; he was still shaky when Arlian returned. Arlian therefore postponed further exploration until he had delivered Uilieh safely back to her home in Arithei, and left Double in Theyani to recover his health while he and Poke ventured further into unknown lands.

All in all, Arlian spent some nineteen months exploring the lands beyond the border before finally concluding that there was nothing more of use to be learned there.

He knew more than he had ever expected to learn about the nature of magic and blood and power and all the myriad forms they could take, but the secret he needed, it seemed, must lie in dragon venom itself. No other still-existent magical essence could produce such consistent results, or bind power so long and so well. No other surviving creature had any equivalent.

A god's blood could apparently engender magical creatures of immense power and duration, if the leech-god of Tirikindaro could be believed, or at any rate bestow longevity on existing creatures, but there were no living gods left in the world, so far as anyone knew, and therefore no possible source. If Arlian could find a god . . .

But he could not, and that meant that if he sought to create something that would restrain the magic of the Lands of Man in a stable, long-term form, the only means available was dragon venom. If he sought to achieve it without the continued presence of dragons, then it seemed he would need to find a way to make their venom produce something other than a new dragon.

That seemed unlikely, to say the least, but it appeared to be his only hope.

And if he was to have any hope of achieving it, he would need to experiment with dragon venom—which, obviously, was not available beyond the border.

Therefore at long last he returned to Arithei, where he re-loaded his battered wagon, hitched up his weary oxen, and late in the warm and snowless southern winter he headed north into the Dreaming Mountains once again, with a fully recovered Double on the bench beside him and Poke walking alongside. No Aritheians accompanied him; Isein, having been warmly welcomed by her clan, had changed her mind about the relative merits of Theyani and Manfort and preferred to remain in her homeland, while Uilieh simply had no business in the Lands of Man, and no interest in going there.

The trio of northerners, now experienced in the ways of the magical realms, made good time. Three weeks took them past Sweetwater, and up the canyon into the Desolation.

27

The Gate at Stonebreak

The first sign Arlian saw of the changes that had taken place in the two years since his departure was the great iron gate, blocking the road in the defile leading down from the Desolation to the town of Stonebreak. The summer sun shone brightly on a black iron framework supporting a stone wall that had been built across the narrow canyon from side to side, to a height of twelve or fifteen feet. At the center two twenty-foot towers flanked two massive iron panels, each some ten feet wide and ten feet high.

Arlian was not pleased.

He had encountered no trace of magic, not so much as a bad dream, since his third day in the wastes; surely, there could be no need of defenses this far north! Nor could the gate be intended to defend against anything *other* than magic; what other threat could emerge from the lifeless desert?

Wasting time and money and manpower to build this thing was foolish; the energy would have been better used in building catapults and carving obsidian spearheads—or in growing crops and raising children, since the Duke's truce with the dragons was presumably in effect.

The wagon rolled to a stop a few feet from the iron barrier, and Arlian tilted back his hat for a better view of the wall. The towers on either side of the gate were simple iron frames, but each was topped with a railed platform, accessible by a ladder on the north side—and neither platform was currently occupied.

"Ho, there!" Arlian called, as loudly as he could manage— his throat was rather dry, as they had been rolling since midday, and his shout was not all it might have been under better conditions.

The call echoed from the stone walls of the ravine, but no one answered. Arlian sat, glaring.

On the bench beside him, Poke leaned back into the interior, groping for something with his intact hand. The guardsman was in civilian garb; the Duke's livery had been stored away out of sight for months. Double was in the wagon behind them; the driver's bench could accommodate only two comfortably.

Poke found what he was after, and handed Arlian a half-full waterskin—their last; their supplies had been rationed carefully to get them across the Desolation, and if they did not get past this gate thirst might quickly become a real problem. Arlian took a healthy swig, cleared his throat, then stood up on the driver's bench and held his hands to either side of his mouth.

"Ho, the gate!" he bellowed.

His shout echoed from the iron and stone, but no one answered.

Double thrust his head out of the wagon's interior between Poke's shoulder and Arlian's hip, and for a moment all three men stared at the gate. Then Double pointed and said, "What's that, my lord?"

Arlian looked where Double's finger indicated, and saw a four-foot lever connected to a heavy chain that vanished into a small opening in the left-hand tower. He had not consciously noticed it before, thinking it merely a crooked bit of the tower's iron frame, but now that Double drew his attention to it, Arlian could see that it was a mechanism of some sort. He stepped down from the bench, jumped lightly to the ground, and strode over to the lever in question. Then he grabbed it in both hands, tested it, and heaved.

Machinery clanked, and the gates sagged open. The lever had released a latch of some kind.

"By the dead gods," Arlian muttered, as he pushed one valve aside. "What do they hope to keep out with *that*?" Clearly, whoever had built this gate and latch assumed that the magical creatures it was meant to exclude were mindless beasts; Arlian concluded therefore that the builders had never encountered wizards or gaunts.

A moment later the wagon was through the open gate, rolling down into Stonebreak. Double asked, "Shouldn't we close it again?"

Arlian growled. "No," he said. "If they're fool enough to leave it unmanned, it's not our responsibility to compensate for their folly."

"Maybe they left it unmanned because they're all dead," Poke suggested.

"Then there's no one to defend, and nothing to be accomplished by closing it," Arlian said—but his tone was milder; the possibility of some great catastrophe having taken place had not previously occurred to him. "I don't see that the gate served much purpose in any case—anything human could get through as we did, and a good many magical creatures are not bothered by iron, nor hindered by such simple barriers. If something *has* slain them all, then the gate did no good."

But then they rounded the final turn in the ravine, and the question was moot—they could see the village ahead, and people going about their business in the street. Everything looked much as Arlian remembered it—save that he could not see the catapults that had stood by the road. He supposed they had been moved to less obtrusive positions.

There had been no catapults in any of the towns beyond the Desolation, but he had expected them to be even more common and more obvious elsewhere than before his journey; he was mildly startled by their absence.

As they had on the way south, the three men stayed the night at the town's only inn, just a dozen yards from where Arlian had slain a soldier called Stonehand in a duel almost eighteen years before, and around the corner from the lot where he had bought the two now-dead horses. Their arrival drew a great deal of attention from the townspeople; apparently caravans were scarce these days.

The locals had been somewhat irritated to learn that Arlian had left the iron gate open.

"The Duke's men said we should keep it closed," one man explained as Arlian ate his supper.

"And how are honest travelers to get through, then?"

"Just as you did," the innkeeper replied, as he delivered the last plate. "That's why we installed that lever."

"Except we had thought they would have the courtesy to leave it as they found it," the other man said.

"Perhaps if you left a man on watch . . . ?"

"That's what the Duke's messenger said we should do," a boy offered.

"But who's got the time to stand out there all day? We have better things to do. Bad enough we had to help the soldiers build it! I spent a good three weeks hauling and hammering iron, without earning a single ducat."

"It wasn't so bad," the innkeeper said.

"*You* weren't out there heaving iron bars about!"

"No, I had an inn full of soldiers and messengers and the like ordering me about day and night, and not a one of them paid for his room. At least you weren't expected to do anything after sundown."

"And at least you were paid for the food and drink."

"What's the point of it?" Arlian asked.

The natives stopped their arguing to stare at him. "The point of what?" the innkeeper asked.

"The point of the gate."

"To keep out the bad magic," the boy said.

"But it's just iron," Arlian said. "That will stop some of the creatures of the earth and air, perhaps. What of silver for the creatures of darkness? Gems for the creatures of dreams and madness? And what of the creatures that can fly over it, or climb the ravine walls around it, or climb down the cliffs? What of humans in the thrall of magic, or wizards, who can work the lever as I did?"

The villagers glanced at one another.

"We wouldn't know anything of that," the innkeeper said.

"Are you a magician, then?" a plump woman asked.

"A dealer in magic, and a dabbler in sorcery," Arlian said. "Not a true magician."

"We have two sorcerers here in Stonebreak," one man said. "Neither of them said anything about the gate not being effective."

Arlian shrugged. "What would a sorcerer know of southern magic? But I've just come from Arithei, and . . . well, that gate won't do much by itself."

"It doesn't have to," the innkeeper said. "I heard the Duke's men talking—they say the dragons will keep out the southern magic. Seems the Duke's made a pact with them, common cause against the southerners. The gate's just to slow 'em down until the dragons get here."

"You trust the *dragons*?" Arlian demanded.

No one answered at first, but as the silence grew uncomfortable one of the barmaids said, "We might as well; we can't do anything about them in any case."

Arlian frowned. "I had heard you had catapults here, with obsidian heads fitted to ten-foot bolts." In fact, he had signed the orders himself, though he had not personally overseen the installation, and he had taken a good approving look at them on his way south. "After what befell Cork Tree . . ."

"The Duke took them back," the boy said. "The oxen that hauled the iron here hauled the catapults away."

"The boy's right," the innkeeper admitted.

Arlian did not like the sound of that at all. "Why?"

Feet shuffled and shoulders shrugged. "We don't know," a man admitted.

Arlian could think of a few possible reasons, none of which he liked. "So you've traded the catapults for your iron gate. Have there been many incursions from the south, then? Strange births, transformed beasts, unnatural plants?"

"No."

"No, nothing like that."

"Nightmares, then, or strange dreams?"

"No."

"But the travelers have brought stories from the Borderlands!" the boy called. "*Terrible* stories!"

"The Borderlands are hundreds of miles from here, beyond the Desolation," Arlian pointed out.

"But the tales all agree the danger is moving north," a man pointed out. "Why leave our defenses until the last minute?"

"Ah, well, then if you're preparing for some possible

danger years from now, the iron gate may be a good start," Arlian acknowledged. "You'll need to do more in time, though."

"Of course," the innkeeper said. "Of course! And we'll do it when the time comes."

"As soon as the Duke sends us orders."

Arlian nodded, and said no more, but his thoughts were not quiet. There were several things that troubled him about this situation.

Firstly, building iron gates so far from the town, and only on the southern side, was useless; if the dragons died and the magic came it would come from all directions, from earth and sky, and a full wall encircling the town would be needed to keep out the worst of it.

And if the dragons did *not* die, then the magic would not come. These people had no way of knowing that, but the Duke's advisors ought to. The Duke himself, although he had gained some sense over the past several years, was still a bit of a fool, and he might not recognize the situation, but surely, some of the people around him would have explained it to him!

If the Duke was trying to build defenses against magical invasion from the south, who was advising him? Why would *anyone* suggest such a course? All this did was to waste time and money that could be better spent elsewhere; what would anyone stand to gain from that?

And why were Stonebreak's defenses against the still-real danger of the dragons gutted? Where were those catapults taken? What had become of the obsidian points? Were the dragons' servants in control, and removing anything that might threaten their monstrous masters? What was happening in Manfort? Was the city, too, being stripped of its defenses? Could even the Duke be that foolish?

And for that matter, why were the people of Stonebreak speaking of the Duke as if he were their lord and master? True, there was no higher authority in the Lands of Man than the Duke of Manfort, and every trading village was expected to pay taxes to the Duke, but that was largely a relic of ancient times. The Duke's ancestors had been the warlords who commanded the human armies in the Man-Dragon Wars, and for seven centuries the Dukes and their troops had been charged with keeping the peace and defending the land against all foes, but they had never been recognized as the final authority in other matters. Local lords and village councils had always set their own rules and made their own decisions—but the people of Stonebreak had built that ridiculous gate at the Duke's command, and allowed their catapults to be hauled away.

Arlian could only guess that they were acting out of fear. In recent years, ever since Lord Enziet's death, the peace had been not merely broken, but utterly shattered—towns and villages had been destroyed by dragons, the lords of the Dragon Society had warred openly against the Duke, and now stories of wild magic rampaging through the Borderlands were everywhere. A village could not hope to defend itself unaided—and the Duke was the only one offering aid. The villagers did not know how to protect themselves against these menaces, and the Duke, it would seem, claimed that he *did* know. What could be more natural than that they would hurry to obey their traditional protector? Why would they question his knowledge?

Arlian finished his chop, scraping the last meat from the bone with his knife, then looked around.

"I thank you all for acquainting me with circumstances here, and I regret any inconvenience I may have caused by leaving the gate open, but I assure you, there is no magic threatening you at present that the gate would keep out. The wild magic has indeed spread into the Borderlands, but is still well south of the Desolation, and does not seem to be encroaching further."

Unless more dragons died, he did not expect it to ever advance, but he saw no point in saying this.

"Is it really bad in the Borderlands?" the boy asked. "Are

there really bloodsucking monsters everywhere, draining the life from the cattle?"

"Not *everywhere*," Arlian assured him, and that casual response unleashed a flood of questions. He spent the rest of the evening describing what he had and had not seen in the south.

And in the morning he and his men headed out while the sun was still red in the east; Arlian wanted to reach Manfort as soon as possible, to see for himself what the Duke was up to.

28

Manfort Transformed

*T*he ruins of Cork Tree were as depressing as ever; no one had yet made any attempt to rebuild, and the trees growing up from empty foundations were taller and sturdier than before.

In Sadar there were no iron gates, but iron posts, not unlike the road markers used in Arithei, encircled the village. The obsidian-throwing catapults that had been built and armed some ten years before were gone; the locals explained that the Duke's men had said they were needed more urgently elsewhere.

In Blasted Oak a protective iron framework had been built around the central shrine, and the catapults were gone.

Jumpwater had no added protections, but the catapults were gone; the same was true at Benth-in-Tara. Arlian found himself wondering what the Duke *did* with all that obsidian.

And then, when he at long last came within sight of Manfort's walls, he saw.

They were rolling through the surrounding towns—Manfort had outgrown its walls long ago, though the streets and shops and houses clustered outside the ramparts were not considered truly part of the city—when they rounded a corner and caught their first good view of the ancient defenses.

At first Arlian thought either his eyes or his memories were deceiving him; the walls seemed higher than he remembered, more shadowed, and they glittered in the late-afternoon sun in a way he had never noticed before.

But then he looked more closely, and understood.

The walls *were* higher. The blacknesses were not shadows, and the glittering was sunlight refracted by black volcanic glass.

Great obsidian spikes had been set into the battlements, hundreds of them; the black iron frameworks of dozens of catapults rose above the spikes, and thousands of wooden shafts tipped with still more obsidian bristled from the catapults.

The Duke might have made a bargain with the dragons, but that did not mean he trusted them; he clearly intended to assure that whatever else might happen, Manfort itself would never fall to the beasts.

"Idiot," Arlian muttered to himself. "What does he plan to *eat* if he lets the dragons destroy everything else?"

"What?" Poke asked, jerking upright. He had been drowsing, half-asleep, on the bench at Arlian's side.

"Nothing," Arlian said. "But look, we're almost home." He pointed.

Poke looked, then blinked.

"What did they *do* to it?" he asked.

Arlian laughed. "Added to the defenses," he said.

Poke did not reply, but stared openmouthed.

By the time they rolled through the gates Arlian was staring somewhat himself. The Duke must have set his entire army to the task within days of Arlian's departure; the city's defenses were truly astonishing. Arlian had not realized there was so much obsidian in all the world; the deposits on the Smoking Mountain must have been stripped clean.

The Duke of Manfort obviously took the possibility of a dragon attack very seriously indeed, despite the truce. Arlian wondered why. The dragons had not dared to attack Manfort itself in more than seven hundred years; why would His Grace feel the need for such elaborate defenses?

Once through the gates the streets of Manfort were much as Arlian remembered them, paved in stone and bustling with humanity—but the crowds seemed even thicker, and there were new shadows on them. The sounds of hammering and men shouting echoed from the stone walls. Arlian's gaze rose to the rooftops.

More catapults. More obsidian—though Arlian noticed that the spearheads on the shafts here were smaller, more delicate, and some appeared to be steel heads with mere chips of obsidian set into them; clearly, supplies of the black stone were running low. Some shafts, in fact, had no heads at all yet. And workmen were still installing more frameworks, more counterweights, more spearshafts, as if the intent was to place at least a dozen shafts atop every building in the city.

Arlian had intended to request an audience with the Duke in any case, but he had not felt any great urgency about it; now he did.

First, though, he needed to stop at the Grey House, to clean himself up and hear the news. He had been gone for two years, more or less, and obviously things had happened in his absence, the city going on about its business without him.

He hoped that Black, Brook, and the children were all well—and that Lady Rime had not passed away. She had seemed healthy enough when he left, but she was not a young woman.

Arlian snorted slightly at that thought; Lady Rime was more than four hundred years old. "Not a young woman" hardly began to describe it! Most of those years had passed while she was contaminated with dragonspawn, and left her untouched; Arlian could not hope to judge accurately her natural age.

The streets were thronged; whatever else might have taken place, the city's population had clearly not decreased. Their progress was slowed by the crowds of pedestrians.

At last, late in the afternoon, the wagon rolled up to the gate of the Grey House. Arlian leapt from the bench, leaving Poke and Double to unload and to attend to the oxen.

He had scarcely handed his hat and cloak to the footman in the foyer when Black appeared. He wore his customary black leather, but incongruously, he held a baby in his arms, a bright-eyed child perhaps a year old, swaddled in fine linen. Black was smiling broadly, beard bristling, and the infant was staring up at him in wide-eyed wonder.

"Ari," he said. "Welcome back."

"Thank you," Arlian replied. "It's good to see you." He glanced at the baby. "Who is this?"

"My son," Black said proudly, displaying the gaping, gurgling child. "Dirinan."

"I see I have missed a great deal."

"Come and join us, and we'll discuss it."

Several minutes later Arlian, Black, and Brook were seated in the gallery, with Dirinan safely in his mother's arms after having demonstrated his eagerness to walk half a dozen wobbly steps before falling, and his ability to make noises that could generously be interpreted as words; these remarkable accomplishments had been appropriately admired by the master of the house. A footman set a tray of wine and cakes on the table before vanishing, leaving the four alone.

Arlian was eager to hear the news, but the others, just as eager to hear an account of his journey, outvoted him, and he spent the next hour giving an account of his explorations beyond the Desolation—though he provided very little detail regarding what he had learned of the nature of magic, emphasizing instead the strange lands and fearsome creatures he had encountered. He did not care to say much about his own plans—or even *make* those plans—until he knew more about the situation in Manfort.

Finally, though, after he had spoken enough to satisfy his listeners temporarily, Black provided a quick summary of how matters had progressed in his absence.

The discovery that killing dragons allowed wild magic to encroach upon the Lands of Man had not merely forced the Duke to negotiate with the Dragon Society; it had shaken the very foundations of his beliefs. He had inherited his title in a time of peace and plenty, when the dragons were rarely seen and no other great dangers threatened his realm. When Enziet's death and Arlian's actions had spurred the dragons to greater activity he had seen it as a temporary problem; Arlian's killing of the dragon that destroyed the Old Palace had brought His Grace to believe that this ancient evil could finally be obliterated, restoring the peace and inaugurating an even greater age of plenty.

The knowledge that destroying the dragons would instead plunge the land into chaos had convinced the Duke that the entire world outside Manfort was, by its very nature, inimical to humanity. He now looked back on those peaceful days before Enziet's death as a lost golden age, a historical fluke, one that was gone forever; he had said as much on many occasions, making no secret of his beliefs.

The dragons, through their human puppets in the Dragon Society, had made demands, and the Duke, rather than struggle against the inevitable, had yielded to most of them. The dragons had agreed to reduce their attacks if no more towns and villages were armed with obsidian weapons, and the Duke had done them one better, withdrawing all the existing defenses outside Manfort itself; in exchange, the dragons had promised that no more than one village would be destroyed each year.

The dragons had wanted the defenses destroyed entirely, but the Duke had balked at that. He had resolved that there must be at least one place kept free of the dragons, one place where men could live without fear of the supernatural evils that dominated the rest of the world, and he intended to insure that Manfort would be such a place.

Word of this had apparently spread; the crowded streets Arlian had noticed were the result of an influx of dragon-wary people who had decided to take refuge within the re-fortified walls.

"I'm impressed," Arlian remarked. "I had not thought His Grace had the will to carry out such a scheme in the face of the Dragon Society's objections."

"The Duke has the unyielding support of his advisors," Black replied. "It was Lord Zaner who proposed making Manfort an impenetrable fortress, and who has overseen the elaboration of the city's defenses. As your representative, I gave him my full cooperation in providing obsidian from the Smoking Mountain; I trust this pleases you."

"Lord Zaner?"

"He is now chief advisor to His Grace," Brook said. She had one finger in Dirinan's mouth, and he had fallen asleep sucking gently on it; Brook had seemed to focus her attention on the baby throughout much of the conversation, but clearly she had been listening, and now she looked up at Arlian as she spoke.

Arlian blinked, but swallowed further comment.

He had wondered for an instant whether Lord Zaner might be part of some elaborate plot to undermine the Duke's position—after all, Zaner had sided with the drag-ons for fourteen years. But then he remembered that Zaner had given up centuries of life, had had himself cleansed of his draconic taint. That could not be a ruse; the dragons would never have allowed one of their offspring to be de-stroyed as part of a political ploy. No, Zaner could unques-tionably be trusted, and his vigorous defense of Manfort was probably the zeal of the convert in action.

Or perhaps he feared for his soul, and wanted to ensure

that when his time came to die he would not feed the hideous appetite of a dragon.

"Dragonhearts are forbidden admission to Manfort, lest they sabotage the defenses," Black continued. "Lady Opal has been expelled. A limited number of untainted ambassadors and representatives are permitted inside the walls, but kept under close watch. Your old friend Lord Rolinor serves as a go-between; the Duke and Lord Zaner prefer not to speak directly to any agent of what they consider the powers of darkness. Restrictions on dragonhearts outside the walls have been lifted, however—not that the Duke was ever able to enforce them effectively in any case."

"Had he been, matters would have gone rather differently," Arlian commented.

"Indeed."

"Then the Dragon Society's members have been restored to full control of their properties and enterprises, and the Lands of Man once again unified?"

Black snorted. "Not at all," he said. "The Dragon Society has openly established their own government in Sarkan-Mendoth, and dropped all pretense of allegiance to the old order. They claim the Duke has gone mad—but they will not fight him openly, save to defend themselves."

"They're waiting for him to die," Brook said. "He has no heir, after all; the line of Duke Roioch ends with him. His wife is still barren, despite Asaf's attempts at treatment."

"I had thought there was a nephew . . . ?"

"There was," Black said. "Lord Balorac. Murdered a year ago by an assassin, a young woman—like his uncle, he had a weakness for a pretty face."

"Though this one was masked," Brook added.

"Lady Tiria?" Arlian suggested.

"Perhaps; she was sought, but not found. To the best of our knowledge Tiria is no longer in Manfort."

Arlian nodded thoughtfully.

He had assumed that he would not find himself welcome in the Citadel, that the Duke and the Dragon Society would have made a real peace that would have cast him as a pariah for his slaughter of so many dragons. From Black's account, though, his position was far better than he had expected—Zaner and the Duke were still defying the dragons as best they could, and would presumably accept him as an ally.

And if he could find some way to bind the land's magic in something other than a dragon, something less powerful, less dangerous . . .

"There are experiments I must conduct," he said.

"Experiments?" Brook asked. She glanced at Black.

"More diabolic machinery?" Black asked. "We *have* catapults now, Ari—probably far more than we need."

"Not catapults," Arlian said. "Nor sorcery, nor obsidian, nor anything else I have experimented with in the past. I intend to experiment with magic."

Brook said, "True magic cannot be made in Manfort, I thought."

"*Southern* magic cannot be made here, but sorcery, while subtle, is still magic, and likewise dragons are magic, and all the inhuman traits of the dragonhearts."

"But you said it would not be sorcery," Brook persisted.

"Nor will it be. I intend to experiment with the magic of the dragons themselves."

"And just how did you intend to accomplish this remarkable feat?" Black asked.

"With their venom," Arlian replied. "I will need a considerable supply." He smiled crookedly. "And yes, I am aware of the irony in this, given how much of that foul stuff I have deliberately burned over the past several years. As we all know, Fate is fond of these little jokes."

"I hardly think this is a fit subject for jokes," Brook replied—but before she could say anything more Dirinan awoke and began crying, delaying further conversation.

29

The Disposition of the Household

*A*rlian's brief explanation of his intentions was interrupted by Brook's departure to attend to Dirinan's needs, but when she had wheeled herself away Arlian finished outlining what he would need.

Black immediately refused to aid in Arlian's attempts to acquire a supply of dragon venom. "The whole enterprise is mad," he said.

"You think *all* my enterprises mad," Arlian retorted.

"Indeed, and this one is madder than most, and I'll have no part in it."

"As you please, then," Arlian said. "Will you at least be so kind as to acquire the other materials I require, then? Traps, cages, livestock, and a husbandman to attend them?"

"I can hardly object to that," Black said. "I will endeavor to have everything prepared for your return."

Arlian blinked at him, and said mildly, "Return? Am I going somewhere?"

"Are you not?"

"I was not aware of any such intention."

"Then how do you propose to obtain dragon venom? I had assumed you would find another lair from your list, and dispose of its occupants."

"Permit me to remind you that His Grace has asked me to refrain from any further killing of dragons until further notice. He may rescind that order when next we speak, but I have no reason to expect that."

"But . . . very well, then, how *do* you propose to obtain your venom?"

"I had thought to purchase it, here in Manfort; it was my understanding that a thriving black market exists."

For a moment Black was silent; at last he said, "Oh."

"Does this alter your decision to refuse me aid?"

"No," Black said.

"Very well, then. Please obtain my experimental subjects, then, and I will see if I can manage the venom without you." Arlian rose, and started toward the door.

"Ari," Black said.

He paused. "Yes?"

"Where are you going? The Duke has outlawed all trade in dragon venom, and you have been two years away; how do you propose to contact the black market?"

"I thought you wanted nothing to do with it."

"I . . ." Black stopped. Then he began again. "Ari," he said, "we have spent most of the past twenty years together. I am your employee, yes, but I like to believe I am also your friend. In either role, friend or servant, I am concerned for your welfare. I know very well your skill with a blade, your knack for improvisation, your determination, and your sheer luck. Nonetheless, you are neither infallible nor invulnerable, and you have just announced your intention of committing a capital crime in a city with which you are no longer entirely familiar. I have refused to aid you in perpetrating this lunatic act, yes—but I can still offer advice on not getting yourself killed in the process, and warn you away from the most obvious threats."

Arlian smiled. "I appreciate your concern, Beron—and yes, I do consider you my friend first, and my steward only incidentally. Likewise, I acknowledge that I have often been reckless. In this instance, however, I assure you I do not plan to take any great risk. I am not entirely a fool—and you are not my only employee, nor the only one who I might expect to have some knowledge of Manfort's criminal element. I am on my way not to the gate, nor the stable, but to the kitchens, to speak with Stammer in regard to both our supper, and whether she might be able to supply the venom I seek."

"Oh." Black hesitated, then admitted, "That would seem sensible enough." Both men were well aware that Stammer had once lived among Manfort's thieves and beggars, and still maintained an extensive network of contacts among her old friends in that unsavory community. In the ordinary course of events she drew on those contacts only to gather news and gossip, but neither Black nor Arlian doubted that she could put them to other uses.

"I am gratified by your reassurance," Arlian said dryly.

Black hesitated again, then said, "My lord, I request permission to remove myself and my family from the Grey House for a time."

Arlian glanced toward the exit Brook had taken. "You are concerned for your children's safety? Perhaps you have a point. In fact, perhaps I should find somewhere else to conduct my experiments."

"No, I . . ." Black stopped.

Arlian looked at him thoughtfully. "I would not want to leave Manfort," he said. "If these experiments succeed in creating an alternative—well, I think the dragons themselves might take an interest, and His Grace has conveniently guarded Manfort against the dragons as thoroughly as I can imagine possible. Nor would I care to operate on anyone's premises but my own, and I own only two parcels here—the Grey House and the grounds that once held the Old Palace."

"Another could be bought."

"Oh, I hardly think it worth that much effort and expense," Arlian said. "No, I think it better after all to follow your own suggestion, and ask the staff to vacate the Grey House temporarily."

"Thank you, my lord."

Arlian studied Black; it was obvious from the formal address that something remained between them.

"I can hardly use the grounds of the Old Palace," he said. "Lord Obsidian's guests make it impossible. To evict them now, after all these years—well, it can't be done without great upset and turmoil."

"Ari—it's not the danger that concerned me," Black admitted. "I hadn't even thought of that at first."

"Are you that appalled, then, that I dare to handle the venom at all?"

"Not appalled, Ari. Tempted."

That had not occurred to Arlian, but now he felt foolish that it had not. Certainly, Black had mentioned the subject often enough in the past.

"You need not recite the litany again," Black said, before Arlian could regain his composure. "I know well enough that you consider the heart of the dragon more curse than blessing, and I have heard Lady Rime and Lord Zaner speak at length of how they have been freed from soul-deadening bondage, how they have regained their ability to love and their joy in life. I know the elixir would rob me of much I value—but time itself will do the same, and far sooner than I like. I am fifteen years older than you, Ari, and in any case you are a dragonheart—you do not feel the cold winds of age chilling your blood, as I do. The prospect of a thousand years of life, even the sort of bitter life you say you lead, is far more appealing than the spectre of death. I can resist that temptation when it is distant and difficult, but if you bring it into my home and ask me to live with it but a few steps away . . ."

"I understand," Arlian said. "You need say no more. You and Brook and the children are welcome to make your home at the Old Palace, or at any of my holdings outside the city, until the temptation has been removed."

Black bowed. "Thank you," he said.

"One last thing, before you begin your preparations for departure," Arlian said.

"Yes?"

"Send a messenger to the Citadel, and inform His Grace of my return and my eagerness for an audience at his earliest convenience."

"Of course." He bowed again.

Arlian nodded an acknowledgment, then turned and headed for the kitchens, where his arrival precipitated much excitement among the servants there. They hurried to make him welcome and assure him that the household was in good condition and that his supper would be ready on schedule, in perhaps another half-hour; he could hardly object to these attentions, after a two-year absence, but he hastened matters as best he could, and finally arranged to speak to Stammer alone in one of the pantries.

"I thi . . . thi . . . think you'll find everything in order, my lord," she said. "I have always no . . . notified your steward promptly about any problems."

"I'm sure you have," Arlian said. "I'm not here to discuss the kitchen staff."

Stammer stared at him silently; he knew she would have asked for an explanation of why he *was* there had she been able to do so without stammering. Rather than prolong her discomfort, he quickly explained what he wanted.

"It's ex . . . expensive," she said.

She did not ask *why* he wanted dragon venom, he noticed. He was not entirely sure whether this was because she trusted him, or because she wanted to avoid a prolonged discussion.

It was odd, he thought, how bad her stammer was when speaking to him; she barely stammered at all when talking to the rest of the staff, instructing them in their duties or choosing the day's menu.

"I'll provide the money," he said. "That's no problem at all."

"It may t . . . take a few days," she said.

"Of course," he said. "As soon as you can manage it will be fine."

She curtsied.

And with that out of the way, he turned his attention to the preparations for the evening meal.

30

Deceptions in Court and Street

*T*he morning after his return Arlian received word that the Duke requested his presence that very afternoon; he cut short his review of his finances and devoted himself to his appearance, as it would not do to go before the Duke with his hair unruly or his beard untrimmed. His coach had stood unused for years and was discovered to have rotted beyond easy repair, so he was unable to ride to the Citadel in appropriate style, but when he walked up the hill he wore his best boots and a new hat, purchased in haste that morning, and thought himself suitably turned out.

He waited slightly over an hour in a small salon before being shown into the audience chamber, where the Duke, looking rather the worse for wear, sat slumped on his throne, his fine blue jacket hideously wrinkled. Lord Zaner stood at the Duke's right hand, and Lord Spider at his left.

There were fewer courtiers than Arlian remembered from previous occasions, and no one in the room was masked—that unwelcome fashion appeared to have finally ended, though whether of natural causes or ducal edict Arlian did not know. He saw no one he recognized as either a member or hireling of the Dragon Society—not Lady Opal, nor Lady Tiria, nor Ferret, nor Wing, nor Lord Rolinor.

He had scarcely finished his formal obeisance when the Duke said, "Lord Obsidian—what news do you bring?"

"No news of great importance, Your Grace, save that I have returned safely from the Borderlands and am once again at your service."

"Your message expressed eagerness for an audience."

"Indeed, I am eager to know what you would have of me. Circumstances in Manfort appear to have changed somewhat in my absence."

"Changed? Perhaps outwardly. In fact, we are much as we have always been—an island of civilization besieged by monstrous magic. The difference is that we now acknowledge this openly; pretense has been abandoned."

"I observed the enhancement of the defenses."

"Yes."

"As your warlord in the campaign to exterminate the dragons, I take an interest in such matters. Might I ask why this was done?"

"Because I won't lose Manfort. I won't let them have it all. Maybe we can't obliterate the monsters, but neither will I allow them a complete victory. I will see Manfort destroyed before I allow them to come here."

Arlian glanced at Spider's face, which was rigid and blank, and then at Zaner's, which was visibly worried.

"I see," he said.

"You were in the Borderlands," the Duke said.

"Yes, Your Grace."

"Has everything fallen to the monsters, then? The wild ones, I mean, not the dragons?"

"Oh, by no means, Your Grace! The border is stable once more, albeit several miles north of where it was of old."

The Duke blinked at him, then straightened in his chair. "Stable?"

"Yes, Your Grace."

"But you killed so many dragons . . ."

"Not enough to have weakened them that badly, it would seem; their power still protects much of the Borderlands. Some of the wild magic does seep through—we had nightmares well into the southernmost portion of the Desolation, near Orange River, and could see abnormalities in the sky—but for the most part, the situation has stabilized and the new border is secure."

"Is it? Remarkable!" The Duke sat up straight, his features animated. "I had assumed . . . well, no matter what I had assumed. Then we have only the dragons to fear here?"

"The dragons and their minions, yes, so it would appear. I saw the gate you had ordered built in the ravine south of Stonebreak; I fear that was wasted effort. Nothing unwelcome will be crossing the Desolation."

"You encourage me, Obsidian. And you . . . tell me, did you visit Pon Ashti?"

"Yes, Your Grace, I did, when first I reached the Borderlands."

"Then what became of it, do you know? We received a report that the Blue Mage had been destroyed, and that the city was open to trade once again."

"The Blue Mage died while I was there, Your Grace; she is indeed no more. Beyond that, I know nothing more than you."

This was not literally true, but Arlian could not honestly be certain of what had happened to her—whether he had slain the Mage, or time had caught up with her, or something else entirely had occurred. He preferred not to try to explain this ambiguity to the Duke.

"We thought it might be a ruse, to draw merchants and guards into her clutches."

"She is unquestionably dead, Your Grace."

"How? Did the dragons do it?"

"No." Arlian hesitated; to claim credit for her death at this juncture would seem boastful. "I believe she simply died of old age; unlike dragons, wizards do not live forever."

"So Pon Ashti is free?"

"Perhaps not, Your Grace; it lies well beyond the current border."

"Oh. And Skok's Falls . . ."

"Gone. Everything we have lost remains lost. The Lands of Man have not regained any territory; we have merely stopped losing it."

"Well, in these bitter days even that might be considered a victory. Thank you for bringing this news, my lord."

Arlian bowed an acknowledgment. When he rose again, he said, "Your Grace, I am uncertain of the situation here, and of what my present duties are. I saw the gate at Stonebreak, and observed that you had removed the catapults from several towns while extensively reinforcing Manfort's own defenses. I understood when I left that I was not to kill any more dragons, but had assumed that I would, in time, be sent to build defenses throughout the Lands of Man. Is this not the case?"

"You know, Obsidian, I'm not sure. I certainly don't want you killing any more dragons, but defending other towns? We withdrew the catapults from the southern towns lest they be captured by wizards from beyond the border—we did not want the wizards to slay the remaining dragons and thereby lay the entire realm open to their assaults. But now you say the border is stable, and the wizards cannot approach?"

"So I have observed, Your Grace." Arlian restrained himself from commenting on the logic in removing the catapults. It was actually a rather ingenious theory, if the Duke had honestly believed the Borderlands to be irretrievably lost and a horde of wizards and gaunts on their way across the Desolation. Having now spoken with a number of wizards, however, he doubted that any of them would have had the wit or initiative to have turned the catapults on the dragons, or that they would have triumphed had they attempted it.

It did explain the Duke's actions, in any case.

"Then perhaps the situation is not as black as I feared," the Duke mused. He glanced up at Zaner. "What have you to say, my lord?"

"I hope Lord Obsidian is right, Your Grace," Zaner replied. "You know I have counseled against despair, as well as against overconfidence."

"Indeed. And what would you suggest our friend Obsidian do now, since he says he is unsure of his duties?"

"That is clearly for Your Grace to decide, but perhaps Lord Obsidian himself has suggestions? He has proven himself resourceful many times, after all."

The Duke nodded, and even managed a smile. "Yes, he certainly has. Have you any plans of your own, Obsidian?"

Arlian bowed again. "If it pleases you, Your Grace, there are certain experiments in magic I would like to undertake. I have hopes, albeit faint ones, of finding some way to guard our lands against the depredations of wizards and monsters without any further need for the dragons."

"*Do* you?"

"Faint hopes, Your Grace, but hopes."

"Are you a sorcerer, then?"

"Not in any real sense, Your Grace, though I have dabbled in the arcane arts. Rather, I have spent these past two years in studying with magicians in the lands beyond the border—Arithei and Stiva and Pon Ashti—and have devised certain theories I wish to test."

"Ah! And can you tell us the nature of these theories?"

Arlian hesitated.

"I fear you would find them tediously esoteric, Your Grace," he said at last.

"Oh, I suppose I would—I have never been one for theories." He pulled at his lower lip, glanced up at his advisors, and then said, "I have faith in you, Lord Obsidian—after all, it was you who first demonstrated that dragons could in fact be slain—but you must nonetheless provide me some assurances. Can you promise me that these experiments will not make matters worse?"

"I can only assure you, Your Grace, that I have no reason to believe there will be any unpleasant results, and that they cannot possibly aid either the dragons or the wild magic of the south. I will do my very best to prevent any of my creations—if there *are* any creations—from doing any harm to anyone in Manfort or the surrounding lands."

"Then I grant you permission to conduct your experiments. Will you require any assistance from me or my guards in performing them?"

The Duke's resources would undoubtedly be helpful, but on the other hand, allowing anyone else to be involved in his trials carried several risks. If word were to spread that he was using dragon venom in strange new ways, he would undoubtedly attract unwanted attention from both men and dragons—men seeking to obtain the venom, and dragons seeking to ensure the failure of his efforts. Even mentioning to the Duke in private might be unfortunate, as despite his protestation of faith he might well have second thoughts upon learning that his hereditary foes' venom was involved.

Better, then, to keep everything as private as possible. He might call on the Duke's services later, if and when it became necessary, but for now he preferred to hold on to as many secrets as he could.

"Thank you, no, Your Grace," he said. "I believe I have what I need."

"As you please, then."

As Arlian left the audience he considered what he had told the Duke. Obviously, he did not yet have what he needed; he had no venom.

But Stammer would solve that problem for him in another day or so, he was sure.

In fact, it was four days after Arlian's return to Manfort that she appeared in his study, holding out a small black bottle. He took it from her gingerly, and pulled the cork, anticipating the familiar stink of venom.

The sickly-sweet odor that reached his nose was strange and powerful, but not the smell of dragon venom. He looked up at Stammer, startled.

"It's not venom," he said.

She blinked at him, her mouth falling open; she tried to speak, but could not get a word out.

He held up a hand. "Stop," he said. "Catch your breath. Think what you want to tell me, then say it."

She closed her mouth, swallowed, closed her eyes and hunched her shoulders. Her lips drew into a thin line as she concentrated.

Then she said, "This is what they sell on the streets as dragon venom, I bought it from the most reliable source I could find, and if it isn't real then the real thing is not to be found *anywhere* in Manfort, my lord!"

"Can you smell it?" he asked, holding out the open bottle and its cork.

She sniffed, then nodded rapidly. "That's . . . they tell me that's the way it always smells, my lord."

"But that's nothing like the smell of real venom," he said. "Any of my men, anyone who has been in a dragon's lair, any dragonheart, would know it to be false in an instant."

She closed her eyes for a moment, concentrating, then said, "They aren't the ones who would be buying it, my lord."

"Indeed they are not," Arlian agreed, looking down at the open bottle. "A very good point. Thank you."

Stammer curtsied, and turned to go, but Arlian stopped her with a word. "Fetch me a magician," he said. "Whoever can be here most quickly."

"A s . . . sorcerer, or an Aritheian, my lord?"

"Either one."

She curtsied again, and hurried out.

Arlian stood for a moment, studying the bottle.

He should have guessed, he told himself. After all, dragonhearts were recognizable, at least to the experienced eye of another dragonheart, and if venom were indeed available in the streets of Manfort at *any* price, would there not have been scores of new dragonhearts making their presence known?

Still, he was curious about what this potion was that was being sold as venom; was it perhaps some potentially useful magic?

The following day's analysis, conducted jointly by Lilsinir and Lady Rime, indicated otherwise. "The juice of the crimson poppy and the white lotus," Rime told him. "From the Eastern Isles."

"And the leaf of the *ko* plant, from the jungles below Skok's Falls," Lilsinir added.

"The combination would *feel* powerfully magic," Rime

said. "The drinker's heart would race, and he would feel a rush of tremendous exhilaration."

"And he would dream strange and wonderful visions, clearer and more powerful than any ordinary dreams," Lilsinir concluded.

"I see; and how, then, would he know he had been deceived?" Arlian said. "There may be a hundred men and women here in Manfort who believe themselves to be secretly possessed of the heart of the dragon."

"Until they fall ill, of poison or disease," Rime said. "That would reveal their folly. Whatever effects this fluid might have would be mere passing illusion, and would cause no lasting change."

"Indeed." Arlian stared at the black bottle for a moment, then set it once again on his desk and turned away. "In that case," he said, "I must fetch some real venom, as quickly as I can. I yet have evidence of the hiding places of another forty or so dragons."

"But the Duke has forbidden you to kill them!" Rime protested.

"Killing them will cost the Lands of Man more territory," Lilsinir said. "Wild magic will encroach further. Another lair might mean all the Borderlands will be lost."

Arlian stopped and stood for a moment, eyes closed. He breathed in deeply and slowly, then let out a long sigh.

"I know," he said, opening his eyes but looking at the door, not at the women. "I know. But if no one learns more, if no one finds ways to divert the land's magic, then we will never be free of these monsters. Our state of affairs will never be better than it is now. I must have the venom to experiment with. If I can take it without slaying the dragons . . ."

He stopped and closed his eyes again.

"I want the dragons dead," he said, jaw tense. "I want my revenge. Even after all these years, I want them to pay for what they did to my parents, my brother, my friends and neighbors, and all the thousands of innocents they have

slaughtered; what I have done has not been enough. I do not
think *anything* will *ever* be enough. I know this for a failing
in myself, that I cannot accept the injustice of the dragon's
existence and nature, that they keep us and prey upon us as
we keep and prey upon cattle; nonetheless, I want them all
dead. To go into their lair and *not* butcher them all goes
against my heart's dearest desire. Still, I do not want the
deaths of still more innocents on my conscience; I do not
want the Duke's truce broken, nor the horrors beyond the
border unleashed upon more unsuspecting villagers. I will
try to restrain myself, I promise you. I will creep into whatever lair I can find only when the weather is cold and bright,
so that the dragons will be soundly asleep; I will catch the
drippings from their jaws and collect the residue from the cavern walls, rather than cut open their throats to take the venom
directly from the sacs there. If they do not wake, I will not
kill them.

"Yet.

"Only when I have an alternative to the wild magic beyond the borders will I feel myself free to slay them all."

He opened his eyes and met Rime's gaze. "Now, are you
satisfied?"

"Entirely," Rime said. "If you need any assistance I will
be happy to aid you in your experiments when you have
once obtained the venom, and should you achieve your goal
I will applaud as loudly as anyone as you exterminate the
dragons once and for all."

"As will I," Lilsinir agreed. "Thank you, my lord."

Arlian nodded an acknowledgment, and swept out of the
room. He would need to notify the Duke that he was leaving
the city to obtain the materials for his experiments, but
more importantly, he would need to determine his destination. The summer was rapidly fading into autumn, and if he
wanted to find his venom this coming winter he needed to
search the records and locate a likely site without further
delay.

The Experiments

31

Into the Lair of the Dragons

*H*e had been three weeks upon the ice, high in the Shoulderbone Range of the Sawtooth Mountains, when he finally stumbled upon the opening.

The centuries-old reports he had followed here were maddeningly vague; all agreed that a pair of dragons had swept down from these peaks long ago and destroyed towns in the valleys below, but no one had seen just where the creatures had emerged from the rocks. Arlian had had years of experience in locating caves and tunnels, but the windswept snows here had smoothed over the sort of cracks and crevices that would ordinarily have provided clues, and he had brought no other scouts or sorcerers to aid him. He had wandered almost aimlessly from one slope to the next, guided by little more than the assumption that the cave mouth was not directly visible from any of the inhabited regions, hoping for some sign.

He was farther to the west than he had ever been before, far enough from the center of the Lands of Man that sometimes, when he was on the higher slopes and looked to the west, he could see the distant movement of unnatural clouds and strange colors on the horizon. He knew that he was seeing magic in the wilderness beyond the western borders, and he wondered whether it had ever been visible from these peaks before he began slaughtering dragons.

That distant wild magic was not what he sought, though, and after the first few glimpses he ignored it and concentrated on matters closer at hand.

His food supplies were running dangerously low, and he had seen no game nor even tracks in over a week, when he noticed the shadow. The snow cover on this particular mountainside was smooth and white, shining bright in the afternoon sun—but one spot seemed slightly less bright.

He turned toward that spot and pressed onward, his boots throwing up a cloud of glittering crystals with every step as he shuffled forward through the ankle-deep powder.

As he drew nearer and the sun descended toward the western ridge that fainter spot grew into a pale gray streak in the whiteness, then into a blue shadow. It was a depression in the snow a few inches deep, with smoothed but definite edges.

The surface was undisturbed; nothing had been digging here, nor had the wind shaped this particular form. From the look of it, the snow here had *sagged*.

Arlian smiled, cracking the ice on his mustache.

The snow cover had sagged because an underlying layer had fallen; no other explanation was possible. Wind would not have carved such a depression, and would have filled it in if it had been there before the snow fell. He did not know what had fallen, or why, but the mere fact of a fall meant there was someplace for it to fall *into*.

No one had ever built anything up here, in the wildest part of the Sawtooth; he was dozens of miles from the mines and quarries, far from the highest pastures. For the snow to fall in, there must be an opening in the mountainside itself.

That did not mean it was a dragon's lair, of course, but the reports *did* indicate a lair in this area. He stumbled forward eagerly.

He paused at the edge of the depression; he did not want to risk plunging through the snow into a cave, perhaps injuring himself, perhaps awakening whatever occupants might lurk therein. He pulled his gloved hands from his pockets and opened the front of his outer cloak.

His long, obsidian-tipped spear was strapped to his back;

at times he had carried it and used it as a staff to help in walking through the deep snow, but today was cold enough that he had preferred to keep his hands tucked away. Now he struggled with the icy bindings, cursing into his frozen beard until he was finally able to free the weapon.

When the heavy spear pulled loose the shift in weight threw him off balance, and one foot slid in the snow, almost sending him sprawling; he went down on one knee but caught himself before tumbling over completely.

When he was stable again, rather than stand up he bent his other knee and knelt at the edge of the depression. Then he jabbed the butt of the spear into the snow, pressing it down as far as he could.

It sank in a good three feet, much farther than he had expected; the powdery snow he knelt in was little more than a foot deep, though of course there was a layer of hard-packed snow and ice underneath.

That three feet was satisfying; it meant there was indeed a hole of some sort. He began digging, being careful not to let himself slide forward.

The sun was below the ridge and the eastern sky indigo when he finally broke through the packed snow and fragments of ice into the cave, a good eight feet below the drifted surface.

Snow trailed down the sloping passage, a tapering whiteness on the dim floor; the stone walls were coated with a thin layer of black ice. Arlian crouched in the opening, peering down into the darkness, considering his next move.

Always before when he had found a dragon's lair he had then retreated to gather his forces, and had returned with at least half a dozen men, all heavily armed and bearing torches, before entering.

And when they *had* entered, it was with the intent of killing everything they found inside; attempts at stealth had been purely to avoid waking the creatures before they could be slain, and if one *did* wake—as sometimes happened—it simply meant that that one was the first to die.

Here, though, he was alone, and armed with only the single spear—he had not cared to burden himself with any additional weaponry.

He did have assorted other supplies, of course. He was reluctant to provide any sort of heat, since dragons craved warmth and a flame might well wake them, but he would obviously need light. He put down his spear, threw back his woolen cloak, and swung his pack around.

A moment later he had a battered brass lamp filled with oil—he had carried the bottle of oil under blouse, vest, scarf, coat, and cloak, with only his shirt separating it from his flesh, so that his body's heat had prevented it from congealing. He found flint, steel, and tinder, and removed his gloves to strike a spark.

By the time the lamp's wick finally flared up his fingers were trembling with cold; he paused for a moment to warm them over the flame before pulling his gloves back on and tugging his cloak around his shoulders.

Then he stood and lifted the lamp high.

Icy stone walls gleamed dimly on either side of a high, narrow passage slanting downward into the earth, so narrow that he wondered how a dragon could fit through it—but then, dragons were not natural beasts. They were magic given solid form, and could compress themselves in a thoroughly unnatural manner.

Of course, he supposed it was possible that this was the wrong cave. He sniffed the air, the cold stinging his almost-numb nostrils.

He could not be entirely sure, but he thought he could smell it: dragon venom.

He smiled, dislodging half-melted ice from his beard. He hefted his spear, raised his lamp, and began moving down into the tunnel as quietly as he could.

The passage was long, and often steep, the floor uneven; it seemed as if the mountain had cracked, and enough dirt and gravel had tumbled down the crack to form a rough surface at the bottom. It was not quite as small as he had first thought; the height had exaggerated its narrow appearance, and the actual width, once he was well inside, averaged seven or eight feet. There was no evidence that anyone human had ever before set foot here, but as he made his way downward the stink of dragon venom became ever more certain, growing stronger with every step. Here and there, particularly in the narrower stretches, distinctive grooves marred the walls or floor—claw marks left by the monsters as they made their way to the surface.

The air grew warmer as he descended into the earth; naturally, the dragons would not have nested there if the cave itself were as cold as the mountainsides above.

He had no way of judging time once the opening to the outside world was out of sight, but he was reasonably certain he had been walking and climbing for an hour or more, and he was beginning to wonder whether his lamp's oil would hold out, when the left-hand wall ended abruptly, half the floor fell away, and the cavern suddenly opened out before him.

It was a jagged, angular space formed by broken layers of granite, without any of the water-smoothed forms of more familiar caves. There were no true verticals or horizontals, but only varying diagonals; he stood at one end of a narrow ledge where one almost-vertical plane had sheared across, and the upper portion had somehow been pressed back.

He could not see the full extent of the cave, as various sections angled off in odd directions, but the far side of the visible portion was perhaps forty yards away. The air here was only slightly cool; he had long since opened his cloak and unbuttoned his coat, but his shoulders were soaked with sweat and his beard wet with melted ice. The reek of dragon venom was so thick that for some time now he had been breathing through his mouth, to minimize its effects, and the lamp sometimes flared wildly as wisps of vapor touched its flame.

And on one gently sloping surface thirty feet below him

slept the dragons. The light of his lamp between flares was dim, and the distances dispersed it, but the gleam of sleek, scaly black hide was unmistakable; the humped, motionless shapes could be nothing else but Arlian's ancient foes.

The records Lord Wither had left him, records carefully collected and compiled over almost a thousand years, had only reported two dragons dwelling in the Shoulderbone Range; in fact, he had chosen this particular area to search in part because the fewer the dragons, the less the risk that one would wake while he was present, and the less damage done if he did find it necessary to kill them.

As Arlian looked down into the lair below, though, he remembered what Lord Zaner had told him at the Grey House more than two years before: The dragons had allowed him to find and slay their old and weak, while the young and strong had retreated to more secure hiding places.

He had never before approached this lair because a mere two dragons had not seemed worth the effort while larger groups remained in more accessible locations. He had chosen it this time not only because there were supposed to be only two occupants, but because it was so isolated that he had no need to worry about mistaking innocent locals for Dragon Society assassins, or vice versa—anyone else up in the Sawtooth Mountains in midwinter *must* be an assassin pursuing him.

It would seem that the dragons had anticipated his logic in choosing his previous targets, but had not anticipated his current mission. He turned the brass knob that extended the wick and raised the lamp higher, trying to count; a sudden venom-flare momentarily blazed up, briefly lighting a much larger area.

At least a dozen dragons lay upon the stone below—at *least* a dozen. When the flare died away he could not see far enough into the shadows and corners to be sure, but he thought he could make out fourteen, and what might be either a fifteenth or an unusually dark and curving piece of granite lurked deep in a nook to one side. Still more might easily be sleeping out of his sight.

Well, he certainly ought to be able to find plenty of venom here!

32

Familiar Faces

*T*he ledge on which Arlian stood narrowed ahead of him; he turned his back to the wall and crept along, looking for a way down. The thirty-foot slope below the ledge was not vertical, but it was far too steep to climb; if he slid down that way he would probably reach the bottom unhurt, but he would never be able to make his way back up.

But then the ledge ended, or at any rate took a sudden downward step—about a four-foot drop to a lower, slightly wider ledge. After a brief hesitation, Arlian lowered himself. Clambering back up would not be especially difficult; if he were fleeing a waking dragon, though, it would be a very unwelcome delay.

This second ledge sloped downward more steeply than the first, and the floor of the main chamber sloped upward; this gave Arlian hope that they met, somewhere in the darkness ahead.

This hope was dashed when he finally came within sight of the cavern's far end—but by then the drop was a mere ten or twelve feet, and he could see a break in the wall below, a crack a few inches wide. With a running start he was fairly certain he would be able to jump up, catch his fingers in that crack, and boost himself up to the ledge.

He eyed the stone carefully, to make sure he was not fooling himself about the distances; he studied the floor below to make certain that his running start would not require stepping on dragons' tails or in pools of venom.

It would not be easy—but he had not come this far to be stopped by so small an obstacle. He sat down, swung his feet out over the edge, and set the lamp on the stone beside him, thinking.

Carrying a lit lamp down would not be easy, but it would be very useful to have it while he collected venom. Leaving it on the ledge would only light this end of the chamber, but would be far safer.

While he considered alternatives he swung his spear over the edge, lowered it down as far as he could, then let it fall; it clattered on the stone below, louder than he had expected.

He paused, waiting to see if any of the dragons stirred, but the only sound he heard was his own breath, the only movement he saw the flickering of his lamp.

He took off his cloak and laid it on the ledge, then unslung his pack and lowered it over the edge, reaching down as far as he could before releasing it. He removed his coat and dropped it onto the cloak.

Then he picked up the lamp, took a deep breath, and jumped.

The lamp's flame flared up wildly as he fell, as much from the wind of his fall as from any drifting clouds of venom, but it did not go out. He landed hard, and sprawled forward, but kept his grip on the brass handle. Hot oil splashed across his glove, but did not ignite.

He lay still for a moment, then pulled himself up and knelt on the sloping stone, raising the lamp high.

His spear and pack lay a few feet away, and the nearest dragon was a looming black presence a few yards beyond.

He got to his feet, reached for his spear—then stopped.

He was not here to kill dragons. He was here to collect venom.

Reluctantly, he left the weapon where it was and instead

opened his pack, finding the blue glass bottle he had carried all the way from Manfort. It had contained wine originally, but he had drunk the last of that a month before,
then rinsed the bottle thoroughly to prepare it for its new
purpose.

He also fished out the smaller brown bottle that had held
his lamp oil; he guessed he would have no trouble filling
both, given how many dragons slept here.

When he stood upright again he had the blue bottle in
one hand and his lamp in the other, the brown bottle thrust
into his vest. He stepped forward toward the dragons, leaving spear and pack where they lay.

He would have preferred to find puddles of accumulated
venom he could dip the mouth of his bottles into, or to collect it from dripping wall formations, but the smooth, sloping surfaces of this unusual cave had not allowed pools to
form, and did not drip. Instead the venom that dripped, spat-
tered, or condensed on the floor and walls trickled down in
shallow streaks, too thin to dip into—though their paths had
been etched into the stone by the venom's corrosive nature.

He followed the slope downward across a good forty
yards of slanting floor, hoping to find a pool at the bottom,
but instead discovered that the venom was seeping down
into a crevice only an inch or two wide, far too narrow to
admit his gloved hand or either bottle.

Tired and annoyed, he made his way back up the slope
toward the slumbering dragons.

They did not, he thought, look very magical, nor did the
trickle of venom oozing down the floor look like the very
essence of magic that he believed it to be, that he *needed* it
to be. Yes, the black scales shimmered in the lamplight, and
the venom gleamed, but no more than any number of natural substances. Simple water would have shone more
brightly than the venom.

He could have sponged mere water off the stone with a
cloth, and wrung it into a container—but venom was far too
corrosive for that. Glass would hold it, as Lord Rolinor's

brandy flask had demonstrated, but cloth would disintegrate at its touch.

The only way he could get venom into his two bottles would be to catch it as it dripped from the dragons' jaws.

He moved carefully up to the nearest dragon. The beast lay curled up, catlike, with its back to him; the ridge of its spine was even with his chin, its unmoving flank far above his head. There was no discernable rise and fall as it breathed—but then, Arlian was not entirely certain that dragons did truly breathe. They were not natural beasts, despite their appearance, but magic made flesh. They ate not meat nor fruit nor grain, but human souls; they were born not of womb nor egg, but from human hearts and blood; why, then, would they breathe? Arlian supposed that whatever analogue of breath they might have would partake of magic, rather than air.

He circled to the right, following the dragon's neck, and found its loathsome head resting upon its right foreleg and the tip of its tail.

And venom dripped slowly from its jaw.

This was not a particularly large dragon; Arlian pulled the brown bottle from his vest and set it carefully on the stone below that dripping jaw, setting it on a handful of dust and turning it to make it as stable as possible on the sloping floor. He carefully held the lamp as far from the venom as possible, to avoid sending a flare into the dragon's unmoving nostrils and waking the monster.

A drop of venom struck his glove as he maneuvered, and a cloud of stinking smoke hissed into being as the fluid burned through the leather. Arlian snatched off the glove and scraped it against the floor until the hissing stopped and the smoke dissipated.

That done, he stepped back and looked at his contrivance.

Venom was gathering along the ridged black lip; as he watched, a drop formed, and fell—missing the mouth of the bottle by inches.

Arlian sighed. He looked at the dragon's face, to be sure

there was no sign that the creature's sleep had been disturbed.

He did not recognize this particular dragon. Like all its kind, its face was strong-featured and unique—perhaps it was a part of their magic, but each dragon's face was memorable in a way no other species, not even humanity, could match. No dragon could ever be mistaken for another, if one once saw its face. Arlian could remember every detail of every dragon he had ever seen face-to-face, regardless of what the circumstances might have been, and regardless of whether he *wanted* to.

This particular dragon was not one he had seen before— but then, the vast majority he had seen were dead. The dragon that had spoken to him sorcerously through a bowl of bloody water was dead; the dragon that had contaminated Lady Rime's blood and destroyed the Old Palace was dead. All the dragons he had found in their lairs were dead. Only the one that had slain his grandfather and sired the abomination growing in Arlian's heart, and its companions in the destruction of the village of Obsidian, still lived.

Another drop of venom fell, and this one struck the rim of the bottle's mouth and split. Half of it trickled down the bottle's side; the other half fell inside.

Light and smoke flared up as the venom ignited the traces of oil lingering in the bottle; Arlian stepped back, startled. He glanced at the dragon's face, then at his spear, lying thirty yards away.

The dragon did not stir.

Arlian let out his breath in a slow sigh of relief, and a second drop of venom fell into the bottle.

There was no second flare, though smoke swirled upward from the bottle's mouth. Arlian guessed there was no longer enough good air in the bottle to feed actual flame.

He left that bottle where it was, and turned his attention to finding a place for the other. He resolved not to simply choose the nearest dragon this time, but to find one producing the best flow of venom. He raised his lamp and began to explore the population of the cave.

The next dragon he passed was unremarkable, and had arranged its jaw on its foreleg in such a way that the venom trickling from its mouth never dripped, but ran down over the black scales to the floor. The third lay with its jaws on the floor itself. The fourth might have served, but Arlian chose to look further.

And when he looked at the face of the fifth dragon, he stopped dead in his tracks, trembling.

He knew that face.

He had seen it looking at him through the burning ruins of his parents' pantry long ago, as a boy of eleven; he had seen it casually spit venom at his grandfather, burning the man's face away.

This was the face that had haunted his dreams almost every night as he slaved in the mines of Deep Delving, that had lingered in his dreams and memories ever since.

This was the dragon he had sworn to kill, all those many years ago. This was the true target of his lust for revenge. This was the focus of all his hatred, the monster that had destroyed his family and twisted his life into its dark and loathsome form. This was the creature that had casually robbed him of the capacity for love and joy, wiped out any possibility of human descendants, and tainted his blood with its own vile spawn.

He stood frozen for a moment, too numb with shock and hatred to think or act; then he turned and ran for his spear, dropping the wine bottle as he neared.

His hand had closed on the shaft, and he was lifting the weapon, when he stopped.

He could kill the beast, here and now; he knew that. He could kill it, and the others would almost certainly wake, and he might kill one or two others before he died. If the other two that destroyed the village of Obsidian still lived, they might even be among those he slew—but he would never know if he had found all three, since he had never seen one of their faces.

He could kill the dragon. He could avenge his grandfather, his parents, his brother, and himself—and die.

For most of his life, that had been all he hoped for.

But if he died now, the other dragons would survive. The Lands of Man would suffer under their dominion, a village destroyed every year. Black and Brook and their children would live out their lives in a world corrupted by the dragons; Vanniari and Rime and all the others, as well.

He looked at the spear, its obsidian head glistening in the lamplight, then lowered it to the floor.

"Later," he whispered to himself. "There will be time later." He released the spear and stood up, then turned to look at the sleeping dragon.

"I know where you live now," he said. "I can find you—and I will." He picked up the blue bottle. "But I have something else to do first—something to live for."

He smiled.

"And I'll use *your* venom to do it."

33

Out of the Caverns

*A*rlian awoke to total darkness.

At first he did not remember where he was. The possibility that he had gone blind occurred to him, or that he had died, but in reality he thought that he was back in the mines of Deep Delving, a slave asleep in his little tunnel, about to be called out for his shift. His escape, his journeys to the Borderlands and beyond, his life in Manfort as Lord Obsidian, his elaborate revenge and his years of dragon-slaying, all seemed nothing more than a fantastic dream.

But the sheared granite wall beside him did not have the familiar texture of hewn limestone or galena, and his memories flooded back. He was in a dragon lair deep beneath the Shoulderbone Range, and the pack pillowing his head held flint and steel, while a lamp with a little oil still in it lay nearby.

He had allowed several hours to fill the bottles. For most of that time Arlian had slept as soundly as the dragons, curled up in a corner with his extinguished lamp placed far enough away that he would not accidentally spill it in his sleep, but close enough he could find it in the dark.

He sat up, pulled the pack to him, then groped for the lamp.

A moment later the wick caught from a sliver of glowing tinder, and he could see his surroundings once more. He hastened to inspect his collections, and found the brown bottle overflowing, the blue nearly so.

Setting the lamp down for a moment, he capped both bottles securely, wrapped them in extra clothing, and buried them deep in his pack, as well protected as he could make them. Retrieving the lamp, he looked around at the sleeping dragons, which seemed completely undisturbed by his stay among them.

The temptation to plunge the lamp into a trickle of venom and set as much of the cave ablaze as possible was very strong, but he resisted it; it would not harm the monsters, perhaps not even seriously annoy them, but it *would* alert them to his presence.

Plunging his spear into the black heart of his family's murderer was an even greater temptation, but he resisted that, as well, telling himself that a better time would come. Instead he returned to the corner where he had descended into the cave, where the ledge reached its lowest point. He set the lamp on the cavern floor, then hoisted his pack up above his head and leapt upward, shoving the pack two-handed up and over the edge before falling back.

The heavy pack barely made it, and the noise he made upon landing worried him; he paused and looked around at the dragons.

They had not stirred.

He picked up his spear and looked at it, tempted anew; then he sighed, backed up, and with a two-step running start jumped for the ledge again, tossing the spear up beside the pack.

It bounced and rattled, and came to rest with the butt end sticking a few inches out over the edge.

That left Arlian himself, and the battered oil lamp. The lamp was a problem—but it was also on the verge of running dry; it flickered every time he moved it, the remaining oil splashing faintly in the reservoir. It wouldn't last for the entire journey back to the surface, in any case.

He could find his way in the dark if he had to, and he could not throw the lamp around as he had the pack and spear—it would spill, and Arlian might find himself awash in flaming oil, or worse, flaming venom. He stepped away from the lamp, preparing to leave it behind. Its glow would see him up the ledge and into the tunnel, and he could find his way from there in the dark. The lamp would burn itself out harmlessly in a short while . . .

He paused.

If he left it, then in the spring, when the dragons awoke, they would know someone had been here. They might well abandon this lair—and that would mean at least fifteen dragons (he never had made an exact count, and was not about to waste his remaining oil doing it now) he would need to track down all over again.

That was unacceptable.

He couldn't fling a lit lamp up onto the ledge, though, and would need both hands to climb up. He doubted he could make the jump in the dark, so extinguishing the lamp for transport would not work, either. He had to carry the lamp somehow, and do it without using his hands.

He wished he had thought all this out *before* tossing his pack up where he couldn't reach it; he had nothing with which to improvise a carrying strap.

Finally, though, he devised an arrangement where he buttoned his vest through the lamp's handle, fastening it to his chest. That put the open flame uncomfortably close to his collar and beard, but he thought he could manage it for the few seconds it would take to get back up to the ledge.

He turned the flame down as low as he could without risking extinguishing it, then paced off a reasonable distance, turned, and ran. At the right moment he jumped, catching his fingers in the crevice in the wall.

He slammed against the stone, and felt the lamp's heat on his chest; his knees struck the granite hard, and he was sure he would have painful bruises there. He had a solid grip, though, several feet off the cavern floor, and the ledge was just a foot or two higher, to his right.

But there was a burning in his fingertips, one that simple strain could not account for; he could see wisps of smoke that did not seem to be coming from the lamp.

Hastily, he scrabbled his feet against the granite, swinging himself to the right; as his right foot found temporary purchase he pulled his right hand from the crack and grabbed for the ledge.

The fingers hooked over the edge, and he heaved himself upward; when he felt his hold was secure he snatched his left hand free and lunged for the ledge.

Then he was hanging by his fingers, the sharp granite edge cutting into the joints, the toes of his boots scraping at the wall below; he heaved again, and got first his right elbow, then his left, onto the ledge.

From there it was easy, despite the burning in his fingers, the smoke swirling in his face, the burn on his chest, and the dim, flickering light; a moment later he stood upright on the ledge, unbuttoning the battered lamp from his scorched and twisted vest.

He stared at it ruefully; the impact with the walls had bent the little lamp out of shape, smashing it almost flat, and the wick adjustment no longer functioned at all. The flame still burned, though, and the remaining oil had not all spilled, and he had left no evidence behind on the cavern floor—that was what mattered.

Then he turned his gaze elsewhere, with unhappy results. The fingertips of his gloves had been burned to smoking tatters; that seam in the wall had apparently collected venom in the bottom, and he had thrust his fingers right into it while climbing up.

If he had known that that reservoir of venom existed, he might have contrived a way to collect it there and never needed to go down among the dragons at all—but in that case, he would never have known that his grandfather's killer lurked here.

The front of his vest had been pulled, twisted, and blackened, and the blouse beneath bore a large black burn. He brushed black soot from his beard, as well; he would need to see a barber at the first opportunity.

Of course, he would have needed that in any case, after so long a journey in the wilderness.

At least his spear and pack seemed undamaged; he glanced in the pack to be sure the two bottles of venom were still intact and unopened, then secured everything as best he could, retrieved his coat and cloak, and made his way up the slope, easily heaving himself up to the higher, narrower ledge, and then leaving the cavern behind and starting up the long tunnel to the surface.

The temperature dropped steadily as he climbed; he paused at one point to eat a hasty meal of crumbling cheese and dried salt beef, and had scarcely finished when the lamp gave a final flicker and went out. He finished repacking in the dark, working by feel, then pulled on his coat and cloak; he did not really need them yet, but he knew he would soon.

He had brought no water, and was thirsty after his long sojourn in the cave, his dry meal, and his various recent encounters with flames, but he knew that once he was back on the surface he could find all the snow he wanted. Drinking water was never a problem in the Shoulderbone Range in winter; he merely needed to get out of the tunnel.

At least there was no danger of getting lost, of taking the wrong passage or the wrong direction; there was only the one long crevice, sloping steadily upward. He set out again.

He could not judge how long it took; counting his steps or heartbeats seemed pointless. Instead he simply marched onward, until at last he glimpsed a lessening of the darkness ahead.

He pressed on, and several minutes later found himself scrambling up through snow and ice onto the blinding whiteness of the snow-covered mountainside in full daylight. The sky above was intensely blue, the air cold and sharp; his fingertips, unprotected by the ruined gloves, stung with the cold.

He scooped a generous handful of snow into his parched mouth to slake his thirst, then pulled his cloak tight, his hands stuffed securely into the warm inner pockets, and began the long trek back toward Manfort.

34

Obsidian House

*A*rlian suspected that an ordinary man might well have lost a few fingers and the tip of his nose to frostbite on the way back down from the mountains, but he was a dragonheart, immune to poison and disease—his nose and fingers ached for days even after he reached the warmth of civilization, but did not blacken or rot.

Winter's hold had begun to weaken by the time he reached Manfort; the streets were clear of ice, and at midday the patter of water dripping from icicles was a constant ripple of sound throughout the city, as if rain were falling from invisible clouds in the clear and sunny skies.

The icicles were more numerous than at any time in Arlian's memory—the forest of rooftop catapults had provided them a myriad of new places to form.

When Venlin ushered him into the Grey House Arlian soon discovered that Black and his family had indeed moved out, and were not there to welcome him; he accepted this without comment, and made no effort to contact his steward immediately. Instead he took a day to bathe, rest, and recover from his travels. He had paid a tavern girl in a village in the foothills of the Sawtooth Mountains to trim his hair and beard, but she had not been trained to the standards of Manfort, and at any rate the journey from there to Manfort had allowed them to grow out again, so he spent his first evening sprawled comfortably in the tub while Wolt struggled to restore a veneer of civilization.

That also served to avoid any wearisome conversation; Wolt was not much of a talker, and no one else dared intrude while the master was bathing. Arlian had already picked up some news on the road, enough to be reasonably certain that nothing earthshaking had occurred in his absence, and he was not in a mood to describe his adventures or cope with household affairs. That could wait.

In fact, he decided as he lay in the tub with Wolt neatly shaving his throat, he did not want to waste any time on household affairs at all. He wanted to proceed directly to his research, and for that he wanted the Grey House to himself, so that the only life at risk would be his own.

But that could wait until morning; he closed his eyes and enjoyed the comforting warmth of the bath.

Accordingly, after he had breakfasted the following day

he first sent word to the Duke that he had returned safely with the materials for his experiments, and asked that he be excused from any duties at the Citadel so that he might proceed immediately with his research. That done, he summoned his remaining guests and the entire staff from the kitchens and servants' hall and upstairs offices, and informed them that the household was to be evacuated.

"Where shall we go, my lord?" Lilsinir asked. "Tiviesh tells me that the Citadel is not particularly welcoming these days."

"Are we all to take up residence in your new establishment, then?" Wolt asked.

Arlian had been about to answer Lilsinir, but now he stopped dead, then turned to stare at Wolt.

"New establishment?" he asked.

"Yes, of course," the footman said, plainly puzzled. "The house your steward has been building for you on the grounds of the Old Palace."

Arlian considered that for a moment.

"Black is building a new house for me?"

Wolt apparently realized now that this was news to his employer, but was not yet certain how it was being received. "Yes, my lord," he said noncommittally.

"Is he, indeed?"

"Yes, my lord. Is this not by your own orders?"

Arlian smiled crookedly. "Let us just say that I had not remembered, for a moment, giving those orders. But yes, I think removing the entire household to this new residence, if it be sufficiently prepared, would be entirely suitable. See to it at once, all of you."

The servants scattered, leaving Arlian standing in the parlor.

"Building me a house, is he?" He shook his head, and addressed the air. "Even after all these years, Black, you can still surprise me."

Naturally, Arlian oversaw the relocation—he did not admit to curiosity, but concern for the welfare of his employ-

ees, and the necessity of ensuring that the new house was fit
for them to live in, required his involvement. Thus he found
himself making his way through the old gardens, past lingering patches of half-melted snow, and across the thresh-
old of Obsidian House, where he stood in the entryway and
contemplated the product of Black's efforts.

The building was obviously still far from complete, but
Arlian liked what he saw. Black had clearly borrowed ideas
from several sources, rather than simply following either
Manfort tradition or the current fashion. The entryway
opened into a large and airy hall, where a sweeping staircase led up to a broad balcony; several rooms opened off
the balcony, and more below it.

There were, as yet, no rugs nor hangings, several of the
doorframes did not yet hold doors, and the many-paned
windows were not yet encumbered by any sort of drapery,
but the proportions of the existing structure were elegant.
This house was far smaller than the Old Palace, occupying
an area that had once been one end of one wing, but it
nonetheless had a feeling of spaciousness and comfort similar to the Palace's, and quite different from the cramped
confines of Grey House.

Black emerged from one of the doors beneath the balcony and saw Arlian standing in the entry. He stopped.

"My lord," he called. "I trust it meets with your approval."

"Indeed it does," Arlian replied.

"You had said we were welcome to make our home here,"
Black said, standing where he was. "I chose to take you at
your word—and of course, as I am your steward, our home
is yours."

The door behind him opened farther, and Brook's
wheeled chair edged out; Black stepped aside to let his wife
past.

"Ari!" she called, wheeling herself across the great hall.
"Welcome!"

"Thank you," Arlian replied, stepping forward to meet her.

"We thought you had been too long in that gray stone

tomb, dwelling in Lord Enziet's shadows," Brook said, as she brought her chair to a stop.

Arlian glanced around at the unfinished walls and smiled. "If my eyes are to be trusted, *this* house is gray stone, as well."

"Ah, but it's hardly a tomb!" Brook said, gesturing at the broad windows. "And we had to use stone—there are still dragons out there, after all."

"Alas, there are," Arlian agreed, taking Brook's hand and bowing.

As he did, he could not help noticing a definite roundness to her belly; apparently, if all went well, Kerzia, Amberdine, and Dirinan were soon to have another sibling. He remembered the two stillbirths before Dirinan's arrival, and the miscarriages between and after the two girls, and hoped this pregnancy would have a happy outcome; he had not expected another so soon after the boy.

As if summoned by his thoughts, Brook's three children came spilling down the stairs from the balcony. Black hurried to intercept them. After a moment of chaos, the entire party was organized for the purpose of giving Arlian a tour of his newest property.

The airy feel of the great hall was maintained in most of the major rooms; Arlian approved of the arrangements that permitted this. Black knew his employer's tastes and habits and had designed the new house accordingly, providing an equivalent of every room Arlian had favored in the Grey House or the Old Palace, while leaving out those features he had neglected.

Arlian particularly admired the lift, with its elaborate system of pulleys and counterweights, that allowed Brook, or any other amputees who might visit, to move to the upper floors without being carried up the stairs. Black had designed this himself, and had ensured that the mechanisms could be worked so easily that even his children could, if necessary, use them.

As they neared the conclusion of the tour Arlian found

himself in the servants' hall, watching his staff bring in their belongings.

"You call it Obsidian House, I am told," he said.

"Of course," Black replied, as he shifted a sleeping Dirinan from one shoulder to the other.

"I did not see any obsidian anywhere in it."

"No, you did not," Black agreed. "The Duke has confiscated all the obsidian in Manfort, and as much as he can from elsewhere, for use in the city's defenses. You will have noticed, I'm sure, the iron frameworks on the roof?"

"I saw them as I approached, yes."

"That stair I pointed out on the upper floor goes to a tower room where the release mechanisms for all the catapults may be controlled. The counterweights are not yet rigged up, and the bolts are not yet in place, but a full system of defenses has been installed. Because it was built in from the first, rather than added later, we were able to make it far more efficient than most; it will require only a single operator to release a full volley."

"And if that first volley misses?"

"Oh, well, reloading will take rather more manpower," Black admitted.

"And more obsidian."

"I am sure His Grace will allot us our fair share, when the time comes."

Arlian reached forward to help Stammer with a large bag. "I had once hoped," he said, "that Manfort would never again *need* defenses against dragons. I find it saddening that the city now bristles with them, and that the Duke seems to consider them a permanent necessity."

"Perhaps we *won't* need them," Brook said. "Still, they're reassuring."

"I suppose they are," Arlian said, lifting Stammer's bag. "Where does this go?"

Three hours later, after a hastily improvised cold supper, Arlian made his way back down to the Grey House.

He had to use his own key, and hang up his own cloak; he

had, after all, sent the staff away. The stone passages were cold, dim, and silent, in stark contrast to the noisy, sunlit bustle of Obsidian House.

He could hardly maintain the entire house single-handed; he decided he would keep the fires lit in the kitchens and his own bedchamber, and let the rest die out. The cold might reduce the pest population, thereby accomplishing through neglect what ongoing efforts with broom and flyswatter had not.

He went through the mansion, closing doors and dousing lamps, then settled at last at the kitchen table to plan out his experiments.

He fell asleep around midnight, his head on the table, the two sealed bottles of venom on the shelf above.

35

Studies on the Effects of Dragon Venom

*A*rlian's first experimental subject was a large rat.

Closing off most of the rooms had driven a good number of rats and mice into the kitchens, and trapping them alive proved relatively easy; he collected several in a variety of cages in one of the pantries.

Mice were too small to handle easily, so he chose a fat black rat for his initial trial. He isolated it from the other captive vermin, coaxing it into its own small cage, then carried it out to the courtyard of the Grey House and placed it upon the pavement. The rat retreated to a corner of the cage in the shadow of the catapults that lined the roof, and it crouched there while he prepared a dose of elixir.

The first question to address was what sort of blood to

use in his preparation. The mix that produced dragonhearts was dragon venom and human blood; should a rat, then, receive the same combination, or a mix of venom and rat's blood?

There was no record of any pets or livestock surviving a dragon's attack; no nonhuman dragonhearts had ever been reported. Arlian suspected that that meant nonhuman blood would not work.

On the other hand, feeding human blood to a rat struck him as somehow unseemly and repellent, and the non-appearance of surviving beasts might mean that the dragons had made a point of slaughtering any beast that might have spawned an inferior sort of magical creature. Since Arlian *wanted* another sort of magical creature . . .

He mixed a single drop of dragon venom with a half-cup of blood drawn from the other rats, then carried the mixture out to the courtyard.

The rat backed away from him into the farthest corner of its cage, but Arlian was able to get a secure hold and drag it out. The animal tried very hard to keep its mouth closed and as far as possible from that foul-smelling brew, but at last Arlian was able to hold the animal in one hand, pry its mouth open with the other, and then hold it open while he quickly poured the seething mixture down its throat.

The rat vomited immediately, but that meant nothing; Arlian had vomited after drinking his grandfather's contaminated blood, and that had not saved him.

Arlian, however, had not then gone into convulsions; bloody spew had not sprayed from his mouth, nor smoke seeped from his nostrils.

The rat lived a surprisingly long time, under the circumstances—almost half an hour. Arlian considered putting the poor thing out of its misery, but that would invalidate the whole experiment; he had to be absolutely certain that the animal would not survive. He forced himself to watch as it weakened and died.

The next rat received its drop of venom in a cup half-full

of Stammer's blood—Arlian could not use his own blood, since he was himself tainted and his blood poisonous, and had therefore prevailed upon his servants to supply what he needed, paying them generously for the precious fluid. The results of this experiment were slightly less dramatic than the first trial, lacking the smoke from the nostrils, but were even more swiftly fatal.

Two more rats produced identical reactions.

Arlian then tried a few variations, first using his own blood for one thin brown rat; that rodent keeled over within a dozen heartbeats, and died almost instantly. Venom diluted in water or wine was more lethal than venom diluted in healthy blood, but not quite so deadly as in Arlian's blood.

At last, after four days and more than two score dead rats, he could think of nothing more to try, and began anew with the two dozen pigs Black had bought. The husbandman Black had hired to tend the livestock, a fellow called Mucker, helped fetch the animals into the courtyard, but once each pig was securely tied to a post the man departed quickly; he made it plain that he wanted no part of these unnatural experiments, which he considered wasteful and dangerous, and that he was only staying in Arlian's employ because Black had promised him truly exorbitant wages.

Arlian might have found another pair of hands useful in administering the elixir, but he saw no need to make the man uncomfortable, and he could manage by himself. He thought he understood something of Mucker's attitude, but did not share it; these experiments were *necessary,* and might do far more to aid humanity than would the pork and ham that the pigs would have otherwise provided. From the pig's point of view it surely could not matter much; he would be equally dead either way.

When the pigs yielded no useful results Arlian intended to move on to other species, but oxen were difficult to force-feed, and presented serious disposal problems; he attempted only two of them.

He tried half a dozen mice, despite their small size, with no more success; nor were a few assorted spiders and insects any better.

He was getting nowhere at the end of almost a month's work, and he knew it. It seemed as if dragon venom, either undiluted or in any combination whatsoever, was invariably and swiftly fatal to *anything* except humans and dragons.

Magic itself was not inherently toxic; he knew that much from his experiences in the lands beyond the southern border. The draconic nature of the venom, he decided, must be the source of its deadliness. If there were some way to separate the magic from the dragonness . . .

But how?

He consulted with Lady Rime, and with all the Aritheians still dwelling in Manfort, but none of them knew even as much as he did about the matter.

The key, he guessed, was in the blood. Dragon venom by itself would kill a man dead; in combination with human blood, though, it created a dragonheart. Somehow human blood allowed the magic to work before the venomous nature could take effect.

He needed something that would remove that venomous nature *entirely*, that would filter it out while passing the magic on—but what? He stared at the half-empty brown bottle.

Perhaps another layer, as it were, might help; he fetched another rat and tried combining a drop of venom with half a cup of human blood and half a cup of rat's blood.

It didn't help.

He tried feeding the dead rat to a dog; the dog died.

He tried feeding some of the rat's blood to another rat; it, too, died.

He tried combining the rat's blood with a fresh drop of venom, thinking that perhaps the two poisons might cancel each other out, and the result killed another rat.

Perhaps rats and pigs and oxen were simply not suitable; in desperation he caught a stray cat in the alleys behind the

Grey House, an unusually plump one, brought her into the kitchen, and fed her a mix of human blood and venom, planning to use her blood for his next experiment. After pouring the mess down her throat he set her down on a bed of rags and sat down to wait beside her.

She promptly vomited—he had expected that—and then lay down, looking weak and tired. That was what had happened with previous animals. But then, a moment later, she began to breathe in great heaving pants, her flanks rippling; no previous beast had done that. Arlian stared, and then realized what he had done.

This cat was not fat, she was pregnant—hardly unusual in the spring. If he had not been so focused on his own concerns, his elaborate experiments, he would have noticed. Now the poison had brought on contractions, and he had undoubtedly killed a litter of kittens along with his chosen subject.

He had not intended that. Arlian was hardly sentimental, and had felt little remorse over poisoning dozens of assorted animals in the course of his research, given its importance in the campaign to free humanity of the dragons, but he did feel a serious twinge of regret at this unintentional waste.

Sure enough, half an hour later the cat had produced two kittens, tiny, mewling things lying helplessly on the rags, eyes closed, their mother too sick from the poison to properly lick them clean or nurse them; the second was scarcely born when their mother gave a final twitch and lay still.

The kittens were still alive, though. One was white with striped gray patches, like its mother, while the other was entirely black. They lay upon the rags, heads moving from side to side, their tiny paws pulling at the rags as they struggled to move themselves.

And they appeared healthy.

Arlian stared. He had expected them to die immediately, but they showed no sign of illness or poisoning at all. Perhaps, he thought, the magic had not had time to reach them. Or perhaps a little magic *had* reached them, but the venom's poison had not. There might be something to be learned from these kittens. This accident might even be just what he had sought. He looked around, aware that Mucker had left for the day and he was alone in the house, with no one to call on for aid, and no idea at all how to keep a pair of orphaned newborn kittens alive.

Obviously, they would need warmth and milk; they needed to be cleaned off completely. Beyond that, he had no idea; he had never kept pets of any sort, and had left the care of the livestock to Mucker.

He had no milk for the kittens, but he could keep them clean and warm; he gathered both of them up in some of the rags they had been born on, wiped the remaining blood and tissue from their fur, and carried them closer to the hearth. He set them down just outside the fender, arranging the rags into a nest, then looked around at the shelves, trying to think what he might substitute for their mother's milk.

Warm water would be better than nothing; a bit of wet cloth would give them something to suck on, at any rate.

They were still mewing, pawing at the rags, pulling themselves along; Arlian was amazed at their vitality. It was not as if their mother had been particularly healthy or well fed, after all.

Perhaps they *had* absorbed a little of the magic.

He hurried to the water bucket, snatched a towel from the rack, and dipped a corner. Then he returned to the hearth, twisted the towel's corner into a crude approximation of a nipple, and tried to direct it into the black kitten's mouth.

The kitten was not having any of it; it spat the towel and water out, quite vigorously. And then it opened pale blue eyes and glared at him.

Arlian stared back.

He knew that wasn't right; a kitten's eyes did not open less than an hour after birth. He was unsure just what was normal, but he knew it took at least a few days. This kitten could not even stand, yet it was glaring at him as intensely as any full-grown cat.

This was beyond him; he needed help.

He did not dare leave these unnatural little beasts unattended, so he could not go and bring help back. Taking newborn kittens out in the cold outside air seemed risky, but he saw no other practical choice. He set a dozen towels warming on the hearth, then found a wooden crate and prepared a portable nest.

An hour later he was in the kitchen of Obsidian House, explaining the situation to Brook and Stammer; Black was out on business, negotiating with drapers for some of the final accoutrements the establishment still lacked.

Brook listened intently, but Stammer was more interested in watching the kittens. Both kittens had their eyes open now, and stared up at her with a very unkittenlike assurance.

"Lady Rime's sorcery may be helpful," Brook said. "I doubt Lilsinir has anything. She's been complaining for some time how little magic she has left."

"She can still cleanse dragonhearts, can she not?" Arlian asked.

"Oh, yes," Brook said. "She and Asaf and Tiviesh are all well equipped for *that*—but the demand has scarcely been overwhelming, especially since the Duke made his pact with the dragons. No, it's the other magic that's in short supply, and I doubt she would have had anything to help study magical kittens, in any case."

"Perhaps I should take them to Lady Rime . . ."

"No, leave them here!" Stammer said, looking up. "I . . . I . . . I mean, I . . ." She stammered herself into silence, gazing pleadingly at him.

Arlian smiled. "They can stay here," he said. "I can bring Lady Rime up to study them here. And I'm sure all the children would be glad to see them, once they're old enough to play with."

"If they live that long," Brook said.

"Indeed," Arlian agreed. "That's hardly a certainty, is it?"

"I'll f . . . f . . . find them some milk," Stammer said.

A few hours later, when the sun was down, Arlian found

himself momentarily alone with the kittens in the kitchen
of Obsidian House, staring at the tiny animals again. They
had emphatically refused the warm milk Stammer had offered them; in fact, they had not eaten nor drunk since their
birth, yet they seemed as strong and alert as ever—more
alert, in fact, as they gazed back at him knowingly.

Lady Rime had not yet replied to his message, but somehow Arlian suspected her sorcery would yield little useful
information about these strange little creatures. They had
clearly escaped poisoning, yet had received at least a portion of the venom's magic.

The possibility must therefore exist of creating thousands
of such kittens, thereby soaking up the magic of the Lands
of Man and allowing the dragons to be slain, but Arlian was
by no means ready to celebrate. This would appear at first to
be exactly what he sought, but the kittens made him uneasy.
While it seemed absurd that magical cats could be as bad as
wild magic or dragons, he was not comfortable with these
unnatural little creatures.

And how many dozens or hundreds or thousands of
such tiny creatures would it take to equal one dragon? Did
the magic consumed correspond to body weight? Would
they grow to the size of ordinary cats, or to the size of
dragons?

They were a mystery, an enigma, and whether they were
a solution remained to be seen.

"Do you know what you are?" he murmured, staring at
the gray and white kitten's strange blue eyes.

Do you? came the reply.

Arlian started back.

He had heard that sort of voiceless communication before, in sorcerous conversation with the dragons; he had not
expected it from a kitten.

These were clearly not true kittens at all.

What they *were* remained to be seen.

It was at that moment that Black walked in; he had been
absent for most of the day, but had finally concluded his ne-

gotiations with the drapers and taken care of whatever other business had seemed urgent.

He found Arlian staring at the kitten, and followed his employer's gaze.

"Kittens," he said. "Stammer told me you had brought a pair of kittens here." He looked at the pair, who looked back, unafraid. "About two weeks old, are they, or three? Stammer said they were newborn."

"They are," Arlian said. "Born this very day."

Black threw him a sharp glance. "You're certain of that?"

"Completely certain. I saw the birth with my own eyes."

"This was one of your damnable experiments, then?"

"Rather, an inadvertent side effect of one. I hadn't known their mother was pregnant until after I administered the elixir."

Black looked back at the kittens and shuddered.

"They're abominations," he said. "So vigorous and alert, eyes already open, in less than a day? It's not natural."

"Indeed, it is not," Arlian agreed.

"Destroy them," Black said.

Just then the door thumped, and Brook rolled in in her wheeled chair. Black glanced at her, then repeated, "Destroy them, Ari."

"These may be the best hope we have," Arlian protested. "These are the only living results of all my tests and trials. They may well hold the solution I seek!"

"Then keep them at the Grey House. You assured us all your experiments would be conducted there."

"And they will be—but I cannot care for these there, and I cannot risk their intrusion upon further experiments. Although it was built by your order and to your design, this is my house, Black, built with my money, on my land, and I want these kittens kept here, at least for the present."

"The children adore kittens," Brook interjected.

Black whirled to face her. "I don't want these things around my children!"

"They're just kittens," Brook replied. Arlian, aware that they were not truly just kittens, said nothing.

"They're magical, unnatural kittens," Black said, "and even ordinary kittens have claws and teeth."

"We will keep a careful watch on them, Black."

Black looked from his wife to his employer and back. "It seems I am outnumbered," he said. "I have never been able to refuse you, Brook. If you wish these furry little pests to stay, then they will stay, and so shall we—but we will indeed keep a close watch on them, and the children will not handle them without one of us present."

"Agreed," Arlian said, relieved that the matter had been resolved to his satisfaction. "Take whatever precautions you like—but the kittens stay here."

36

The Spawn of Magic

*T*he kittens were only ten days old when their strangeness became so obvious that even the doting children could not deny it. The specific occasion was when the gray-and-white, now known as Patch, stretched out what should have been tiny paws and instead revealed fingers—thin, furless fingers, with knuckles and nails, utterly unlike anything a cat should possess.

That was enough to send Amberdine shrieking from the room, crying for her father.

A few moments later it seemed as if half the household was crowded into the kitchen, watching intently while Black and Arlian studied the two little creatures.

"Toes," Arlian said, holding out Smudge's hind foot.

"And fingers," Black agreed, holding Patch.

"No scales, though," Arlian said, looking down at the squirming kitten-thing. "But the fur . . ."

"The fur's thinning," Black said, "but why would there be scales?"

"Because it was dragon venom that made them into whatever they are," Arlian said.

"Dragon venom and blood," Black corrected him. "What kind of blood did you use?"

"Human," Arlian said. "Wolt's, I believe."

Several of the observers turned to look at the footman, who was watching from the doorway.

"You drew some of my blood that morning, my lord," Wolt acknowledged. "But you took blood from all of us at one time or another."

"Hold out your hands," Black ordered.

Wolt complied. Black held up Patch's tiny paw, fingers spread, and looked from the kitten to the footman and back.

"Fingers are fingers," Brook said. "*I* can't tell whether they're alike."

"But Mother, cats aren't supposed to *have* fingers!" Amberdine replied.

"Obviously, these two aren't true cats," Arlian said, looking at Smudge's inscrutable little face. The cat looked back, but no voiceless words appeared in Arlian's mind.

Neither of them had repeated that stunt of speaking silently since that first instance, on the night they were born, and Arlian had begun to wonder whether he had imagined the whole thing. He was not given to flights of fancy, but it hardly seemed reasonable that a newborn creature of *any* kind, even a magical one, should be able to communicate in such a fashion.

He set the kitten-thing back in the box, then straightened up.

"Whatever they are," he said, "I am responsible for them, and I want to know everything out of the ordinary that any of you might observe. Please keep me informed of any abnormalities—but for now, let us all return to our usual concerns." He gestured at the surrounding throng.

Most were reluctant to leave, and of course some had legitimate business in the kitchen, but eventually he managed to coax a semblance of normality.

He and Black made their way to Arlian's still-unfinished study, where they settled onto a pair of out-of-place chairs that had been brought from the Grey House.

"You know," Black said, "those things have done more than all your warnings to convince me that I do not, in fact, want to taste that elixir."

"Then at least *some* good has come of my experimentation," Arlian replied.

"Experimentation you had agreed to keep at the Grey House. This may be your house, Ari, but as I told you the night you brought them, I do not appreciate having those two little monstrosities here, reminding me of what you were doing half a mile away, and possibly endangering my family."

"I needed help in caring for them!"

"Did you? They seem to be thriving without food or water; if starvation has no effect, I wonder whether *anything* can kill them."

"A good question," Arlian asked, glancing uneasily in the direction of the kitchens. He had not yet considered the matter—but then, he had still been thinking of them as kittens, and killing kittens was so very easy that the idea that these two might be difficult to dispose of, should they prove dangerous, had seemed absurd.

"At least you seem to have abandoned your experiments, and have brought no more furry little horrors here."

Arlian shook his head. "I have not abandoned anything," he said. "I am merely waiting until the results of this trial are complete before beginning the next."

"You intend to continue?"

"Oh, certainly—I am obviously getting close to a solu

tion! These strange little catlings may be just what we need. Create an army of them to drink up the natural magic of our homeland, then exterminate the dragons, and we have . . ."

"You have an army of strange little monsters," Black interrupted. "You can't possibly mean to trust these things, can you? Ari, they're *cats*—sneaking, bloodthirsty little thieves. And that's the part we *know*; we have no idea what form their magic may take."

"They're *not* cats, though," Arlian protested. "You saw that as well as I did. They're partially human."

"Or partially dragon," Black retorted. "There are no scales *yet*, and those fingers and toes were the color of yours or mine, but they could easily become a dragon's claws in time."

"Those fingers looked human to me."

"And are humans any more to be trusted than cats?"

"If born of good parents and brought up properly . . ."

"As Lord Hardior was, or Lord Enziet?"

"I know nothing of their parentage or upbringing, Black, and neither do you."

Black conceded the point with a wave. "Nonetheless," he said, "it would seem we have at least four parents for these kittens of yours—their mother, the tom that covered her, the dragon whose venom you stole, and poor Wolt. Even if we grant both the felines to be of good character, and have faith in Wolt's reliability, it would seem to me that their magic comes directly from a notorious monster."

"The magic derives from the earth and air itself," Arlian protested. "The dragon was merely its previous possessor."

"And do you know that it will not have taken on some part of that possessor's nature?"

"I do not," Arlian acknowledged. "And that is why further experimentation is required. These two appear to be acquiring human traits, rather as dragonhearts acquire draconic traits, but far faster; it will be interesting to see how far the process goes. And clearly, another experiment is called for to determine what will happen if another litter is subjected to a similar transformation, but with cat's blood rather than human."

"I would recommend that you not create any more monstrosities until you are certain you can destroy the two you already own."

"I have no intention of destroying those two."

"I doubt you *can*. Enziet needed six hundred years to find a blade that could pierce a dragon's hide; we may well need as long to find a weakness in these kittens of yours."

"Black, they're *kittens*. Or rather, they . . ." He frowned, and left the sentence unfinished.

"They *appear* to be mostly kitten," Black corrected. "We don't know *what* they are."

"Indeed. But if we create another litter with no human blood involved, and observe whether *they* grow fingers, we will have more information to work with."

"And if you create kittens imbued with pig's blood, will they root and grunt before they rip your throat out? Will horse's blood give us hooved kittens standing fifteen hands at the shoulder? What new abominations do you propose to create?"

"I don't know," Arlian admitted. "I intend to experiment, and let the results of each trial guide the next."

Black sat back and considered Arlian for a long moment. Then he said, "I have told you almost since we first met that you're mad, but I always tolerated that madness. I understood your loathing for the dragons, and your carelessness of your own life, or at any rate I believed I did. This willingness to plunge headfirst into the unknown, though, and tamper with powerful magic you do not even begin to understand—*this* madness is beyond my comprehension. That venom you waste in your experiments is worth a fortune; it could allow a hundred men, women, and children to extend their lifetimes tenfold or more, and instead you are feeding it to cats and cattle. What's more, you are draining their very blood from your friends and servants to feed to these beasts." He shuddered. "It sickens me, Ari. These experiments belong in the Grey House; they're very much in Lord Enziet's tradition."

"Lord Enziet's experiments gave us the secret of obsidian," Arlian pointed out.

"And cost us Dove and Sweet, and probably any number of others, not to mention Enziet's own humanity."

"He lost that to the dragons long before," Arlian said.

"Because he was tainted with the same elixir you now use to create fingered kittens—yet you expect these kittens to be harmless and cooperative?"

"They show no trace of dragon nature," Arlian insisted. "Only cat and human. I believe the dragon's evil was filtered out by their mother's womb."

"On what do you base this belief?"

"There are no scales. Only fur and skin."

"They do not purr, Ari. They do not care to be petted. There is no love in them, any more than there is in an ancient dragonheart."

"They're only ten days old!"

"Then wait and see whether I am right."

Arlian rose to his feet. "How long must I wait, then? Months? Years? No, better to experiment further, and watch them develop simultaneously."

"Better to leave well enough alone!" Black retorted, also standing up.

"Black, if you think those catlings so dangerous, why do you allow your children to play with them?"

"Because I am a softhearted fool who can deny his women nothing, no matter how much I know I should!" Black shouted. Then he turned on his heel and marched out.

Arlian watched him go, surprised and dismayed; then he shrugged.

"You'll see," he said. Then he began gathering up his notes and preparing to return to the Grey House to resume his experiments.

37

Kittens from Hell

*F*inding more pregnant cats in the spring did not prove particularly difficult, especially when one was willing to pay extravagant sums for them. Managing to be present when one began to deliver her get proved trickier; nonetheless, Arlian eventually succeeded.

A mixture of cat's blood and dragon venom poured into one queen's mouth between the arrivals of the first and second kitten in her litter resulted in the death of the mother and all the kittens but the first.

Several further attempts were made, trying other variations, and fared no better. Arlian discovered that any mixture containing dragon venom, but *not* containing human blood, was swiftly and invariably fatal to both mother and offspring. The presence or absence of cat's blood, pig's blood, bull's blood, wine, or beer proved irrelevant; venom and human blood formed the magical elixir, while venom without human blood remained an incredibly virulent poison.

He had not expected that, but it did fit with what he had been told by the thing in Tirikindaro—men and dragons were somehow interrelated. The elixir could be made only with *human* blood; any other sort simply diluted the poison without altering its nature.

His methodology in this series of experiments had the side effect of producing numerous ordinary kittens, born before the venom mixture was administered and therefore unaffected by the elixir. At first he tried to bring these kittens to Obsidian House to be raised in the kitchens there, but it soon became clear that Patch and Smudge did not approve, and he instead began delivering them to Lady Rime's home, where her adoptive grandchildren were delighted by these new pets, and happily gave them the careful attention they needed.

Not all of them survived, but Arlian felt he had done his best for them, and told himself that most would surely have died in the alleys and cellars of Manfort if he had never intervened in their mothers' lives.

That the mothers would have lived—well, he preferred not to think about that. The importance of his efforts made such losses tolerable.

As he continued his experiments at the Grey House he also walked up the hill to Obsidian House periodically to check on the results of his earlier trials, and confer with Black and Brook regarding their own observations. He watched as Patch and Smudge grew into misshapen parodies, miniature cat-men like nothing ever seen in Manfort, though there were certain similarities to the gaunts and nightmares of the south. The pair ceased to be cute—quite an accomplishment in creatures that had begun life as kittens, and were not yet two months old. They walked awkwardly on either two legs or four, and gracefully not at all; their tails shrank to mere stubs, their ears moved down the sides of their heads, and their fur grew thin and patchy everywhere but the tops of their heads.

They did retain some kittenish traits, though—they were active, impulsive, and inquisitive, frequently startling the inhabitants of Obsidian House by turning up in unexpected places or suddenly dashing across the floor in front of unsuspecting humans. They were given the run of the house, since their agile little fingers could defeat almost any lock or barrier, but they stayed mostly in the kitchen and pantries.

Despite their choice of residence, they did not eat or drink; like dragons, they apparently subsisted entirely on air and magic.

When a later experiment—one involving Stammer's blood—produced another live magical kitten, Arlian delivered the creature to Obsidian House, where Patch took an intense interest in the new arrival, prodding it gently with those unnatural fingers. She did not spit or claw, as she had at the ordinary kittens Arlian had brought in.

Others were less enthusiastic. Smudge ignored this new kitten entirely—which was a more positive reaction than he had had to the ordinary ones, but still not especially welcoming. Kerzia and Amberdine watched it warily from a safe distance; Dirinan refused to be in the same room with it, shrieking at the sight of it. Stammer reluctantly accepted responsibility for its care, and named it Bee when it managed a faint buzzing purr as it lay curled in her hands.

"How . . . how m . . . how many more?" she asked, as she cautiously petted the kitten.

"I don't know," Arlian said, glancing at Patch. "I'm trying to understand why these creatures are as they are, and I don't know yet what I need to know."

Patch turned her head to stare at him.

Don't you?

"No, I don't," Arlian said, glaring at the creature.

Stammer was staring at her as well. "It spoke," she said.

"I know," Arlian said. He looked from the cat-thing to the newborn kitten, then at Stammer and at the two girls standing a safe distance away. "They can do that."

"They can?" Kerzia said.

"What else can they do?" Amberdine asked. "They're magic, aren't they? Can they work spells or glamours?"

"I don't know," Arlian said. He looked down at Bee, frowning—it seemed such a small, helpless thing to be the result of so much effort and blood, and to be a possible hope against the dragons.

Patch still crouched at the edge of his field of vision; she was already at least three times Bee's size, and far more formidable. Perhaps the hope was real, Arlian thought—but he was not happy at the form it took. Patch and Smudge had never done anything obviously malicious or intentionally cruel or destructive, but Arlian could not deny that the creatures made him uncomfortable. They were so very unnatural, so mysterious—they could communicate, but did so only very rarely, so rarely that Black's children had not known the ability existed. Arlian had not realized their words were *that* rare; he had attempted to converse with them a few times, with little result. They never said much, and never answered his questions when he asked whether they knew anything of their own nature.

The possibility that the kitten-things might prove as unacceptable in their own way as the dragons had crossed his mind, but he had dismissed it. They were new and strange, and very young, that was all; when they had matured and learned a little more there would be time to insist on answers to his questions.

He rose. "I have more experiments to conduct," he said, as he turned and marched out. Half an hour later he was back at the Grey House, going over his notes and trying to ignore the lingering stench of ordure and death that hung over his work area despite his best efforts at cleaning and airing.

For his next planned trial he intended to combine human blood, pig's blood, and venom and see whether the kittens took on any porcine characteristics. He had a sealed jar of Wolt's blood and another of pig's blood on hand, and his two bottles of venom—though the brown one was now mostly empty. He made his preparations, keeping a careful watch on the cats he had caged and waiting.

It was past midnight, and he was dozing in his chair, when something woke him; he turned to see that his middle cat was laboring.

He snatched up his waiting vial of elixir and opened the cage—then became aware that something was watching him, something other than the three cats. He turned.

Patch was crouched on her haunches in the corner of the

room, her forepaw-hands folded beneath her chin, staring intently up at him.

"How did *you* get here?" Arlian said, as he uncorked the vial.

Followed you, came the reply.

Then the struggling of the mother-to-be distracted him, and he turned his attention to the arrival of the first kitten. When it was clean and safe, Arlian grabbed the mother's head and forced her mouth open.

Stop, Patch said.

Arlian did not stop; he emptied his preparation into the thrashing animal. That done, he tossed his feeding vial aside and turned as the mother began to vomit. He had seen this before, and had no desire to watch another death—but the presence of the kitten-thing was new. He looked in the corner.

Patch was no longer visible.

"Where are you?" Arlian asked.

She is dying.

He could not locate the source of the unspoken words. "I know that."

You have killed her. Poisoned her.

"Yes. I am trying to learn how the magic works, so I can take it away from the dragons."

You killed our mother this way, then?

"Yes." He hesitated, then added, "I'm sorry."

You say you are sorry, yet you do it again.

"Yes. I need to know, to understand."

Why?

"You would not understand; you don't know enough of the world."

I may know more than you think. Answer me—why do you need to know?

"So I can destroy the dragons without unleashing wild magic on the Lands of Man."

You wish to destroy?

"Only the dragons. To save innocent lives."

How is one life better than another? Why should the dragons die, rather than those you call innocents?

"The dragons kill people."

You kill.

"But . . . it's not the same. I kill only for important purposes. The dragons kill because they enjoy it. They slaughtered my family on a whim. I must destroy them so they cannot kill others as they did my parents."

You killed our mother, and are still killing. Must we destroy you, then?

"I killed your mother to create you! To make something that could contain the dragons' magic without becoming a dragon."

I do not know what a dragon is. What do dragons have to do with cats?

"Nothing." He remembered all the failed experiments with blood other than human; whatever the connection between men and dragons might be, cats did not share it. "Cats were just convenient." He stared into the dim corners of the room, trying to locate the little creature; behind him the dying cat gave a final heave, and expelled a second and final kitten.

If you seek allies in your battle with these dragons, should you not find ones you can recruit without killing their parents? You slew my mother—do you think I should help you, when you have done this to me? Blue eyes appeared in the gloom, staring at him.

"I didn't know it would kill her, at first," Arlian said. "I was trying to find a mixture that would transfer the magic without harming anything."

The eyes vanished. *You know now, yet you have just killed another cat. If you want allies, find something that your poison won't kill.*

"I tried," Arlian said. The cat-thing had made no threats, nor was the tone of its unspoken voice noticeably angry, but Arlian's hand had fallen to the hilt of his sword.

Did you? And you found none?

Arlian did not answer; instead he turned at a flash of movement.

The second kitten had been born as its mother died—and now tiny hands gripped its head and twisted, displaying far more strength than any creature so young should possess, and fangs flashed as they plunged into the mewling little thing's throat. An instant later the newborn was dead.

"What are you *doing*?" Arlian demanded.

No more, Patch replied, glowering at him as she stood on her hind feet over the dead kitten, the live firstborn squirming blindly a few inches away, groping for its dead mother's breast. *You will make no more of us.* It held out a handlike forepaw. *Look at this, at what you have done—this is not right. I am neither feline nor human.*

"Indeed you are not," Arlian agreed. "You are more than either, a product of this land's magic. Where is the wrong in that?"

You killed my mother to make me what I am; is that not wrong enough?

"Dragons are born of death; the wizards and monsters of the south, too."

And did you not seek something better?

"I seek an alternative, yes—and you are a possible alternative."

I am a monstrosity. I forbid you to create more.

"Forbid? You are a kitten, scarcely larger than my hand—how do you think to argue with a grown man, and one possessing the heart of the dragon?"

I am, as you have just said, an embodiment of the land's magic—and these are the Lands of Man, the Dragon Lands, not the kingdom of the cats. There are greater powers here, and for the moment I give them voice, and in that voice I tell you, kill no more beasts in your foul experiments.

"I will do as I must," Arlian said angrily.

The cat-thing did not reply, but instead leapt at him, tiny

fingers outstretched, in a leap that should have been impossible for so small a creature.

Arlian easily knocked her aside, but she vanished before she struck the floor. Arlian blinked, and drew his sword. Clearly, the experiment called Patch was not a success, and would have to be destroyed before she killed anything else as she had the newborn kitten.

Fangs suddenly buried themselves in his calf; he twisted, and saw the cat-thing behind him, its teeth sunk into his flesh through his trouser leg. He did not brush it away, though; instead he took careful aim and plunged his sword's point toward its tiny heart.

The blade skidded across the thin fur as if he had struck at granite.

Arlian had seen that happen before, long ago, in a cave beneath the Desolation, when he broke two blades on a newborn dragon. "Damn," he said. He tossed the sword to his left hand, then reached down to grab the creature.

She released her hold and danced aside, vanishing again the moment she reached a shadow.

This was ludicrous, Arlian thought as he straightened and sheathed his sword. He stared into the shadows, but could not see Patch anywhere. Obviously, her magic enabled her to hide preternaturally well—an amplification, perhaps, of a cat's natural talents.

The sword had not touched her, any more than ordinary steel could harm a dragon; Arlian had half expected that, and had come prepared when conducting his experiments. He reached into his coat and pulled out an obsidian dagger.

"Patch," he called, "where are you?"

She did not reply—but he heard a crash, and whirled.

The almost-empty brown bottle of venom had been knocked from the table and smashed on the stone floor; foul vapor was swirling up from the scattered shards. Patch was on the table, looking up at the still-full blue bottle on a nearby shelf.

"Damn!" Arlian said again, lunging for the kitten-creature.

Patch leapt, an impossible monkeylike leap that left her hanging by her fingertips from the shelf, her toes scrabbling at empty air.

Arlian ran, and grabbed the blue bottle before Patch could pull herself up; then he stepped back, bottle in one hand and stone dagger in the other, and watched as the kitten dropped to the floor, righted herself, and turned to face him.

"I will not take orders from a kitten," Arlian growled.

Patch charged.

The dash at his legs was so unexpected he almost dropped the bottle to fend off the attack, but he caught himself at the last instant. He let her lock her fingers around his ankle and sink her fangs into him once again. Then he bent down and stabbed at her with the obsidian dagger.

To his astonishment, it was no more effective than his steel had been; the needle-sharp point slid and skipped across her fur without piercing. Those blue eyes glared up at him, and then she began climbing.

He dropped the dagger, raised the blue bottle above his head with his left hand, and looked about for a weapon. He remembered Black's suggestion that it might take six hundred years to find a way to kill the kittens—but Patch had killed the newborn with nothing but her own paws and fangs.

That was presumably a part of her magic.

He grabbed Patch by the throat and pulled her free of his trousers; she squirmed wildly, flexing and twisting in his grip. He squeezed, unconcerned with whether or not he harmed her, as he would never have done with any ordinary kitten.

She did not seem to be bothered by the pressure on her throat; her gyrations did not slacken in the least.

While holding the cat-thing at arm's length, he set the bottle carefully on the table; then he took a firm grip with both hands and tried to wring Patch's neck as she thrashed and clawed at him.

He could not do it. Even his full strength was not enough to snap the little creature's spine. The best he could do was hold her relatively still.

He held her at arm's length again, and stared at her, trying to think what he could do, as she struggled desperately. It was probably too late to try to calm her or bargain with her, and killing her . . .

Well, steel and strength and obsidian had failed, but there were other possibilities. He looked down at the floor, where spatters of venom had eaten holes into the slate. He knelt, and shoved the kitten's face into the smear of venom that had collected in one such hole.

There was no effect; she continued to struggle and squirm as strongly as before.

That was interesting, that his new creation should be immune to the dragon's poison; venom was the one toxin that *could* scar, sicken, or kill a dragonheart.

But of course, it did not trouble the dragons themselves. By analogy, then, Patch's kind were not mere ambulatory incubators that would someday spawn new magical creatures, like dragonhearts, but were themselves, like dragons, the magical end-product.

Neither iron nor obsidian nor venom . . .

Still clutching the struggling cat-thing, Arlian made his way out through the servants' entryway to the carriage house, where his trader's wagon still stood; he had never bothered to empty it completely after returning from the Borderlands. Now he climbed up into it, pressed Patch down solidly onto the bench where she could be secured with one hand, and groped inside with the other.

A moment later he held up what he sought—a silver dagger.

Patch stopped struggling.

Strike, then, she said.

He struck.

38

An Audacious Proposal

*A*rlian disposed of Patch's remains, and the other corpses produced by the night's experiments, in the ash pit where he had disposed of so many others; he observed that Patch had decayed with unnatural speed, like a dragonheart, though not as thoroughly as would a dragon.

By the time that was done dawn had begun to lighten the eastern sky, and he had a live, normal, but very unhappy kitten to deal with. He wrapped the poor little thing in a warm towel, then set out to bring it to Lady Rime's family.

As he closed the door of the Grey House behind him the silver dagger was tucked inside his coat, where the obsidian had been before, and the towel-wrapped kitten was cradled in his arms.

As he attended to these matters, and again as he walked down the still-deserted street, Arlian thought over the night's events and everything Patch had said.

She had said he should find a species where the elixir would not kill an expectant mother, and of course he did know of one such species, the obvious species for further experimentation—but he had not dared to think of experimenting on humans. The risks and unknowns seemed very high, too high to ask any woman to face, for either herself or her child. In a thousand years of records there were no reports of any pregnant woman surviving a dragon attack or becoming a dragonheart; he could not be sure that the mother would survive, let alone an unborn child.

And of course, if the mother *did* survive, she would be a

dragonheart. She would never again bear children. Even if the Aritheians were to cleanse her of the taint, remove her heart and leach the venom from it, she would probably be sterile—in all the years since the method was first developed, none of the handful of former dragonhearts had ever managed to sire or conceive a child.

And on the other hand, if the experiment *worked,* what would the child be like? There would be no confusion of cat and human, but only human. The dragon portion did not seem to make the transition from mother to offspring, though the magic did. Would the child be a wizard, perhaps? Or a powerful natural magician, but otherwise human?

Or something else?

He could only carry out such an experiment on a willing pregnant volunteer—if then, since an unborn child was hardly in a position to consent to it. This was not something he could force anyone into; the potential consequences were too severe. And who in the world would volunteer for such a thing? What mother could be so heedless of her child's welfare?

Perhaps someone sufficiently desperate might be found—but taking advantage of someone's desperation in such a fashion seemed wrong.

He was mulling it over carefully when he arrived at Lady Rime's estate, where he was distracted by the swarm of children eager to see the new kitten.

"This will be the last," Arlian explained, as Bekerin readied a milk-soaked rag and Rose took the shivering kitten from Arlian's hands. "I will be doing no more experiments on cats."

"That's just as well," Rime said, smiling. "I think we have quite enough kittens now."

Arlian looked at her thoughtfully. At one time he would have consulted with her about his plans, but they had spoken so rarely in recent years, and she had seemed so entirely concerned with her adopted family, that he no longer felt comfortable discussing greater issues with her.

And Black would have been another advisor, but he had
been sufficiently distressed by Arlian's recent experiments
that they had drifted apart. And given Black's horror at experimentation with animals, he would surely be appalled by
any suggestion of experimenting on an unborn child.

Lord Zaner might have an opinion, and could provide a
useful sounding board, but should he disagree with Arlian's conclusion he might bring the Duke's soldiers
sweeping down from the Citadel to intervene; Arlian did
not like that prospect. He intended to make his own decisions, and carry them out or not as he chose, rather than as
the Duke instructed.

When the kitten, a gray one now named Fog, was properly settled Arlian politely declined an offer of breakfast
and headed up the street toward Obsidian House, thinking
deeply.

Patch had turned on him, and been killed—in fact, the
cat-creature had seemed to *want* to be killed. He had poisoned dozens of cats and pigs and dogs in the past few
months; now he suspected he might need to kill Smudge
and Bee, as well. He did not like killing animals, but it did
not particularly trouble him; after all, as a man who happily
ate beef and pork and mutton, he could hardly object to
killing animals on general principles.

People were another matter.

If he were to turn a pregnant woman into a dragonheart,
and the baby survived and proved to be a new sort of magical creature, then he might have his way of diverting the
land's magic away from either dragons or chaos—but if the
new creature proved maleficent, could he bring himself to
kill a child as he had slain Patch?

He shivered and pulled his coat more tightly about him;
although the spring was well advanced, early mornings
could still be chilly on occasion. He glanced up at the pale
blue sky.

Summer was coming; the dragons would definitely be
waking soon, if they were not already active. The Duke had

granted them one village a year; any day now, they might sweep out of their caves and slaughter a town full of men, women, and children. The weather in Manfort was still too cool and bright for them, but there might be areas elsewhere in the Lands of Man already suffering under the oppressive heat and thick clouds of dragon weather.

A town a year, every year, for the rest of eternity, if the dragons were not stopped—and the only way he knew to stop them, now that their secrets were all known, was to kill them.

And if they *were* stopped, all their kind destroyed, then chaos would overwhelm the Lands of Man as it had the realms to the south and west.

Arlian still could not accept either possibility. He needed a third alternative as much as he ever had. Patch had demonstrated that magical cats were not an acceptable choice. What if magical children were no better?

Arlian had killed men before, several of them—he had no exact count, but from the first bandit in the southern slopes of the Desolation to the last magician in Kaltai Ol there had easily been a dozen or more. He had never slain a child, though.

But if the new creatures were truly children, he told himself, then he would have no *need* to kill them. They could be brought up to be compassionate and kind.

Couldn't they?

At Obsidian House he made his way to the kitchens, to find himself the breakfast he had disdained at Rime's; there he discovered Brook and her three children at the table, talking quietly.

Arlian could not help noticing that Brook's pregnancy was well advanced now; if all went well her fourth child would be born before the summer was far advanced.

And if she were to drink a cup of blood and venom before then . . .

"My lord," Brook said, upon seeing him enter, "have you seen Patch this morning?"

"Oh," Arlian said.

At the tone of his reply Brook took one look at his face, then told her children, "Go find your father. All three of you, right now."

Amberdine promptly trotted away; Kerzia took a moment to catch Dirinan by the hand and tow him along as she followed her sister.

Arlian sat down across the table from Brook, and said, "Patch is dead, I'm afraid, by my own hand."

"What happened?"

Arlian hesitated, trying to decide what to explain and what to leave out, and then, without really intending it, found himself telling her everything.

He was just explaining how the obsidian dagger had glanced harmlessly off Patch's back when Black appeared in the doorway with a daughter on either side and Dirinan riding on his shoulders.

"You sent the children to find me, my dear?" Black asked.

Brook looked up, startled. "Oh," she said. "Yes, I did, but I'm afraid it was a mistake—I had misunderstood something Lord Arlian said."

Black glanced curiously at Arlian, who said nothing.

"Could you take the children outside, please?" Brook continued. "They should enjoy this weather while they can."

"Of course." Black looked from his wife to his employer and back, then down at the girls. "Come on," he said. "Why don't we take a walk down to visit Lady Rime? We could see what Rose and Bekerin and the rest are doing."

"They have a new kitten," Arlian said. "He's named Fog."

"Kitten!" Amberdine exclaimed, jumping up and down.

"Haven't you seen *enough* kittens lately?" Black asked, smiling.

"No," Amberdine answered, very definitely.

"This is the last," Arlian said. "I've finished my experiments with cats."

Black looked at him with an expression that might have been relief. "Then we'll go meet this one last kitten," Black said. "Come on." He turned, and herded the girls away.

When they were gone, Arlian resumed his narrative. When he had completed a bare outline of the night's events, he tried to explain his thoughts about what had occurred; throughout all of this Brook provided an attentive audience.

It took some time. In the course of Arlian's explanation Stammer and some of the other servants looked in occasionally, but upon seeing the room occupied by Lord Obsidian and the steward's crippled wife deep in conversation they quickly departed.

Finally, though, Arlian finished speaking, and sat silently, gazing across the table at Brook.

She gazed thoughtfully back, then said, "The dragons destroyed Siribel five years ago. They burned it to the ground, and smashed the stone piers into the sea, because the town fathers refused to pay taxes to Lord Hardior on top of what they paid the Duke."

Siribel, Arlian knew, was the coastal town where Brook had been born and raised. Her family had died in that attack, much as his own had died when the dragons attacked the Smoking Mountain more than twenty years earlier. "I'm sorry," he said.

"My parents were dead to me before that," she replied. "They were dead to me when they never inquired after me in Gan Pethrin, where Sarcheyon sold me to the slavers. But my sisters, the neighbors—the dragons killed them all."

"I know," Arlian said.

"I want the dragons dead—perhaps not as much as you do, Triv, but I want them dead, all of them. Every time you came home and reported how many of their nests you had cleaned out, how many you had slain, the sun shone a little more brightly for me, my heart was a little lighter, my children's future seemed a little more hopeful. When the Duke made peace with the Dragon Society and forbade you to kill more, the world darkened again." Her hand fell to her swollen belly. "I want you to go on killing dragons, Triv," she said. "I will risk this child inside me if that's what is required to send you and your men out there with your black spears again."

Arlian stared at her. He had not asked her, and to have her volunteer like this was more than he had hoped for. "I cannot promise . . ." he said.

"If you do not perform your experiment on a human child, will you kill any more dragons?"

"I don't know," he said. "The Duke has forbidden it, and the wild magic is . . . If it came, our civilization would not survive it."

"And you think that the child would be human, and not a monster?"

"I . . . I don't know," he said. "I believe it would be human in *appearance,* certainly, but then wizards are often human in appearance, while they are not inwardly human. And I cannot be sure of anything, anything at all."

"Any child is a risk," Brook said. "I have lost two, and every time I have conceived I have lived with the possibility that my baby would be deformed, hunchbacked, harelipped, dwarfed, blind, or deaf, that I might bear a drooling idiot with missing limbs. Each time I was pregnant I lived in dread that the child would be born without feet, and be as much a cripple as I am—oh, I know that that was unlikely, but no one truly understands how these things happen. Adding magic to the terrors I face does not seem so very dreadful."

Arlian considered that for a moment, trying to understand her feelings and failing. At last he said, "You understand, though, that if we do this you will be, at least temporarily, a dragonheart? That this will then of necessity be your *last* child?"

"Arlian, I am forty-two years old; this would quite probably be my last child in any case."

"You may be unable to suckle the babe."

"A wet nurse can be found easily enough."

"And you will need to undergo the Aritheian cleansing rites eventually, if you are not to give birth to a dragon. The venom will eat away at your soul, at your heart, if it is not removed."

"I have spoken to Lady Rime often enough, Arlian, and Lady Flute has been kind enough to attend me on occasion; I helped nurse Lord Zaner back to health. I know what is involved."

"Thank you, Brook." Arlian was seated and could not bow properly, but he lowered his eyes in respect. "I am honored by your offer."

"Then fetch your venom, my lord, and let us proceed without delay, before anything can interfere—and before the baby arrives. I am in my final month, I think, and although it should still be a few weeks, and I do not feel anything to indicate otherwise, babies come on *their* schedule, not ours."

"I am more concerned about the meddling of magical forces, or of Fate, than of a premature birth, madam, but I agree that some haste is appropriate." He pushed back his chair, rose, and turned—and found himself meeting the gaze of two small, blue, slit-pupiled eyes.

You killed my sister, Smudge said from his perch on a shelf beside the hearth.

Brook's head jerked around, startled, and she, too, saw the kitten-thing.

"I did," Arlian agreed, his hand creeping toward the silver dagger in his coat. "She attacked me."

Do you intend to kill me?

"I am perfectly willing to, and will do so if you threaten those I care about."

And if I do not?

"I bear no ill will toward you."

Perhaps it would be well if I left.

"Perhaps it would," Arlian agreed.

And then Smudge had vanished. Arlian was unsure whether this was some trick of natural feline stealth magically exaggerated, or outright invisibility, but there could be no question that the creature could disappear in the shadows far more effectively than any ordinary cat.

For a moment he stood silently, waiting to see whether the strange little beast would reappear; then Brook said, "There's Bee to worry about, but I think we have a few weeks before that one can cause any trouble. Right now I really think you should fetch that venom."

The possibility that Smudge intended to spill or smash the blue bottle, as his sister had smashed the brown, could not be ignored. "At once," Arlian agreed, as he strode toward the door.

By the time he left the grounds of the Old Palace he was almost running.

39

A Father's Objections

As Arlian hurried down the avenue he glimpsed Black returning, without the children; he waved, but did not wait for his steward, nor take the time to speak, before he turned the corner onto Cutler Street.

He reached the Grey House in good time and found the bottle of venom undisturbed; there was no evidence that Smudge had been in the vicinity, and Arlian guessed that his concern had been needless. As an added precaution, though, he wrapped the bottle in several layers of toweling and packed it in a leather shoulderbag before departing the Grey House, locking the doors behind himself and heading back up the slope toward Obsidian House at a brisk pace.

The sun was perhaps an hour past its zenith when he

rounded the corner and saw the old palace gateposts ahead—and saw Black standing between them, a sword bare in his right hand, his left on the hilt of a swordbreaker. Arlian slowed, and looked around for some reason for Black's unsheathed steel—as a steward, rather than a lord, Black did not ordinarily carry a sword or swordbreaker at all. The ones he now bore were a set Arlian kept for his use in practice.

Arlian saw no enemy, no need for a blade—and Black was not moving, not turning to face a foe. Instead he stood between the stone pillars, staring directly at Arlian.

Arlian glanced over his shoulder to be sure no assassin lurked behind him, but saw only the bare cobbles of the street, the high brick wall of Lord Dehellen's estate, and a few workmen pushing a cart some twenty yards away.

The workmen did not look like assassins, and in any case were moving away. Had Smudge perhaps slipped out, or made a threat of some sort? "Ho, Black!" Arlian called, turning his gaze forward once more and picking up his pace.

"Arlian," Black replied, raising his sword to guard. His voice was low and harsh.

Arlian stopped dead, twenty feet from the tip of the raised blade.

Black did not call him "Arlian." Black called him "Ari." Under certain circumstances Black might perhaps call him "my lord" for emphasis, or "Lord Obsidian" as gentle mockery, but never, so far as he could recall, "Arlian." Something was very wrong.

"Beron," Arlian answered. "What is it?"

"You are not going to poison my child," Black replied.

Arlian understood the situation immediately, and cursed himself for not having anticipated this. He had been so caught up in his own concerns, so encouraged by Brook volunteering unasked, that he had forgotten how Black would react.

"I sincerely hope not," he said.

"You are not going to poison my wife."

"Beron, please . . ."

"You are not going to bring that filth into our home."

Arlian frowned. "*Your* home?"

"I saw what those kittens became," Black continued. "You are not going to do that to my baby."

"I don't intend to," Arlian said. "The effects should be . . ."

"*I don't care what you intend!*" Black bellowed, advancing on Arlian with his sword at ready. "I don't care what you think the effects are!"

Arlian raised his hands in what was intended to be a calming gesture. "Black," he began, "I . . ."

"You will dump that bottle out, here and now," Black ordered, before Arlian could say more. "All of it. Not a single drop passes this gate."

"I will not," Arlian said, stepping back, his hands falling to the hilts of his own sword and swordbreaker.

Black's swordpoint was at his throat. "You *will*," Black growled.

Arlian's left hand flashed up as he twisted sideways, and his swordbreaker knocked Black's blade away; then he drew his own sword and faced his steward in guard position.

"Don't do this, Black," Arlian said.

"You are not going to destroy my family," Black said, making a quick advance—one intended to intimidate or wound, not kill. Arlian sidestepped it easily and did not riposte, but simply resumed his guard.

He was aware, as he circled slowly around his opponent, that they had acquired an audience; several people who had been going about their business a moment before had stopped to watch the duel.

"You have destroyed one thing after another all your life, Arlian," Black said. "You destroyed Enziet's bargain with the dragons, you destroyed the Old Palace, you killed Drisheen and Stonehand and the rest, you destroyed the Blue Mage. You plunged all the Lands of Man into chaos, from Sarkan-Mendoth to the Borderlands, in pursuit of your insane dreams of vengeance. And now you propose to destroy my wife and child, and I have had *enough* of destruction."

And then he attacked, moving just off the beat that would have followed the rhythm of his speech.

Arlian knew that trick; Black had taught it to him many years ago, when they had been caravan guards crossing the Desolation. He was ready, and turned the sword easily.

But then Black's swordbreaker came around unexpectedly and slashed at the sleeve of his coat before he could pull away and bring his own weapon into play on that side. Arlian twisted, dodged, and countered, thrusting his sword at Black's chest.

Black parried, sending Arlian's blade up to the left, to pass harmlessly over his shoulder. The momentum of the attack threw the two men up against each other, chest to chest, for an instant before both sprang backward.

"Don't do this," Arlian said again.

"Pour out the venom," Black replied.

"Black, I *can't*," Arlian said. "I need it. It would take months to get more, even assuming I dared attempt it before next winter, and Brook's babe is due in mere weeks."

"Don't you say her name!" Black said, making a sudden two-handed whirlwind attack. Arlian fell back, too busy defending himself to speak. The two fought silently for a moment, the only sounds their breath and the whickering and clashing of steel. Their audience watched quietly, clearly unsure of what the fight was about; Arlian guessed half of them didn't even know who he and Black were.

At last they stepped apart for a moment, eyeing each other, swords and swordbreakers raised.

"Black," Arlian said, "I don't want to hurt you, and I certainly don't want to harm Brook or your child, but I need to test the effects of the elixir on an unborn babe if I am ever to have any hope of freeing this realm of the evil magic that haunts it. I need a pregnant woman as my subject, and your wife has volunteered. I did not *ask* her, Black—she *volunteered*. And where else am I to find a volunteer?"

"She did not!" Black snarled, feinting. "You coerced her, as you coerce everyone. You have the heart of the dragon, Arlian, and you influence those around you without even knowing it, without intending it."

"I . . ." Arlian realized he could not deny Black's charge; he honestly did not know whether there was any truth in it. Certainly a dragonheart had a charm, a charisma, that no ordinary man could attain. "Black, I'll find someone else," he said.

"No," Black said. "Pour it out. If you keep it, I know that sooner or later you will feed it to her. You have her under your spell now."

"Black, I promise you, I have not enchanted your wife."

"Of course you have!" He lunged, then reversed swiftly; Arlian barely countered the second attack, and a slash appeared in his linen coat. "You have enchanted her as you enchanted me, all those years ago, when we met outside the Blood of the Grape." A third attack was less deft than the first two, and steel rang as Arlian's swordbreaker caught Black's sword—but the blade slipped free before Arlian could twist his hand and snap it. "You do not *mean* to enchant anyone, but how else can you explain it?"

"I cannot," Arlian said. "Perhaps it is Fate, though, rather than enchantment. Perhaps I was meant to be here purely to bring this unborn child to its proper destiny."

"If so, then I defy Fate," Black said, twisting around for an extraordinarily risky backhand attack. Arlian turned it easily, and circled to the left.

"Perhaps it is neither Fate nor enchantment, but simply the vagaries of the human heart," Arlian said. "Perhaps you befriended me because your heart was big enough to encompass the needs of the desperate boy I was then. Perhaps Brook volunteered because *her* heart is big enough to take great risks for the good of all humanity."

Black made a high slashing attack that Arlian blocked easily, but then brought his swordbreaker in for a jab at Arlian's belly; Arlian barely avoided it.

"Her heart?" Black said. "The *human* heart, you said? But if she drinks your foul brew, her heart will be the heart of a dragon, not a woman. The love that fills it will be corrupted and eaten away—you told me so yourself. Even if she is not poisoned, she will no longer be the woman I love—and once transformed, she *cannot* love me, or our children. Would you rob them all of their mother?"

Arlian's defenses faltered at that, and Black's swordbreaker cut his side before the two men pulled apart again.

"For more than sixteen years I have resisted the temptation to buy myself a thousand years of extended life, largely because you told me how cold and loveless your own existence was," Black said. "I was never certain I believed you—until now. What you propose to do to my wife demonstrates that you *are* the heartless monster you have always claimed to be."

"No, Black," Arlian answered. "I am damaged, beyond question, but I am not utterly heartless—perhaps because it was not my own blood I drank, but my grandfather's, so that the dragon growing inside me has consumed *his* soul rather than my own. I did love Sweet until she died—and I love you, my friend. Please, put up your sword."

"Empty the bottle, and I will put up my sword. Not before."

"Black, Beron, remember that Brook's heart will be cleansed once the child is born; she will be whole again, as Rime is. Surely, you cannot think Rime incapable of love!"

"And what if she refuses to submit to the cleansing, as so many other dragonhearts have refused?"

"Why should she refuse?" Arlian asked, genuinely puzzled.

"A *thousand years of life,* Ari! Had you forgotten?"

Arlian frowned, and almost missed turning a low jab. He *had* forgotten, for the moment.

"And hours of agony as the magicians *cut out her beating heart,* Arlian—had you forgotten that, as well?"

Arlian had no good answer to that; he knew that the cleansing operation was indeed excruciating. He hesitated, then said, "Black, loath as I am to do so, I will give *you* a dose of the elixir as well, if you allow Brook to take it; the two of you can, if you choose, live out a thousand years together."

"Oh, now you offer me the poison, after all these years of preaching its evils to me?"

There was a quick flurry of steel, and Arlian could not spare time or breath to reply immediately. When the two broke contact it was Black who spoke first.

"A thousand loveless years, to end when a dragon bursts from my chest and devours my soul? Watching my children grow old and die, knowing I can never sire more?"

"You have three fine children," Arlian said, "and a fourth on the way. Is that not enough?"

"I don't *know,*" Black snapped. "If I let you bring that bottle into Obsidian House, there may never be a fourth, and there will *certainly* never be a fifth."

"You have a son," Arlian said, "and two fine daughters. Your fourth child may well be something far more than human, if all goes well . . ."

"Something like a dragon, perhaps? Or a wizard, like the Blue Mage?"

"No! Something like . . . like . . ." Arlian groped for words. "I do not *know* what, Black; if I knew, perhaps I would not even need to make my experiment."

"You are not *going* to make your experiment!" Black closed for a fresh attack. "I will *not* be the father of a monster!"

Arlian defended himself, but did not counterattack; he was hoping that Black's fury would spend itself, and they would be able to talk the problem out and arrive at a solution. Black's rage, however, showed no sign of abating; in fact, Arlian found himself struggling to fend off the assault.

Black was older, and lacked the superhuman stamina of a dragonheart, but he was the more skilled of the two; after all, he had been Arlian's sole teacher in the arts of swordsmanship. In the early stages of the duel Black had been holding back, trying to force Arlian to yield and dump out his supply of venom, but now he had worked himself up into a frenzy. He was fighting for blood—not necessarily to kill, not yet, but aiming to spill his opponent's blood and weaken him until he could fight no more.

Arlian, on the other hand, was still fighting defensively, hoping for a chance to disarm his opponent without hurting him. That gave Black an additional advantage.

And, Arlian realized, Black was winning. He had cut Arlian's side, and then his upper arm, and his shoulder—in time, if this continued, blood loss would more than make up for the heart of the dragon.

He tried retreating, thinking Black would stay near the gate to block his path, but Black pursued him relentlessly. The gathering crowd of watchers stepped aside to make room for him as he backed away down the avenue.

Apparently, Black would no longer be satisfied with keeping him out of Obsidian House; he wanted a conclusion. He wanted the venom spilled. Arlian was glad that he had slung the bottle on his back, securely wrapped, where Black's blade could not smash it.

The fight moved down the street, away from the gateposts, and Arlian considered his options.

No ordinary citizen would intervene; tradesmen and workers would never interfere in a duel between lords, or between a lord and an underling. That was simply not done. Another nobleman might choose to join in, should he recognize that Black was not a lord but a mere employee—but that would not do; the lord would certainly do his best to kill Black for his effrontery, and while Black was a talented swordsman he could not hope to fight two skilled opponents at once for long.

Guardsmen might be convinced to act, especially if they recognized their warlord; they could be ordered to restrain Black.

In his present fury, though, Black might well kill one or two soldiers, and *that* would get him an arrow or two—or a dozen—in response.

But there was another possibility. Black was so focused on the duel itself that he had neglected other concerns. Arlian stood his ground for a moment, fending off Black's attack, and then deliberately left an opening—a real one, as he knew Black would not be fooled by anything less.

Black took the chance he was offered, and lunged, his sword slicing through the tattered remains of Arlian's coat, through the blouse beneath, and into Arlian's skin—but Arlian had expected this, and spun away so that the blade scraped at him but did not cut deeply. He turned, and suddenly he and Black had changed positions and stood at right angles to their former line.

And that meant that Black no longer stood between Arlian and the gateposts, nor between Arlian and Obsidian House. Arlian did not give his opponent time to realize his error; instead he broke and ran, full out, for the gateposts.

Black gave a wordless bellow of rage and set out in pursuit.

Arlian rounded the nearer gatepost and ran up the old path, then veered aside, heading across the gardens toward his new residence.

Black was close on his heels, but Arlian was the younger, taller man; he stayed out of reach of his steward's sword.

And then he was on the path leading up to the front door of Obsidian House, but there was an obstruction; he almost fell as he struggled to stop himself before running into it.

Or rather, into *her.*

Brook sat in her wheeled chair, her face grim, as Arlian

staggered to avoid colliding with her. He veered to the side and stepped around her, then turned.

Black had stopped, as well, and now the two men faced each other over Brook's head, panting, blades ready. Although they were within reach of one another, neither dared make any attack; while they could easily avoid striking Brook directly, they both knew that a parry might send a blade downward, momentarily out of control.

"Allíri," Black said, "move aside and let me past."

Arlian had never heard Brook's true name before; he hadn't even realized she had one. But of course she did; she had been fourteen before she was sold into slavery.

"No, Beron," Brook replied.

"Allíri, please."

"No. Put down your sword. This is ridiculous."

"I won't let him harm you," Black insisted.

"Triv isn't going to hurt me," Brook replied.

"I won't let him feed you that poison. I won't let him poison our child."

"And do I have no say in this? The child is in *my* body, and we live in Lord Obsidian's house—I do not think the decision is entirely yours to make."

"He's ensorcelled you, charmed you."

"Or the dragons have seduced and deluded *you*—had you not considered that?"

At that, for the first time, Black hesitated. Then he looked over Brook's head and called, "Let us settle this between us like gentlemen, my lord! Step out from behind the woman!"

Arlian looked past Black and saw that a portion of the crowd that had gathered to watch their fight had followed them through the old gate and up the crooked path. He wondered whether Black had seen them and was now playing to the gallery, hoping Arlian would be unwilling to be seen hiding behind a pregnant cripple's skirts.

Black should have known him better than that; Arlian had never cared what anyone thought of him. He had been called a coward in public before, and had survived it without being drawn into a pointless duel.

"This is *not* between you," Brook announced loudly. "This is *my* decision."

Black's frustration and fury were plain on his face—or at any rate, plain to Brook and Arlian, who both knew him well; a stranger might not have realized the depth of emotion indicated by his thinned lips and furrowed brow. "The child is mine, as well as yours," he said.

"Can you prove that?" Brook retorted. "Do you have any evidence of that other than my word?"

That shook Black more than anything previously said; he blanched.

"Am I a free woman, or do you intend to keep me a prisoner until the child is born? Will you watch over me, day and night, to see that I obey your orders?"

"I am not giving you orders," Black said, his voice unsteady.

"If I am any man's slave, husband, I am Lord Arlian's. He took me from Lord Toribor at the risk of his own life—and then he set me free, and as a free woman I choose my own path."

"I am not giving you orders," Black repeated. "I . . . I am *concerned,* Allíri, for your welfare and your child's."

"Concern is addressed with words and welcomed actions, husband, not with threats and bared blades."

Black hesitated.

Arlian, too, hesitated. The possibility of making a gesture, of sheathing his blades and exposing himself to Black's mercy, occurred to him—but he rejected it.

There had been times when he had made such gestures, times when he happily risked his life, but this time the stakes were too high. His research had shown him that magic could take new forms; he had a chance to destroy the dragons and shut away the chaos beyond the borders, and if he died, who would continue that research? When he had risked his life before, it had been either at times when his goals appeared so hopeless that he had little to lose, or at times when others were ready and willing to take up his campaign against the dragons; this was not such a time. His blades stayed ready.

"We will discuss it," Arlian said. "I did not mean to exclude you from my counsels, old friend, but you had drawn away, avoiding contact with my efforts."

"And you could not allow *that,* could you, my lord?" Black said. "No, I must ever be involved in your madness."

"You are always free to leave my employ, Black."

"Am I?" He shook his head. "I have been caught up in your fate since we first met." In a sudden movement he sheathed his swordbreaker. "We will discuss it," he said. "And in all probability you will convince me to allow you to pursue whatever insanity you choose, just as you always do. I will fall under your spell again." He lifted his sword and pointed it at Arlian's throat. "But let me tell you now, Ari, that whatever I may say, whatever I may agree to, if you harm my wife or child, if you have misjudged your experiment and kill or maim either of them, then I *will* kill you. The Dragon Society has tried to do that for sixteen years now, but they do not know you as I do. You understand revenge, Ari—you have lived your entire life for little else. If you harm Brook or our baby, you will find that I, too, understand revenge."

"I know," Arlian said quietly.

Black stared at him for a moment, and then looked down. With the sword still directed at Arlian, Black addressed his wife.

"We will need to discuss a great deal as well, Allíri. I am not your master, but I am your husband and the father of your children, and you are putting everything that exists between us at risk."

"All the world is at risk, my husband," Brook replied. "That is the nature of life."

"Some risks are greater than others," Black said, dropping his blade. "Let us hope we have not misjudged the ones we have chosen today." He sheathed the sword.

Arlian sheathed his own weapons, as well—and heard someone weeping. He shifted his gaze as Black turned.

Kerzia, Amberdine, and Dirinan were standing at the front of the little crowd of watchers, staring somberly at their parents, and Amberdine was weeping miserably.

40

The Final Experiment

*A*s he stumbled through the central passage of Obsidian House Arlian tried not to think about the rumors that would be spreading through Manfort like mold through damp bread. He did not remember either Black or himself saying anything really detailed about the nature of their dispute, and the crowds had stood far enough back that they could not have heard everything clearly in any case, so the stories would probably bear only the vaguest resemblance to the truth of the situation. Whether that imprecision was good or bad, Arlian was uncertain.

Whatever their nature might be, the one fact beyond question was that there *would* be rumors. There was nothing he could do to prevent that. He could not even think of anything he could say to turn the tales to his advantage, and therefore he said nothing to the servants who stared in silent horror at his bloody clothes as he found his way to the scullery sink.

After cleaning and bandaging his half-dozen worst

wounds, Arlian waited in the kitchen while Brook and Black calmed and comforted their children and sent them upstairs with some of the servants. He used the time to unwrap the blue bottle of venom, and to find a sturdy wooden cup and a good sharp knife. He wanted to be ready if an agreement was reached.

If they could not come to terms, if Black was able to persuade Brook to rescind her agreement, it was not the end; he still had the venom, and there were certainly other expectant mothers in Manfort. Surely, one could be found who would agree to the experiment—yesterday he would have thought that impossible, but hearing Brook's words had convinced him otherwise.

In the absolute worst case, he thought, he could buy a pregnant slave.

He had never bought a slave; he had freed every slave he had ever acquired through other means. He would certainly free any slave he purchased for this purpose, as well—but only *after* feeding her the elixir.

Such a course of action would violate his own principles, but nonetheless, he knew he would resort to it if he had to. Everything he knew of magic, everything he had learned from his experiments or from the Blue Mage or the leech-god or the southern magicians, led him to believe that this final experiment was the route to what he sought.

At last Brook came down in her lift, and Black marched down the stairs, and the three of them sat down to talk.

They spoke for hours, and while any number of opinions on lesser issues were adjusted by the exchange, the core positions of the three did not change: Arlian intended to offer Brook the elixir, Brook intended to drink it, and Black hated the idea, but acknowledged that he could not prevent it without bringing even greater personal catastrophe on himself and his family.

The possibility that Black, too, would drink was discussed, and shelved; he would wait and see what the effect on Brook might be. Arlian promised to allow him access to the remaining venom should he later choose that path.

"You know, Ari, I think that promise, more than anything else, tells me how important this is to you," Black remarked.

"I believe it may be the most important thing I have done since I first plunged an obsidian dagger into a newborn dragon's heart in the cave beneath the Desolation."

"Then let us do it," Black said, pushing himself back from the table. "Enough talk; let us be about it." He pulled at his sleeve, baring his left forearm. "I believe you need blood. If my wife is going to drink human blood, then let it be mine."

"I thought I would use my own," Brook said.

"You need your strength," Arlian said, taking hold of Black's wrist and raising the knife.

A moment later, while Black was bandaging his arm, Arlian let a few drops of venom fall from the bottle into the cup of blood; the mixture bubbled and smoked, but Brook snatched it up.

"Before my courage fails me," she said, gulping the stuff down.

Black went rigid, staring at her. Arlian hastened to cork the bottle and pull it away.

Brook gagged, then spasmed; the cup tumbled from her hand and shattered on the floor. She jerked, choking, and tumbled from her chair; one elbow caught on the table but failed to hold her, and neither man had his hands free to catch her before she fell.

Black released the half-knotted bandage and dove for her, barely in time to keep her head from hitting the stones. He lifted her to a half-sitting position and turned her so she did not choke on her vomit.

Arlian made sure the bottle was safe on a shelf before he returned to the subject of his experiments.

"By the dead gods, that's foul!" Brook gasped, between heaves.

"Allíri," Black said, brushing her soiled hair away from her face. "Allíri, I love you." He looked up at Arlian. "You've poisoned her."

"It's the same thing I drank, the same thing *every* dragonheart drank," Arlian said, as he fetched rags to wipe up the vomit and collect the shards of the cup. "Yes, it's foul, but she'll live, and the baby will live."

"You don't *know* that," Black growled. "That stuff may have gone rancid in that bottle you've been carrying around—all the rest of you got it fresh from the source."

Arlian opened his mouth, closed it again, and then said, "Why did no one mention that possibility until *now*?" He knelt beside Brook, wiping her face gently with a clean rag. "It smelled no different, but that may mean nothing. If that's why all my animals died . . ."

"I'm not going to die," Brook whispered. Then she closed her eyes.

"Allíri?"

She did not answer—but she was still breathing.

"I think she's sleeping," Arlian said. "I lost consciousness when it happened to me, but I awoke well enough."

"Help me get her to bed," Black said.

Arlian obliged.

An hour later Brook was safely in her bed, sleeping normally, with Black at her side; the kitchen had been cleaned, and Arlian was in his own chamber, preparing to retire. The strain of helping transport Brook had reopened the wound in his side where Black's swordbreaker had cut him; Arlian dabbed at it with the bandage, then tossed the bloody linen on the nightstand before applying a fresh cloth. When he was done he dipped his hands in the basin by the bed.

A thin swirl of blood stained the water, but Arlian paid it no heed as he pulled off his boots and stockings. He glanced at it as he began to lie back on the bed, and froze.

The meager trace of blood had shaped itself into a faint and shadowy image, the image of a face Arlian recognized.

The face of the dragon that had killed his grandfather.

What have you done? the dragon asked.

Arlian grimaced wearily. "We won't know that for some time yet, I'm afraid."

You are meddling in the workings of Fate.

"Fate is meddling in *my* work," Arlian retorted.

Then he tapped the bowl, shattering the fragile image; he blew out the bedside candle and lay down to sleep.

41

Unwelcome Guests

*B*rook slept through much of the following day, but by the day after she had returned to normal—as had her child, it appeared.

Arlian had used the time to hire half a dozen guards for Obsidian House, and give orders that the rooftop catapults were to be loaded and made functional as quickly as possible. He did not really think a dragon would dare venture so far into the heart of Manfort, past the encircling defenses, but it did no harm to be cautious. The hired guards would be of little use against dragons, of course, but the dragons could well send human agents—in fact, such a tactic was far more likely than the monsters coming themselves, and that was the entire reason for employing these men.

Arlian had not called on any of the Duke's guards for this duty because that would have required too much explanation, and because such men would have divided loyalties—they might be withdrawn at the Duke's whim. Instead he had hired men who were experienced caravan guards, and dressed them in his own livery.

He had also made certain that everyone in the house understood that Brook's unborn child might prove to be of very special importance, and must be protected at all costs, even more than any other unborn babe.

And now, it seemed, all was well, and Brook and the child recovered from the elixir's initial impact.

"I felt it kick," Black told Arlian, smiling, as the three of them moved down the upstairs hallway, Brook in her chair and the two men walking behind her. "It's still alive."

"Of course it is," Arlian replied. He glanced at the back of Brook's head, and debated mentioning his brief sorcerous exchange with the dragon. He had, as yet, said nothing of it.

He now regretted his haste in breaking that contact; had he not been so exhausted, mentally and physically, he would have asked a few questions, tried to elicit more information. As it was he could barely recall any of the exchange. The dragon had asked him what he had done, he remembered that, but what else? Something about meddling with Fate . . .

Well, wasn't that what he had intended to do? And hadn't the dragons themselves meddled ten thousand years ago? The thing in Tirikindaro said the dragons had betrayed and killed the gods then, and that it had drunk the blood of a god.

It belatedly occurred to Arlian to wonder how the dragons had accomplished this, and what had been able to tear open the throat of a god. He remembered Patch's fangs opening the throat of that last kitten.

Could the creature growing in Brook's belly eventually become some monstrosity capable of ripping out a god's throat? Was it something so terrible that even the dragons feared it?

What *had* he done?

He decided he would continue to say nothing of the image in the bowl—and he might attempt to contact the dragons again, when he had an opportunity. He had not spoken to them directly in more than a decade, nor had he tried to, but perhaps the time had come to reconsider.

He stepped out onto the balcony overlooking the great hall and gazed down over the rail. The construction was complete, and the furnishings largely in place; the room was elegant, yet inviting. The sky outside the broad windows was dark with gathering storm clouds, but even so the hall was brighter and airier than any part of the Grey House.

This was a far more pleasant residence than the Grey House could ever be, and now that his experiments were apparently complete Arlian thought the time had come to relocate and dispose of Enziet's old home once and for all.

"Black," he said, "I want you to arrange to transfer the remainder of the household from the Grey House to Obsidian House, and to find a broker to sell the Grey House. I'd say this should be done before the birth—I suspect you may be too busy for some time afterward to give the matter your full attention."

Black hesitated. "Are you certain, my lord? We do not yet know just what you may have done to the child—how do we know we will have no use for some of the facilities Lord Enziet installed?"

Arlian glanced at him warily. "You mean the barred rooms and the chains?"

Black did not answer.

"If we need anything of that nature, we will provide it here," Arlian said. "I have had my fill of Lord Enziet's legacy."

Black glanced upward, a glance Arlian knew was not directed at the innocuous vaulted ceiling, but at the obsidian spearheads that now adorned perhaps half the iron catapults on the roof, and at the dragons that obsidian was meant to pierce.

"I know I will never be free of my inheritance from Enziet," Arlian said, "but I need not cling to all of it. Let the

Grey House be sold, and my soul freed of that particular burden."

"As you wish, my lord," Black said. He turned and headed for the stair.

Brook, for her part, headed down the corridor toward her special lift.

Arlian remained on the balcony for a time, thinking.

If his experiment succeeded, and Brook's child possessed a dragon-sized share of magic but was otherwise healthy and to all intents and purposes human, then he would still need to create more of these new beings before he could continue his campaign to wipe out the dragons. The Lands of Man would need one of these magical people, these fey folk, for each dragon slain.

That would mean contaminating dozens, perhaps hundreds, of pregnant women, putting them through the same brutal illness Brook had just survived, and later cutting the hearts out of new mothers so that they could be cleansed of the draconic taint. That would not be a pleasant undertaking. He knew Rime still bore a gruesome scar on her chest, and Arlian supposed the other former dragonhearts did, as well.

He glanced back toward the lift. It seemed horribly unfair that poor Brook would have to suffer through that, and would bear the scar until she died; were not her missing feet scars enough for one lifetime?

Arlian sighed and turned back to the rail, still thinking. Henceforth when he killed dragons he would need to gather venom from the dead in each lair, as Lord Rolinor had, to ensure an adequate supply. He would need to recruit women to bear the magical children.

This plan's resemblance to the loathsome practices of Kaltai Ol struck him, and he frowned. He did not like that.

But these children would not be murdered, would not be fed to monsters; they would be cherished for their part in freeing humanity of the dragons. They would be useful only alive, not dead.

But that brought up another question he had not yet considered—how long would the children live? And could they reproduce themselves without dragons to provide venom, or would their children be merely human? It might be necessary to keep *one* dragon alive, to ensure that the supply of venom was maintained.

That was hardly an appealing prospect.

And what would the children be like? What if they proved as dangerous in some way as the dragons?

Well, he knew a silver blade had killed Patch easily enough; presumably silver would be able to kill the children, as well, should it prove necessary.

Arlian could not imagine that it would. This child would be magical, yes, but it would be the child of Black and Brook, sibling to Kerzia and Amberdine and Dirinan; how could it be anything that needed to be killed?

That a member of Black's family might prove unacceptably dangerous or evil seemed incredible—but what would he do if it was?

What if the experiment failed entirely, and the child had no magic, or was just another dragonheart? What would he do then?

He could go back to poisoning cats, he supposed, and create a swarm of monstrous kitten-things, then kill the ones that seemed dangerous or unbalanced. He wondered where Smudge was, and what would become of him and of Bee. Patch had been mad, and had seemed eager to die, but Smudge had shown no such tendency. Bee was still too young to judge.

Bee was beginning to show human traits, though, exactly as Patch and Smudge had—apparently the admixture of cat's blood had made no great difference.

Arlian sighed. The kittens were, to say the least, not a great success; he certainly hoped Brook's child proved a superior alternative.

He wandered along the balcony and down the stairs, glancing out the windows at the sky. The clouds were thick and dark, so dark that it looked more like twilight than mid-morning, but so far no rain had fallen.

"My lord."

Arlian turned, startled, to see Wolt holding out a folded scrap of paper.

"A messenger just brought this. He says it's urgent."

Arlian accepted the paper and read, "Must see you at once, at the Citadel." It was signed, "Rolinor."

He frowned, puzzled. What business would Rolinor have with him?

But then he remembered the image in the bowl, and who Rolinor now represented. It seemed that the dragons wanted to talk to him, and if he would not speak to them directly then their agent would serve.

For a moment he considered going back upstairs, drawing a little blood, and seeing whether he could conjure up an image—but then he decided that no, he did not particularly want to talk to a dragon.

He did not particularly want to talk to Rolinor, either, but he might learn something if he did. He might find out whether the Dragon Society knew anything about his experiments. He might get a sense of whether or not the dragonhearts were in full accord with their masters about recent events.

And while he was at the Citadel he might speak to Lord Zaner, or even the Duke, about the nature of his experiments. He had not kept them informed of his progress, lest they interfere, but perhaps the time had come to let them in on his little secret. Perhaps they would want to elaborate on the city's defenses still further if they knew something the dragons feared was soon to be born here.

They might well already know something of what had happened, of course; the Duke had his spies, and the kittens had been known to everyone in Obsidian House.

"The messenger is waiting, my lord," Wolt said.

Arlian looked up.

"He says his instructions are to wait and accompany you to the Citadel."

That did not sound as if Rolinor merely wanted to talk; that sounded as if this was setting up yet another inept assassination attempt.

Well, Arlian had no objection to ridding the world of another would-be assassin. "Fetch my sword, and the steel-lined hat," he said.

Half an hour later the obviously nervous messenger ushered him into a small bare chamber in the Citadel's outer wall, where Lord Rolinor sat waiting. No assassin had struck, a fact that troubled Arlian. Why ask him to accompany the messenger if not to regulate his pace and mark him as the target? If the business was *truly* urgent, Rolinor could have come to Obsidian House in person. If there was a third party Rolinor wished him to meet, or something Rolinor wished to show him, he saw no sign of it in the empty meeting room.

Rolinor, too, appeared nervous as he gestured for Arlian to sit.

"I prefer to stand, my lord," Arlian said. "Now, what is this urgent business you have with me?"

"First, my lord, let me say how very pleased . . ." Rolinor began.

Arlian, suddenly concerned, interrupted him. "What is this urgent business, my lord? I have business of my own to attend to."

"Ah, of course. It would seem, my dear Lord Obsidian, that you have taken something that does not belong to you."

A thought was growing in the back of Arlian's mind, but he suppressed it long enough to ask, "What are you talking about?"

"I refer to a quantity of dragon venom. I am informed that . . ."

He stopped in midsentence because Arlian had turned to go.

This was obviously not urgent. This was not something that required an immediate meeting. This was an excuse to ensure that Arlian was in a particular place at a particular time. He had thought that was to locate him so that assassins could strike, but now he realized there was another possibility.

They wanted him here so he would not be somewhere else.

The timing gave it away; the messenger from Rolinor had arrived mere minutes after Black had departed. He had probably been waiting in the street, watching for that departure.

They wanted both Black and Arlian out of Obsidian House. The hired guards were still there, but presumably Rolinor's employers knew that and had planned accordingly.

Arlian was not absolutely certain what the target was, but it didn't really matter; he strode out the door before Rolinor could react.

"Stop him!" Rolinor called after him. "Stop that man!"

Arlian broke into a run.

At the Citadel gate he bellowed "Follow me!" and beckoned to the guards as he passed. He did not pause to see if they obeyed, but he could hear one of them asking the other "Was that Lord Obsidian?" as he passed.

They would follow, he was sure, but perhaps not immediately, and perhaps not certain whether they were aiding him or pursuing him. In any case, he did not trouble himself about that, but ran full-tilt down the street. He drew his sword as he rounded the old gatepost, and by the time he reached Obsidian House had his swordbreaker out, as well.

He could see as he approached that he had been right in his concern; the front door stood open, and one of the front windows had been smashed in. The hired guards were nowhere to be seen—and he saw one of the livery jackets discarded, as if tossed aside by someone fleeing.

He ran inside, calling, "Wolt! Venlin! Brook!"

No one answered, but he heard voices and a great clatter

ahead. He followed the sound across the great hall, under the balcony, and down the passageway toward the kitchens.

There were men in the Duke's white-and-blue uniforms there, men with drawn swords, and lying motionless on the floor by the wall was a figure in Arlian's own household livery, one of his footmen. He could not see the fallen man's face; the intruders' boots blocked his view. There was no sign anywhere of his caravan guards, no sign that anyone but the footman had opposed this invasion.

Arlian saw now a flaw in his own defenses—without their employer or his steward to rally them, his hirelings had not dared to defy the Duke's men. They might have fought well enough against ordinary assassins, but when confronted by the Duke of Manfort's own soldiers, they had apparently fled. No one had told them they might face Manfort's own defenders; the possibility had not occurred to Arlian.

These soldiers had no legitimate business here, though, regardless of their uniforms.

Arlian did not bother to give a warning or challenge; there was no need for questions. These men had invaded his property and struck down a member of his staff, and no matter what livery they wore he had the right to defend what was his. Instead of speaking, Arlian simply ran the nearest through as the guardsman turned to face the new arrival. His sword slid easily into the man's side, behind the breastplate, but as the man twisted and crumpled the armor tugged at the blade, and pulling it free took a few precious heartbeats. By the time Arlian had extracted his weapon and recovered his balance the entire party had had time to realize he was there.

So much, he thought, for the element of surprise. It had removed one foe, but he counted five still standing.

He was not motionless while counting, though; even as he pulled his sword free he was slashing with his sword-breaker, keeping the nearest unwounded invader off-balance. The man was still just beginning to bring his own blade around, fending off the swordbreaker, when Arlian's sword cut his throat. The intruder fell back, sword flailing, as his other hand clutched at his severed jugular. His slow collapse, combined with the motionless soldier on the floor, served to force the two sides apart momentarily.

The swordbreaker had been an effective distraction. Guardsmen were not ordinarily trained in two-bladed dueling tactics; their duties did not generally include fighting noblemen. Arlian knew that, and hoped to exploit it further.

All the same, right now he was standing in a corridor perhaps eight feet wide, facing four angry guardsmen alone, and there was definitely room for two of them to attack at once—perhaps three, if they coordinated their assault. The two he had taken down were not actually dead yet, and if the second could stanch the bleeding he might well be able to rejoin the fight. And all six wore breastplates.

Arlian had thought he would be facing assassins in the street, so he was not totally unprepared; he wore a mail shirt beneath his blouse, and his hat was lined with a steel cap. Still, his foes were better armored.

He wondered whether they were bright enough to keep him busy while one or two went down the corridor, up the back stairs, out to the balcony, and then down again, to surround him. So far they showed no sign of doing so.

"We've got him," one man said, as he faced Arlian. "You get on with it."

And that was the even worse possibility—that two of them would keep him busy while the others finished their assignment. It was possible that they were merely looking for the bottle of venom that stood on the kitchen shelf, but far more likely they were here to kill Brook and her unborn child.

But then why were they all bunched in the passageway? Arlian tried to peer past them, to see if Brook was there, perhaps caught between the soldiers and the kitchen door, but he could see no sign of her.

Then he realized where they were. The soldiers were standing in front of the lift that carried Brook and her wheeled chair from one floor to the other.

Then he had no time to worry about Brook as the two men nearest him attacked, almost simultaneously.

They weren't very good at it, fortunately; he was able to parry one sword with his own, the other with his sword-breaker, as he fell back a step. As they lunged again, not quite in unison, he turned sideways, letting one go past while catching the other's blade on his swordbreaker again. He had no good opening at side or head, and the breastplate protected the chest, but his own counterattack plunged his sword into the meaty part of the soldier's thigh.

"Damn you!" the man grunted, swinging wildly. Arlian, with one blade in the man's leg and the other fending off the other attacker, was unable to completely avoid the strike; the sword's tip slashed at his right arm just above the elbow, shredding the linen sleeve and scraping across the mail beneath. He was forced back a step, his back to the corridor wall.

Then the wounded man went down, his leg no longer able to support his weight. Under other circumstances Arlian would have given him a chance to surrender, or waited to see what happened, but with three more attackers he could not afford mercy. He thrust the point of his sword through the fallen man's eye.

Then he turned to face the others.

Two of them were coming after him, while the third was doing something at the door of the lift. He was reaching upward, jabbing his sword through the opening, and Arlian realized that the lift was between levels, its floor perhaps six feet up.

That had been clever of Brook, he thought, taking refuge there—but then he was too busy defending himself to think about anything but staying alive.

One of his opponents, the one who had been facing him all along, was no great threat, but the other proved to be the

best swordsman of the lot. Only Arlian's mail saved him
from one particularly smooth lunge at his heart; he was able
to turn so that the strike glanced across the rings instead of
penetrating, but had the metal not been there the blade
would have pierced his left lung.

The presence of the stone wall behind him was both good
and bad; it meant he did not need to worry about an enemy
behind him, but it limited his own movement, as well. He
could only retreat in one direction, toward the great hall.
That did give him an escape route if he needed one, though.

He heard movement from that direction, and wondered
whether it was some member of his staff coming to help.
None of them were trained swordsmen, but perhaps one
could go for help.

But who would they go to? These intruders were ostensibly the Duke's men, and Arlian's relationship with His
Grace had been sufficiently uneven that the staff could
scarcely be sure that the Duke had not sent them.

Arlian was quite sure that the Duke hadn't sent them; no,
if they were indeed the Duke's men, they had been bribed
by the Dragon Society. The Duke would have no reason to
want Brook dead; neither would any of his present advisors.
When last Arlian had spoken to the Duke they had parted on
good terms, with the Duke hopeful about Arlian's mysterious experiments, and Arlian had heard not the slightest hint
that the Duke's attitude had changed.

But Wolt and Stammer and the others wouldn't know
that.

Someone might fetch Black, though. That would be just
one more trained fighter, but Arlian had already cut the initial six-to-one odds in half, and one more might well be
enough to take them all. Black would certainly fight as
fiercely for his wife's life as anyone would ever fight for
anything.

If the servants were there this might be a good point to
break off the fight temporarily, retreat to the great hall and

regroup, perhaps hear whether Black was on the way—if Brook was still alive in the lift, as he fervently hoped, she could surely hold out another few seconds. His muscles tensed. He retreated a step, and risked a glance toward the great hall, hoping to see a familiar face there.

His heart sank.

There were three more of the Duke's guards, approaching with swords drawn.

He was surrounded.

42

A State of Siege

To one side were three live foes, two facing him and the third busily thrusting a sword into the lift; four men lay on the floor in that direction, either dead, dying, or dazed. To the other side three more enemies were drawing near. No help was in sight.

He had taken out three of them, but that was not a great comfort under the circumstances; there were still more than enough to kill both him and Brook. It seemed very likely that he was about to die.

The one comfort he did see in the situation was that this would clearly demonstrate to anyone who cared to investigate that someone—and that someone could only be the dragons or their servants—emphatically did not want Brook's child to be born. Somehow, the baby was a serious threat to them.

Black would know what had been done, and he could speak to Lord Zaner, to Lady Rime, to the Duke of Manfort; the scheme might still succeed even if Brook and Arlian died. Black would be devastated by the loss of his wife, but he would also want revenge. He had sometimes mocked Arlian's vengefulness, but losing Brook would surely be enough to ensure a ferocious desire to retaliate, even if it did not reach the level of Arlian's own obsession. He had said as much when they fought, just two days before.

But that assumed Black would survive, and Stammer or one of the others had almost certainly slipped out to fetch him. He might well walk directly into a trap. The Dragon Society would not have sent nine men just to intimidate a few servants and kill an unguarded pregnant cripple . . .

The Dragon Society would not have sent *nine* men at all; the Duke's guards worked in pairs. And where had these other three been when he first arrived?

All this had passed through Arlian's mind in a fraction of a second, and his instincts and training had simultaneously been preparing his next move—he turned and charged the new arrivals, shouting "Now!" as if he were leading a dozen men.

The three hesitated, as he had hoped—they presumably had no clear grasp of the situation, did not know what had happened or how many foes they might be facing, only that they had heard fighting and come to investigate. He was able to slice one man's neck, almost decapitating him, and then he was past them and out in the great hall.

He did not wait for them to react; instead he headed directly for the stairs.

That had to be where the three newcomers had been, and where a tenth man was, or perhaps several more men—upstairs, trying to get in the upper part of the lift as the half-dozen downstairs were trying to get in the lower. Arlian went bounding up the steps and into the corridor.

Sure enough, a soldier knelt at the lift door, thrusting a sword into the opening. Arlian did not hesitate, but charged forward and cut yet another throat. Blood sprayed across the floor and into the lift, and the man gave a ghastly croak as he crumpled.

"Damned breastplates," Arlian muttered, as he kicked the sword from the dying man's hand. Then he ducked down and peered into the lift.

It was dark, but as he had expected Brook's chair was wedged into a back corner, and Brook was crouched awkwardly upon it. She was on her knees on the seat, rather than in her usual sitting position, to keep her legs away from the sword thrusting at her from below; her swollen belly was clearly affecting her balance, and she had one hand on the wall, steadying her.

Arlian dropped his swordbreaker for a moment and grabbed up the sword he had just kicked away. He turned it, and shoved it hilt-first through the opening. "Brook, here!" he called. "Quickly!"

She looked up, startled. "Triv?" Then she saw the hilt and grabbed for it, reaching as far as she could without toppling over. Her fingers had barely closed on it when Arlian released it and withdrew again.

He would have liked to say something more to Brook, offer her encouragement, perhaps ask a question or two, but he did not have time; three soldiers had pursued him up the stairs. He snatched up his swordbreaker and rose to meet them.

They did not charge recklessly in, though; at the sight of him and their dying comrade they stopped, swords ready.

"He killed Sham," one of them said.

"He killed half the fellows downstairs, too," another agreed.

"Who is . . . Is he Lord Obsidian?"

"Of course he is, you fool!" the man in front said. "Who did you *think*?"

"Maybe that steward of his, the one who always wears black leather. We were warned about him."

"That's not leather, is it?"

"So he's Lord Obsidian," the leading soldier said. "He's still just one man, and there are three of us."

"There were *ten* of us a minute ago."

"And half of the others are still downstairs! Yes, he's dangerous, but we have him trapped."

"Trapped? Where does this corridor go?"

"He's the warlord. He's a dragonheart and a dragon-slayer." The soldier lowered his sword and stepped back. "I may want to live a thousand years, but I'm not going to if I get myself killed here. I'm out of this." He turned and walked away.

"Come back here!" the leader shouted.

"Rot with the dead gods," the other replied, as he started down the stairs at a trot.

"He's right," the next man said to the leader. "He can retreat down the back stairs and go to the Citadel. If we stay here we're dead."

"Filth is coming up the back stairs!" the leader shouted. "Just wait, and we'll have him . . ."

He didn't finish the sentence; Arlian knew an opportunity when he saw one, and attacked.

As he had hoped, the other soldier broke and ran, leaving his superior on his own.

The leader was a surprisingly good swordsman, though; he parried Arlian's thrusts easily, and even managed a riposte that sheared through a few links of mail before being deflected.

He had only the single blade, though; Arlian locked swords and closed, then stabbed his swordbreaker into the man's side, behind the breastplate.

The soldier's eyes went wide.

"Oh," he said. "But . . ."

Then he collapsed, and Arlian pulled his blade free, looking up and down the corridor.

Six dead, two fled, two still unaccounted for, he thought.

"Bitch," he heard someone say. He smiled. He headed for the back stairs.

When he opened the door and stepped into the passage-way he saw the two soldiers there; one was clutching his arm, trying to stop the flow of blood from a deep cut, while the other had a comforting arm around his shoulders. The wounded man was unarmed; the other still held his sword.

They looked up at the sound of the door, and saw Arlian standing there, both his two blades covered in blood. Then they looked at each other.

Then they broke and ran.

Arlian watched them go, then stepped up to the lift. "Brook?" he called. "Are you all right?"

"I think so," she said. "Are they all gone?"

"All the ones who can still walk," Arlian replied. He looked down at the bodies on the floor. None of them were moving; he did not see anyone breathing. Here was the one he had taken down with his first attack, stabbed in the side; his eyes were closed, so he had probably not died instantly, but he appeared to be dead. There was the first one with a cut throat, who seemed to have bled to death quickly; his blood-soaked hand was still pressed uselessly to the wound, his eyes star-ing sightlessly at the ceiling.

And there was Wolt, lying dead with stab wounds in his chest and gut, and a surprised expression on his face. He still held a kitchen knife in one hand.

"Damn," Arlian said. Then he looked at the lift. "They killed Wolt."

"I know," Brook said. "After your guards ran and the sol-diers broke in, he defended me, giving me time to get the lift moving."

"Oh." Arlian looked down at Wolt. The man had been a competent servant and a pleasant fellow, but Arlian had never suspected he had the courage to do such a thing.

"I'm sorry," he said. He looked up and down the passage, trying to decide what to do next.

This assault had failed, but it was by no means certain that there would be no more. The four surviving soldiers might regroup, or there might be a second enemy out there.

Arlian had survived dozens of assassination attempts, but Brook could not walk, could not fight—at eight months pregnant it sometimes seemed as if she could hardly move. If there were assassins, or more soldiers . . .

"We need to get you out of here," he said.

"Arlian," Brook said, "where are my children?"

Arlian turned, horrified. He had forgotten the children. "I don't know," he said. "Where were they?"

"I sent them to their rooms when the soldiers broke in," she said.

"Then that's almost certainly where they are. The soldiers didn't threaten them?"

"No. They probably just hadn't thought of it yet."

"Well, go on upstairs, then, and we'll check. I'll take the stairs and meet you . . ."

"I can't."

Arlian stopped and peered into the dim interior of the lift. "Why not?"

"Because I got out of my chair to use that sword you gave me, and I cut that man's arm with it, but now I can't get back up, and I can't reach the controls from down here."

"Oh." Arlian looked about helplessly.

The lift was a sort of open-sided box six feet on a side, and right now it was stopped about six feet up, its base four feet below the corridor's ten-foot ceiling, its roof a foot above the floor upstairs. The opening to the passage had a stone arch closing off the top portion, but that left a fair-sized gap where the soldiers had been jabbing at Brook.

"Can you fit through?" Arlian asked. "I can catch you and lift you down."

"What about my chair?"

"I don't . . ."

Just then he heard footsteps, and then Black's voice called, "Brook?" Arlian could hear a note of desperation.

"Here!" Arlian answered. "She's safe!"

Black appeared in the passage, not even glancing at the bodies on the floor; Stammer was close behind him.

"Help me get her out," Arlian said, gesturing at the lift. "Then we can lift Stammer in, and she can bring the chair down."

Black hurried to assist.

A few minutes later Brook was back in her chair, her children around her—Dirinan and Amberdine were crying uncontrollably as they clung to their mother, but they were otherwise unhurt. There was a small gash on Brook's shin where a sword had reached her, but that had been bandaged.

"You needn't worry about infection, at any rate," Arlian said. "The heart of the dragon does that much good."

Then he looked down the passage, at the corpses and the blood. "We can't stay here, though," he said. "We were lucky this time."

"Where will we go?" Brook asked, looking up from wiping Amberdine's tears.

"Someplace defensible," Arlian replied.

"Outside Manfort, perhaps?" Black suggested. "Where they can't find us as easily?"

"They can find Brook anywhere," Arlian said. "That's another thing about the heart of the dragon."

"They can? How?"

"The dragon that provided the venom will know. It must have known when she drank the elixir, and told Rolinor or some other agent through sorcery; there's no other way this could have happened. I'm sorry, Brook; I hadn't thought of that. I should have."

Black frowned at this, then said, "But still, here in Manfort . . ."

"Look out the window, Black," Arlian interrupted.

Black blinked. He glanced out at the great hall.

"Look at the sky. Feel the air."

"A storm is coming. What of it?"

"No storm," Arlian said. "Darkness and heat. They're preparing the way."

"The dragons?" Kerzia asked, her voice hushed. "The dragons are coming?" She looked from her mother to her father to the windows, then back to her father.

Arlian nodded. "And there are no defenses outside Manfort. We can't leave the city."

"Oh," Black said. "Well, they can't come here—the whole city is ringed with obsidian spearheads. It's men we need to fear."

"The Grey House?" Brook asked. "Are we going back there?"

Arlian gestured at the shattered window on the far side of the great hall. "They couldn't do that at the Grey House. It's a fortress."

"Agreed," Black said. "That should be safe." He glanced at his wife's belly. "And it shouldn't be for very long."

Arlian glanced as well, but said nothing.

The child would be born soon, yes—but wouldn't it need to grow up? Surely a mere baby could not be a serious threat to the dragons.

Black and his family might be hiding behind those fortress walls for years.

And there was the weather to consider—dragon weather. Yes, Manfort was heavily defended, with much of the world's supply of obsidian carved into weapons and bristling from the walls and rooftops—but the dragons *knew* that, yet the weather had turned hot and dark.

How desperate to kill Brook's child *were* they?

43

The Blades of the Dragon Society

*I*t took three hours to move Black, Brook, and their children back to the Grey House, but three days to clean up the mess at Obsidian House and relocate the remainder of the household. On the second of those days Arlian's presence at the Citadel was required by the Duke.

That was hardly a surprise; after all, half a dozen of the Duke's soldiers had died in Arlian's house, and the Duke knew that he had not ordered them there. It was only natural to want an explanation.

The explanation began in the audience chamber, but after a few minutes the two men retired to a private room, by mutual consent. Arlian gladly agreed to leave his weapons, and to submit to a brief search; under other circumstances he might have resented the lack of trust evident in such a request, but in this case he would have thought the Duke a fool *not* to want his guest disarmed. There had been altogether too many betrayals and assassins around of late.

Arlian had in fact considered the Duke to be a fool when first they met, but his opinion had moderated—or perhaps the Duke had gained a little wisdom with his years. Arlian still did not consider His Grace to be an intellectual master, but admitted the city's ruler had a modicum of common sense.

When the heavy oaken door had closed solidly behind them, the Duke turned to his guest. "Now, my lord," he said, "suppose you tell me what is happening in my city, and why you have not seen fit to keep me properly informed."

Arlian bowed. "My apologies, Your Grace. I have neglected my duties, as you say. In part I did so simply for lack of time to produce appropriate reports, but far more importantly, I feared that any word sent to your court, however you and I might endeavor to keep it private, would reach ears we would prefer not to hear it, or eyes we did not want to read it. I did not want my experiments compromised."

"You say my court is riddled with spies and traitors, then?" The Duke settled onto a blue-upholstered chair as he spoke.

"Alas, Your Grace, I do." Arlian took the room's only other chair, upholstered in deep red.

"And have you any evidence to support this accusation?"

"The corpses removed from Obsidian House would seem to be precisely that. These were men in your service, but *someone* had promised them the dragon-venom elixir if they slew my steward's wife."

"Your steward's *wife*? They were not assassins sent to kill *you*?"

"Indeed they were not."

"Why would anyone want to kill your steward's wife?"

Arlian explained, in detail.

When he had finished the Duke sat silently for a moment. Then he asked, "Do you *know* what this child will be?"

"No, Your Grace. I can only guess. However, the dragons may know—their servants certainly seem to be determined to prevent the birth."

"You assume it was they who sent those soldiers?"

"I do. One of the men explicitly mentioned that he had been promised dragon venom in payment for his services."

"The dragons may have good cause to fear this magical baby you have created. *We* might, as well, if we knew what it will become."

"Your Grace, can this child be any worse than a dragon or

wizard? We have the means to destroy any dragon or wizard. The kitten-creatures could be slain easily with a silver dagger."

"You are dragging all the Lands of Man into the unknown, my lord."

"Yes, Your Grace, I am. I feel the risks are justified. Imagine if all our realm's magic were held by our own children, children brought up in loving homes, taught everything we know of justice, of mercy—would not such a future be infinitely preferable to the reign of the dragons, demanding the annual sacrifice of an innocent village, or to the unpredictable chaos of uncontained magic?"

"Of course it would—I think. Or . . . We don't *know*, Obsidian."

"And the dragons are determined we never *will* know. I would prefer to see this third possibility, and make our own choice."

"Yes. Perhaps, yes." The Duke tugged thoughtfully at his beard.

"I have moved my steward's family to the Grey House, which is more easily defended than Obsidian House."

"You might bring her here, where we can all keep . . ."

"Your Grace," Arlian interrupted, "we have just discussed why the Citadel is not safe. Simply because you must permit so many people to come and go, you cannot know the heart of every man here, and the prospect of living for a thousand years is enough to tempt many who might otherwise be trustworthy."

The Duke considered that unhappily, then said, "We will post guards around the Grey House. They will not enter— you and your staff will see to that—but they will add another layer of safety."

Arlian was not entirely convinced of the wisdom of this, given that one group of the Duke's guards had so recently been suborned by the enemy, but he did not think it advisable to argue too strongly with the Duke, and certainly his own hired guards had proved completely worthless; accepting this measure would soothe the Duke's feelings. "That would be very welcome, Your Grace," he said.

"I will want to see this child, when it is born."

"I . . . Allow us a few days to be certain it is safe, and for the mother to recover her strength, and I am sure that can be arranged."

The Duke nodded, then grabbed the arms of his chair and pushed himself upright.

The audience was over.

By the third day of the relocation the first squad of guardsmen had taken up positions on the surrounding streets. Black had taken to wearing a sword and sword-breaker at all times; Arlian had always carried a sword when venturing out in public, but now he kept his weapons close at hand even in the house.

The first assassin was intercepted and killed on the fifth day.

It was on the sixth day, when the perimeter was solidly in place, that the first serious mass assault began.

The attackers had moved into position gradually— tradesmen leaning in doorways as if waiting for customers, whores standing on corners, farmers and merchants stopping wagons here and there. The soldiers, unsure of the nature of the threat they were there to confront, did not notice anything out of the ordinary until midafternoon, when the coach rolled up to the gate.

Then a lace-cuffed hand gestured from the window of the carriage. "You, sir," a voice called, "is this Lord Obsidian's home?"

The guard nearest the coach stepped up. "It is, my lord."

"Excellent." The carriage door opened and a man stepped out, a muscular figure clad in a fine green silk jacket, white lace at his throat, a jaunty wide-brimmed hat shading his features. "Open the gate, would you?"

"I cannot do that, my lord," the soldier said uneasily. "Let me send word of your arrival." He beckoned to the footman inside the gate, who stepped forward but did not lift the latch.

The nobleman frowned. "Is this really necessary?"

"I fear it is, my lord."

"Oh, very well. Tell Lord Obsidian that Lord Rhiador must see him at once, on a matter of great urgency."

The soldier bowed, and gestured to the footman. "You heard him."

The footman bowed, and hurried across the narrow fore-court.

Within the house, Brook and Arlian had been debating.

"I am not going to let you trap me up there!" Brook insisted.

"But on the third floor we can bar the door of your room, and any intruders will have to fight their way up the stairs past us."

"Bar the door? Do you mean to put me in *that* room? Sweet's prison?"

"I . . ."

"And will you remember to feed the prisoner, and make certain my chains do not chafe?"

"You will not be chained, nor in any way a prisoner . . ."

"If you bar that door I most certainly *will* be a prisoner, my lord! The bar is on the *outside*—had you forgotten?"

"I had thought that it might be relocated."

"Ari, this house has no lift, and I cannot take my chair up and down stairs without assistance. I tolerated that for years, but now that I have had a taste of life elsewhere my tolerance has worn very thin indeed. I appreciate the necessity for staying in this house, but I do *not* see why I should not remain on the ground floor, where I can move about as I please, where I can dine with my family, where I can, in the event of an emergency, call out a window to the Duke's guards."

"They are all outside the wall," Arlian pointed out. "I did not allow them in the yard."

"I can shout loud enough to be heard, I assure you."

Arlian glared at her for a moment, but before he could say anything more he was distracted by a polite cough. He turned to see a footman standing in the door of the room. "Yes?"

"My lord, a gentleman giving his name as Lord Rhiador wishes to speak to you."

Arlian frowned. "Rhiador?"

"Yes, my lord."

"I don't recognize the name."

"He said it was a matter of great urgency."

Arlian sighed. "I will be out in a moment," he said. He looked at Brook, then at Black, who stood nearby. "You have said little, Black."

"My wife can speak for herself, my lord."

"Then you agree with her?"

"I do. She is a capable woman, not something to be locked away in a vault."

"Capable? She has no feet!"

"She has a brain and two good arms. She has never learned the sword, but she has considerable skill with a knife."

"She is heavy with child, and consequently clumsy!"

"Ari, she survived the previous attack well enough."

"Because I returned in time!"

"I could have held out for some time in that lift!" Brook protested.

"Fine!" Arlian flung up his arms. "Fine. Do as you please. I will go speak with this Lord Rhiador, and see what new complications have arisen." He turned, and marched toward the gate.

A moment later he looked out through the bars at his visitor. He did not recognize the green-coated nobleman, though something about him seemed uncomfortably familiar. "Ah, Lord Obsidian!" the new arrival said, holding out a hand. "May I come in?"

"You have the advantage of me, my lord," Arlian replied. "I do not recall your face."

"Oh, I have not previously had the pleasure of your acquaintance, my lord; I have only seen you from a distance, in the Citadel and in Ethinior."

"Ethinior?"

"At the masked ball."

"Indeed." Arlian still did not reach for the proffered hand, and Rhiador let it fall. "And why have you come to see me?"

"I believe I have news of certain activities that will be of great interest to you."

"Oh?"

"Yes."

"Whose activities?"

"Lord Shatter's. Could we go inside, perhaps, and speak in private?"

Arlian considered this—he had no particular reason to distrust Rhiador, but at this particular moment he was inclined to distrust *everyone,* and he had no recollection of ever encountering Lord Rhiador or his name prior to this meeting, so he had no reason to trust him. This person could well be an assassin.

And quite aside from such rational concerns, something about the man simply made him uneasy.

Arlian was, however, curious as to what Lord Shatter, nominal head of the Dragon Society, might be up to, and the house was surrounded by the Duke's guards—men chosen for their trustworthiness, and in such numbers that they could not *all* have been suborned.

"No," Arlian said. "However, I will come out to your coach, if you like."

Lord Rhiador was visibly disconcerted, but then spread his hands. "Of course," he said. He stepped back from the gate, to give Arlian room.

Arlian opened the gate left-handed, keeping his right hand on the hilt of his sword, and stepped out—and as he did, Rhiador bellowed, "Now!"

Arlian whirled, astonished, his sword in hand. He had half expected Rhiador to draw a blade, and in fact the nobleman did draw both sword and swordbreaker, but all around them other weapons appeared, as tradesmen, whores, and beggars suddenly brandished knives and clubs and fell upon the unprepared soldiers. Arlian had not anticipated *that*.

And then the rooftop archers began to shoot.

Arlian ducked, blade coming up to defend against Rhiador's attack—but Rhiador was circling, not attacking.

Other people were attacking—the coach's driver had jumped down, sword out, and charged Arlian, and two footmen had appeared from somewhere behind the vehicle, as well. Arlian's back was to the gatehouse wall as he drew his swordbreaker and met this assault.

His sword crossed with the driver's blade, parrying a slash that Arlian judged either was intended merely to intimidate, or indicated that the man was no swordsman. He attempted a riposte, and discovered a third possibility—that the blow had been meant to lure him in. He ducked and twisted as the driver's sword struck where his right eye had been an instant before, then countered with a thrust that put his own sword's tip through the driver's left shoulder.

The man stepped back, but kept his sword up, while the two footmen moved in with their own blades. These were not the finely honed and balanced swords used by dueling lords, but the shorter, heavier, clumsier weapons wielded by hired guards or simple thugs. They would be little real threat to Arlian individually, but facing three men at once was a serious challenge.

And then he remembered that he had been facing *four* men, and he quickly glanced to his left.

Lord Rhiador, whoever he really was, clearly had his own mission—he had slipped out of Arlian's reach and opened the gate. The footman who had been tending it, a man named Hendal, had tried to stop him, and now lay on the ground, red spreading across his chest as he gasped out his life. Rhiador was running across the forecourt.

The door of the house was closed, but Arlian could not

recall whether he had locked it. He had thought he was coming out here to speak to a guest, not fend off an assault, and he had been distracted by his argument with Black and Brook—*could* he have left it open?

An arrow snapped loudly against the gatepost above his head, and he remembered that the house had been surrounded by the Duke's soldiers. He could not see much from his sheltered position in the gateway, but he could hear orders being shouted, men screaming, metal striking metal and flesh and stone.

The guards had not been instantly overwhelmed, at any rate—from the bellowed orders, they seemed to be holding their own.

And they were all there for a single purpose—to protect Brook and her child. That was Arlian's own purpose, as well—and Rhiador was inside the wall, and in a moment would be inside the house.

Arlian feinted, then turned and ran into the narrow stone-paved yard, breaking off his duel with the other three men from the coach; the driver promptly pursued him. The footmen hesitated; then first one, then the other, followed.

Rhiador, his hands made awkward by the blades he still held, was struggling with the door latch; at the sound of running feet he turned to see what was happening—and saw Arlian suddenly turn aside, running *across* the yard, rather than toward him.

He plainly had no idea why Arlian would do that, but he accepted the gift, and turned his attention back to the door.

Meanwhile, Arlian had looped back toward the wall as the driver charged after him, and was now able to approach the gate from the other side, stepping over his dying servant's body to slam the heavy iron framework shut. He threw the bolt, and called through it, "Captain! Guard this gate at all costs!"

There was an instant's hesitation, and then the commander of the defenders replied, "Yes, my lord!"

Then Arlian turned toward his attackers, fending off a quick thrust by the coachman's blade.

He stood with his back to the gatepost again, but now he was inside the wall, in the narrow yard of the Grey House, with the only gate securely closed, facing just three opponents.

The fourth, Lord Rhiador, had finally managed to force open the door and slip inside, and Arlian hoped desperately that Black and the rest of the staff would be able to deal with him. For the moment Arlian had quite enough to keep him busy here.

He looked at the driver, wrapped in a dark gray cloak, and at the footmen, and belatedly recognized the latter's livery.

These were Lord Hardior's men.

Rhiador. Hardior.

Arlian cursed his own stupidity as he launched an attack on the coachman. "A glamour," he said. "He bought a glamour." He made a lunge at the driver's already-injured left shoulder, and the man shied away, leaving a brief opening; Arlian's swordbreaker came across and slashed a deep cut into the coachman's belly.

Then the lefthand footman came up, sword slashing; Arlian turned aside from the driver long enough to feint at the footman's belly with the swordbreaker, and when the man stepped back, lowering his blade to defend himself, Arlian's sword caught him in the throat.

The tip of the blade caught in a fold of flesh, and Arlian ripped it sideways, slashing the man's neck. The footman's scream was drowned in a gout of blood, and he fell backward, thrashing in agony, as Arlian turned his attention back to the other two.

The driver was seriously wounded now, in both shoulder and gut, and the other footman was clearly not as recklessly brave as his companions; they did not attack.

Both of them were inside the gate, though, and Arlian could not afford to leave them alive. He feinted toward the footman, who backed away obligingly; then Arlian jabbed his swordbreaker backhanded into the driver's upper arm.

The coachman's sword fell from his hand, and he sank to his knees.

Arlian left him kneeling on the stone, weeping and bleeding, while he chased the footman down and ran him through the heart. The man fell against the side of the house, the heavy sword tumbling from his hand; then he crumpled to the pavement, dead before he reached the ground.

Arlian turned, to see the driver struggling to his feet and reaching for the gate.

"Damn," Arlian said, sprinting back.

The coachman heard him coming and turned, and as Arlian watched, his face seemed to melt and reshape itself. He, too, had worn a glamour, one that had now been broken.

He was unarmed; his sword lay on the stone, and he had had no swordbreaker. He raised empty hands above his head.

Arlian really did not much care at this point whether or not the coachman wanted to surrender; the man was much too close to the gate, and others were still fighting just the other side of the bars. He prepared to skewer the man—but then he recognized the face that had been revealed when the spell broke, and turned his killing stroke at the last instant, instead placing the blade across the invader's throat and forcing him up against the wall.

"Lord Shatter, I believe," he said. "How long has it been—sixteen years? Seventeen?"

"Obsidian," Shatter gasped, clutching his belly with blood-soaked hands. "I'm bleeding."

"Yes, you are," Arlian said. "You're bleeding poisonous blood I offered to cleanse for you."

"I didn't want to die."

"Oh, you are *going* to die, Shatter; the only question is when. Unless you want it to be right here and now, you will answer every question I ask."

"I'll bleed to death."

"Quite possibly. If you answer me quickly enough, there might still be time to bandage yourself."

"I'll answer anything, please. . . ."

"What are you doing here? Why is Lord Hardior here? How did you get here from Sarkan-Mendoth?"

"We've been near Manfort for weeks," Shatter gasped. "When the dragons awoke and found you had visited their lair without killing them, they demanded we learn why. We sent spies, but then when the first reports came the dragons demanded we come ourselves, to oversee . . ."

"What did they want?"

"The venom you took."

"Why?"

"To prevent . . . to prevent what you've done."

"And what have I done?"

"You've . . . you've re-created their ancient foe, they said. I don't know what they mean. Please, Obsidian . . ."

"Re-created?" Arlian considered that. He had assumed that Brook's child would be something *new,* and that the dragons either feared the unknown or knew somehow what that new thing would be and feared it—but instead, he had *re-created* something the dragons feared?

How could that be?

"I don't know what they mean," Shatter said, "but if we hadn't come to kill the woman they would have destroyed *us.* I've never seen them like this. I don't know what you've done, but the dragons are willing to risk everything, *everything* to stop you—they had us use every agent and spy and traitor we had in this attack . . ."

"I'm sorry, Shatter," Arlian said, as he drew his sword across the dragonheart's throat and plunged his swordbreaker into the man's heart.

The blood that spilled from Shatter's heart smoked and bubbled in a thoroughly unnatural fashion; Arlian knew that to be a sign that that heart had become more dragon than man.

Arlian still did not entirely understand what was happening, but if Shatter had told the truth—and how could Arlian doubt it?—then preserving Brook's life was even more important than he had realized, and he could not afford to waste another second here.

Nor could he leave Shatter alive behind him, to open the gate or slip a blade into someone's unguarded back.

He turned away from the agonized, betrayed terror in Shatter's dying eyes, and ran for the door.

44

To Defend the Grey House

*R*hiador—or Hardior, as he almost certainly was—had left the door of the Grey House standing open; Arlian dashed inside, bloody blades at the ready, and closed the door behind him, dropping the bar into place.

He did not need to guess where to go from there; he could hear the clash of steel. He hurried through the archway, around the corner and down the gallery.

A chair was overturned, a rug kicked aside, but the gallery was uninhabited. A smear of blood stained the floor, and the sound of swords echoed from the walls. Arlian ran its length, then turned left, into the large salon in the northwest corner.

Hardior whirled to face him.

The glamour had broken; this man wore the green silk jacket and lace at the throat, but his face was Hardior's familiar features, rather than the Rhiador mask. He had lost his hat somewhere, and a slash across one cheek was bleeding, but he showed no other sign of injury. He held sword and swordbreaker, with blood on both blades.

Behind him stood Black. His left hand hung lifeless and empty, covered in blood, but his right still held a sword at the ready. His black silk blouse was in tatters, his black leather vest hanging open and loose.

Brook was nowhere in sight, which relieved Arlian. She must have fled farther into the depths of the house.

Arlian had no breath to spare for words; he lunged.

Hardior parried and stepped aside, turning his back to the nearest wall, but not in time; Black's thrust took him in the side and sank deep.

Hardior's swordbreaker swooped down, quillons locking around Black's blade, and before Black could withdraw the sword Hardior twisted his weapon.

Black's blade snapped off short, and a chunk of bloody steel flew across the room and rang from the stone of the far wall. The hilt and a foot-long stump remained in Black's grasp, and a few inches were still embedded in Hardior's body, but the middle portion was gone.

Black staggered, and Hardior jabbed at him with the swordbreaker while his sword fended off Arlian.

"Are there any more?" Black asked, gasping.

"Not yet," Arlian said, "but there were more outside the gate, and they may get through."

"Can you hold him while I find another sword?"

"Do we *have* another sword?"

"A spear, then—can you hold him?"

"Yes."

"Good." Black flung the broken stump at Hardior, then staggered away, toward the door to the north corridor. Hardior lunged for him, but found Arlian's blades intervening and retreated again.

"You might find a dropped sword in the yard," Arlian suggested.

"I might, at that," Black agreed, as he vanished through the door.

"I doubt he'll live that long," Hardior said. "He's losing a great deal of blood."

Arlian made a quick, low attack, which Hardior countered easily. "I'm surprised," he said. "I had thought Black to be a good swordsman."

"He has the skills," Hardior replied, as he made a swift series of feints, "but he is slowing with age, and he was at a disadvantage in that he was constantly diverted by his whore. He could not circle around, or do anything that would allow me past and through the door."

Arlian's wordless riposte took the tip off Hardior's right ear. He remembered how he had maneuvered past Black himself, not so very long ago, and mentally cursed himself.

"Clever, that chair of hers," Hardior said, as his attempted counter sliced the air by Arlian's hip.

"Black's invention," Arlian said, as his swordbreaker slipped past Hardior's defenses—but at such a reach that there was no power behind the blow, and the tip penetrated no more than half an inch into Hardior's chest, scraping futilely across a rib.

After that they fought in silence for a time, exchanging blows but inflicting no real damage upon one another. Arlian was dismayed; he had thought himself the better swordsman, but Hardior was holding his own well.

The knowledge that this battle might not be decisive, that even if he killed Hardior the mob outside might overcome the guards, force the gate, and storm the house nagged at the back of Arlian's mind; he ignored it to concentrate on the fight at hand, since after all, if Hardior won it would not matter whether the mob got in—the dragonheart was quite capable of killing Brook himself.

"Why is this so important to the dragons?" Arlian asked at last, as yet another thrust was turned aside. "What are they afraid of?"

"I don't know," Hardior said. "I don't care. I know where my interests lie."

"You were not always so certain."

"I learned my place." Another exchange of blows sent a table tumbling and sliced into an embroidered drapery. "I am the Duke of Sarkan-Mendoth, Obsidian—I know which side I am on."

"You call yourself a duke, yet you are running errands for the dragons as if you were no more than a lackey."

"The dragons are the masters of this land, Obsidian—since the gods died they have been the greatest power we know. We all live at their sufferance."

"Not in Manfort," Arlian retorted. "*Our* duke, a duke by right and by birth and not merely in self-proclaimed name, has seen to that. He has defended us against them, rather than giving us over into their power."

"And do you think those stone weapons will stop them, if they choose to come?" Hardior retorted. "You have slain the old and sick among dragons, the newborn, and the mad—do you think your obsidian will be enough against their best?" And as he spoke, he stumbled.

That was the opening Arlian had awaited; he thrust, knowing he was leaving himself open as he did so. Hardior's sword speared upward through Arlian's shoulder, but Arlian's blade ran the elder directly through his heart.

Hardior was at least a century younger than Shatter; there was only the faintest wisp of smoke, no sickly rippling, but the blood that ran up Arlian's blade did seem to twist and flow oddly at first.

"Yes," Arlian said, as he pressed the sword home. "Yes, I do think obsidian and human courage will be enough." To be sure of his victory, he sliced Hardior's throat with his swordbreaker before pulling the sword from his foe's heart.

Hardior's collapse pulled the sword from Arlian's shoulder, and Arlian was suddenly aware of the pain; he dropped his own weapons, staggered back, and sat down hard on a nearby sofa.

He was struggling to catch his breath, trying to stanch the bleeding with his hand, when he heard the unmistakable cry of a woman in pain.

"Damn," he said, forcing himself back on his feet. He stumbled through the door to the corridor, then realized he was unarmed. He turned, retrieved his dropped sword, and then headed down the corridor, wiping the blade on a handkerchief as he went. He left the swordbreaker where it lay; with his wounded shoulder he could not wield a second blade effectively in any case.

The cries had stopped; he paused in the corridor, then called, "Brook! Where are you?"

He could not make out the words of her reply, but he was able to follow the sound well enough, and found her slumped, panting in her chair in the courtyard.

"What are you doing out here?" he asked, looking around. "What's wrong?"

"Avoiding being cornered," she said. "Ari, where's Black?"

"He went to check the gate. Are you wounded?"

"Send for the midwife," Brook answered.

"Oh." He had thought the baby was not due for at least a fortnight, but he knew that babies came when they chose, and Brook was experienced enough to know the signs; he did not waste time arguing. He glanced around, then bellowed, "Venlin!"

"*You're* wounded," she said, staring at his shoulder and the blood seeping around his hand.

"I was aware of that," he said. "Venlin!"

The ancient footman finally appeared. "Yes, my lord?" he asked.

"Where is everyone?"

"Forgive us, my lord—we took refuge up in the servants' hall."

"Good. No one's hurt?"

"Only Hendal, the gatekeeper."

"I saw him; I'm sorry. Send someone for the midwife, if you can get someone out safely. Is the fighting still going on?"

"I don't know, my lord."

"Find out. Send for the midwife. Is Lilsinir with you?"

"I believe she is upstairs on the third floor, my lord."

"Send someone up to fetch her and her physician's supplies; my steward's wounds need immediate attention."

"Yes, my lord." Venlin turned and trotted away. Arlian called after him, "Send Stammer out here to stay with Brook!" Then he turned to Brook and said, "I must go, but I'll return as quickly as I can." He managed a sickly smile. "I want to see this child of yours that has our foes so concerned!"

"Go find Black," Brook said. "And the midwife."

Arlian nodded, and then winced as the pain in his shoulder worsened. At least, he thought, he need not worry about infection; dragonhearts were immune. That did not lessen the discomfort, though.

He turned and hurried toward the nearest door to the gallery.

A moment later he was in the forecourt, where he headed for the gate. A step from the door he broke into a run—Black was sitting on the pavement, his back against the gatehouse.

Even as he ran, Arlian's ears registered the comparative silence—no screams, no clashing blades, no rattle of arrows. The battle was clearly over.

Men were still shouting orders to one another, though.

"Lord Obsidian!" someone called.

"Just a moment," Arlian said, as he knelt at Black's side.

Black was still breathing, but that breath was shallow and unsteady. Arlian frowned unhappily. He looked up through the bars.

The captain of the guard company was standing there looking worried. "My lord," he said, "what's happening?"

"The house is safe," Arlian said. He glanced at Hendal's body, still lying untended a few feet away, and the bodies of Lord Shatter and Hardior's two footmen. "Four men got through the gate, and all four were killed, as was one of my own men. My steward is grievously wounded."

"You're bleeding, too," the captain said.

"Lord Hardior's blade went through my shoulder," Arlian agreed.

"Your steward came out and asked our situation, but then he sat down . . ."

"He's unconscious," Arlian confirmed, as he tugged the bloody remains of Black's shirt away from the wounds and studied them. "And yourself and your men? What's happened?"

"Whoever those attackers were, they turned and ran," the captain said. "We killed a few, captured a few, and lost eleven of our own. Most of my men are out trying to apprehend the foe's archers as they come down from the rooftops."

"Good. Do you have a physician, perhaps? Bandages? Water?"

"I'll see. But my lord, you must open the gate."

Arlian looked up, startled.

For a moment he wondered whether this was a trick, whether the captain was in the pay of the Dragon Society, come to kill Brook—but no, he told himself, they were not *that* clever, to stage this entire battle and sacrifice Hardior and Shatter merely to get their man through the gate. In retrospect, it amazed him that they had been so careless with the lives of two senior dragonhearts.

The dragons clearly did not merely fear Brook's child; they were apparently in absolute terror of it, to risk so much.

"I want it heavily guarded," Arlian said. "And none of your men are to enter the house under any circumstances save my direct order."

"The physician cannot work through the bars; I have no need to allow anyone else beyond the gate."

"Good." Arlian rose, and with trembling fingers slid back the bolt. He stepped back, opening the gate—and kept his sword ready in his hand.

The captain stepped in, took one look at Black, then turned and bellowed, "Leather, where's the physician? We've got a badly wounded man here!"

"Thank you," Arlian said, letting his sword drop. "Thank you, Captain."

Then, overcome by weariness, he sat down suddenly on the stone of the forecourt, staring at the blood on the pavement and realizing that some of it was his own.

That stirred him to a final effort. "Captain," he said, "the blood—some of it is tainted."

The captain had been cleaning Black's wounds, but now he snatched his hands away. "Dragonhearts?"

Arlian nodded. "Myself, and that one," he said, pointing at Shatter.

"Not your steward?"

"No." Arlian smiled. "He's no dragonheart; he's about to be a father."

Then he closed his eyes and rested.

45

An Exceptional Birth

Despite Arlian's concerns and Brook's urgency, the next few hours were calm. The midwife arrived in good time, and while Lilsinir and the guards' physician attended to Black and Arlian, the midwife saw to Brook, getting her out of her chair and onto a bed.

The children were permitted to visit briefly with their parents, just to be reassured that both Brook and Black were still alive, and were then hustled off to the kitchens in Stammer's care, to await the arrival of their new sibling. Amberdine was clearly aghast at her father's condition and broke down in tears; Kerzia attempted to comfort her while fight-

ing back her own tears, and Dirinan took one look, then
buried his face in Stammer's shoulder and refused to hear
or see anything more.

The household staff removed Hardior's remains and began the unwelcome task of cleaning up the salon and
gallery. Venlin, with the aid of a few carefully chosen soldiers, removed the corpses from the yard, as well—Hendal,
Shatter, and Hardior's two footmen. This labor, which
would not have been pleasant under any circumstances, was
made worse by the oppressive heat and heavy overcast; the
lamps were lit half an hour before sunset, as the skies were
already as dark as night.

More soldiers were cleaning up the surrounding streets,
and questioning the prisoners they had taken—most of
them rooftop archers. Arlian was very interested in hearing
what these interrogations produced, but could not partici-
pate, or even spare the time to hear reports; there were more
immediate concerns occupying his attention.

His own injuries were inconvenient, but not life-
threatening; as a dragonheart he had no fear of infection, of
fever or gangrene. The wound in his shoulder was the only
serious one, and even that would undoubtedly heal in a fortnight or so; for the present it limited the motion of his right
arm, restricting any attempt to swing the arm above the hor-
izontal and making any sort of lifting painful. Blood loss
had left him mazy and weak; the physician had treated this
by feeding him three pints of thin beer, to replenish the fluids he had lost, which undoubtedly helped his body but did
not initially make his thoughts any clearer.

Black's condition was more serious; he had lost more
blood than Arlian, and had no real protection against fever
or decay. Further, he was not conscious and could not drink
anything of his own volition; Lilsinir managed to force
some water down his throat without choking him, and thoroughly cleaned the numerous wounds, but could do little
more. After some debate among Brook, Arlian, Lilsinir, the

guards' physician, and the midwife, Black's unconscious body was arranged on a couch in Brook's bedroom, a few feet from his laboring wife's side.

"When he is past the worst, I have healing herbs, some minor magicks, that will help," Lilsinir told Arlian. "For now, we wait."

And Brook was definitely in labor, the baby descended into position, contractions coming at steadily narrowing intervals. She had been through this before, and knew what to do, but nonetheless she looked at Arlian with fear plain on her sweat-drenched face.

"What if it's a monster?" she said, when the midwife was out of the room fetching towels. "I lost two babies, and that was horrible, but they were just babies—what if this is something else? I'm not sure whether I'm more afraid that it will die or that it will live. Ari, what have we *done*?"

"We've terrified the dragons," he said, holding her hand.

"What?"

"We've frightened the dragons. Shatter and Hardior said as much."

"Shatter?" She snatched her hand away. "Lord Shatter, chairman of the Dragon Society? Was he here?"

Arlian nodded. "I cut his throat," he said. "He's dead."

"And that really was Lord Hardior? His face changed, and I didn't know which one was real."

"That was Lord Hardior. He used a glamour to disguise himself, so he could enter the city safely, much as I did when I rescued you in Cork Tree." He paused, then added, "He's dead, too. A thrust through the heart."

"But why were *they* here?"

"The dragons sent them. They didn't trust any mere hirelings or henchmen; they sent their own best men. We have the dragons terrified."

"But *why*? What am I bearing? What is so terrible . . ." She was interrupted by a contraction; she grimaced.

"Shatter said we have re-created the dragons' greatest foe," Arlian said.

"But what *is* it?"

The midwife returned just then; Arlian glanced at her, and said, "I cannot be certain—but I do not think we need fear it."

"Don't frighten her," the midwife said briskly. "She has quite enough to do without worrying about anything but herself for the next few hours."

"I know," Arlian replied. He patted Brook's hand. "All will be well, Brook. You do what you must, and let others deal with the rest."

The hours wore on, and Arlian remained nearby, ignoring the midwife's obvious disapproval. Lilsinir and the guards' physician stopped in to check on Black once or twice, but were too busy attending the other wounded from the battle outside the walls to stay.

Arlian listened uneasily to Black's breathing, which seemed to stay dangerously shallow.

And then, late in the night, when Arlian had lost track of time and dozed fitfully, the baby finally arrived.

Arlian had somehow expected something to go wrong, something else to intervene, or at the very least signs and portents to accompany the birth, but none of that happened; instead Brook gave a final gasp, and the midwife held up a wrinkled, blood-smeared boy, so red he seemed to glow in the lamplight. She hastily toweled the babe off, and he let out a strong, healthy wail as the midwife handed him to Brook.

The child was small, but seemed well formed, with the appropriate number of fingers and toes. Arlian, standing by the bed, stared at mother and child, looking for any sign that the infant was something other than human; then he turned to the father.

Black was still sleeping, though he had stirred at the child's cry. The boy was silent now, nuzzling at his mother's breast, though he did not take the proffered nipple.

Brook looked up at Arlian. "His name is Ithar," she said. "Beron and I agreed."

"Ithar?" Arlian said. "That's fine."

"It's a good name," the midwife agreed, as she tidied up.

"He seems . . . I don't see anything . . . He's just a baby," Brook said. She looked down at her son, then back at Arlian. "What were the dragons afraid of?"

"I don't know," Arlian said. Then he turned at a sound behind him.

Black had awakened, and sat up on the couch; he was staring at Brook.

"Don't get up," Arlian warned.

"Wasn't planning to," Black mumbled.

Arlian turned back to Brook and held out his hands; smiling, she handed him the baby.

Ithar opened his eyes and looked up at Arlian, and for a moment Arlian was transfixed.

The baby's eyes were intensely blue, and gave off a soft, pale light. This was no optical trick, no mere illusion; the boy's eyes were glowing.

Arlian blinked, and then remembered where he was and what he was doing; he turned and took two quick steps, then held the child out for Black to see. "You have another son," he said.

Ithar looked solemnly up at his father with those glowing blue eyes, then reached out one tiny, unsteady hand. Black smiled weakly and leaned forward, letting the little fingers brush his beard.

The weariness suddenly seemed to fall away from him; color rushed back into his cheeks. He swayed, then looked down. He and Arlian watched as the bandages fell from his wounds, and the flesh beneath healed as they watched. The glow from Ithar's eyes and hands was unmistakable, undeniable—the newborn infant was working powerful magic.

Healing magic. Benign magic.

Arlian's experiment, it would appear, was a success.

Ithar gurgled, then closed his eyes and fell asleep in Arlian's arms.

"By the dead gods," Black said, looking down at himself.

And Arlian remembered what Shatter and Hardior had said, how the experiment was re-creating the dragons' greatest foe, and remembered also what the leech-thing in Tirikindaro had told him almost two years before about how the dragons had betrayed and murdered their greatest foes ten thousand years ago.

Black lifted his hands, and Arlian handed him his sleeping child.

"Not the dead gods, but the living," Arlian said.

Black looked up at him. "What do you mean?"

"Congratulations," Arlian said, grinning. "You're the father of a god."

The Gods

46

The Final Assault Begins

It was on the day following Ithar's birth that the second and final mass assault began.

The day had started quietly, with various people coming to admire the new baby, and with some exploration of the newborn's supernatural abilities. Ithar's touch, they found, could heal his father's wounds, or the injuries of soldiers and servants, but did nothing for Arlian's shoulder, nor for the aftereffects of his own birth—the midwife had tended to Brook unaided by divine magic.

"We're dragonhearts," Arlian explained to Brook later that morning—a morning as hot and sunless as any Arlian had ever seen. "His natural enemies. Tainted."

"But I'm his mother!"

"Tainted nonetheless."

"Then get Lilsinir in here and purify me!"

"When you have your strength back."

Brook reluctantly accepted that, then returned her attention to Ithar, asleep at her breast. "I have no milk," she said. "I suppose that's from the venom, too."

"Almost certainly."

"We'll need a wet nurse; I'm surprised he hasn't been crying about it."

"He may not need a wet nurse, nor milk," Arlian said. "He is something more than human, after all."

"A god, you called him."

"I think he is, yes."

"That seems . . . audacious, even for you, Arlian. He's so

tiny—I think he's smaller than his brother or either of his sisters was. How can he be a god? A god, born of man and woman?"

"A god born of man and woman, and of a dragon and the land's own power."

"Is that what you expected, when you gave me the elixir? That my child would be a god?"

"No; I thought he would be a magician, of sorts. It was not until the dragons' own men came to kill him that I began to suspect he would be more."

Brook glanced at the room's one narrow window, which gave so little light that even at midmorning the oil lamps were still lit. The air was hot and heavy, thick with the odors of smoke and sweat. "I think the dragons will be sending more than men to kill him."

"I am not at all sure how he can be killed," Arlian said, "but I agree—they must certainly know he has been born, but the clouds have not dispersed, nor the weather moderated. This is undeniably dragon weather. They killed the gods long ago, and must intend to kill Ithar in the same fashion. Still, how can they hope to get at him, here in Manfort, behind the city walls? The Duke's catapults are everywhere; a hundred tons of obsidian blades guard us."

Black had entered the room as Arlian spoke, and asked, "But are the catapults manned?"

Arlian turned, startled. "Are they not?"

"They were not yesterday, else the attackers could never have placed those archers on the rooftops without being seen. I doubt the Duke has the manpower to keep even the outer catapults manned on a regular basis; I think he's assuming we will have warning of any impending threat."

"Warning?" Arlian gestured at the window. "Is not that sky warning enough?"

"The Duke's men are searching the city for the Dragon Society's agents, following up yesterday's action," Black said. "I doubt anyone has given the possibility of a direct attack from above much thought."

"Damn!" Arlian turned and almost ran from the room.

He had not yet reached the Citadel's gates when the screaming began; he took one look at the sky to the northwest and turned back, running toward the Grey House. He paused at the gate to order the surrounding cordon of guards to spread the word and man the catapults, then burst in the door shouting, "The dragons are coming!"

The household came alive with shouting and scurrying as Arlian hurried down the gallery toward Brook's room.

Black emerged as Arlian approached the bedroom door. "What's happening?" he demanded.

Arlian still found it slightly disconcerting to see Black upright and active, so soon after his miraculous healing, so his answer was not as coherent as he might have wished.

"Dragons," he said. "Four of them."

"Where?"

"Northwest," Arlian replied, pointing and almost whacking his hand on the stone wall of the passageway as his injured arm failed to obey him properly.

Black blinked at him. "Flying?"

"Yes, flying," Arlian said. "How else would they come?"

"The rooftops of Manfort are covered with obsidian-tipped spears," Black pointed out. "Four dragons do not seem so very great a menace when we have those defenses. No, they are not all properly manned, but surely enough will be ready to handle four dragons! I had thought perhaps they might approach by land—the catapults cannot be accurately aimed into the streets, and we would need to fight them with spears."

"They are flying, nonetheless," Arlian said. "And I fear I have less faith in the abilities of the people and machines defending us than you do. I have been fighting dragons my entire adult life, and I think I know something about the job, and I do not care to rely entirely on the catapults."

"And what do you propose to do, then? Were you coming here to ask my son to use his divine powers to protect us?"

"Of course not," Arlian said, startled. "God or not, he's

still a newborn babe. And he's also what the dragons are coming to kill—to bring him more directly to their attention would be insane."

"But Ari, you *are* insane, are you not?"

"By the dead gods, even I am not so mad as *that*! No, I've come to move Brook and Ithar to the cellars, where the dragons cannot get at them even if they pass the walls and avoid the spears."

Black nodded. "The other children, too," he said.

"A good thought. I'll take Brook and Ithar; you fetch the others." Then he hesitated, looking at his arm. "No," he said, "you take Brook—I can't lift her with my shoulder like this. I'll bring the others."

A few minutes later the two men were on the stairs leading down from the kitchen into the cellars; Black held Brook in his arms, while she held Ithar. Arlian was leading Dirinan by the hand, while Kerzia and Amberdine wrestled their mother's wheeled chair down the stone steps. Stammer had gone ahead with a candle.

"At least it's cooler down here," Brook said, as she wrapped Ithar more securely in his blanket.

It was, indeed, cooler in the cellars than in the unseasonable heat above, though perhaps not as cool as Arlian might have expected. As they reached the foot of the stair Arlian paused and looked around. He had almost never been down here before, though it was his own house; the cellars were the domain of the kitchen staff, not of the master of the house. He saw barrels of beer and kegs of wine, racks of bottles, shelves lined with jars, wax-coated wheels of cheese . . .

A sudden queasiness struck him as he remembered once before, when he had ventured down into his family cellar on a hot, dark summer day, a day when dragons were on the way.

He had been only eleven then, a mere village boy, rather than a man nearing forty. Now he was Lord Obsidian, the warlord, the dragonslayer, the swordsman, the fabulously wealthy dealer in foreign magic, the man obsessed with revenge—but he was still the same person in many ways. He still remembered the dusty black wheels of cheese in his parents' cellar; he had been counting them for his grandfather when the dragons arrived, when his world had disintegrated around him.

He shuddered at the memory, at the remembered taste of his grandfather's envenomed blood, at the sound of Grandsir's voice shouting at the dragons. He struggled to recall the exact words the old man had used.

"May the dead gods curse you and all your kin, dragon," Grandsir had said. "Your time is over! You have no place in the Lands of Man!"

That had not been true—but Arlian had been fighting ever since to *make* it true, to ensure that the dragons would never again have a place in the Lands of Man. He glanced at Ithar.

Perhaps the gods were not *all* dead anymore. He glanced upward, at the stone ceiling. At least for the moment they were not all dead—and he wanted to keep it that way. If new gods arose, beneficent gods, then humanity might be given a new chance, a new world of peace and justice. Brook's baby was the harbinger of that world.

He was not going to trust in anyone else to protect humanity's future. "You stay down here, all of you," he said. Then he turned and hurried back up the stairs, leaving the three children calling after him.

Worried maids were standing nearby when he emerged. "Anyone who wants to leave may go, with my blessing. Any of you who would prefer to take refuge in the cellars are free to do so," he said, as he marched through the kitchen toward a certain storeroom. High-pitched voices, rustling skirts, and running feet behind him told him that his staff was taking him up on his offers of flight and refuge.

Years before, before he had told anyone else of the dragons' vulnerability to obsidian, before he had become the Duke's warlord, before he had supplied obsidian for the spears and catapults that armed the city's soldiers, he had had an assortment of obsidian weapons made for himself. Before *that*, Lord Enziet, the former master of the Grey House and the sorcerer who had first theorized that obsidian might pierce a dragon's hide, had also attempted to make obsidian blades. A few of these assorted weapons were still stored away. Most of Arlian's obsidian armory had been turned over to the Duke's forces long ago, but a few of the earliest, crudest weapons had been left behind.

Arlian selected the longest spear in the collection; he knew from experience just how far through a dragon's flesh a spearhead had to go to reach the monster's heart. With the weapon in hand he trotted up two flights of stairs, then made his way out onto a balcony overlooking the barren central courtyard. He looked up.

He could hear distant screams, and other sounds he did not immediately recognize—thumps and rattles and rustles. The square of sky overhead was dark with heavy clouds, but he could not see any dragons. He could see the catapults on the roof—catapults that were not manned.

It would have been pleasant to have blamed the Duke for this failure, but Arlian knew better. This was his house, and he had installed those catapults long before the Duke began his intensive fortification of the city.

He and Black had also assigned Ferrezin and Wolt to see that they were manned, in the event the dragons ever came to Manfort—and Ferrezin was long since departed, while Wolt was recently dead. Black had been somewhat distracted of late, and was now in the cellars with his family, hardly in a position to help.

Arlian had stored a ladder on the balcony for exactly this purpose; he swung it into position and climbed.

A moment later he stepped onto the tile roof, then up onto the narrow platform below the catapults. The wood sagged slightly in places, and he suspected that the underside was partially rotted—he had not thought to ensure proper maintenance.

From this new, elevated post, Arlian looked out over Manfort.

To the north and slightly east stood the Citadel, which despite its name was a palace, with broad windows and wooden galleries; around it, and all through the Upper City, were more manors and mansions, built in a variety of styles and of a variety of materials. Many of these elegant homes were now topped with elaborate frameworks, most of them ugly mismatches for the architecture below—catapults with long throwing arms and hanging counterweights, equipped to fling obsidian-tipped projectiles at approaching dragons. Most of these devices, alas, were not manned.

Some of the mansions were already ablaze, the flames lighting the sky orange and adding black plumes of smoke to the unnatural overcast.

To the south and west lay most of the city, the lower, older areas built entirely of gray stone, the streets paved in stone; there was little there that would burn, little that a dragon's venom could penetrate. The Upper City, though, had been built during the Years of Man, the long centuries when the dragons slept in their caverns, bound by Enziet's bargain to emerge as rarely as they could tolerate; the buildings there had been designed for appearance and comfort, not fireproofing.

The breeze blew from the Upper City and smelled of smoke—not the normal odor of cookstoves and hearths, but the reek of woodsmoke and charred tiles.

The Grey House, on the edge of the Upper City, was the oldest mansion still standing, dating back to the previous Man-Dragon Wars; it was as fireproof as anything below, and considerably more defensible than most, as well as having the oldest catapults in Manfort, each ready to shoot four ten-foot spears.

Arlian paid little attention to the city itself, though; he was looking at the sky above it.

He had seen four dragons approaching before; two of

them were still airborne over the Upper City, spraying flaming venom on the rapidly emptying streets below, but three or four spearshafts dangled from one monster's flank. As Arlian watched, more catapults thumped and more projectiles flew around the beasts without striking.

A third dragon was sprawled across a mansion roof, perhaps a quarter-mile away; one of its wings had apparently been torn apart by a volley of black-tipped missiles, and it lay wounded, spouting flame and smoke. Arlian could not see the details at such a distance.

The fourth dragon had vanished, presumably slain.

That did not seem so very dreadful, but then Arlian looked out beyond the city walls, and saw more distant black shapes, almost invisible against the clouds.

More dragons. Those first four had been only the vanguard; now the main body was approaching.

They were soaring nearer, moving swiftly, black against the dark clouds, coming from every direction. He began trying to count them, but then quickly abandoned the effort as they veered back and forth, passing in front of one another, or slipping out of sight behind towers and rooftops.

He remembered that at the end of his last hunt he had estimated the total surviving population of dragons at forty-six, and a bark of bitter laughter escaped him. There were more than forty-six in sight. There were *many* more than forty-six. His quick estimate was that perhaps two hundred dragons were approaching—and who knew how many more might be lurking beyond the horizon, or still safe in their caves? Exterminating the dragons was a far greater task than he had realized—but he had no intention of abandoning it.

For now, though, he was primarily concerned with surviving the coming battle. He lifted his spear in his left hand, and his right reached for the release lever of the nearest catapult.

47

A Sky Black with Dragons

*W*aiting until the last minute increased the chances of a killing strike, but it was perhaps the hardest thing Arlian had ever done, standing there holding the lever as the first dragon swooped down at him, talons outstretched, spraying a flaming cloud of venom. He ducked down, avoiding the flames, feeling the heat singe his sleeve but keeping his hand on the release.

And then the monster was right on top of him, a great black figure towering into the sky above him, and he pulled the lever down.

The latch slipped free, the weights dropped, and the throwing arm snapped forward, launching four heavy bolts at the dragon. Arlian did not pause to see the effect; he was already running to the next catapult.

The dragon screamed, and Arlian risked a glance back in time to see the creature flailing its wings wildly; three of the four bolts had struck its chest, clearly wounding it deeply.

None had penetrated to its heart, though; it still lived. Claws raked at the roof, sending shards of shattered tile spraying upward.

And then a sound behind him provided an instant's warning; Arlian threw himself sideways off the platform as an immense gout of flame roared past his ear.

He had forgotten where he was; his action sent him tumbling down the steep slope, and he barely caught himself before rolling off the edge. He lay on the roof and looked up.

The wounded dragon was rampaging across the northeast corner of the roof, on the other side of the ridgepole, thrashing about as it tore at the spearheads in its chest.

Another dragon now perched on the northwest corner, smiling at him, smoke trailing from its nostrils, venom dripping from its jaw. He recognized its face—this was one he had seen in the cave in the Shoulderbone.

Three more dragons were settling onto the southern side of the roof, on the far side of the central courtyard; their spread wings overlapped, the six extended membranes easily reaching from one corner of the mansion to the other. A shadow passed overhead, and Arlian looked up to see still more dragons flying above the Grey House. The sky was black with them.

This, of course, was where they were headed—*all* of them were coming to the Grey House. They had not come to destroy Manfort; they had come to kill Ithar, and to ensure that no more like him were created.

Arlian scrabbled up the roof as quickly as he could, trying to act before the dragons could react; the pain and stiffness in his right shoulder slowed him, but he was able to leap up and grab the release lever on the next catapult.

He yanked down, not bothering to aim. The mechanism thumped, the weights dropped, and air whistled across wood and obsidian as another four projectiles flew.

One glanced off the wing of the nearest dragon while the other three sailed past it, and Arlian realized that he had no hope of inflicting real damage, or even surviving, if he remained on the roof—the dragons were too close, and too many. He dropped, and let himself slide down the tiles, barely catching himself on the waiting ladder.

A great black claw reached down after him but missed, breaking half a dozen tiles and tearing a gouge in the roof. As Arlian half climbed, half slid down the ladder he found himself thinking foolishly that the roof would probably leak now, with all those tiles broken.

Then he was on the balcony, but he knew that provided

no safety; one of the dragons on the southern side of the courtyard was stooping, stretching its long neck down into the square and preparing to spit venom. Arlian grabbed up his heavy spear and ducked through the door into the house as the toxin sprayed toward him.

The fluid failed to ignite—that sometimes happened, he knew, and when it did the foul stuff would dissolve or corrode whatever organic material it touched, instead of burning.

But it would also be recoverable from the stone pavement below—if he and the city somehow survived this, that would be another few ounces of venom that could be collected, mixed with human blood, and fed to pregnant women to create more godlings.

And that was what must be done, he realized as he hurried toward the stairs—more godlings must be made, as quickly as possible. Ithar was precious at present because he was unique, but if there were a hundred baby gods and goddesses, or a thousand, how could the dragons hope to kill them all?

He stumbled, then, as a thought struck him—surely, the dragons knew that was possible. They needed to destroy not just Ithar, but all knowledge of his existence and the means of his creation.

That meant they would try to kill every single person in Lord Obsidian's household; Arlian had not kept Ithar's nature and origin a secret. On the contrary, he had boasted of it.

He had not only told his own staff; he had informed the Duke of his experiment. He had sent word to Lady Rime when Ithar was born, and her entire household undoubtedly knew, just as Arlian's did.

Did the dragons know that?

Word had probably not spread much beyond those three residences—the Grey House, Rime's estate, and the Citadel. The Duke would almost certainly have said something in confidence to his more trusted advisors, such as Zaner and Spider, but most of the court would not have heard any details. If the dragons destroyed those three buildings and their inhabitants, the knowledge might well be lost.

But did the dragons know that?

They might think killing Arlian and Black and Black's family would be sufficient—or they might think all of Manfort must be destroyed.

The sound of his own feet on the stone as he ran down the stairs was almost lost in the roaring chaos outside; he could hear dragons bellowing, flames crackling, men and women screaming, and a thousand other noises.

He tried to think what he could do, how he could help. He could simply join the battle outside, try to kill as many dragons as possible before they killed him, but he doubted that would end well; he was not in his best shape, as he was reminded every time he grabbed at the balustrade with his right hand and felt his shoulder tear. He could try to get out of the city, to spread the word of Ithar's birth throughout the Lands of Man—but that felt like abandoning his people, and besides, how could he hope to make his way out of Manfort without being found by the dragons? He was a dragonheart, and he had come to believe, after years of experience in dealing with the beasts, that that meant the dragons could locate him anywhere, could sense the whereabouts of the thing growing in his blood—perhaps not *all* the dragons, but certainly the one that had first contaminated him, the one that had killed Grandsir so long ago. Even if he somehow got outside the walls, the dragons would hunt him down. Their hired assassins had always been able to find him; now that the dragons themselves had emerged and joined the fray, he suspected he did not have long to live in any case.

But if he could get *Ithar* out of the city—or at the very least, knowledge of how he had been made—there might be hope.

A gigantic crash sounded somewhere above him, and the entire house seemed to shake; plaster dust sifted down the stairwell. The dragons were trying to tear open the house to get at him.

He headed for the kitchen and the cellar stair as the rumble of falling stone echoed down the passageway.

Lord Enziet had lived in this house for centuries, Arlian remembered. Arlian had thought that Enziet had liked it because he believed even the dragons would not be able to penetrate the thick stone walls, but if so, then going by the sounds overhead Enziet had been wrong.

And Enziet was rarely wrong, Arlian admitted to himself. He had probably known that these stone walls would not stop a determined dragon.

And Enziet always prepared for every eventuality. Arlian slowed his pace as a thought began to form.

Enziet had always prepared for contingencies, always. And he had slipped out of the city unnoticed when the Dragon Society had summoned him for an infraction of the Society's rules. Had Enziet had some secret means of escape from the Grey House? Was there a hidden tunnel, perhaps?

That would be entirely in keeping with Enziet's character, and the man had certainly had plenty of time to build one. The logical place would obviously be the cellars . . .

Arlian renewed his speed and hastened to the kitchen, and to the cellar door.

As he descended the dark stairs, though, another thought struck him. If there *was* a tunnel, and he sent Black and Brook and Ithar and the rest out through it, he did not dare go with them—as a dragonheart, his presence would give away their location.

And, he realized, *Brook* was a dragonheart, as well . . .

"By the dead gods," he murmured to himself. Separating a mother from her newborn child, in order to protect the child?

But what choice did they have?

And Brook had no feet. Her wheeled chair, clever as it was, could not traverse stairs or rough country, and there was no way of knowing where the tunnel, if it existed, might lead. She would almost certainly have been an un-manageable burden in any case.

But would she accept that? Would *Black* accept it?

Black was waiting for him at the foot of the stair, candle in one hand and sword in the other; in the gloom behind him Arlian glimpsed several of the household servants, Brook in her chair with her children clustered about her and her babe in her arms, Lilsinir with a heavy bag slung over one shoulder—Arlian had no idea how the Aritheian had gotten there, but was relieved to see she was alive and well, and he recognized the sack as the one she used for transporting her magical and medical supplies.

That was good; if they lived through this, those medical supplies might be important.

"Ari," Black said, "what's happening up there?"

"Dragons are attacking Manfort," Arlian replied. "Hundreds of them—quite possibly all that are left alive in the entire world." He pointed at Brook and Ithar, barely visible in the shadows. "They're after the baby. We need to get him out of here."

"It's more than a mile to the city gates," Black said.

"I know," Arlian said. "But it occurred to me—do you think Enziet might have had an escape tunnel down here?"

Black stared at him for a moment, his face impossible to read in the dim and flickering candlelight. "Of course he would," he said at last, sheathing his sword. "He was Enziet. That's exactly the sort of thing he would do." He turned and shouted, "Children! All of you! Look for a door or a tunnel—perhaps hidden behind something!"

There was a great scurrying, and lamps flared as Kerzia and Amberdine, and Stammer and Lilsinir and the maids and footmen, began searching the cellar walls. They scattered, leaving Brook hesitating in her chair, holding Ithar and watching her husband and Arlian.

"There's something else," Arlian said, as Black started to turn away to join the hunt.

Black paused. "Yes?"

Arlian beckoned, and led his steward over to Brook. There he knelt and whispered, "The dragons are tearing down the house above us." He pointed upward, and the crashing of falling stone confirmed his words. "They want Ithar."

"I know," Brook said.

"They know where I am," Arlian said. "Because I'm a dragonheart. The dragon who poisoned me, all those years ago, can sense where I am because I bear his spawn in my heart."

"Then how . . ." Brook began, but Black held up a hand, and she fell silent.

"If we find an escape tunnel, then Black and the children and servants must take Ithar and flee—but I will stay here, and fight any dragon that finds its way this far down. I mustn't go, or the dragons will be able to follow."

"Ari . . ."

"You said Black and the children," Brook said, interrupting her husband.

Arlian looked her in the eye. "Yes," he said.

"Because I'm a dragonheart, too."

"Yes. And the venom came from that same dragon. If it can find me, it can find you."

"So I must stay, too." She spoke calmly, but Arlian could see her hands trembling, could see how wide her eyes were.

"Or flee by another route, perhaps," he said. "I can scarcely ask you to fight at my side. I can carry you up the stairs . . ."

"Ari, are you mad?" Black growled. "Leave Brook here? Take Ithar away from her?"

"You need to save the baby, take him where the dragons cannot find him, tell everyone how to make more like him. If there is just one godling, the dragons will hunt him down, sooner or later; if there are a thousand, what can they do? Take him, to show everyone what can be done, how we can use our land's magic to make the world a better place, how we can have magic that heals rather than poisons us."

"Ari, Brook is my *wife*. Yes, I want to save Ithar, and all my children, but I am not going to leave my wife!"

"Yes, you are," Brook said, thrusting the baby toward him.

Black blinked. "What?"

"Save the children. Leave me. Better Arlian and I die and the rest of you live than that we all die."

Black stared at her.

"She is a dragonheart," Arlian said quietly.

"So I see," Black replied, taking Ithar in his arms. He looked down at those calm, softly glowing blue eyes, then at Brook's cold brown ones.

Then, without another word, he turned away and headed for the far end of the cellars, where the children were calling to one another.

Brook watched him go, then asked, "What if the dragons can sense Ithar, as they sense us?"

"Let us hope they cannot. Ithar is a creature of magic, yes, but unless there is some far deeper game here than I can comprehend, he bears no dragonspawn. You took that upon yourself for him. Still, it is possible, and we can just hope for the best."

For a moment they were silent, and then Brook asked quietly, "What if there is no tunnel?" Arlian noticed a quaver in her voice, and looked down to see a tear welling in her eye.

"Then we *all* die," he said. "I'm sorry, Brook." He glanced up at the ceiling, then after Black's retreating figure. "I'm sorry for everything." Somewhere above them a wall collapsed with a tremendous crash, and Arlian could hear the crackle of flames. He hefted the spear in his left hand.

"Brook," he said, "do you want to stay down here, or should I carry you up to the kitchen? I'll need to make a second trip for your chair."

"I'll stay here," she said. "I am trying my best to be brave, my lord, but I am not ready to deliberately go any closer to the monsters that have come to kill me."

"Fair enough. I intend to go up there, though, to hold them off as long as I can." He turned toward the stairs.

At the bottom step he paused, listening, as he realized that he could no longer hear the girls' voices. "Black?" he called.

"We found it, Ari," Black's distant voice replied. "Goodbye, my lord—and Allíri. May the dead gods keep you safe."

Then he heard a faint thump—a door being closed.

Arlian swallowed.

Behind him he could hear Brook weeping, but he did not look; instead he turned and marched up the stairs, the spear ready in his left hand.

48

A Final Meeting of Old Foes

The Grey House was afire—but this was hardly the conflagration it might have been elsewhere. There were no wooden beams here, no tarred roofing; the entire structure was stone and metal, down to the mullions in the windows. Even when dragon venom had been liberally sprayed in every direction, all that burned were the doors, the draperies, and the furnishings. The walls might be blackened by soot, but they did not burn.

All the same, it was scarcely a pleasant environment Arlian found when he emerged into the kitchen; the acrid smoke blinded and choked him as he tried to locate his enemies. Sound was no help, as the roar of the flames and the crashing of stone was all around him; he could smell nothing but smoke; his eyes stung and his vision blurred. Still, he squinted into the gloom.

Streaks of burning venom were seeping through cracks in the ceiling, like streamers of orange fire; smoke swirled and danced overhead. The table was smeared with soot and char, but had not yet ignited; so far, of the kitchen's substance and contents, only the doors were burning, a slow, smoky smolder—but through the one door that stood open he could see the dining hall awash in flame, the tapestries and chairs ablaze, the ceiling fallen in.

For a moment he wondered what he was doing here. What could he hope to accomplish, one man against a horde of dragons?

He could buy time for Black and Ithar and the others, he told himself. He could buy a little time for Brook. And he could perhaps take one or two dragons down with him.

And then the world seemed to shake, and one corner of the ceiling fell in, a great black claw smashing down into the kitchen. Arlian turned, spear raised, as the talons ripped at the stonework, crumbling solid limestone as if it were cheese.

Then an immense black head thrust into the opening, filling it completely and widening it further, and two golden eyes stared down at him from an all-too-familiar face. Arlian stared back, and then said, "You!"

I know you, the dragon replied soundlessly. *You carry my seed.*

"Damn you, yes! You killed my family, burned our home, and poisoned me!"

The dragon seemed utterly undisturbed by this accusation. *If you would flee, flee. I am not here for you this time. I would prefer to let you live to bear my offspring.*

"I won't flee—don't you and your kind know me better than that after all these years?"

The dragon's eyes seemed to smile at that, and for a horrible instant Arlian thought he recognized something of his grandfather in that smile. *All these years?* it said. *Your entire life has been just a few heartbeats. You are a child. A troublesome child, but still merely a child.*

"A troublesome child?" Arlian asked, lifting the spear in his left hand. "Well, at least I've troubled you!"

Indeed. The smile vanished. *You have helped to create a godling.*

"I have helped to butcher more than four score of your foul breed!"

The old and infirm—and our numbers were higher than was entirely wise, in any case. We permitted ourselves such excess when we first conquered this land that we diluted our own magic through overbreeding.

"What?" Arlian was distracted by a crashing somewhere nearby—clearly, other dragons were in the area. He was also having difficulty breathing as the stench of venom mingled with the smoke, rendering the air even more toxic, and thinking clearly was becoming a challenge. "When you first conquered this land? When was that?"

When we took it away from your gods—the sort you hope to restore. And where is the godling?

"That was ten thousand years ago!"

Yes. I remember. Where is the child?

"Gone. Somewhere safe. Somewhere you can't find him."

The dragon stared wordlessly at him for a moment, but did not seem to be seeing him; Arlian looked for some way to get the spear at its heart, but could not find one. Only the monster's head was in the kitchen; the rest was still apparently on the next floor up, in what Arlian estimated had been the servants' quarters before this invasion—though it surely would not all fit there, and its tail might extend almost anywhere in the house.

He is still nearby, but . . . hidden.

"You're lying. You don't know where he is."

Oh, but I do. I can sense every sort of magic, not just my own.

Arlian's heart sank, but he bluffed, "No, you cannot—we have magicks you cannot imagine!"

No.

"Yes!"

You have the black stone. You have sorcery. You have some simple magic brought from the southern wilderness, and you have your godling. That is all.

"It's enough!"

It may be. I cannot feel exactly where the child is—you have indeed hidden it well. Beneath the ground? In a cavern, like our own?

"A deep one."

No. Rather, one so narrow I could not fit through it. To reach the child we would need to dig through the stone of the earth.

The entire house shook, and somewhere an avalanche of crumbling stone roared; dust sifted through the smoke. Something screamed, a deep, inhuman shriek.

Arlian trembled; he could see the point of his spear wobble. The smoke and venom were sapping his strength; his eyes were tearing so much he could hardly see. His imagination supplied all too vivid a picture of the dragons ripping up the streets and digging down to Enziet's tunnel. "If you do that you'll be trapped," he said. "Easy targets for our spears. You would be digging through your own dead before you reached the child."

There is considerable truth in that. Already more than a score of us have been struck down by your missiles, and twice that number injured but not fallen. Some have already turned and fled. To land in the streets, relinquish the freedom of the skies . . . The dragon's expression turned thoughtful. *It would seem we may be defeated. I had not thought it possible.*

"It is *inevitable*!" Arlian shouted, trying to sound as if he believed it.

Listen, man, the dragon said, *you know not what you are doing, protecting this creature.*

"We are freeing our land of evil and chaos—the evil of your kind, and the chaos of wild magic."

And what are you imposing in its place? Do you have any idea what this godling will become?

"Not really," Arlian admitted. "But we still swear by the gods you destroyed, while dragons are so feared and hated that our ancestors were reluctant to even say your name. The child's first act was to heal a wounded man, while a dragon's birth kills its host. I think we have reason to choose the child."

And what if you are wrong? No black stone will pierce its heart.

"Silver will."

Silver will not. Those pitiful half-formed creatures you created were mere twisted shadows of the power that dragon venom and a human womb produce. The godling is not so easily slain as they.

For a moment Arlian wondered whether the dragon was lying. Did the creature hope to play on the human fear of the unknown, and coax Arlian into letting it reach Ithar for fear the child would be otherwise indestructible? "Yet you propose to slay it; what weapons do *you* carry?" he asked. "I see no dagger in your talon."

We have ways.

"And you will not tell me what they are? Why do you fear this child so?"

The gods were our . . . our rulers. We prize our freedom.

"As we prize ours—and while you live, and the gods do not, we have none."

So you would rather be the gods' cattle than our prey?

"If the gods prove worse than you, we will have time to change our minds."

Not if you have slain us all.

"We can still choose chaos!"

No. Who will tell you how to kill the gods, when we are gone?

"We will find a way. Perhaps the thing in Tirikindaro will tell us—it was there, it knows what you did."

And if it did, that would not help you. You do not have that which can kill a god.

"We'll find it."

No. Not if we are gone.

"Why not?"

Perhaps if I tell you, you will let a few of us live, the dragon mused. *Perhaps you will allow my spawn in your heart to live to maturity.*

"Why should I?"

Because only dragonbone can harm the gods, the dragon said. *Our teeth, our bones—nothing else. As we alone can create them with our venom, we alone can destroy them. We came seeking this little one ourselves, rather than sending our human servants, because once it had been born they and their weapons could not harm it. We can.*

"Then why do you fear the gods so? If your teeth can tear their flesh, why should you risk your own lives to attack Manfort? Why would you fly directly into a wall of obsidian blades to get at a single child? Why is it so very important to you that no gods should exist?"

They are our natural enemies, our antithesis.

"Your rulers, you said—but if *you* can harm *them,* how could they rule you?"

The dragon hesitated—and as it did the house shook again, and a wall of the kitchen was torn open. Arlian fell backward, away from the cloud of dust and the rush of air—air that could not be called anything but hot, but that was nonetheless cooler than the sweltering heat of the smoke-filled, flame-riddled kitchen.

A second dragon's face appeared in the opening, its attention focused on the first. Arlian blinked at it through the smoke and haze.

What are you doing? it asked. *Have you found the abomination?*

It is in a tunnel beneath the earth, where we cannot reach it.

Where? We can dig it out.

Arlian recognized this new arrival. This was another of the three that had destroyed the village on the Smoking Mountain—he had glimpsed its face as it flew by.

If we dig, men with spears will slay us while we work, and it will flee farther down the tunnel.

Then are we doomed? The fatalist faction was correct?

This human can fetch it for us.

The second dragon turned its head toward Arlian. *It is the boy from the volcano. The heir to the bargainer. The killer. The maker of the godling. He will not aid us!*

He may be convinced.

How?

He prizes freedom, and truth, and justice. Perhaps if we tell him the truth he will understand our own need for our freedom and our justice.

"Perhaps I will," Arlian said. "But I will never give up the child until I know why you fear him so!"

We fear what he will become, a year from now.

"A year? He's a newborn babe!"

In a year he will walk and speak.

"But . . . what of it?"

Do not tell him.

We have little choice. If we do not, how can we reach the godling?

"You said something of freedom and justice . . ."

We cannot be free when a god lives. They are our masters.

"I don't understand—you can destroy them. Why would they be your masters?"

We were their pets, their playthings, their slaves, the second dragon said. *We will not be slaves again.*

"Slaves?"

Slaves.

Slaves.

When a god speaks, we must obey. We have no choice. It is a part of their magic.

In the old days they allowed only a handful of us to exist. Once every thousand years a young woman would be chosen to bear a godling, then to serve a thousand years as their high priestess until the dragon burst from her heart. One, only one, at a time. Only when the dragon's red had faded to gold was the next woman chosen.

And that handful was kept as half-starved servants, allowed nothing to eat but the souls of those few who had offended the gods. The gods ordered us about as if we were dogs guarding their thrones.

Do you wonder that we do not wish to return to that?

"And do you wonder that we do not want to be your slaves, any more than you wished to be theirs? We do not wish to be your prey, your food supply, your playthings."

Then you will enslave us?

The question shook Arlian's conviction.

"How did you free yourselves? If you're telling me the truth, if a god's word could not be defied, how did you ever escape from this bondage?"

We waited and planned for centuries until we could strike at all of the gods at once, so none had time to speak, to order us to stop. We lured them into position, and then we struck.

We rebelled, as slaves will anywhere.

And that reaffirmed Arlian's own position. Humanity had been slaves to the dragons, and had rebelled against them—as the dragons had rebelled against the gods.

To force the dragons back into slavery would be wrong—but *must* the gods enslave them?

For centuries, under Enziet's bargain, the dragons had allowed humanity its freedom. Could not the gods do the same, forever?

"We will teach him," Arlian said. "We will teach them all. To enslave another is wrong, whether one is a god, a dragon, or a man. To kill an innocent is wrong, as well, and the child is innocent—as I am not, and you are not."

For a moment none of them spoke; then the dragon that

had killed Grandsir said, *You will not bring the godling to us?*

"No," Arlian said. "Perhaps you can live your own lives far from here, if you harm no one; a treaty can be made, perhaps, and we will thereby tell Ithar not to seek you out. But I will not let you kill him."

Then die. And the second dragon surged forward, smashing its shoulders through the stone wall of the Grey House as if it were paper, and spraying flaming venom from its jaw.

49

Vengeance Considered

Arlian dodged the gout of burning poison as best he could, but the flame singed his hair and sleeve and left his eyes stinging. He ducked sideways, into the corner by the hearth. The dragon tried to turn its head to pursue him, but could not maneuver in the cramped quarters of a human kitchen; Arlian was able to get to one side of its jaw, where it could not turn its head far enough to strike at him with teeth or venom, and the other dragon could not attack him without going through its companion.

That did not stop the dragon's claws, though; a taloned foreclaw smashed through the stone wall and struck at him.

He struck back with the spear, meeting the blow halfway; the obsidian spearpoint tore through scale and armor, punching entirely through the dragon's foreclaw, slowing the attack to a mere shove.

The dragon screamed with rage, filling the kitchen with a fog of sparks and toxic vapor, as it tried to twist around to get a look at its foe.

Arlian, meanwhile, tried to pull the spear back out and realized he could not; instead he dove forward, grasped the jagged black spearhead, and pulled it *through* instead, as the dragon thrashed and squirmed.

Where is he? Help me!

He carries my spawn, the other replied uncertainly.

The spear came free, and Arlian climbed up on the monster's pierced claw, then scrambled up its foreleg.

Get off!

Arlian had had experience at this—there had been occasions when a dragon or two awoke before he and his men could thrust a spear in its heart. Those dragons, though, had been old and weak with age, and sluggish from their deep sleep and the winter cold. *This* dragon was young and strong, awake and angry, its blood hot with fire and magic. It jerked and struggled, and at one point would have flung Arlian aside had he not bounced off a jagged chunk of wall and regained his grip at the cost of a backache and an immense bruise.

His right shoulder was still stiff, as well; he could not raise that hand up to grip properly.

Still, he was able to crawl up the dragon's shoulder and onto its back, and there he raised the spear in his left hand—and jammed it against the ceiling before he could bring it up to a vertical position.

But then the much-abused ceiling gave way completely, crumbling around him; stone glanced from his head, shoulders, and back, and the spear swung upright. He jumped to his feet, grabbed the shaft in both hands, and thrust it down into the dragon's back.

The dragon screamed and thrashed, and Arlian's feet went out from under him, but he kept his grip on the spear; the added weight only drove it deeper into the beast, and his knees scraped on black scales again. He could feel the throbbing of the dragon's heart as a vibration in the spear, deep and strong, slower than a human heart but faster than any other dragon's he had ever felt.

He moved his hands up the shaft, squeezed, and thrust downward again.

Thick dark blood welled up around the shaft, then spurted up on his hands and face, and the dragon collapsed beneath him.

Bravely done, child.

Arlian turned to see the other dragon still watching, still making no hostile move. He took a shuddering breath, then asked, "Will you attempt to kill me now, or will you continue to let me live for the sake of your offspring?"

I think that Fate chose its agents well.

"What?" He coughed as he pulled the spear from the already-decaying body of the dead dragon.

What would I gain from your death? I came to destroy a godling, to preserve the freedom of my race; you have made that impossible. If Fate is working to restore the gods, then it is nearing its goal. Oh, I could eat your soul, and I would surely relish so rare a person as yourself, but then my own child would be lost.

As it finished this speech it began to withdraw its head. The collapsed kitchen ceiling was gone, and Arlian could see that the house above was entirely gone as well; he could see the dragon rear up its long neck and spread its gigantic wings.

"Wait!" he called.

He knew it was madness. He knew this was utterly insane. The dragon had just said it would let him live. It had just agreed to depart, to give up its attempts on Ithar—and he was *calling it back.*

But he had a reason, a reason he had lived with since boyhood. This was not just any dragon. This was the dragon that had killed his grandfather. This was the dragon he had sworn vengeance upon a hundred times over the years. This was the dragon he had dreamed of for more than twenty years— and had dreamed of *killing* for more than twenty years. This was the dragon whose poison had robbed him of his humanity, replaced his own heart with obsession and hatred.

He had let it live once, in the cave in the Sawtooth Mountains, for the sake of a greater good, but now, here, there was no such reason for restraint.

The dragon, however, did not wait. It sprang upward, wings flapping, and the wind from its ascent knocked Arlian from his perch atop the dead dragon's spine; he tumbled and slid down the rotting black flesh to the broken flagstones of the kitchen floor, his head whacking hard on the stone.

He lay dazed for a moment, staring up at swirling smoke and streaks of fire against a background of thick black clouds.

With the dragons gone and the kitchen open to the sky much of the smoke had cleared away, and after a moment his head cleared, as well. He sat up.

The Grey House was a ruin; scattered fires were still burning here and there in the wreckage. The dead dragon towered before him, filling half the kitchen, all of the kitchen yard, and a portion of the demolished stables, but its flesh was already shrinking and falling away, exposing corners and edges of bone.

Arlian remembered what the dragons had said about killing gods; he would want to save some of those bones, just in case.

Over the crackling of the flames he could hear screaming, roaring, crashing, shouting—the dragons had obviously not yet all departed Manfort. Some might have abandoned the hunt, but others apparently had not; presumably there were factions among the dragons, as among humans, and at least one faction still fought.

And the dragon that killed his grandfather was still out there. It might be flying back to the Shoulderbone, or to some new, as yet undiscovered lair. It might be wheeling to attack the Duke's soldiers, or digging for Enziet's escape tunnel.

And Arlian intended to find it and kill it. He had sworn as much over and over. The beast had let him live when it could have killed him, but that didn't matter—he had to kill it. He *had* to.

He could not get out through the kitchen yard; the dead dragon blocked that route completely. He would have to go out through the rest of the house. He turned, and stumbled toward what remained of the arched doorway into the passage to the dining hall.

The little corridor was surprisingly intact, but the dining hall was gone—and he discovered then that there was more than one dead dragon in the wreckage of the Grey House.

This one had been dead a few minutes longer, by the look of it; the catapult bolts that bristled from it were sagging, twisting the rotting skin, dropping free. The stinking mass nonetheless formed an impassable barricade. He retreated to the kitchen and tried another door.

That one was blocked by fallen stone.

He tried every possible route, and all were barricaded by either debris or decaying dragon. He looked up at the fetid remains of the dragon he had slain and considered trying to climb over, or at least clamber up its skull to get up atop the piles of stone, but then another thought struck him.

The dragon he wanted had surely gone by now—but so had Black and Ithar and the rest, and the hidden tunnel was a way out of this ruin.

He could help Brook out, as well.

With that, he turned, shoved aside a few blocks of stone, and found the cellar stairs. "Brook!" he called—or tried to; the smoke and strain had finally gotten to his throat, and he could not manage much more than a croak.

No one answered. Arlian swallowed, trying to clear his throat, as he staggered down the stone steps.

At the bottom he called again. "Brook!"

"Ari?"

He turned, and saw her in the shadows, rolling her chair forward slowly. "Yes," he said.

"What's happened? Are the dragons coming?"

"I don't think so," he said. "I think we should find that tunnel and get out of here—the house is a ruin."

"Are you sure? We won't be leading them to Ithar?"

"They can sense him—but they know they can't reach him in the tunnel. As long as Ithar is underground he's safe."

"Then we need to warn them!" she shouted. "They'll bring him out at the other end of the tunnel if we don't!"

"Oh," Arlian said, suddenly feeling extraordinarily stupid. "They might." He looked around the cellars. An oil lamp was mounted on a wall bracket by the stairs, and Brook held a thick candle, but beyond that everything was dark—if the dragons had broken through from above anywhere, Arlian could not see it. "Where was the entrance?"

"I don't know," Brook said. "That way, maybe?"

Arlian peered into the gloom in the direction she indicated, and tried to remember where he had last heard Black's voice. "Maybe," he said. He moved behind Brook's chair and pushed.

The two of them searched the cellars for what seemed like hours, investigating every dark corner and disturbed cobweb, before finally stumbling upon the butcher's cupboard with the double latch. Releasing the first latch let the cupboard door swing open, revealing a tin-lined interior where a rack of hooks held nothing but dust; releasing the second latch let the entire cupboard swing forward, revealing a door-sized opening in the stone wall behind it.

As they searched, the house and city above them gradually quieted. When they finally inspected the butcher's cupboard for the third time they could no longer hear anything but their own breath and a distant muttering.

Had Brook not finally noticed the child-sized fingerprints on the mechanism, they might never have discovered this entrance.

"It was fortunate that your daughters are inquisitive little creatures," Arlian remarked as he stepped cautiously into the opening. "I doubt an adult would ever have found that second latch." He held up a candle and studied the passageway.

It was, indeed, a tunnel, dark and cool and smelling of stone, its walls seamless black. It measured perhaps four feet wide and six feet high; Arlian had to stoop slightly to avoid hitting his head on the arched ceiling. It did not, however, lead directly away from the cellars, as he had expected; rather, it paralleled the cellar wall, extending out of sight in both directions, offering him two choices.

And to his surprise and dismay, the cobwebs had been torn away and the dust on the floor smeared by many feet in *both* directions. He knelt, candle in hand, and studied the footprints.

There appeared to be more of them to the right, and those were pointed in both directions; to the left all seemed to head away from his present location.

"Ah," he said. He stood up and explained to Brook, "They went that way at first," pointing to the right, "but then turned back for some reason and came back and went on that way," pointing to the left.

"The tunnel was probably blocked," she suggested.

"Probably." He pushed her chair over the sill into the tunnel and turned her to the left. "Come on, then."

"Hello!" she called into the darkness ahead. "Black? Kerzia?"

No one answered, and Arlian pushed the chair forward into the gloom.

The tunnel seemed endless. There was a bad moment when they reached an intersection where a side tunnel ran off to the right, but a quick look at the undisturbed cobwebs in that direction convinced Arlian and Brook to continue straight along the passage, following the footsteps of the others.

Then, abruptly, Arlian stopped. "Listen," he whispered.

Brook leaned forward in her chair, then smiled and shouted, "Here! We're here!"

"Mother!" a distant voice replied, followed by the sound of running feet. Arlian made out a dim light, far down the tunnel but nearing rapidly.

A moment later Amberdine was climbing into her mother's lap, while Dirinan clung to Brook's leg and Kerzia stood nearby. Behind her Ithar slept in his father's arms, and beyond that Arlian could see Stammer, Venlin, Lilsinir, and three or four others.

"What happened?" he asked Black.

"I would ask you the same," Black replied, with a crooked smile.

"Your tale first, then mine."

Stories were exchanged. Black's party had chosen to turn right at first, and had followed the tunnel for some distance before emerging into the burning ruins that they had only with effort identified as the remains of the Citadel. The defenses had been demolished, and the main structures burned to the ground; dragons were everywhere. Black had immediately turned the party around and led them back down the tunnel, through an opening in a structure so thoroughly devastated that he could not say with any assurance how the tunnel had originally been concealed.

There had been some argument about whether or not to return to the Grey House, but the consensus had been to continue down the other way—a decision that had been assisted significantly by the discovery that they did not know how to open the butcher's cupboard from the back; there was no obvious mechanism.

The left-hand tunnel had eventually brought them out in an empty house in the lower part of the city, not far from the wall; the exit was through the back of a large fireplace, and they had propped it open before emerging.

Almost as soon as they emerged, however, the house came under attack. There were still loaded catapults in that part of the city, so Manfort's defenders had put up a fight, but Black had seen no point in staying where the dragons might eventually reach them, and had led most of the group back down into the tunnel. A few of the servants had scattered, with Black's blessing, to make their own way.

"We were going to try the side tunnel," Black said, "and if that was no better we would simply stay down here until the fighting was done."

"Wise, very wise," Arlian said. "It would seem the dragons can track Ithar, as they can track Brook and me. They are reluctant to dig down to this tunnel, however, as their size works against them in confined places." He glanced back the way he had come and did some quick estimating. "I would guess that the side tunnel leads to a certain abandoned establishment on the Street of the Black Spire," he remarked.

"You could be right," Black said. "Now, though, tell us what happened at the Grey House."

Arlian quickly explained, though he made no attempt to convey the entirety of his conversations with the two dragons.

"Wh . . . wh . . . what do we do now, my lord?" Stammer asked.

"*You* wait here—you, and Ithar, and Brook, and the children. I am going to go aid in the battle you describe, down by the wall, and see if I, as warlord, can give a few orders. And when the fighting is done I will return for you, if I can, or send someone, if I live but cannot come myself—or if I die, I would suggest you wait here until thirst and hunger become a serious issue, and then find your way out as best you can."

"Yes, my lord."

"I'm going . . ." Black began. Then he looked at his wife, his four children, and the long, empty tunnel. "I'll stay here, if you don't mind," he said.

"I entirely approve," Arlian said. "You have always been a protector, not a dragonslayer. Guard your family, and see that Ithar lives."

Then he pressed past Brook's chair and children and trotted quickly down the tunnel.

50

A Harvest of Death

A rlian emerged from the cold fireplace into yet another
firelit ruin—one face of the house had been torn away,
and the stinking black remains of a rotting dragon, bristling
with spears, now lay across the broken stones of what had
once been an entryway, one of its tattered wings stretched
upward to where the tip of the wingbone had caught on a
jagged fragment of cornice.

The rest of the house was largely intact, and the effect
was somewhat disorienting—dusty drapes hung undisturbed, and closed doors guarded rooms that were now open
to the street.

Arlian picked his way across the scattered stones and
past the dragon's staring dead eyes, then stopped in his
tracks as a drop of venom fell from its jaws and hissed on
the pavement. He stared for a moment, then turned and
headed back into the house, searching.

A moment later he returned with a glass jar in his right
hand and a kitchen knife in his left, and knelt to slit open
the venom sac at the base of the dead monster's jaw. He
filled the jar, then stood and made his way carefully out into
the street.

The fighting had moved on again, as he had expected—
the dragons were tracking Ithar, flying above the city out of
catapult range, waiting for the infant to emerge again. He
could neither see nor hear any actual combat at present,
though he could see flames and smoke rising from the Upper City, and there were still soldiers hurrying through the

streets, their white and blue uniforms bright against the gray stone and black smoke, black-tipped spears in their arms.

"Ho!" he bellowed, as best he could with his dry throat. "You there, guard!"

A soldier stopped and demanded, "Who are you?"

"I am Lord Obsidian, the Duke's warlord," Arlian replied. "I have new orders."

"Orders?" The entire party of half a dozen soldiers had stopped now, and turned to listen. "We don't have any orders; we're just fighting the dragons and the fires wherever we can, and gathering up spears we can bring back up for the catapults to use anew."

"Good man! I commend your courage and initiative. I have instructions, though, that might put an end to the dragon's attacks."

The guards traded uncertain looks.

"How do we know you're the warlord?" one of them asked.

Before Arlian could reply another said, "That's Lord Obsidian. I was with him at Norva eight years ago."

"I've seen him in the Citadel," another confirmed.

The others did not appear to be completely convinced, but they turned their attention to Arlian without further protest.

"You live in Manfort, all of you?" Arlian asked.

The uncertain looks became more hostile. "Yes, we live here," one man replied. "What of it?"

"You have family here?"

"Some of us. Why?"

"Are any of your wives or sisters expecting children? I have a magic that may drive the dragons away, but it requires pregnant women—as many of them as we can find."

The soldiers stared silently at him for a long moment; then one said, "My aunt is expecting a child."

"Excellent!" Arlian lifted the jar of venom. "Take me to her."

"What will this spell of yours do?" the soldier asked, not moving.

Arlian hesitated.

The temptation to lie was strong, but he resisted. He was trying to create a new and better world from the ruins that surrounded them; to found that world on a lie would be wrong.

"It will make the mother-to-be a dragonheart," he said, "and it will make the child a god."

The disbelief was plain on their faces. One turned away in disgust.

"I have done this before," Arlian said hastily. "I have made a god of my steward's child—that is why the dragons have broken the truce and attacked Manfort, because they fear these godlings above all else. They sought to destroy the one I made, and kill me before we could make others."

The departing soldier ignored him, but the others exchanged glances. "*You* caused this?" one soldier demanded, waving his spear at the surrounding chaos.

Arlian glanced around at the tumbled walls, the scattered spearshafts and shards of obsidian, the broken shutters and shattered tile strewn in the streets; he took a deep breath of the smoky, dusty air. "The *dragons* did this," he said, "and whatever my part in it, it is too late to undo it. The dragons have come, and they seek to kill the child, even at the cost of many of their own kind." He gestured at the rotting black hulk behind him. "But if there were *many* children— dozens, or hundreds, spread through the city—the dragons could not destroy them all before they, themselves, are slain, and in a few years we will have divine assistance, gods who will guard us as the dead gods did thousands of years ago."

"I don't believe in the gods," another soldier said.

Arlian grimaced. "Whatever you believe, at least offer your aunt the chance to become a dragonheart, and transform her child into something magical and new."

The guards exchanged glances again.

"I want no part of this," one of them said, turning away.

"This is all madness," said another, "but the *world* has gone mad."

"How do we do it?" asked the man with the pregnant aunt.

Arlian smiled, and explained.

"Tell others," he said, when he had finished. "Tell everyone. There are dead dragons scattered across the city, and each holds enough venom to make a hundred new gods." If the word spread far enough, fast enough, the dragons would be unable to contain it, unable to suppress it. "You understand?"

The soldiers nodded. Arlian handed over the jar of venom; then he went in search of more recruits, more bottles and jars, more venom.

For hours he ranged through the city, picking his way across fields of rubble, dodging scattered fires, avoiding flame and venom, occasionally hiding from swooping dragons—but everywhere that he found the corpses of dragons he harvested their venom, and everywhere he could find anyone able to listen he explained and cajoled, and distributed the venom he had gathered. Evening wore on into night, and the first hint of dawn, faint behind the thick layers of smoke and cloud, touched the eastern horizon.

Arlian was on a rooftop, speaking to the crew of a catapult, when a dragon screamed high overhead, wheeled and plummeted—not randomly, but clearly aiming at a specific target. The catapult crew heaved the heavy mechanism around and fired.

"There," Arlian said, pointing, as the missiles flew. "Perhaps someone has done as I directed; it may be that the dragon senses the creation of its most feared enemy."

Most of the spears missed the hurtling dragon, but one tore through its wing, sending it spinning out of control. Another barrage of obsidian struck at it from another rooftop catapult, and it fell.

"If someone has contaminated a woman, as you say, then

that means another dragonheart," one of the soldiers said. "And in a thousand years, another dragon."

"Perhaps, perhaps not; we have the means to prevent it, and a thousand years is a very long time," Arlian said, satisfied, as he gazed down over the parapet at the streets below.

He remembered that he had intended to find and either kill or cleanse every dragonheart, once he had killed every dragon, yet here he was, cheerfully creating more—but he considered the bargain entirely worthwhile. For every god created, there was a dragonheart, yes—but the god would arrive in no more than nine months, the dragon not for a millennium. Dragonhearts could be cleansed. Dragons could be slain—or if his foes had spoken the truth, controlled by the words of a god.

A thousand years from now the world might look very different indeed. The arrival of dozens or hundreds of new dragons might well be of no great consequence by then, in a land protected by dozens of gods.

And it would certainly be no worse than the past. Arlian now knew that when he was born the caverns beneath the Lands of Man had held perhaps three hundred dragons, perhaps more, perhaps *many* more—but he had slain more than eighty of them, and now dozens had perished in this desperate attack on Manfort. Unless there were hundreds still lurking in caverns, hundreds that had never joined in the attacks, then roughly one-third to one-half of the dragons' entire population must have died in his lifetime. Allowing a replenishment centuries in the future did not seem unforgivable.

Hundreds of innocent men and women had undoubtedly died as well, and much of the city had been destroyed, but there was little Arlian could have done—he had had no way of knowing the dragons would be so desperate as to attempt a direct assault into the massive defenses the Duke had built. He had not known that little Ithar would be so great a threat to them.

They had come to Manfort inviting death, and they had

received it—and that meant that more of the land's magic would be free. More gods *must* be created, not merely to control the dragons, not merely for the sake of future generations, but to absorb that magic so that the borders of the Lands of Man might hold.

Arlian watched the dragon tumble into the street, where a dozen spearmen waited, then turned to the ladder. He had delivered his message to the crew, as he had to scores of others throughout the city, and he was on the verge of collapsing from exhaustion; he had been awake and active for almost twenty-four hours now. He descended from the rooftop and looked around, then up.

The number of dragons weaving in and out of the low-hanging firelit clouds over the city was greatly diminished; many of the survivors were tiring of the attack, and the less determined had already departed, returning to their lairs. Only a scattered handful still seemed determined to strike, flinging themselves desperately earthward despite the obsidian defenses, trying to strike what blows they still could against their multiplying unborn foes.

It was time to return to the tunnel, to bring Black and his family and the rest of the staff some food and drink. Arlian had collected supplies from military stores and abandoned houses in the course of his wandering; now he hefted a heavy pack onto his back, picked up a long spear he had found in the street, and headed for the house where the tunnel entrance lay.

He was climbing past the skull of the dead dragon when he heard a rush of air and looked up.

Another dragon, very much alive, was swooping down toward him; spears protruded from its flank and one wing was torn.

And he recognized its face.

You have betrayed us, it said. *Already there are twenty, thirty new godlings in the wombs of this city's women. You could not wait another few years? You could not give us time to prepare?*

"Betrayed you?" Arlian shouted, raising the spear. "How can I betray a sworn enemy? I made no promises to you—indeed, I swore long ago to destroy you, as you destroyed my home!"

The dragon's reply was a burst of venom—but the fluid failed to ignite, and Arlian easily avoided most of the spray. Despite his exhaustion and the heavy pack on his back he sprinted across the shattered room to a stairway, and ran up the steps.

The dragon dove into the house after him, and the floor shook beneath Arlian as he turned the corner at the top of the stairs, doubling back toward the open end of the upstairs hall.

The dragon had thrust its head into the downstairs room, not realizing what Arlian intended; it was unable to withdraw or dodge in time. Arlian charged off the end of the broken floor, and landed atop the dragon's shoulders.

No! The dragon's single word seemed to echo in Arlian's mind as the monster lifted its head, smashing the remainder of the upstairs hall, sending stone and wood flying in all directions.

It was too late; Arlian plunged his spear into its back, sliding the obsidian point between two of the beast's ribs. He jumped, putting his entire weight onto the shaft, and the spear sank through a dozen feet of flesh and into the monster's black heart.

Blood bubbled up, and the dragon thrashed briefly, then died, eyes open and staring blindly at a crooked sconce that still clung to one wall of the ruined house.

Arlian stood atop the dying beast for a long moment, looking down at it.

"Grandsir, you are avenged," he said.

But it felt no different than the slaying of any other dragon—empty. His taste for revenge was gone.

He had thought that this one might be different. This was *the* dragon, after all, the one he had sought for so long, the one for which all those others had been inadequate substitutes—but his strongest response to its death was merely a faint disappointment.

When he had killed the other dragon in the kitchen of the Grey House he had been too busy to think about what he had done, to realize that he had finally killed one of the three dragons that had destroyed the village of Obsidian so long ago, and when the realization had sunk in later he had thought the lack of immediacy explained the emotional void, the lack of satisfaction he felt.

This time, though, he had known exactly what he was doing, what he was killing, what oaths he was fulfilling—and he still felt little more than fatigue and a dull sense of relief that he had survived.

He thought that perhaps he could blame this on his nature as a dragonheart, on the taint in his heart and blood, on the diminution of his soul—but he did not entirely believe that.

The truth was simply that the flame of hatred, the need for revenge, had faded with time, until vengeance had become merely a habit.

Perhaps now, with this particular dragon gone, he could break that habit. He looked up at last—and saw three more dragons dropping toward him from the clouds.

"Damn," he said. He tugged at the spear, but it had lodged against a rib, and he could not free it; he released it and half scrambled, half slid down the dragon's flank.

There were other spears dangling from the monster's shriveling flesh, but there were *three* dragons coming toward him; he abandoned any thought of fighting, and instead ran for the fireplace.

He had passed through the fireplace itself, and through the wedged-open stone door, and was beginning to think himself safe, when the great gout of burning venom swept down upon him, knocking him off his feet and burning the hair from his head, burning his clothing from his arms and legs, burning away much of his flesh. Only the massive pack on his back protected his head and body and kept him alive.

He felt it all. He felt the skin tearing and peeling from his limbs, felt his blood burning from the exposed flesh, felt his hair flare up like a torch as his legs weakened and he tumbled forward. He had time for a single scream, and then the agony became unbearable and he fell unconscious to the tunnel floor.

51

Aftermath

*A*rlian blinked, trying to understand what he was seeing and feeling.

He was lying on his back on something hard, looking up at a pattern of dark squares edged in gold. He could smell lamp oil and dust, and the light on the ceiling, if it was a ceiling, was the orange of lamplight. He felt no pain, no weariness, though his last memory was of exhaustion and agony.

He was, however, desperately thirsty.

And he felt *strange*, in a way he could not describe, as if his blood had somehow become simultaneously warmer and cooler.

This made no sense. He had been burned in dragonfire; he should be suffering horribly, but he was not.

He cautiously lifted a hand, expecting a jolt of pain, but there was no pain. He turned his head carefully to look, to make certain his hand had actually moved. It had—and beyond it he saw a cabinet with a row of human skulls arranged atop it, and he knew where he was.

He was in the hall of the Dragon Society, in their old headquarters on the Street of the Black Spire, deserted since the Society was driven from the city by the Duke's orders. The dark squares overhead were the coffered and gilded ceiling.

And he was lying on a table.

"What . . ." he said, his voice a croak.

"He's awake!" Kerzia's voice called. "Look, he's awake!"

Clothing rustled, chairs scraped on the floor, voices muttered, and a moment later Arlian found himself being helped into a sitting position, surrounded by familiar, concerned faces—Black, Brook, their children, and Lilsinir. None of the other servants were there.

And now there *was* pain—faint discomfort, really, as if from a very old injury—in his chest. He looked down, and for the first time realized that he was naked, his lower body covered only by a sheet.

His chest was bare, and a long, thick scar ran down the center. He could not see the top, but the bottom was at the base of his rib cage.

He had seen such a scar before. He turned to Lilsinir. She nodded.

Then Black was handing him a waterskin, and he put aside further questions long enough to drink deeply.

When his thirst had been assuaged he swallowed, coughed, and asked, "What happened?"

Several voices spoke at once, but he raised his hands for silence—noticing, as he did, that his right shoulder was entirely healed—and then gestured to Black.

"What happened?" he asked again. "How long have I been here?"

"Two days," Black said. "Almost three, really."

Arlian looked down at his chest again, then at Black. He did not bother to put his question into words; the meaning was obvious. The scar on his chest gave every appearance of being weeks or months old, not mere days.

"Ithar healed you," Black explained.

Arlian closed his eyes, then opened them again. "Start at

the beginning," he said. "The last thing I remember is running into the tunnel, and being caught from behind by dragonfire."

"You screamed," Black said. "We heard you, from farther up the tunnel, and found you dying of your burns—from the venom, more than the flame, I suppose, but whatever the cause the flesh had been eaten down to the bone in places, your blood boiled away. Any ordinary man would have been dead before we got there, but you, of course, were a dragonheart—and that was both your salvation and your doom. Ithar would or could do nothing for you, because of the heart of the dragon—at least, so we assume; he cannot tell us why, but he would not touch you. Lilsinir could keep you alive for a time, but could not heal so much damage. She removed your heart and cleaned it of the dragon's taint, and when it was restored to your body, *then* when we brought Ithar to you, his touch healed you."

"Clever," Arlian said. "Thank you." He looked around, and spotted Ithar sleeping in his mother's arms, tiny and peaceful, a picture of divine serenity. "Thank you," he repeated. The baby did not stir.

"We used the side tunnel to bring you here," Black continued. "It seemed the safest place at the time."

"Indeed," Arlian said. "Well done. I take it, from Ithar's presence, that the last few dragons broke off their attack?"

"Few dragons survive, so far as we can tell," Black replied. "The clouds broke yesterday, and it rained half a day; today the sun is out, and the weather is cool. There is no sign of the remaining dragons."

"Many fled before the battle was over," Arlian said, remembering. "They have their factions and quarrels, just as we do, and not all of them chose to fight to the end. I have no doubt that many survive—but I would assume the fighters, the troublemakers, were the ones that died."

"That would make sense."

"Are there many dead ones?"

"Scores of them, strewn about the city and the surrounding towns. There is a trench above the tunnel where we hid that's filled with them, like the offal pit in a butcher's shop—they tried to burrow down to us, and Quickhand brought a party of spearmen who slaughtered them while they were confined there."

"Quickhand?"

"Yes—he took charge of much of the defense, since so many officers of the guard died in the destruction of the Citadel, and since he had experience in slaying dragons."

"Ah! Good for him. And there were dead dragons as a result."

"Scores of them, as I said. We have been collecting their venom, trying to get as much as possible before the sacs rot away, so that we can create more beings like Ithar, and we have been successful; I think almost every mother-to-be in Manfort now carries a child that's more than mortal."

"That should be enough, I would think," Arlian said. "After all, we need merely ensure that the land's free magic is not permitted to reach unsafe levels; there's no need to create an entire population of gods."

"The remaining venom may have its uses, all the same," Black said.

Arlian nodded. He felt no need to argue the point. "Save some of the bone, too," he said. "The fangs in particular."

"Why?"

Arlian glanced at Brook and Ithar. "I'll explain later," he said. He looked around. "Where are Stammer and Venlin and the rest?"

"Safe at Obsidian House. They had no reason to stay here, and the damage there was slight."

"And why did *you* all stay?"

"Lilsinir and Ithar stayed in case you needed further healing, and the rest of us stayed to be with Ithar. We are all a single family, you know."

"Of course." He looked at Brook and nodded. "Has the babe . . ." He stopped, unsure how to complete his question.

"He sleeps most of the time," Brook said. "Like any

baby. He does not nurse; when he wakes he looks about himself, and if he sees anyone in pain—well, anyone but a dragonheart—he reaches out to touch and heal. And when he has healed, he goes back to sleep. It is as if he drinks the pain of others as his mother's milk."

"We have told others," Black said. "But Ithar has his limits; he can only do so much before dozing off, and if awakened he cries like any other infant and will do no more until he has rested. Since the dragons departed and we emerged from the tunnel we have taken him among the injured, and allowed the injured to be brought to him, but we save his touch for those who need it most, those who would die without it, or whose suffering seems greatest."

"Those like me."

"Yes. And even then, there are too many for him to attend them all."

Arlian considered that, and considered Ithar. He was just one godling—but there were others on the way.

The world would be a different place with such beings in it, there could be no doubt of that. Arlian tried to imagine what it would be like. Miraculous healing might be only the beginning of the gods' power; the world might be transformed into a paradise.

Or not. After all, while the ancient legends spoke of the days of the old gods as a golden age, those days had ended long ago and legends often exaggerated. There were the darker elements—the fact that the gods could not exist without dragons, that the dead gods had once fed their dragons human souls.

Dragonbone could kill gods, if it ever became necessary. He would want to make certain that secret was never lost—but he hoped it would never be needed.

The next few years would be interesting, with dozens of newborn gods growing up in and around Manfort, and Arlian was intrigued that he would be there to see them.

For now, though, there were more mundane matters to

consider. He looked down at himself again. "By any chance, have I any clothing?"

"I'm afraid all yours was in the Grey House. What little we found in the rubble had all been ruined by the fires," Black said.

"Are there any tailors left alive? How fares the city?"

Black exchanged glances with the others.

"It's hard to be certain how Manfort fares," he said. "I spent most of yesterday inquiring after its well-being, though. Most of the population seems to have survived; after all, the dragons were not particularly trying to kill anyone but us. The Upper City, though, was largely destroyed. The Citadel is embers and ash—and the Duke of Manfort is dead, along with his wife and most of his court, with no known surviving heir. He died valiantly, commanding his soldiers, Arlian—I always thought him a fool and a wastrel, but I will never deny his courage, as he made no attempt to flee."

Arlian nodded—but he could not help wondering how much of the Duke's courage had been despair, a conviction that there was nowhere to flee to and no purpose in flight.

"The remaining nobility are planning to convene a council to arrange for the city's governance and assign command of the army," Black continued. "I am not certain who is involved."

"Lady Rime? Did she survive?"

"Alive and well, though her mansion burned—she fled before the fires reached her. She and all her family are safe—the servants and children carried the cripples and their chairs." Black hesitated. "In fact, I offered her the use of Obsidian House until other lodging can be arranged. She has estates outside the city, of course, and I suppose she will rebuild in time, but for the moment she needed a roof."

"And Obsidian House still stands, you said?"

"I had its exterior built entirely of stone," Black said. "I saw what became of the Old Palace, and did not care to see a repetition. And no dragon bothered to break in and set the interior ablaze—after all, it was empty."

Arlian nodded. "Excellent. You've done very well, Beron; thank you. And Rime and her family are welcome to remain as our guests as long as they choose."

Black bowed.

Arlian turned to Lilsinir. "You cut out my heart?" he asked.

"Yes, my lord."

"You acted without my consent."

"I acted to save your life."

Arlian nodded. "Thank you," he said. Then he turned back to Black. "About that tailor . . ."

52

Homecoming

Over the next few days Arlian's wardrobe was gradually restored—not to anything remotely resembling its previous extent, but to the point where he could go out in public without embarrassment. Two tailors, a seamstress, a hatter, and a cobbler saw to the task of outfitting him.

He did not, however, go out in public, embarrassed or otherwise—rather, the clothiers were brought to him. Ithar's miraculous healing had removed the pain and restored his flesh, but he was still weak, and did not feel ready to face the outside world. He remained in the dusty, windowless halls of the Dragon Society while he recovered.

During those days, as he underwent the various measurings and fittings and alterations, he spoke with whoever he could find, asking endless questions. He learned that although Black's family had stayed at the Society's hall at first in case Ithar's healing abilities were needed again, now that Arlian was clearly on the road to recovery they were moving back to Obsidian House—though Brook and Ithar would continue to visit the hall and other points about the city so that Ithar's healing abilities might be available to whoever needed them. Stammer and the other servants had already returned home, and were preparing the house to receive its master—although it had not burned, there was incidental damage from stray sparks, from stray catapult bolts, and from panicky neighbors.

Lilsinir was making arrangements to perform the purifying ritual on Brook—having experienced the heart of the dragon, Ithar's mother was now more than willing to return to her former self.

"I do regret losing all those centuries of life," Brook said, when Arlian commended her on her decision. The two were sitting by the shelf of skulls, Arlian in one of the ordinary chairs and Brook upon her wheels. Ithar lay asleep in his mother's arms.

"They are not worth what they cost," Arlian said.

"Perhaps, as the mother of a god, I might somehow manage longevity without the loss of my soul," she suggested, smiling.

"I have no idea whether that's possible, but it would certainly please me," Arlian said, smiling in return.

"And what are your own plans, my lord?"

"I have no more plans," Arlian replied. "My vengeance is complete, and my heart is whole again—still patched together in places, still pained by the loss of so many I loved, but human and healing. The dragons are defeated, if not yet annihilated, and a worthy form has been found to succeed them as the land's magic. I am done. There is nothing left to do but live out my life."

"You could hunt down the remaining dragons, when you have recovered."

"I will leave that to others—perhaps to Ithar and his kin, when he comes of age. I have done my share."

"Indeed you have, and more—but you will not continue for your own satisfaction?"

"No. I have had enough, and more than enough, of slaying dragons." Arlian knew that not long ago he would have considered it unthinkable to give up his campaign while a single dragon still survived, but now, as he said, he had had enough. He was unsure whether it was the loss of the heart of the dragon that had transformed him, or killing the beast that had killed his grandfather, or something else entirely—perhaps Ithar had healed his soul as well as his body, and cured him of his need for revenge, or perhaps the mere presence of a living god in the world was enough to change his mind. Whatever the reason, he had indeed had his fill of vengeance.

He had sworn to destroy the dragons or die in the attempt, and he felt that he had fulfilled his oath—although dragons yet lived, he had set in motion events that would inevitably render them powerless and impotent. That was destruction enough to satisfy him.

"Then perhaps you might find other ways to spend your time that are worthy of a man of your accomplishments," Brook suggested. "You could offer your name to the council of nobles—I think a good case could be made that you should retain the title of warlord, or perhaps even become the new Duke. After all, what did Roioch accomplish that you have not equaled?"

"Duke?" Arlian grimaced. "I would rather go dwell in the Desolation as a hermit. Better Zaner, if he yet lives, or Spider, or Quickhand." Lord Zaner was among the missing—no one knew, as yet, whether he had died in the Citadel with so many others, or escaped and gone into hiding.

"Might you study sorcery, perhaps?"

"I have but a single lifetime in which to learn now, and I suspect that the nature of magic may be changing in the years to come, as the gods grow in strength. I doubt I could gain enough skill to be worth the effort."

"There is nothing that interests you, then? Nothing to hold your attention?"

"Perhaps in time there will be."

Brook was hardly satisfied by that, but did not press the issue further.

Finally, when Arlian felt himself up to the walk and had once again been outfitted in a manner appropriate for a lord, he clapped his new hat on his head and marched up the Street of the Black Spire, then made his way to the Old Palace grounds, taking in the devastation around him.

The older portions of the city were largely intact—roofs had been caved in or torn away here and there, catapults ripped from their mountings or smashed to bits where they stood, but most of the gray stone walls still stood, the gray stone streets had been largely cleared of debris, and the tradesmen and laborers were going about their business just as they always had. Shop doors stood open, and the odor of baking bread mingled with the lingering woodsmoke.

At least half the Upper City, though, was a wasteland— mansion after mansion had been burned to the ground, leaving occasional upright slabs of stone or brick thrusting up from heaps of still-smoldering wreckage. Ragged figures were moving across the rubble of some estates, picking out scorched books or china cups that had somehow survived.

Arlian knew he was partly to blame for all of this—the destruction, the chaos, the hundreds of deaths. If he had never interfered with the dragons, if he had never tried to create a better world, then none of this would have happened. If he had not experimented with the dragons' venom then Ithar would have been an ordinary child, and the dragons would not have attacked Manfort—but every year a village somewhere would have been destroyed, so that the souls of its people could feed the dragons.

If he had not slain so many dragons, then wild magic would not have encroached on the Borderlands.

If he had not revealed the secrets of draconic reproduction, the fourteen years of war between man and dragon might have been avoided—or perhaps not. Lord Enziet would have died soon in any case, and he would have had no heir in place to hold the dragons to their old bargain or teach humanity that obsidian could pierce a dragon's hide.

If Arlian had not intervened, then hundreds or thousands of people would not have died beneath the dragons' attacks—but the dragons would rule the Lands of Man as they had for thousands of years, and at least as many would have died in time, over the next several decades or centuries.

He had caused vast destruction, but in doing so he had created the hope of a future free of the dragons. Dreadful as the situation before him was, and much as it pained him to see so many people hurt and so many homes destroyed, he still believed he had done the right thing.

At least, he *hoped* he had, but there was no way he could ever know with any certainty.

He would just have to live with that.

He neared the crest of the hill, and the site of the Old Palace. Several of the structures erected on those grounds had been burned or crushed—Arlian paused briefly to look at the extent of the damage on his land.

It was not as bad, in truth, as most of the other destroyed areas. It occurred to him that Lord Obsidian's surviving guests would have their pick of dozens of new sites if they chose to rebuild their homes.

It could have been far worse.

He ambled past the remaining gatepost, one having been demolished in the fighting, then around to the left and up the path to Obsidian House.

The new house was virtually untouched. The stone walls stood clean and strong in the sun—whatever repairs had been needed were not readily visible. The iron catapults on the roof were empty, their bolts spent, but were otherwise undamaged. Arlian smiled at the sight.

He hoped those catapults would never be needed again—and he knew that he had helped create in Ithar a far more effective defense.

He lowered his gaze to the front door, and quickened his pace.

"He's coming!" someone called.

And then the doors and windows opened, and children poured out. He saw Kerzia and Amberdine and Dirinan, Kuron and Bekerin and Rose, Halori and Selsur and Fanora, running and dancing around him as he strode in.

Waiting inside the door were Hasty and Cricket and Lily and Musk and Kitten and Brook in their wheeled chairs, three on either side of the entrance, with Dovliril and Stone and Stammer and Venlin and a dozen other servants lined up behind them.

And directly ahead of him, in the center of the great hall, stood Black, holding the infant Ithar in his arms, and Rime, supported by her cane and her granddaughter Vanniari.

"Welcome home, Lord Obsidian," Vanniari said. "Welcome home."

Arlian looked about himself at Rime's gathered household and his own, and felt a welling in his heart he had not felt since childhood.

He could no longer remember its name with any certainty, but he thought it might be love—or perhaps simply happiness. It was not the devotion he had felt for Sweet, but a warmth and yearning akin to childhood memories of his love for his family, directed at all those who stood around him, welcoming him.

He had felt nothing like it since his parents died, and had never expected to feel it again, but now he was no longer a dragonheart. He was, for the first time in his life, just a man.

And he was home at last.

Praise for The Obsidian Chronicles

DRAGON VENOM

"In Watt-Evans's stirring conclusion to his high fantasy Obsidian Chronicles (after *Dragon Weather* and *The Dragon Society*), the swashbuckling story line builds to a twist ending sure to leave the author's fans smiling."

—*Publishers Weekly*

"Watt-Evans concludes his formidably complex and intelligent trilogy about Arlian the dragon-slayer. This book is as rich in incident and idea as its predecessors. It is challenging enough to raise some questions about the ethics of some classic devices of high fantasy within the context of a very good high fantasy: this one." —*Booklist*

DRAGON WEATHER
*Named The Best Fantasy Novel of 1999
by *Science Fiction Chronicle*

"Watt-Evans explores the theme of whether any man can single-handedly right all the wrongs in the world, and whether any man can know what true justice is. This—plus a unique concept of the nature of dragons, how they come into being, and their true relationship with humans—makes *Dragon Weather* exceptional." —*Hartford Courant*

"This wonderful character study is easy to read, highly descriptive, and fast paced." —*VOYA*

THE DRAGON SOCIETY

"[With] plenty of intrigue and magic, this book is sure to satisfy the author's many fans, as well as lovers of epic fantasy in the tradition of L. E. Modesitt and Terry Goodkind."

—*Publishers Weekly*

"Watt-Evans always delivers a good story, and this is one of his best. Watt-Evans proves once again that he has few rivals in the art of intelligent, serious-minded fantasy adventure." —*Science Fiction Chronicle*

Tor Books by Lawrence Watt-Evans

THE OBSIDIAN CHRONICLES
Dragon Weather
The Dragon Society
Dragon Venom

LEGENDS OF ETHSHAR
Night of Madness
Ithanalin's Restoration

Touched by the Gods
Split Heirs (with Esther Friesner)